'Eerily atmospheric, pulse-pounding and unputdownable'
SARAH PEKKANEN

'I had no idea that a story could be both so beautifully written and so unbelievably terrifying'
ALAFAIR BURKE

terrifying descent into my deepest maternal fears . . . One of the most haunting, gripping novels I've read'
KATIE GUTIERREZ

'Triumphs in a gripping and convincing finale'
DAILY MAIL

'You'll want to gulp it down in one sitting, if you're not too scared to turn the page! Everyone should read this book!'
LAUREN NORTH

'An extraordinary book with a unique voice which caught me from the first line'
JANE CORRY

'Sierra's plot is propulsive and is literally heart-pounding . . . It will enrage you, it will scare you and it will definitely make you want to discuss it'
GLAMOUR

'A whip-smart snapshot of marriage, motherhood and the female experience in a man's world'
GILLY MACMILLAN

'So tense, so thought-provoking. I felt my heart rate rising as I read it . . . The definition of can't-put-down'
ARAMINTA HALL

'Almost unbearably tense, suffused with fear without ever exploiting it'
SUNDAY TIMES

'A scalpel-sharp thriller'
NIKKI SMITH

LEY AUDRAIN

'Tender and terrifying' **ABIGIAL DEAN**

'Breathtaking' **SOPHIE HANNAH**

. . . AND THAT READERS CAN'T STOP TALKING ABOUT

'What a stunning piece of writing'
★★★★★

'A must-read'
★★★★★

'I was desperate to know how it ended!'
★★★★★

'I have no doubt this will be one of the most talked-about books of the year'
★★★★★

'I read this book months ago and I still can't get it out of my head'
★★★★★

'This was absolutely brilliant'
★★★★★

'Wow, wow, wow'
★★★★★

'This book blew me away!'
★★★★★

'This book creeps up on you, reels you in and keeps you hooked'
★★★★★

'From the first page of this book I was addicted'
★★★★★

'After finishing *Nightwatching* early in the morning, the next day I had an all-day book hangover'
★★★★★

'Read it – you won't be disappointed!'
★★★★★

NIGHT WATCHING

NIGHT WATCHING

Tracy Sierra

PENGUIN BOOKS

PENGUIN BOOKS

UK | USA | Canada | Ireland | Australia
India | New Zealand | South Africa

Penguin Books is part of the Penguin Random House group of companies
whose addresses can be found at global.penguinrandomhouse.com

Penguin Random House UK,
One Embassy Gardens, 8 Viaduct Gardens, London SW11 7BW

penguin.co.uk
global.penguinrandomhouse.com

Penguin
Random House
UK

First published in the United States of America by
Pamela Dorman Books/Viking 2024
First published in Great Britain by Viking 2024
Published in Penguin Books 2024
001

Printed and bound in Great Britain by Clays Ltd, Elcograf S.p.A.

The authorized representative in the EEA is Penguin Random House Ireland,
Morrison Chambers, 32 Nassau Street, Dublin D02 YH68

A CIP catalogue record for this book is available from the British Library

ISBN: 978–0–241–99927–1

Penguin Random House is committed to a sustainable future
for our business, our readers and our planet. This book is made from
Forest Stewardship Council® certified paper.

For Catherine

My mother

———○———

I have a very general acquaintance here in New England.

THE MAN, "YOUNG GOODMAN
BROWN," NATHANIEL HAWTHORNE

There was someone in the house.

She stood in her son's dark bedroom. Through its open door and down the long hallway, the landing at the top of the steep kitchen stairs was lit by the dim glow of a plug-in night-light.

The light was there so the children would be able to see the stairs in their nighttime wanderings. To prevent them silently, helplessly falling as they padded from their rooms to their parents' bedroom overnight seeking water, or comfort, or after a wet bed.

The old house let the wind hiss through and crack its ribs. The sounds of it bracing against the storm, its staggered breathing, were familiar. But through it all came noises that rooted her to the spot. Also familiar, but not at this time of night. Not when she had been sure she was the only one awake.

In the brief hush between the frozen gusts came the wheeze of weight on the stairs.

You're imagining things.

Her daughter lay asleep in the next room. Her son was already sleeping again a few steps away from her.

For a moment the hope that it might be her husband lifted her.

Stop it. That's impossible.

But it could be her daughter sleepwalking again. They'd bolted the door of the girl's room that led to the old front stairs—a place too dangerous to let her sightlessly wander. But it was possible her daughter had gone out the other door to her bedroom. The one they left unlocked despite the girl's sleepwalking and the danger of the kitchen stairs. The door they left open so she could use the bathroom at night, so that she understood she was still a big girl, they trusted her and she should trust herself.

Yes, that could explain it! And you wouldn't have heard the baby monitor go on.

Her husband had mounted a motion-activated baby monitor outside their daughter's unlocked bedroom door after three nights of finding the little girl standing at their bedside, still and unwakeable in the darkness.

"What can I say?" Her husband had shrugged. "Cameras are what I know."

Click, fizz, beep! The monitor would spring to life in their bedroom, and their daughter would pass on the screen, looking blurry and bleached on the night vision, retinas giving an animallike mirror flash. One of them (her, always her) would get up and intercept their daughter before the girl had a chance to accidentally hurt herself. She would guide her little girl back to bed, stroke the dark hair away from the empty open eyes, away from the slack mouth, sit with her daughter until she lay back on her pillow.

That must be it. Sleepwalking.

And yet, she couldn't make herself move. Couldn't unfasten her eyes from the distant night-light. A part of her remembered that the sound of her daughter on those stairs was simply different. A part of her acknowledged that in all her daughter's nighttime drifting, the little girl had never actually gone down the stairs. And the sounds were coming from the stairs.

A twisted bit of nursery rhyme echoed through her head, one of the endlessly reread child things that now permeated her consciousness.

If wishes were fishes we'd have some to fry. If wishes were fishes we'd eat and not die.

A low thump, a pause. A complete and instant switch in her thinking.

He's hit his head.

It sometimes happened to people who were unfamiliar with the eccentricities of the old house. Anyone taller than six feet had to tilt their head or duck to avoid the low cut of the ceiling at the turn of the kitchen stairs.

There were thin, scraping sounds as this person readjusted. Recalculated. Moved again.

She saw fingers wrap the banister like white spider legs.

The intruder pulled himself up slowly until he stood at the top of the stairs, features washed to invisibility by the darkness and the way the night-light shone low behind him. For the briefest of moments looking at that silhouette, she saw her husband. Opened her mouth to call to him, ask how he'd gotten home.

But your husband wouldn't hit his head. Not tall enough.

With this thought came clarity. The figure went wrong around the edges and unfurled into a stranger.

It's a man.

He was tall. His arms hung loose and long. His presence had the distantly familiar rancidness of something wrong and rotten she'd tasted before but couldn't quite place.

Do you recognize him? Who is he?

He tipped his head and stared directly at the pool of darkness down the long hallway where she stood shrouded.

She knew objectively, logically, that it should be impossible for him to see her. How many times had she stood in his precise spot, in his exact pose? How many times had she looked down the dark, off-kilter hall toward the oldest part of the house, where she now stood in her son's room? Trying to tell in the middle of the night if the door was open, if her little boy was standing there, never once able to see anything but shadow. Because that night-light on the landing, close to the floor and faint as it was, blinded her to anything beyond its dim reach. Always, every time, she had to be almost at the boy's bedroom door before she could be sure that yes, there was her son, back out of bed, silently watching her. Instead of safe asleep.

The light has to—it must—blind him.

The man's face was made a skull by the shadows. Solid black where eyes should be. The light snagged on his lips to cut an over-grinning smile. His whole self seemed to her so huge it was beyond the bounds of reasonable. So substantial it was as though even his mouth, his nostrils, his ears, must be filled with flesh.

She struggled for air. It was the reality of him, the human de-tails, that choked her. His short, sandy hair stuck out sideways the way a child's does after pressing flat against a pillow overnight. His dark shirt was only half tucked in. He shifted his weight. Scratched at the side of his nose, then rubbed at the spot where he must have hit his head.

Her eyes went wide. Her blood surged thick and pounded her ears to deafness. She realized she was shaking, had a flash of shame at her total inability to control her own body. She remembered this shame. Saw in memory a linoleum floor. No fight, no flight, just complete and utter shuddering immobility.

And time. *Tick, tick, tick,* a clock must be saying somewhere. *Tock, tock, tock,* uncountable seconds passing.

One minute, two? Ten? Breathe. Think. He sees you. Can he see you?

The man's size was a suffocating reminder of how small she was.

His shadow stuck to the ceiling, cast high by the low glow of the night-light.

He's in your house. Your house!

This was why her ears were deafened by blood. Why terror hollowed her out weightless.

Someone who would take that step, someone who would snap aside that curtain?

Oh yes. Someone like that is serious.

But—maybe he isn't real? Maybe you're seeing things.

This idea melted through her. The man could be a vivid nightmare. Or one of the fears she rubbed between thumb and forefinger, one of the worries she would rumble and burnish to smooth morbid fantasy staring sleepless at the bedroom ceiling.

Where do you come up with these awful things? That's it, that's all. Overactive imagination. A dream. One-two-three, air in, air out, open your eyes. Then, poof! He'll disappear. You'll see.

But when she forced her eyes closed, forced them open again, the man hadn't vanished. For the first time she noticed he was wearing sneakers.

She understood the implications somewhere deep and visceral. He couldn't have walked through the blizzard in those sneakers. She imagined him sitting on the bench in the entryway downstairs. Taking off his snow boots. Placing them neatly on the floor, side by side. Pulling the sneakers out of a bag and putting them on. A conscientious houseguest. Planning to stay a while.

He is very, very serious.

Her eyes skittered to the side to see the snowflakes still falling. Their whiteness was the only thing visible outside, touching then spinning away from the sliver of window glass visible between the curtains, resting in and softening the corners of the panes. Before the nor'easter began, there'd been at least a foot of accumulation. By bedtime there'd been almost two feet on the ground. Now—well, she couldn't tell from where she stood. But she knew that her house, the whole property, the whole world, was wrapped tight.

Next to the window was her son's bed. The little boy was curled into a tiny, soft, sleeping lump, his chest moving ever so slightly up and down under his green blanket. A bit of hair and a curve of his ear were the only things discernible in the darkness.

As she looked at her son's shape, her heart was squeezed by such love and panic she nearly groaned with the pain of it. She thought of his soft, full cheeks, how they intersected with the tiny bone of his chin. The sweet, cartoonish proportions of his little self. The tender, potbellied gourd of his torso. His thin limbs and straight hips. Her own small, perfect boy who was fully and completely a person, however tiny. However new here.

And now?

What's going to happen to that little person now?

She dragged her eyes back to the man.

Ten seconds? Ten minutes?

He'd been there for just a moment. He'd been there forever.

But it can't happen. This can't happen. Not to you.

These things happen. These things happen every day.

It must be your fault. What did you do?

A pull of despair tugged the back of her tongue.

You did everything right, didn't you? You locked the doors. The windows.

What did you do to deserve this?

But she knew better than most that deserving had little to do with getting. She was sure almost no one got to give permission for the worst things that happened to them.

The man stood patiently in the splash of weak light. So awfully, jaw-achingly patient. She watched as he listened for even the lightest sounds of life. She watched him choosing his next steps.

2

In her son's dark room, she keenly felt the presence of the door behind her to the top landing of the front stairs. Once upon a time, they'd been the home's only stairs. On the other side of that landing was the door to her little girl's bedroom that they kept bolted from the landing side for her safety.

Her mind's eye saw each of them as a component in a schematic. Her son here, her daughter asleep in her room. The man waiting at the top of the stairs that led down to the kitchen. He stood between her and the modern addition attached to the back of the old house. Between her and her bedroom, her office, the garage. Which meant he stood between her and her phone on her bedside table. The car in the garage. The gun locked snug in its wall safe. The bullets for that gun hidden high in her husband's closet. Between her and her computer, set up in the guest room that doubled as her office. There he stood between her and all possibility of help and aid and rescue and communication and strength.

She felt a need to claw at something.

Hold still, hold still! He'll see you.

In wonderment she realized she was soaked completely in sweat. A viscous amphibian flop sweat that let the cold cling to every bit of her skin with aching pressure. Already the dampness of it soaked into the T-shirt and underwear she'd worn to bed. It made the robe she'd thrown over herself as a barrier against the house's perpetual winter chill stick to her, clammy.

The man fished something out of a pocket on his immense chest. He let it dangle from a hand. An oblong object, heavy yet loose, a slight swing to it.

SLAP! He swung it and it hit his other palm. The unexpected noise, the weight, the reality, the implications of the unidentifiable weapon he held, swept the tension from her knees so that she had to fight to stand.

That the man wasn't wearing a mask turned things all the more surreal in this new world where everyone did. And him here, doing this, with his face exposed?

But he was wearing gloves. White plastic gloves that glowed from the dim shine of the night-light.

Fingerprints matter but not if we see his face, because he's going to kill us.

She shook her head so quick and tight she heard the ocean.

Stop that! Don't be ridiculous, calm down, think clearly.

No. You are thinking clearly. This is serious. There are stakes. Everything is at stake. Don't pretend otherwise. Look at him. No mask. Gloves. Dry sneakers. Weapon. He's prepared. He will hurt them. Hurt you. Anything else is a fantasy. You know it. You know the lines he's crossed already. Being nice, thinking positive—no.

With a wave of despair she saw it was already over. What could she do but offer up a soft neck and pretend she was elsewhere? There was no way to fight him. No weapon, no help. Two small children and her short, weakened, waifish self. There was no way to win, defend, protect. She folded inward with the hopeless acknowledgment that she'd done the calculations, sketched out all the options, and was simply not equal to the task.

The fear of pain, the terror of what he could do, was an unbearable anticipation. The surging panic in her frozen body turned her into a live wire stripped bare but unable to release a charge.

This is the part of the movie you aren't allowed see. What's about to happen is what forces them to cut to black.

The man leaned back and cracked his spine like a runner preparing to start a race. The peculiar weapon seemed to pull at his hand with a limp heaviness.

The wide face slowly turned as the man looked away from her toward the hall of the modern addition. His shifting weight made the floor groan beneath him.

Still wishful, still deeply hoping that she was slipping into madness, that it was all imagination, she told herself, *That's a nice touch, brain, remembering how the floor creaks right there.*

He took one step, then another. She blinked in disbelief as he moved away from her. He went down the hall of the addition before walking through the door of her bedroom and disappearing.

Because he turned away from instead of toward her, a razor-thin hope zapped and fizzed to life at the base of her neck.

Do something.

She was awake in the middle of the night because of her son. He'd woken her as always in a most disturbing way. Scratching a fingernail along an eyelid. Poking his thumb into her ear. Deftly pulling out a single hair. Tonight, he'd pinched her nose shut until she woke with an inward gasp, batting hands pathetically at empty air. She'd followed her little boy down the hall, his tiny, capable body barely visible in the deep darkness. She knew better than to ask about the nightmare that had caused him to wake her. Her son had almost always already forgotten it. All that was left was the feeling of horror, a residual strangeness, a need to have someone else awake. Tonight, as usual, she'd lightly scratched his scalp to soothe him to sleep.

The little boy's nightmares had started a few weeks after lockdown began.

You think you hide your fears from your children, but they absorb them like they absorbed your blood.

"Does anyone get any sleep in this house?" her husband complained. On his fingers he counted out the issues. "Sleepwalking, night terrors, insomnia, nightmares, too warm, too cold, too wet, too thirsty. Too tired!"

"Well"—she yawned—"at least *you* don't have any trouble sleeping."

"That's true," he said. "I've got the mama wall protecting me. Why wake lame old Dad when you can wake the mama bear? Bring out the big guns?"

"Who are you calling a 'bear'? And that's the first time anyone's ever called me 'big.'"

Her husband shot her his charming, hooked smile. "The little mama, then. Better to wake up the little, tiny, *attractive* mama."

So her son would wake her, never her husband, and she'd follow him silently through the darkness, bundle him into bed, *Twinkle, twinkle, little star, how I wonder what you are.* She'd brush the black hair away from where it stuck to his long lashes, away from the corners of his already-sleeping eyes. And she'd be left wide awake sitting at the end of his bed, waiting to see if the absence of her touch woke her little boy, as it so often did, requiring she repeat the process. Then she'd pad back down the hall, lie down, and stare at the ceiling, wondering at the strange new fearfulness of the world. Thinking of the things she'd done wrong. Of the things she might have been able to control if she'd thought far enough, carefully enough, ahead. She would imagine other worlds where things had gone differently. Better. Worse.

It's not your fault.
It's all your fault.

The man disappearing through her bedroom door was like waking from her little boy's dream. A nightmare shuffling off, leaving behind an uncannily empty quiver of air.

Yesterday, upon the stair, I met a man who wasn't there.

Her skin cracked. Her teeth unclamped.

What are you going to do?

She had a vision of waking the children, pulling them into the snow out the old front doors down the stairs behind her, a five- and eight-year-old, both barefoot, in pajamas, her in a robe and slippers, because shoes, coats, the car, everything—*everything!*—was on the other side of the house.

He'd catch us. Easily. Immediately. Crossing the house or, if we tried to run, through the snow. And it's so far to the nearest neighbor. Half a mile? At least. At least! And in this storm. And through those drifts. Record cold, they said. Record snowfall.

No time, no time. Do something.

She was briefly awed by the realization that for the first time in a long time she felt alive, and even more astonishing, she desperately wanted to stay alive. But her surprise was paired horribly with deep fear. Fear of the man's kinetic violence. What he might do with that strange weapon. Fear of that potential energy released on her children. Fear of pain. She had never dealt well with pain.

Does anyone?

Then, a possibility. In the gripping swirl of her animal frenzy, adrenaline and helplessness, she remembered the hidden place.

L ater, she'd think of it like being possessed. When she saw the man go through her bedroom door, when she remembered the hidden place, it felt as though she'd been plucked out of her body. She watched herself from the outside, confused by her own actions, thinking, *Hey, look at what she's up to. You couldn't do that.* Yet despite the remove, she still felt her hands shake. Still tasted acid terror.

She watched herself put the sippy cup her son used for bedside water into one robe pocket, shove Fuzzydoll into the other. Watched herself carefully fold the blanket back, lift the sleeping boy in her arms. He stirred, then relaxed against her body. His small, pudgy legs dangled free, head solid on her shoulder. He breathed familiar mama sweat in and out, arms loose and trusting.

Her son smelled like drool. Like warmth. A smell unique and universal. "I love you," she whispered muffled into his hair as she held him, already hurrying to her daughter's room. "I love you."

She slid open the sleepwalking bolt on the outside of her daughter's bedroom door and went in. Her daughter was snoring. Flash of the girl as a baby, she and her husband suppressing giggles over a series of massive farts, of honking snores, all coming out of such a tiny, angelic little infant.

"Takes after her father," she'd whispered with a teasing grin, and her husband had put his hands on his hips, released a blasting snoring noise, and said, "Better believe it!" She'd nearly woken the baby with the sudden bleat of her laughter.

She sat on the girl's bed. With her son resting on her lap, she reached out and touched the little girl's shoulder. Her daughter immediately rolled over, balling her fists to rub both eyes roughly, the same way she always did.

"Mommy?"

"Shhh, shhh, angel," she said, stroking her daughter's hair too fast, too feverishly. "Quiet. Please. I need your help. We need to go downstairs. Down the front stairs."

Her daughter looked up, big eyes confused and searching.

No comfort in your hands, your voice. Can't be helped.

"Why, Mommy?"

Why, why, always why, all they ever ask is "Why?" Why can't they just do what you say? Why can't they just listen?

She wanted desperately to lie. To shield the girl from fright. From reality. But she stood up, holding her boy tight, and heard herself say, "There's someone in the house. Someone bad. We've got to hide. Now."

The girl's face started to crumple into crying.

"No, no!" She managed to grip the girl's shoulder. "There's no time for that."

Her daughter nodded and lifted back the blanket. The covers had pulled her long red nightgown up to her thighs, showing skinny legs and bulbed knees. The patches of white skin where the pigment had faded from the girl's feet and ankles appeared luminous even in the storm-thinned moonlight. On standing the nightgown fell into place. The girl clutched her tattered Pinkbunny to her chest.

She swallowed a fresh lump of fear at seeing her daughter's beauty. The girl had a willowy loveliness that hovered at the edge of that awful, quaking bridge leading out of childhood.

It's a problem.

This was not a new worry, but in these circumstances it was more urgent, more manifest. More terrifying.

A big problem.

Her daughter trailed her to the landing, softly closing the bedroom door behind her.

She hardly ever used this stairway, because she so rarely needed to go from her husband's office or the other front room they used as a playroom up to the kids' bedrooms. But the children often used it to go from their bedrooms to their playroom, and signs of them were everywhere. Clouded moonlight through the window at the top of the stairs and the transom panes above the door below allowed for a dim visibility. A Lego knight stood proud on the railing. A stuffed bear was face-planted in a corner, had clearly fallen from lounging on the windowsill. A ribbon wove in and out of the banister rungs. These things stabbed her in the heart as if her children had been lost, as if she'd already failed to protect them, and these objects were all that was left of them.

Her skin prickled in the cold air that wafted up the stairs. The blizzard blasted frozen bits of its violence through the gaps around the old doors below. She watched herself and was shocked to find that tucked somewhere in the folds of her memory was each weak spot on these little-used stairs, each place that might make a noise. Carrying her son, she stepped on light slippered toes from strong spot to strong spot on the treads, a kind of dancing descent, even deftly stepping over the loudest stair.

How strange, how strange, how'd you do that? That's not something you can do.

But her daughter's foot landed squarely in the middle of the first step. The noise of it surrounded them, an echoing doom.

With the bedroom doors to the landing closed, with the low

sound of the wind scraping through the house, maybe the man hadn't heard it? How close was he now? There on the other side of the house, he must have immediately seen her covers thrown back, her empty place in the bed, the phone on its charger.

He might be moving this way already to find you. Or he's searching down-stairs, thinking you fell asleep on the couch.

"Quiet, so quiet, step to the side of the stairs, tiptoe," she whispered at her daughter. "It's okay, angel, you can do it!"

"Okay, Mommy." The little girl descended carefully, avoiding the middle of each stair.

Yes. What a good kid. What a brave little girl. The best little girl.

They took a right at the bottom of the stairs and went into her husband's office. He liked its dark moodiness. She preferred her setup under the blindingly bright overhead lights of the guest room. Out of every window was snow. Drifting, blowing, collecting.

She laid her son gently on the armchair in the corner, and he curled into a warm ball, still asleep.

In the darkness she groped at the wall around the fireplace to find the panel that hinged inward when you pushed it just so.

It's here, isn't it? Wait—it's lower. Now, how do you do this?

On her knees she padded fingertips around the panel until she pushed at the just right spot in the just right way. It swung open to walled-in emptiness.

The space was irregular. It began behind the beehive oven set into the living room fireplace and ended under the stairs. She tried to map it out of her memory but couldn't recall its dimensions well. Not quite three feet wide. Tall at the back, low near the entrance where the front stairs made up its ceiling. Maybe nine feet long.

She'd been inside only once. The sellers showed them the hidden place the day they closed on the house. They demonstrated how to push open the panel with a firm press on its bottom left corner. How to hook your finger on a slightly warped part of the top left to yank it closed. A special, secret gift.

This reveal of the hidden place had relieved her. In that nearly three-hundred-year-old part of the house, her mathematical brain had measured the rooms, and aside from a little sagging, a little bowing, each had the same dimensions as the room immediately above or below. The rooms were so identical stacked above each other, so even, there was something unnerving about it. Something unexplainable and hard to pin down that tipped all that rationality into the irrational.

When the sellers opened the panel, she'd understood. The massive center chimney branched out its messy flues, efficient as the veins and arteries of a human heart. The home's long-dead builders had disguised this unbeautiful, suspiciously animal anatomy by walling in the twisting brick. This left behind a pleasing, even column—and empty space.

She remembered from history class the way early Americans rooted out the native, the organic, the wild. They breathed the ash of the Pequot and understood it as a reminder of their own anointment. They watched witches go limp and knew their acts righteous because God permitted them. Old New England preached efficiency and thrift, but those ideals were secondary to purity. And purity requires waste.

So behind those Puritan walls, dead space waited. A knock on the old wood paneling, and she heard hollow reverberation. Pull out a chink of plaster, poke a finger through, and she'd find it wriggling in nothingness. And behind that panel, under the stairs, around the chimney's intertwining arteries, the builders left the largest, most mysterious space.

"Why do you think they put in this room? Put in a secret door?" her husband had asked.

"The Underground Railroad, or maybe a place to hide from natives," the sellers had guessed. "Our kids, of course, say it's haunted."

Her husband's eyes had lit up at imagining the protected families, the besieging natives, the watchful dead.

She'd said nothing, but thought otherwise. Access like this made any patching of bricks and mortar easier, should the need ever arise. The house predated the Underground Railroad. And in this part of New England, conflict with the natives had moved elsewhere long before the house was built.

"Why seal it?" those early builders asked in her imagination. "It could be useful, someday."

After moving in, her husband hauled out a shop vac. The space had been littered with mortar dust, curled paper, general rubble, and a few desiccated mice. Being so much smaller, she was the one to crawl in and vacuum out the mess while he screwed the hinges of the panel in more securely. She remembered she hadn't been able to stand, but that it had been easy enough to move around the space on hands and knees given the amount of floor between the rough face of the chimney flues and the splintered side of the pine wall paneling.

She had called her husband's attention to an old electric heater that vented out the stairs, wires frayed and insides blackened with signs of burn damage. He awkwardly jimmied his wide shoulders into the hidden place to disconnect it and rip it out, rumbling and happily raging over the unsafety of the thing. Always anger over the irresponsibility of others. Always pleasure over fixing something, making it safe. Protecting them, after all, was such a part of the way he saw himself that tangible evidence of such purpose was a sparkling and beautiful thing. Never mind that she'd been the one to find the problem. To diagnose it. He was the one to say proudly on the phone to his parents, "You'll never believe the fire hazard I tore out from under the stairs. . . ."

"I don't know what we'll ever use the space for," her husband mused. "Given the temperature these bricks likely heat to when you get the beehive oven going, I dunno. Probably we should leave it alone."

The other hidden spaces created by the walled-in chimney had been filled over the centuries with things that increased comfort. Ducts, wires, and pipes were visible through smaller, less hidden access doors. With this one exception, practicalities like closets, shelves, indoor plumbing, and electric lighting had done away with the secret spaces that accumulated superstition, speculation, and imaginings.

That snowy night, the hidden place seemed altogether different than it had on the sunny day they'd cleaned it out. The face of the open passage was purest black. So black that even in that midnight room, she saw it as a darker pit. A dead mouth with a throat deeper than flint.

Somehow, the depth of that darkness made the rest of the room more visible. She saw her son stirring on the chair in the corner. She lunged, but before she could get to him, the little boy woke up and wailed. She slapped her hand over his tiny mouth. Her son's surprise and hurt was a tangible thing that vibrated out of his body and socked her in the stomach with shame.

"Shhh, it's all right, but we have to be quiet, quiet! Look, your sister is here, see? And we all have to be brave, and quiet."

The little boy's face kept on with its melt.

Oh no, oh no.

She recognized the beginning of screaming, of pained fearfulness, loud and bawling. The injustice of waking up, in the dark, and Mama putting her hand over my mouth, so mean, I'm cold, where am I? Yes, all that readable in the curl of her little boy's face. Her hand pressed tighter, and her son grabbed and scrabbled at her wrist.

"We have to be quiet," she whispered. "We have to be quiet! If we're not quiet the monster will get us!"

Both children reacted as though her words hurt. If she'd said it at any other time, one of them would've pulled a smile, said, "Nooooo, Mama, you're teasing! There's no such thing as monsters!" But waking them up, bringing them downstairs to the office they weren't allowed to play in, putting a hand over a mouth, pleading for quiet, surrounded by the darkness, the cold, the storm, sensing the pulse of her fear. A mother's fear. It came together in a kind of horror that made them recoil. And they were silent.

Thank goodness. Thank God.

She took her hand away from her son's mouth, illogically terrified that because of his silence, his stillness, she'd somehow suffocated him. But no, he made small snuffling noises.

Then both children began to whimper, to cry. Frustration rolled over her.

There's no time for this.

"No! No! Look, here's the hiding place, here's where we hide to be safe." She pointed to the open panel. "See? Look! And, see?" She snatched the blanket, the pillow off the armchair, held them up. "These will be cuddly, right? And we've got Fuzzydoll, and Pinkbunny, and we're going to snuggle in here and hide until the monster's gone. Cuddle with Mama. All right?"

Clutching the blanket, the pillow, she looked down at their wide-eyed, fear-filled faces.

This is a tough fucking sell.

How long had it been since she'd first seen the man? Minutes? Only minutes. But still far too long. What was he doing now?

Move. Move! You have to hide.

Anytime she showed impatience, urgency, the children reacted with suspicion and slowness. She saw herself in their eyes. Keyed up, whispering, drenched in sweat, shaking in a way she couldn't control, trying to lure them into a dirty and unfamiliar place.

Because what, you've got a throw pillow? A couple of stuffed animals? Act calm. Get them inside.

Behind them she saw her husband's computer on the desk. Grimaced resentfully at its unhelpful bulk. He'd somehow disabled the internet on it. Said otherwise it was too tempting to browse, connect to the wi-fi, procrastinate, to take himself out of what he called "work mode." He wouldn't even bring his phone into the office.

"I don't wanna go in there." Her daughter stared at the gaping maw of the hidden place, which seemed to exhale a dusty breath. The girl crossed her arms over her chest, hugging herself warmer, protecting the soft places.

I don't want to go in there, either, kid, Christ.

Move, hide!

Be patient. Be patient and calm and they'll listen. That's how it works.

"I know," she whispered. "But we're going to be brave and safe together, okay?"

"No, I don't wanna." Her daughter backed away a step.

"No," said her son, hiding behind her leg. He peeked out at the opening as though something could spring out of it at any minute. Eat him up.

In her desperation, her impatience, she understood the impulse of mother prey animals to devour their children to protect them, feeling a horrible need to swallow them whole, to hold her children inside her again.

I'll eat you up I love you so.

Then, simultaneously, all three looked up at the ceiling. From above them came the unmistakable sound of footsteps. A familiar noise in the house, but twisted. Because it was an un-family sound.

The man was in her daughter's room.

Together, they stopped breathing. They listened, heads tipped up, eyes unblinking as if that would let them see through the ceiling. All three frozen in the fearful reality of the moment.

She knew it was impossible, but drifting down like dust loosened from the floorboards came the certainty that the steps had a personality. They were strong. Impatient. Angry. They were the movement of someone who had been promised total control, and was being denied what he saw as his due. Someone who wanted to tinker with the things that really mattered. Wanted to play a game with stakes.

They heard a soft thump of something being dropped—*thrown?*—as it landed on the too-small area rug. They heard it roll onto the wood floor with a metal clatter.

Then, a roar, a guttural fury.

Because her daughter's room was empty. Because the little girl's bed was still warm.

"Get in," she hissed, "right now."

This time they didn't hesitate.

She threw the blanket and pillow through the dark opening, vanishing them. Crawled into the hidden place and reached hands out to help her son, then her daughter, inside. Told the quietly crying children to move farther in, to make room so she could clear and close the panel, frantically shushing them. She swiveled on hands and knees to pull the panel shut. But she turned too fast and hit her head hard on the corner of something invisible. Hit it violently enough that she thought she'd be sick. Brutally enough that she saw colors.

Anger, pulsing anger, dripped down her body. It made her fingertips spasm and her spine throb deep the way it always did when she hit her head. Stubbed a toe. Whacked a shin. The need to blame something, anything, for her own thoughtlessness. For the pain. Anything other than herself.

Goddamn stupid . . . thing.

You have to move. You have to get it shut. Did you bite your tongue? No. Then why do your teeth hurt? Why do you taste copper?

She put one hand in front of her forehead to protect herself, moved slower this time, and hit nothing. She pushed the panel closed. In the stunningly complete darkness, she slid her fingertips around the panel's edges to check it was lodged just right, felt its tight and even seal. She was grateful at how unexpectedly easy it had been to shut. Recalled how difficult it was to close the panel from the outside.

We're invisible now.

She leaned the unhurt side of her forehead on the rough wood of the hidden door, exhaling with relief.

A little rest.

How long had it been? Time stretched and pulled.

Think it through. You heard him, then it was less than a minute before you saw him. He stood maybe two minutes on the landing before walking away from you. And you grabbed the kids. What, another two, three minutes before you got down the stairs, got them in here? That's all it was. The whole world shattered in less than ten minutes.

"Where are you?" she whispered.

"Here, Mama."

She stayed low, stretched out her arm, and flailed blindly to protect herself from any other unseeable things that could hurt her.

"Don't stand up," she whispered. "Try and stay still. Snuggly. You don't want to hit your head like Mommy did. Here, let's wrap up in the cozy blanket."

"Snuggly." "Cozy." Yes, calm, safe words. How can you speak so quietly and be heard?

The children flanked her. She wrapped her arms around them and brought them close.

"Ow, Mama."

"Sorry, sorry."

Calm down, be gentle, you're scaring them.

Scaring them more.

"Mama's here, Mama's here," she whispered as they snuffled.

I'm here. You're here. This is real.

"No more whispering now, okay? No more crying. We have to be quiet as mice."

She thought of the loud *scritch-scratch* sounds of rodents in the attic.

"Quieter than mice," she said.

Together, buried behind the wall, absorbed into the ancient empty place, they sat and listened.

It felt to her that things were settling around them. The dust, the house, the darkness. At first, there was only the pulsing *thwap, thwap, thwap* of blood in her ears, of blood hammering the growing tenderness of the knot on her head. She blinked, disoriented by the fireworks of her eyelid undersides, how there was more light when her eyes were closed than when they were open. It made her remember touring a cave with her mother as a child, a roadside attraction somewhere along the highway. The guide had turned out his light to this kind of darkness and given a speech. Before too long, he'd said, such lack of light would cause your eyes to die, retinas zapped by disuse. "Bullshit," her mother had muttered to her in the complete blankness of that darkness. The profanity had made her smile, feel so adult, so much smarter than the guide. But in this particular moment, this particular place, losing her ability to ever see again felt like a certainty.

Three blind mice, three blind mice.

The pained throb of her head expanded outward, and she resisted the urge to touch the bump. The quiet grew thicker around them as the sound of her blood abated. The hitches of the children's crying slowed. It was difficult, so difficult, to resist the urge to crush them close again.

Babies, my babies.

It's so cold in here. Need to wrap the blanket around the kids better. What's that lump? The sippy cup in your pocket, right, yes. Can you lean back? Feel around a little. The floor is cold, but with the blanket—

Then, the footsteps began again. Together, the three of them stiffened and drew in their breath.

When did the footsteps stop? How did you not realize that? He's been quiet. Listening?

Her son let slip a "Mama!"

"Shhh."

The little boy buried his head against her, fuzzy and familiar in the robe. Nosed himself to deafness between her arm and middle. She pulled the blanket up around his shoulder awkwardly. That her little boy so clearly, so incorrectly, thought she could protect him, that he felt safer the closer he was to her, stabbed her in the heart.

How is it possible all they have is you?

Boom. Crick. A long crackle traveled from behind them, crossed above them. Yes, she knew these sounds. The origin of each noise, each weak spot, was clear in her head. The thousands upon thousands of everyday sounds were burrs, picked up and stuck to her memory during her innumerable overnight trips to the children's rooms over the last two years.

Don't wake them. Don't step here or there, close the door like so, watch out for that hinge, careful of the latch. If you wake them up, you have to get them back to sleep.

The man had left her daughter's room and was walking to her son's room. He'd stepped on the patched upstairs floorboard above the living room that always gave an empty echo. Then he'd put a foot on the long, thin board that ran nearly the width of the house. Every time she stepped on it in the hall, she'd hear it buckle ten feet away. On moving in she'd woken her son a handful of times before muscle memory set in. Trained by the house to avoid its weak spots.

It felt repellent to be able to track him this way. To feel him walking over things that were hers, triggering memories of creaks and middle-of-the-night mother's missteps.

Her daughter flinched lower and lower with each noise, a turtle drawing its head incrementally into its shell.

She leaned down to where she thought her daughter's ear must be in the dark and quietly breathed, "It's all right, you're very brave." The girl clung to her. She nuzzled her daughter's hair where she knew the gloss of black met the shock of white that framed one side of the girl's face. She greedily smelled the honey shampoo her daughter liked, and underneath it the thick baby musk of scalp and oil and skin that hadn't yet been scrubbed away by age.

When does that smell fade? Maybe for a mother, never. And he wants to snatch it away.

Next came the thudding muteness of steps on her son's carpeted floor, vibrating like a distant earthquake. That strange shuffle in the air, was that him opening the closet? That rattle—he might have bumped into the side table that didn't sit level.

You're grinding your teeth.

She opened her mouth wide to stretch her pained jaw. She rolled her head to release the creeping tension in her neck. It was useless with the pounding knot dizzying her.

A distant *whoosh*. A vague rolling noise. She couldn't identify these sounds, and she strained to hear better, to understand.

Her daughter breathed slower now. Calmer. Up and down, in and out. Listening.

She was flooded with gratefulness that they were here, hidden in this little den, instead of out there, with that intruder standing over her daughter or her son, like he would've otherwise been this very minute. Using that vague weapon. Other weapons.

But now you're trapped.

Her chest felt as though it were being crushed by some enormous hand.

You've trapped them.

The walls moved closer.

There was no other choice. No other choice but to hide.

She stretched and searched to hear anything more.

Maybe somehow things didn't creak and he walked out. Out of the room, out of the house, gone, gone, gone.

If wishes were horses then beggars would ride. If wishes were fishes we'd eat and not die.

BOOM.

They all three startled like deer, flanks jolting to stiffness. The little girl cried out weakly, dove her face deeper into her mother's robe.

The man was immediately above them. The sound was a foot on the same step that had made such a racket under her daughter's only a few minutes ago. An eternity ago. Inside the hidden place, it was like a thunderclap after a just-missed lightning strike, overclose and deafening.

Had he heard her daughter's thin wail? The man stood still, soundless.

And then there was light. On went the single candelabra bulb that hung in the little chandelier dangling at the top of the stairs. Maybe he'd turned it on to avoid hitting his head again. Maybe without her familiarity with the stairs, with only the cloud-choked moonlight through the windows to guide him, the man had been taken aback by that first booming sound, surprised by the unmodern shallowness of the treads.

The light dripped through chinks between stair steps and risers. Fell through cracks here and there around wood knots. Flowed brightest of all through the vent, the one that had been connected to the dangerous, burnt-out heater her husband had proudly torn out. The vent they'd left lodged in the stair riser, because why not? Even though there was no heater, even though it was just a window into the hidden place, might as well let air circulate. Might as well be sure the useless space didn't get moldy, become a problem. A pain to patch, anyhow, if you don't really need to.

The light seemed to her an awful, world-ending thing. It hurt the way light did when a quick sweep of curtain woke her, drawing an arm up to shield her face like a black-and-white movie vampire. Hiss and burn.

Will he be able to figure it out, now that the light's on? Will he be able to see us?

The rectangle of light through the vent splashed onto the edge of the blanket. Slowly, watching her hand shake so heavily she could barely pinch its corner, she pulled the blanket toward her so that the light illuminated only brick and dust. Nothingness.

She could feel her daughter's fear, the shaky heaving the girl was silencing against her, against her soft robe. Her son's heart beat like a tiny caught bird's. He was crying. But quietly.

Quietly enough?

BOOM. BOOM. BOOM. BOOM.

Down he came. Each footstep a press on her heart, her lungs. Her stomach twisted, bubbling and sloshing so loudly she was certain it would give them away.

You need a bathroom.

How ridiculous. How urgent. Hold it. Like you have a choice?

BOOM. BOOM. BOOM.

Dust sifted down on them from between the stair treads.

Don't sneeze.

BOOM. BOOM.

She saw his sneakers through the vent cover.

His feet were so large on the shallow stairs he had to walk sideways down them, like an elderly man descending a steep hill. The sneakers were yellowed and lightly fissured. She saw a faint Union Jack on the side. Drooping grayed laces.

The light could be a good thing. Blind him again. Even if he noticed that vent, even if he peered through it, it would be hard for him to see anything.

BOOM. BOOM.

She kept her arms around the children as gently as she could, rubbing their backs with hands so quaky each felt like its own separate animal. With the light she could see the children trembling, tight and fearful. She leaned close to one ear, then another, and whispered below sound.

"Shhhhh . . ."

BOOM.

The man was down the stairs. She saw bits of him hatched and fragmented through the vent. Dark pants. A dark shirt. Pale skin. The back of his head, dirty blond and messy.

Again there was a clawing somewhere deep in her brain, a whiff of something familiar in his immense size, his shape, the sense that the man was someone she'd known long ago. It was the same feeling she got when she saw someone across the street whose face she recognized but couldn't place.

Where's his coat?

She pictured him taking off a jacket, hanging it neatly above the snow boots he'd changed out of. So polite.

He faced away from the vent, toward the old double doors on the front of the house. There was a lump in his back pocket.

The weapon?

Bright pink, rectangular.

Your phone. He has your phone in his pocket.

She rubbed her mouth, her lips, to try to make it feel more real.

At least you saw it. At least you know. Because what if you made a run for it, tried to get to your phone, only to be cornered in the bedroom, no escape, no way to phone anyone?

Cold comfort.

He stood still. He was probably noticing that the double doors were locked and bolted from the inside. Dead doors, unused due to their obvious impracticality given the larger entry at the back in the modern addition. The man pulled the thick iron bolt with a loud *chunk*. Fiddled with the ancient latch. Swore in a quiet whisper so normal and human it disoriented her.

She knew the problem, of course. The house was full of different antique latches, each irritating in its own way. These particular doors were fastened together with a latch locked by a little iron bar that hung on a nail. It was always frustrating to deal with, that bar loose on that nail, because if you didn't keep holding the bar up with one hand while lifting the latch with the other, the bar would fall, swing down on its little nail, and interrupt the lift of the latch so you couldn't open the doors.

The man gave a loud grunt of annoyance before figuring it out and swinging the doors open. The freezing air whooshed through the vent and hit them in the hidden place, the shock of it making the children startle and shiver.

He leaned out into the storm as flakes swirled around him. Then he straightened and closed the doors.

Click, went the latch. *Clunk*, went the bolt.

Her index finger tore rapid and rough at the cuticle of her thumb, and her stomach twisted sickeningly.

Who is he? You can't know, because you can't even see him. Not fully. Didn't see his face, so shadowed in the dark upstairs.

The man moved, vanishing from her view out of the vent grate. She heard and felt him open the door to the small closet next to the stairs and rummage through whatever was hanging there with a swishing noise. Apparently done, his sounds traveled toward the playroom. There was a waterfall clatter of Legos swept aside by the sweep of the door. A *click* of the light switch, and they were again thrown into darkness.

She recognized the sound of toys kicked aside. Over the last two months, detached and finding it difficult to care about much at all, let alone how clean the house was, she'd stopped making the children tidy regularly. As a result, the playroom had grown well beyond the bounds of its usual mess. She knew the frustration of stepping on toys, of trying to navigate that room. But the man's passage through that child's space was different. For her, indifferent annoyance. For him, seething indignation.

A smash. Something bursting into pieces against the wall. Something else fractured into the floorboards with a crunch.

"My creations!" her daughter breathed.

Yes, probably.

The man had most likely destroyed one or more of the special, oversized Lego constructions her daughter kept assembled around the perimeter of the room. The castle that tapered and widened again, the ship peopled with fantastical creatures, the spiral rainbow stairs that climbed high as her daughter could reach, tiptoed on a stool.

She imagined these flights of imagination leveled. Felt a surge of impotent anger as she remembered the quiet hours her daughter spent, head tilted, chewing her lip, building and enlarging and spinning the pieces out of patient fantasy.

It was an evergreen pain, knowing that things that took so long to build had been, could be, so easily destroyed.

She drew the children closer.

"They're things, and things can be fixed," she whispered. "I'll help you fix them. Shhh."

"That wasn't Daddy," her daughter said so low it might have been meant only for herself. "I thought it might be Daddy."

Her throat tightened with longing, with the illogical hope her husband might somehow come home through the storm to rescue them.

Don't cry.

"It's not Daddy," she agreed.

"That is a big man."

The pit in her stomach cratered deeper. She urgently needed to use the bathroom, to expel everything, her whole churning gut.

You've been thinking of yourself as the lone witness. But you're not. You're not! The way they stared at the ceiling, tracked those footsteps. Remember how they hopped to, right into the hidden place?

You've been hoping you're just crazy, all this time, part of you has still been hoping you were just losing it. Closing your eyes and wishing it away.

"It's all right," she whispered. "Mommy's here. Shh."

How nice it would be, to be crazy instead of correct. For it all to be a psychotic break. To have her husband come down those stairs. She'd pop out of the hidden place, relieved—elated!—to meet his look of confusion. She'd watch his expression transition into horror as she babbled explanations. How could she lock her children away behind walls? Frighten them in the middle of the night? She faded warm into picturing those plodding, everyday consequences. Anger, and psychiatrists, and divorce, and a padded cell. How lovely, how comforting, to live in that alternate reality a moment, where her mind had unhinged and there was no danger of violence from anyone but herself. Those stakes were so low! So beautifully low.

Reality can be more disorienting than dreams.

"Mama?" Her son's voice had a watery sound, quaver of suppressed tears.

What a brave boy. The best boy.

"Mama, you said monsters didn't exist."

She lowered her head, feeling a great weight descend. "I'm sorry," she whispered. "I lied."

inding herself walled into her own home wasn't the first time she'd been forced to acclimate to a new reality, wishing that her own mind was the problem.

Nearly two years before, her husband hung up a call with his parents and told her, "My mom has cancer."

She felt as though she'd stepped out of herself. She blinked at him stupidly.

No, not that word. You must be hearing things. Imagining things. Something wrong with you.

"What? She's—what?"

Her husband paused a long time, staring into middle distance before adding, "My dad'll be a nightmare."

"Your—your poor mom," she managed to stammer.

Her husband rested his head in his hands. "A nightmare. He doesn't even know how to run the washing machine."

Her own father lived alone. Her mother had been proudly thrifty, repairing broken appliances, computers, and bicycles for friends and neighbors. But after she died, he focused obsessively on fulfilling his wife's "waste not, want not" admonitions. He collected broken things, clogging his house with them as if he thought that the right thing, the perfectly imperfect thing, might lure his wife back from oblivion. Over the years his walls of split wicker chairs, speakers bristling fuzzed wires, dusty motherboards grew so impenetrable that when she took the children to visit, they stayed at a hotel, pushed from the house by the piles of his beloved, moldering memorials.

Yet even her father knew how to use a washing machine.

"Your dad was a successful lawyer. He's capable. Maybe he'll rise to the occasion?" She knew this was pure denial, and her voice faltered. "Not that we shouldn't help your mom, obviously, I'm not saying that."

Her husband shook his head. "He's not going to lift a finger."

She nodded. She knew. For years she'd silently observed her father-in-law, trying to understand him, trying to comprehend the vicissitudes of his moods. She'd focused close, as if the older man were a specimen under a microscope, acting and reacting to this or that stimulus. She'd eyed him from afar, hoping to get a whole, telescopic picture. She'd experimented with questions about his childhood, his beliefs, the older man a cow heart, a fetal pig laid on a metal lab table, in need of dissection to make sense of him.

When her husband (then boyfriend) introduced her to his parents senior year of college, a fluttering hope pounded her heart.

A real family. Mother, father, child.

Physically, her husband, compact and dark like his mother, barely resembled his tall, fair, thin father. But at that first meeting she recognized clear similarities.

Both talkative. Athletic. Confident. Loud. Quick to laugh. Able to wick a smile out of even the most pinched-faced stranger.

"You know what I like about you? You've got conversation enough for the both of us," she'd teased her husband early in their relationship.

But it was true. Next to her gregarious husband she felt a part of things, despite being quiet. Despite being chronically incapable of small talk.

Her mother-in-law was quiet, too, only chiming in to compliment the food. Note the weather. Prompting her husband and son to discuss their day.

Is she the opposite of you, quiet because she's only capable of small talk? Or is she like you, instinctually holding her cards close to her chest?

A few weeks after he introduced her to his parents, she was studying in her husband's room when he told his father over the phone he wouldn't be applying to law school. *Crack!* went the superficial, candy-colored veneer of her first impression as the older man screamed admonitions about expectations, wasted money, his bellowing tinny over the phone. "You've lost all respect! What the hell am I supposed to tell the men at the club?"

A month later her husband told his father he'd switched his major from political science to photography—a decision effectively made years before as he'd accumulated art credit after art credit. The calls became a constant, the phone vibrating with the older man's fury.

"You don't know what real work is. You want to swan into— what—some wussy little art world? Be famous? It's humiliating."

Why did her husband always answer the phone?

"He'll get over it. He's all smoke and no fire."

But her husband's father refused to pay his tuition. When his son still didn't back down, still didn't agree to go to law school, took out loans to pay for his last year of school himself, his father refocused his venom.

"I didn't raise you like this. We've worked toward you being an attorney your whole life. You never behaved this way before you met *that girl*. Christ. She's disfigured!"

Her husband hung up on him. But even then, fuming and pacing, he picked up the phone when the man instantly called back, apoplectic.

"How dare you interrupt me?"

If that's what his family thinks of you, it might end this relationship. His father might wear him down. Or wear you out. And do you really want someone like that in your life?

"They're my family. I'm their only son. Once I start earning money, he'll relax."

Her husband had to be right. Family must be worth it. What did she know, really? There were the nine beautiful years her mother was still alive, idealized, she was sure, to a luminous sheen of perfection. There were the stable years when Grandma moved from Alabama to live with them, full of strict, loyal love and clear expectations. But ever since Grandma's death, she'd been alone, her father dedicating himself to the shattered fragments of things he'd never repair.

To her surprise, the conflict redoubled her husband's commitment, as though she were the symbol of his newly grown backbone. And despite her own reservations, she closed her eyes to see family hovering aspirationally in a beautiful future.

Every relationship has challenges, she told herself, which was true. *Family is earned*, she told herself, which, she'd come to learn, was more complicated.

And always there was her husband. The way he kissed her forehead. Wiped the corner of his eyes after laughing at her jokes. Bragged about her work, framing and hanging his favorite of her patent illustrations. His arm rested light around her waist when they entered a crowded party, and she would think, *I belong.*

Her husband didn't judge her because of her dad's fortresses of wreckage. Why should she end things over his father's blazing volatility?

After college, father and son reached a détente that required everyone to tensely pretend there had never been any conflict, an approach diametrically opposed to her straightforward arguments with her own father.

Invariably when her in-laws visited, she and her husband would seize gratefully on the banality of discussing the rain. The PGA Tour. Cleaning products.

Eventually she tacitly understood the boundaries of their civility. Understood why her mother-in-law only seemed capable of small talk, taking refuge in its dull safety. Her husband's progress with his photography was off limits. Securing her job at a large firm as a patent illustrator was similarly a forbidden topic, her father-in-law's face hardening at the reminder of her career being better paid and more intellectual than his son's attempts to sell his photos. Years later, her husband's success, the way his aerial photography became their main source of income and allowed her to go freelance, to pick up their children from school every day, couldn't be acknowledged; it was untouchable proof of the old man's fallibility.

Sometimes they'd accidentally stumble across the unmarked margins of a conversational minefield. Her father-in-law was certain that something unidentifiable was being slowly stolen from him, imperceptibly siphoned away. The lightest reference to any news caused him to sputter vagaries about the way certain people had become unacceptably shrill, over-righteous, uptight, perverse— an endless list of often-conflicting euphemisms that did heavy lifting.

At any darkening of his weather, her mother-in-law's voice dropped to a soothing register. "You are so right, dear. Of course you are."

Unlike his mother, her husband silently let his father rage, waiting out his storm.

Ignoring him is probably better than trying to argue, isn't it? Anyway, your husband fought for the most important things. Partner. Career. Life.

Over the course of years, the yearning for family, for acceptance, incrementally wore away, a stone eroded by waves.

"Sometimes there just isn't any water in a well," Grandma's remembered voice reminded her in its southern drawl. "You gotta draw your bucket right on up, hon."

When her daughter was born, her mother-in-law's joy was visibly tainted by the old man's irritation with the baby's crying, over how the baby's mere existence constantly interrupted him. Within half an hour of their visit to the hospital to meet their grandchild, her father-in-law wordlessly strode out into the hall, red-faced as the infant, her mother-in-law hurrying after him, apologizing.

"We should've made him feel more welcome," her husband insisted.

Good riddance. There's no water in that well.

At her son's third birthday party, her father-in-law eyed his grandson through narrowed lids as the little one cuddled in her arms, sucking his thumb and giggling as she made silly faces.

"Quite the mama's boy, isn't he?"

"I mean, yeah," she sputtered. "He's a toddler."

Her father-in-law raised a knowing eyebrow. "You can't spoil him like the girl. Boys will rip a wuss to shreds."

White-hot fury burned any response out of her throat.

Her husband sighed. "We aren't spoiling anyone, Dad."

She saw the older man's words had been designed to stick a knife in her side. Twist it. Worse, she recognized that her father-in-law had sliced open a worry about the future she'd shoved away, embarrassed at how it chewed at her heart, insidious. Since the day he was born, her son had been soft and pliant. He nursed easily. Snuggled close. Stared up at her adoringly, tiny hands reaching for her, a little arm tightening behind her shoulder in a hug, his head resting blissfully against her neck like it belonged there. He slept with one of his sister's discarded dolls. Carried it with him everywhere. Wept when he saw anyone hurt or if she raised her voice. He cried at every pre-school morning drop-off, sad to see her leave. And she loved it, she did. His open affection. His sensitivity. His unselfconscious need for closeness.

But she worried about the world.

Mama's boy. Wuss. They'll rip him to shreds.

She seethed with the possible truth of the older man's words as she turned away from his gaunt, goading face.

Don't let him bait you.

But her father-in-law had found a bruise to press. Every visit, she'd sweep her son away from the old man's gravelly voice, his wagging finger. "You need to man up. Stop crying."

She felt the moldering decay of hatred sprouting in her skull.

Don't let him make you a worse person.

"You're my tough little guy. And you're kind, too. You can be both at the same time," she'd tell her teary-eyed son in the wake of his grandfather's eviscerations.

The space between visits allowed her to pretend the older man didn't exist for months at a time, a relief that untensed her jaw joints, let her hatred go dry. But there was no more pretending after hearing, "Stage four. Aggressive but operable. Years left, with luck and proper care."

She'd tasted bitter resentment at the news. Because just like her husband, her first reaction wasn't concern over his mother's coming pain, fright, and even death. No. Her first thought was that she didn't want to deal with her father-in-law, the way he would inevitably pull all gravity in his direction.

This isn't about him. Or you.

At her husband's urging, they looked at real estate close to the senior living community where her in-laws were ensconced, out where suburban met rural. They'd discussed moving before—the kids were getting big, good schools, room to play—but the cookie-cutter suburban homes they'd toured had never been enough to lure them out of the city. Then, not so unusually for New England, on a meandering street of large properties populated by nineteenth-century farmhouses, 1980s split-levels, and pre-crash McMansions, they discovered a blackened center chimney colonial, built in 1722, situated on five acres of open pasture rimmed by woods, complete with its own graveyard.

Everything proportional but nothing square. Wrinkled window glass distorting the outdoors to the flux of water. No floorboard the same width, same length. No stair level. Unique, beautiful, worn.

Of course you like it. It's as marked as you are.

Yes, the house was creaky, impractical, hard to heat. Yes, she and her husband were both nervous about the caregiving ahead. But the prospect of being part of the home's history, patching its broken places, gave her a purpose for moving apart from her mother-in-law's illness.

So they bought it. They moved. They dedicated themselves to helping her mother-in-law while they slowly made the house their own.

And now the wood, brick, and mortar of the house's innermost refuge was all that stood between her and the intruder.

6

After the swish of the door, the destruction of her daughter's creations, the man's footsteps faded.

A locker-room reek hit her, and she realized it was the smell of her own sweat. That she was still sweating while miserably trembling with the freeze of the hidden place was yet one more bit of unreality. The children were the only warm thing in the world, bodies nuzzling close against her. Their hummingbird hearts vibrated in their tiny chests. Her mouth filled with dust and terror as she imagined the man with an ear to their wall, listening.

He might be in the office. He might be right on the other side of the paneling. You can't know that, don't be ridic—

Then came the distinct crackle of the weakest floorboard in the house, worn so thin over the centuries that every time she put a foot on it she'd think, *You'll have to replace that, it'll only get worse.*

That floorboard was at the entrance to the office. The man's unseeable presence crawled through her heart, her blood.

How thick is this wall? Just simple pine boards, the decorative paneling nailed over it. Yes, the hidden door's surround was about an inch deep when you crawled through, maybe a little more.

An inch of wood between us and him.

Another step, then quiet. She tried to picture what he was doing. Taking in the details of the room. Looking for where they could be hiding. Rifling through the file drawers. Going through the prints her husband stored in the oak map chest, the larger ones rolled in the corner, the framed patent illustrations and photos of the vacant highways, the empty cities on the walls. Maybe he was sitting in the armchair. Taking a load off. Having a breather.

A light twang traveled clear and warm through the wood of the wall. He'd brushed the strings of her husband's guitar, propped on its stand next to the desk. Not accidentally, either, but the way a person who knows how to play a guitar did when they saw one. She imagined his flat thumb on the strings. Intimate. It forced her eyes closed. A thousand happy memories of her husband's firm, strong hands traveling those strings, those same sounds, and here was this man, claiming it, capsizing all that beauty.

"Hello?" he said.

The children rustled in surprise, as if out of habit they wanted to answer and were resisting. She choked on her own spit and shock. Her thoughts ran in panicked circles, and her bones felt empty as a bird's.

He knows we're here!

"Hello?" he said again, louder.

How?

"Shhhhh," she said to the children, so low she wasn't sure if they'd hear her.

"I see you," he said, voice a singsonging lilt.

No, no, no.

Her daughter groaned into the robe, muffled. Her son started to quietly cry. She rubbed his back, shushing under her breath.

Of course he's found us. Of course he knows we're here! Once he saw the front stairs, he must have figured out we came down that way from the kids' rooms.

The despair cracked over her head, trickling down through her brain.

So it's over, it's all over. It'll begin now. You've failed them.

"I see you! Time to stop playing this little game." Again the childlike warble of the man's voice, all this just for fun, all this to amuse, was so incongruous with the misery of her reality that she squeezed her nails into her palms until the half-moons dug deep enough to hurt.

This is real. You are here. Breathe. You need to get ready. You'll have to wedge yourself between the bricks and the hidden door. That will make it almost impossible for him to open. And he's big. He won't be able to get in easily even if he destroys the panel. Keep him out as long as you can. Kick him in the head. That's it, that's all that's left. And if he gets in—scratch his eyes out.

But she couldn't move. Couldn't make herself unhook the children from her robe, couldn't force herself to risk revealing where they were hiding. Not until she was sure they were lost.

The man's voice was soft and round, as though he were talking to a beloved dog. "I don't want to hurt anyone. Of course not! It's just that a little birdie told me you had a safe, that's all. Just want you to open that safe, give me a little money, and I'll be on my way. Okey-dokey?"

Although she desperately wanted this to be true, *just money, here you go and bye-bye*, up popped the memory of a long-ago coworker who had been robbed.

"We woke up and our laptops were taken," the coworker told the group that gathered to hear the story. "Wallets, even prescription pain pills gone. The scariest thing, though, was they stole our phones, his and mine, both plugged in right next to where we were sleeping, on our nightstands."

Yes, they could all see it. The objects lifted from beside the sleeping faces, pulled away from dreaming breaths. Just that close. Just that vulnerable.

The coworker had nervously twirled her long hair around a finger, said, "The police told us it was good we didn't wake up. The police said when a homeowner wakes up, that's when you get trouble. Burglars want to take things in the easiest way possible. They don't want witnesses. Imagine? Imagine if we'd woken up?" Faces had gone blank with that imagining. That vision of violence. "In a way," the coworker said weakly, "we were lucky."

He must know we've seen him. No way he just wants money. If that's all he wanted, he'd be hiding his face. He wouldn't have a weapon ready. And he probably saw the safe upstairs. It's not like it's well hidden. He's using that as an excuse.

Liar.

"Little ones?" the man sounded plaintive, even lonely. "Won't you come out? I'm not a bad guy. I just need some help. I'm not as lucky as you. My mommy never looked out for me. Just want your mama to help me with some money and then I'll go."

The words shot through her body with an electric hum. The man knew her husband wasn't there—he was speaking only to her and the children. But the children's bodies relaxed slightly. She imagined their feeling the same hope she had fought, thinking this wasn't a monster after all. Just someone who would leave if he got what he wanted.

"Shhh," she whispered close to one ear, then another.

Next came the familiar squeak of the old lounge chair in the corner, its springs complaining of the man's enormous weight as he sat down. After a long pause, he said sullenly, "I don't like it here anymore. This place crawls when it's empty. Every room has too many doors, and all the stairs are uneven. There are voices, noises, and no one's there." He waited a moment, then added loudly, "I just want to get what I'm owed and leave."

After a long, silent pause, she was only barely able to hear the man say almost wistfully, "This isn't how it's supposed to go. It should all be happening."

Another wheeze and crack from the chair—the man getting up. Light creaks penetrated the wall as he walked back and forth across the room.

"You don't want me to bring out the bad guy, do you?" She could almost see him giving a showy tilt of his head, an overexaggerated shrug, the way she did when she explained to the children the consequences of their actions. *You don't want a time-out, do you?*

"If I have to, I can bring out the bad guy. I don't want to, but you just aren't listening." The man sounded acutely regretful, as though this were a thing beyond him, the inevitable result of their noncompliance.

As her children trembled and buried their whimpers against her, etching deep through her mind came the thought, *He's very good at scaring children.*

She pulled her son and daughter closer as if it were possible to comfort them in advance of whatever he might say next. She waited, straining to hear through the quiet. He took so long to speak again that time pulled around and over her like a wet sheet, dragging and catching on every creak, every groan of wood and brick, collecting awful anticipation and snagging on the illogical hope that he had left.

At last, so close to their wall and so loud it made the children startle like fawns against her body, he called out, "Come out, come out, wherever you are!"

His voice had ticked down an octave and rasped with impatience. Its sound was so changed, so otherworldly and full of taunting malice, that she had to shake off the sudden conviction that a different person entirely was speaking.

"Don't you want to come out, little piglet? Away from that dirty old sow?"

Her fear forced something simultaneously solid and soft, the size of a pea, from her stomach into the back of her throat. She swallowed it back down and tasted bile.

Please, please let them stay quiet.

She lightly rubbed the children's shaking bodies with her shaking hands. She tried to protect them from this new strangeness by muffling the barbed-toothed horror of that voice, embracing them so that each had an ear pressed to her side, each had her arm over their other ear.

"Stuck-up old pig," scratched the curled tinfoil of this new voice. "Just like all the rest. Don't see what's right in front of you. Think nothing watches you from dark corners. A strong man watches from a corner. He sees everything. The tender little piglet. The old spotted sow walking on two legs."

Her daughter moaned aloud into the robe, as if these words pained her.

Then, a slippery, skipping noise, the sound of infected lung laughter.

A slew of her grandmother's Southernisms jumped up unbidden. *He's half off plumb. He's nuttier than a five-pound fruitcake. Loony as all get-out. Mad as a wet hen.*

Yes, the man must be splitting apart, his marbles tumbling out and around him.

"A strong man sees piggies are delicious. He sees all the rest for what they are. Weak men with weak desires. Urges tied up. Defeated. Civilized."

A forked tongue stroked over the word "civilized."

"A weak man whimpers at the slimmest female obstacle. He thinks she's something more than the used-up nothing she is."

She buried her face for comfort close to the scalp of one child, then the other.

Of course he's crazy! Who else would be here, doing this? Who else would have hunted us down except someone not right in the head? Twisted and warped and strange.

"But a strong man? He steps over. Steps over all your prissy little rules. Free. A gentleman? He takes what he's owed. What he deserves."

Her head swiveled involuntarily to track the path of the voice. Its frantic, disembodied route penetrated the wall here, then there, high then low, in a way that dizzied her.

He's pacing, that's all.

She imagined the voice slipping out of flabby lips, a stretched rictus smile that matched the cruel joy of the instructive tone.

"All these things you do to try and make me soft, to make me a sheep. To take my pill and like it. No. I step over. I've stepped over."

He's stepped over rules. Sheep and pigs. That's what you are to him. Oh God.

Silence. Silence from the children, silence on the other side of the wall. Her head pounded in pain, swam with disorientation; her heartbeat reverberated in her ears as she listened, fighting the sureness that the man had transformed into some unknown creature that could match the horror of that voice and its bizarre words. She tried to shoo away the conviction that she could physically feel this monster listening ever closer for her and the children.

Stop it. It's just a man. Don't let him scare you. He's trying to scare you into making noise.

"Little gir-rl? Little pig-gy?"

Her daughter's fingers tightened around her arm to the point of pain in response to the summoning lilt of that voice. Her protectiveness flared, and she felt the depravity of the man's intentions bumping like braille under her skin.

"Don't you know you should be grateful? Once it starts you'll see. It's in your nature. Don't you know the whole point of little piggies is to be *delicious*?"

The word "delicious" was exhaled with such a drawn-out sibilant hiss of deep desire that her heart contracted. She plunged her face to her daughter's beloved cheek, inhaled the girl's smell, hugged her narrow hip bone and trembling, birdlike limbs. She pulled the soft and bony body closer to prove that her daughter was present, real, safe, alive.

Maybe he's crazy. Maybe not. He's trying to frighten us into giving ourselves away. Don't let it work. It's not a monster. It's a man.

"Enough of quietness." His voice was a low, threatening rumble. "A woman learns in full submission. I'll find you. You're mine, and that's all you are. I'll find you. Because you want me to."

The words were so steady, so filled with predatory resolve, she closed her eyes against them.

Footfalls moved heavy across the rug. The needs-replacing board groaned as the man left the office. She became aware of the silent, still attentiveness of the children beside her.

How do you explain this? How do you keep them quiet after that? Breathe, breathe.

She could feel the space the man had stood in on the other side of the wall. She had a clear picture of his demon smile. Could smell his inhuman reek.

Instinctively she flinched, registering the voice again. But it was distant; it traveled from another room. She slouched with relief. She made out the word "piggy." The word "delicious."

Stop. Stop thinking of him as some creature. He's a man. Which is worse. He's doing a voice. "I'll get you, my pretty!" "Why so serious?" "My precious." That's all. That's it. Playing the part of the bad guy. Which he is. He's very, very bad. Is he in the kitchen? Is it possible that he never knew you were here?

That he's going to do that same fucking terrifying song and dance in every room to try and scare you out?

Yes. Because he doesn't know where you are. It's all right. It's all right.

But as the walls pressed in around her, as she felt her mind disjointed by terror, felt how tightly she and the children were wrapped, dead ended, no escape, the way time expanded so horribly long and narrow in front of them, she knew that nothing was all right.

Things might never be all right again.

7

Her daughter pulled at her sleeve. Breathed into her ear, "Mommy, what is he?"

Into her mind's eye sprung a fully formed image of the man turning inside out to reveal matted fur, yellow eyes, needled teeth.

Stop it.

"It's just a man," she whispered. She rested her cheek on the part of her daughter's hair, pulled her little boy close, inhaled their precious familiarity. Felt her son rub his wet, dribbling nose dry on her robe. "It was just the man doing a scary voice."

"But I know him." Her daughter's voice dripped desperation. "I know that voice. The man in the corner. From my dreams."

Her head throbbed. No matter how she forced her thoughts toward reason, she felt overtaken by the nightmarish strangeness and physical discomfort. The otherworldliness of that voice, describing how it was owed, how it was better, clung to her like an oily film.

"From a dream?" she whispered. "What do you mean?"

"It's his voice." Her daughter gripped her wrist tightly now, terror lapping contagiously through the darkness. "He said he watches from the corner, Mama! Just like the man in my dreams. The Corner man."

Dreams, not one dream. A recurrent monster that had been haunting her little girl.

"I have bad dreams, too," she said, thinking of her own night-mares and the shadows that stalked her there. "We all sometimes dream scary things. But this, it's—he's—a man."

"No. The Corner—he sounded different."

Her daughter was right. The scraping threat of the Corner was altogether unlike the bizarrely childish patter of the voice that had preceded it.

Don't be crazy, letting yourself get sucked into a little girl's dreams. Stop thinking of him as this Corner. He's a person.

"Mama," her son softly cried, "Mama, I don't like it. Is it a ghost?"

"Shhhhh, please, loves. We have to be quiet. There's no such thing as ghosts. It's not a ghost. Not a nightmare. Not this—Corner—thing, from your dreams. It's just a man. I'm so sorry, so sorry this is happening. But we're here, together."

"You said it was a monster," her son sniffled. "It's a monster."

You shouldn't have said that. Why did you say that?

Because it's true.

"I—it's not a real monster," she said. "It's a bad man. A mon-strous man."

"He hides in the corner," her daughter insisted. "He said so. I know him. He watches me from the corner when he thinks I'm asleep. When I'm sleeping."

Why didn't she tell you this before? She can't know him. But don't you know him? There's something familiar, something—what is it? Isn't there something?

Her sense that yes, she'd seen this Corner man before, heard that voice, ripped at the base of her neck like a pin left in fabric.

She felt sick with the horror of the voice's unidentifiable familiar-ity, of the dark room, of being stalked, the unreality of the situation. The way things felt like themselves but also not, familiar but utterly different, as in dreams.

It is like a dream. But it's real. And it's happening to you.

And you have to make them be quiet.

"I know it was scary. I know it didn't sound like the same person talking, but it was. He's not a monster or a ghost. Not a dream. No Corner man. He's a person. An angry person. It was scary, like nightmares, but it was just him doing a scary voice."

"Why? Why would he do that?"

"Honey, he's a bad guy, like he said. He's trying to frighten us. So that we make noise. So he can find us. We have to be quiet."

Delicious.

"Is he trying to hurt us?" her daughter whimpered.

She was afraid that if she told the truth, the children would dissolve into fear, cry, give themselves away, and in the inky blackness she couldn't speak.

"Is he going to hurt us?" her daughter asked again. "Mommy?"

It was always difficult, lying to the children. Her husband had gotten angry when she'd matter-of-factly explained what had happened to her mother after her daughter asked why they'd never met their "other grandma." He'd been even angrier when the children blithely recounted to him her detailed description of where babies came from. He couldn't understand why, without any discussion with him, she'd answer direct questions honestly, risk having a five- and eight-year-old informing their friends about the birds and the bees, about violent grandmother death, yet still keep up the farce of the Easter Bunny and Santa Claus. She couldn't explain it, either, just found herself oddly incapable of lying to those gentle, upturned faces when they asked her straightforward questions about things so fundamental.

She rubbed her mouth, hand gritty from the grime of the hidden place. The children stiffened when, from a different part of the house, far enough away words were impossible to make out, again came the rumbling sound of the Corner trying to frighten them out of a new room.

"He won't hurt us, because he won't find us, okay?" she at last managed to say.

"Was the Corner man talking about me, Mama?" Her daughter's voice wavered. "Was the little girl he talked about me?"

She shouldn't have to think about these things. She's so little. So little.

"I think so, love." She stroked her daughter's back. She tried to keep the sob out of her voice. "We all need to stay quiet and safe together. We're a team."

Her daughter thought a moment, then said, "Okay, Mama."

Such a brave little girl. And he was talking about you, too, wasn't he? The "female obstacle," he said. The "old sow." That's you. "I step over," he said. You're one of the obstacles he's stepping over to get what he wants.

Her son's voice burbled with tears. "I want him to go away."

"I know, love." She ran fingers through her son's hair as steadily as she could manage.

The windows rattled in their frames. The storm was picking up. Frozen air came rushing down the chimney, forcing dust through the masonry around them. The whole stack seemed to sway, surrounding them with the crunching sounds of brick on old wood.

He watches from corners. Hides in nightmares. Watches her sleep, she said. Of course it's nightmarish to her. Of course she's afraid. You have to be the calm one. Think of next steps. Don't let him win.

You need to get the children comfortable so they can stay quiet.

"Let me move the blanket so I can wrap you two up," she whispered. "So you can sleep. We need to stop whispering, though. Stop talking."

She guided them slowly, blindly. On all fours, she dragged the blanket as deep into the hidden place as she could, as far away from the opening of the vent as possible, one hand up to protect her pulsing skull from further damage. She spread out the blanket. Patted hands around to find the pillow, and placed it.

It was narrower where the space backed up to the domed shape of the beehive oven set into the living room fireplace. Feeling with her fingertips, she got an idea of how tightly they were tucked between the paneled wall of the office, the curve of the oven, and the tall climb of the chimney.

A den, not a tomb. A den, not a tomb.

"Come here, crawl, please, carefully," she whispered. She spread fingers wriggling in blackness until she felt one child, then the other. One of them kicked her in the breast, another poked her in the eye as she helped them to the center of the blanket. She blinked the poked eye. Rubbed the bruised breast.

She couldn't stop touching the children. Stroking their hair, squeezing a hand. Her arm around a shoulder, lips kissing a forehead. The quiet, the blackness, was so all-consuming, made them so unseeable, that without that touch she feared her children might disappear. Be eaten. Again a line from one of the children's books she'd read and reread aloud to them flitted through her mind.

I'll eat you up I love you so.

She folded them in the blanket, stroking it to be sure their soft little limbs were covered, heads sharing the pillow. Found Pinkbunny, found Fuzzydoll. Knocked the dust off them. Made sure the children weren't so close they'd go straight to shoving each other. Were close enough they'd warm each other.

"It's a little blanket burrito. Not so bad. A snuggly little burrito," she said.

She curled her body around them. Felt the cold air freeze her legs in the exposed place between her slippers and the robe. Felt it creep along the back of her neck, down her sternum, chilling her sweat.

Again and again, she told herself this was all real, it was no nightmare, that no fanged Corner had crawled out of dreams or shadows to devour them.

He's a real man. A real person.

Which is much worse than anything else.

8

I could never spend a night in this house," the chimney sweep said.

A few months after moving in nearly two years before, she'd hired the sweep to assess the six fireplaces branching from the house's center chimney. He was tall, and though she warned him about the stairway height, he'd hit his head there, and again on an upstairs doorframe.

"People were shorter hundreds of years ago," someone had told her, "that's why these doors are so low."

She'd fact-checked and found that heights hadn't changed in the nearly three hundred years since her house was built, let alone in the two hundred years since the nineteenth-century addition—the kitchen downstairs and the low-ceilinged stair leading to the useless half room, half hallway upstairs—had been inelegantly sewn onto the back side of the place. Given the addition's original purpose had been to house servants, most likely ceilings and doorways were low because it was easiest to build and cheapest to heat.

Same as it ever was.

She assumed the sweep's hesitation was because he was clearly far too tall to live in the house comfortably. But then he side-eyed her, said, "Have you seen anything yet?"

"Like what?"

"You know." He rubbed his arms as though chilled. "Ghosts."

He shuddered, visibly shuddered, and she followed his gaze around the room, trying and failing to imagine what the chimney sweep saw among her belongings. Jealousy wiggled in her skull that the sweep was able to believe badness, hauntedness, was isolated to this or that building; pain sealed in the past instead of lurking inevitably in the future.

Wouldn't that be comforting?

"Least the chimney is in good shape," he conceded.

The sweep leaned inside the iron door of the beehive oven, bits of light from his flashlight escaping around him. As he pulled himself out, she was reminded uncomfortably of a breech birth, the oven a round womb, and looked away from the odd intimacy of it.

"You used the beehive yet? It's been restored at some point. Modern firebrick. Good stuff."

The sweep irritated her. He worked slowly, chatting and expecting her attention yet ignoring her warnings about the stairs and doorways. Worse, his unhurried visit had interrupted her focus on illustrating a client's elegant pollination drone, its tiny motors that angled for roll, pitch, and yaw. So she found herself needling him, saying, "You know, I haven't seen anything. But there *is* a graveyard out back."

"A graveyard? Not really?"

"Really."

"I couldn't do it." He shook his head dolefully. "I couldn't live here."

For the first four months at the outskirts of suburban New England, she regularly thought about that chimney sweep as she floated around her in-laws' apartment, silent and invisible as one of his ghosts. Any word she said was met with her father-in-law's resentment, as if she'd pushed into his home with an unwelcome "boo."

With the children placed in front of a television so as not to disturb their grandfather, she did her in-laws' laundry, made dinner, prepped breakfast and lunch for the next day, tackled bottomless dishes, made sure the chocolate-flavored Ensure was waiting chilled in the fridge, the only thing her mother-in-law could stomach. All while the old man pointedly read his paper. Watched golf with his feet leisurely crossed on the ottoman. Assessed what she'd accomplished with a derisive snort.

She flitted away from her mother-in-law's "you don't have tos" and "I'm fines." Because despite her protestations the older woman would fall asleep on the couch under the light of her grandchildren's cartoons, their soft limbs draped around her, waking to repeat, "Thank you. Thank you."

As she assisted with intimate things—the bathroom, the bathing, the physical reactions to treatments—her father-in-law would break his malevolent hovering and flee, revolted by the physicality of these tasks. In his absence, the older woman shed small talk like a worn-out skin.

"Dear, would you tell me about what happened to your mother?" she'd say, or "My father was an unkind man, which somehow made it more difficult when he died. Unresolved problems . . . they fester," and "I've always been a 'go along to get along' girl. What a waste."

As pieces of horrible news landed at doctor's appointment after doctor's appointment, her mother-in-law sat calmly, saying, "I see. I understand. That's not what we'd hoped, is it? I know this must be hard news for you to deliver, but thank you, Doctor."

Yes, the older woman stared the Grim Reaper straight in the eye and didn't show a trace of fear, just marveled, "Really? You're bothering with me?" as he lowered the scythe a little closer.

She admired her mother-in-law's resilience. Wondered at the still-hidden depths that might have created it. What her own regrets, her own strengths, would be, when her time came.

"Your mother is one tough lady," she told her husband. "Sick as she is, she's still thinking of everyone else."

"Yeah, I'm sure she's pretty loudly being the noble sufferer," her husband grumbled. "She's an expert martyr."

"Or it's grit. I mean, I'd be wallowing and snapping at everyone. Or, I don't know, crying all the time."

He shrugged. "You'd feel differently if you'd grown up with her."

She thought of her father back in Utah, clinging to his broken junk tighter than he had ever held on to her. Thought of the way her husband ludicrously insisted that she was too hard on her dad, that he was unwell, had possibly even felt the life-shattering impact of her mother's loss more deeply than she had.

"Maybe you're right," she conceded. "Family does have a unique way of getting under your skin."

But every time her mother-in-law hugged her goodbye, the older woman's affection was so genuine, so enveloping, it filled that void of love her own father never poured anything into. She would close her eyes, inhale that nearness, that acceptance, and for the first time since she was a child wordlessly breathe, *Mother, Mama, Mommy.*

Her mother-in-law particularly enjoyed hearing about their house, chuckling at stories of people like the chimney sweep. There were plenty of them, true believers who preached about ghosts in the attic, spirits under the stairs, the fingernails of ugly, vengeful history clawing from the floorboards. The older woman nodded along as she recounted how they'd decided not to install an alarm system after the installer had explained false alarms would be a problem in the oldest portion of the house, with the way the windows rattled. They'd have to shell out some real cash, pay for a monitoring service, exterior cameras and outdoor wiring, to make any system functional. Given that the few break-ins in their area in the last decade had been seekers (drug or thrill), her husband had decided it was all a waste of money.

"Nothing ever happens out here," he'd huffed. "What would someone steal? We don't even have a nice TV."

She'd frowned at him, thought, *And yet, you won't get rid of that gun.*

"That alarm man," she told her mother-in-law, "stood right out on the lawn looking up at the house, and, dead serious, was like, 'The best security you've got is that this place is really fuckin' spooky.'"

Her mother-in-law rolled her eyes. "I swear, it's always the burliest-looking men who are the biggest babies." She paused. "Even so, I don't know if I'd want to live in that house. Too many reminders of unpleasant things."

For the true believers, there was too much of the supernatural about the place. For people like her mother-in-law, there was too much reality.

The people enslaved by the family that built the home back in 1722 had painted murals on the attic walls, drawings that instantly undermined the lessons she recalled from grade school history class. There, only the Salem witch trials, Lizzie Borden with her ax, and other female insanities had interrupted the ball of New England righteousness that bounced from pilgrims to revolutionaries to Union soldiers.

Her father-in-law had sneered at the drawings as though they were a personal insult, wrinkling his nose as if smelling something sour.

She hated the spiders and wasps and mustiness of the unfinished attic, how it was invariably miserably cold or swelteringly hot, but always paused by the painted wall. Her own calling was technical, but she believed this gave her a unique appreciation for the fluid.

Although the lines were faded with time and lightly water damaged, all the portraits—the drawings of Black figures near the ceiling who floated in a kind of heavenly judgment above the pale, wigged men and their rouged wives painted near the floor—were shot through with personality, had clearly been based on real people.

Despite her mother-in-law's flinty ability to face down death, the older woman had grimaced at the time-tilted stones of the home's graveyard, the oldest each topped with a carved skull flanked by wings.

"It's just so maudlin, dear, having it right by the children's swing set."

"Mmm," she'd hummed, busy reading the original enslaver's epitaph.

> He lived a long unblemished life.
> Virtue and industry, he practised and taught.
> Reader, if this be pleasing to God and beneficial to man,
> do thou likewise.
> 1702–1778

Is there anyone who thinks they're evil? Or does evil always see itself as superior?

As her mother-in-law thinned, became pained and sleepy and distant, her husband's appearances at the apartment dwindled.

"That girl's keeping him from us," she heard her father-in-law complain in the next room. "God knows what she tells him."

Her husband's protestations that he was the one who got groceries every week, picked up his mother's prescriptions, drove her to see this or that friend, lacked conviction. He knew as well as the rest of them that he was fleeing to the skies, leaning out of his two-seater

Super Cub airplane to capture a God's-eye view of New England. His photos were seasonal: glowing foliage; hundreds of colorful people on beaches, around pools; tiny dots of humanity rushing down ski hills. Photos that sold well to interior designers, specially printed in massive sizes and delivered to similarly massive vacation homes of the beach, country, and mountain type.

"Look how easy death is to defy," the headstrong tilt of his chin said. "I do it every day."

Yes, she saw that terror crouched behind her husband's bravado. In the loving beam of his mother's fading gaze, he short-circuited. This was why his dangerous work had become all-consuming, leaving her and the children to travel to the apartment alone.

"We didn't raise him like this," her father-in-law groused in the next room. "He's being manipulated by that girl."

When the older man received nothing but her curt, silent nods in response to his imperious criticism of her cooking (salty), the way she folded things (crooked), or how she hadn't used distilled water in the iron (ruinous), he began pick-pick-picking at his grandson.

"Hell, kid, you throw worse than a girl! Your sister can throw. Sister's more of a boy than you are," and "What's this? Are you *crying*? Over a TV show? Christ almighty," and to her exhausted mother-in-law, cuddling the three-year-old in her lap, "You need to stop babying him. It's one thing for the girl to be a tomboy. But you're going to turn him all wrong, too."

"I don't want to go back to Grampy's," her son said in the car.

"Why not?"

"Dunno." The little boy looked out his window, lip trembling.

She hired a babysitter and left the children with the teenager in the evenings, her son returning to his perpetual cheerfulness without his grandfather's insults as part of his daily life.

"I'm sorry," her mother-in-law said, wringing her hands. "He's just worried I baby the little one too much. And I do, I really do. It's probably not good for him, and—"

"I'll bring them whenever you want," she said. "You let me know."

"It's genetic," she overheard the old man seethe to his wife. "I warned him—I warned him his kids might look just as awful. And now the little girl's got it on her face! Did it have to be the girl? On a boy it would be bad enough, but a girl?"

She unthinkingly stroked the white patches around her neck, the drips of pale that tripped along her cheeks, the places where the pearl of her hands met the pigmented skin of her arms.

"Stop that, please don't say that," her mother-in-law shushed, words that only made her father-in-law grow louder, tip into righteous outrage that blinded him to irony.

"Don't you order me around in my own home!"

"Dear, it's nothing, that vitiligo. Just a little color." Her mother-in-law's tone aimed for soothing, but was shot through with a current of distress. "I think—I think it's beautiful."

Isn't it beautiful? Isn't it just beautiful? echoed her mother's voice in memory.

She felt tears rise, retreated to the bathroom to hide them.

Her mother-in-law, eyes rheumy, tummy sunken, skin yellowed, asked her if she believed in God. In heaven.

She knew what she was supposed to say. But instead, she told the older woman about standing in the garden signing the chimney sweep's check, impatient to return to her drawings of the robotic pollinator.

"Good luck with this place," he said, breaking through her thoughts of piezoelectric actuators flapping micro-thin ceramic wings. "Better you than me."

When he finally left, she turned to go inside and noticed the bees.

They rolled in the petals and around the stamens of the wide-open roses. Flew to the lavender, legs and bodies collecting pollen from invisible filaments. She listened to their hum. Watched the perfection of their engineering. An immensely efficient, infinitely adaptable, pre-programmed, fully biodegradable, self-replicating pollinator that produced not only useful, clean-burning wax, but honey. Pure and utter elegance. The robo-pollinator, however advanced it had seemed moments before, was all at once eons, millennia, behind.

What a narrow place the chimney sweep imagined the afterlife to be, she'd decided, souls waiting only to frighten the living. If there was some great beyond, didn't nature prove it would be more astonishing than people were capable of conceiving? After all, though a person had invented the robotic pollinator, nature had evolved the bee itself—a creation that outstripped all human capability.

"That's lovely, dear," the older woman said. "But it doesn't really answer my question."

She'd been the one to find her mother-in-law dead on the brand-new adjustable bed her in-laws had gotten as part of their buy-in to senior living. She'd found her on that pricey bed, the apartment so new she could smell the paint, the flooring planks of plastic pressed to look like wood. Not a place anyone would walk into and ask about ghosts. But in that bedroom her mother-in-law was cold, her mouth opened in a grotesque mime of a scream, eyes fixed on the ceiling, their whites shot through with blood, skin purpling.

Although she tried to close the mouth, the eyes, to disguise the horror of her mother-in-law's final moments, rigor had set in and she couldn't manage it. The soft towel she draped over the older woman's face sank into the eye sockets, the open mouth, giving an effect so disturbing she'd immediately removed it. Instead she closed the door and quietly called the funeral home her mother-in-law had pre-selected. Her body was wheeled out before her father-in-law woke from a nap in the guest bedroom ("I can't sleep in the same room, not with all the groaning"). On seeing her nervously hop up from the couch, the man ignored the visible signs she'd been crying and immediately began complaining that dinner wasn't ready.

Voice fracturing, she told him she was sorry, that his wife had died sometime that day, in her own bed, just as she'd wanted.

He took two rapid steps toward her and slapped her across the face with an open palm so violently it knocked her down to that pressed plastic floor.

"You," he said standing over her, pointing an accusatory finger, "can't be the one to tell me this."

She scrambled up and backed away toward the door, grabbed her bag while keeping her eyes trained on him as though he were a snake, a venomous predator.

As she left, through the pain, the shame, the fury, the humiliation, all she said was "No."

Her husband's anger bloomed with her bruises. He fought with his father on the phone, the older man unrepentantly claiming she'd sneered at him, been cruel, had appeared happy.

The men didn't speak at the funeral.

Her bruises faded. Her husband began saying things like "We're all my dad has now" and "Do you really think Mom would've wanted him to be so alone?"

But there's no water in that well.

About two months after her mother-in-law's death, her husband focused somewhere above her shoulder and said, "I know you can have a hard time—responding—to my dad. Was there something you did? Something you maybe said that set him off?"

His words branched inside her in an endless fractal root system, nearly impossible to pull out once planted.

"What could, what could I have done? Done to deserve that?" she stammered.

"Right. You're right. But—maybe?"

She burst into tears, and he apologized. But her husband had granted his father the benefit of the doubt, had elevated pleasing him above her safety. Even as her thoughts reeled in the spin of this betrayal, she understood that she blamed herself, too. Blamed herself in a way she could never explain to her husband because if she did, it would cut in a way irreparable.

You saw your father-in-law for who he is a long time ago. You let him into your life anyway. And what happened? Exactly what you always thought might happen. So it is your fault. It is.

Blaming herself imposed a reassuring cause and effect, a sense that she had power to prevent further violence. She told her husband she wouldn't ever speak to her father-in-law again. That the children weren't allowed to see him.

Maybe that satisfying sense of control was why, hunted in the cold darkness behind the walls of her own home, what rattled in her mind under every other thought, every motion, frantic as a rodent in a trap was a search for how she might somehow be at fault for all of this. That there was something she had done, or should have done, or should still do that she couldn't quite yet pinpoint, some way to bring it all into focus that would allow her to prevent harm.

What did you do? Why is this happening? Why is this happening to you? What next? What next?

9

You can't stay in here forever. Will he leave? How can you know if he does?

In spite of the cold, the discomfort of the hard floor, in spite of her muscle-tightening fear, an immense weight pulled at her eyelids.

Coming down off the adrenaline, or else maybe you shouldn't be lying down at all with that egg on your forehead.

She sat up. The blood drained from her vibrating skull. After a moment's intense sureness she was going to vomit, she felt slightly better.

No, shouldn't be lying down like that with your head hurt.

She tucked her legs into her robe to warm them. Her child-kicked, newly bruised breast ached in a way that made her wonder as she always did with the children's accidental hurts how someone so small could inflict such pain. Made her remember the misery of breastfeeding, the swollen bite of mastitis. She leaned against the bricks of the chimney, causing grit to slough down her back.

When she closed her eyes, her exhausted mind distilled all her internal criticism into her husband's voice, his tone the same as when he'd asked, "Was there something you did?"

"You should've just gone downstairs," this voice said, "pretended to be asleep on the couch, left the children sleeping. Maybe then he'd have thought no one saw him, and would just take your things. Leave you alone."

But you know what he wants. Or maybe wants. No! No maybe. He's said it now. You heard him. He came here because he thinks he deserves whatever, whoever, he wants.

"You should've run down the stairs right away, run for the car keys while he was in your room, driven away, gotten help."

But the snow. Remember last year, the time we couldn't even pull out the cars, had to wait for the plow? If you got stuck, what then? Him dragging you by the hair, screaming, back into the house.

She thought of that unidentifiable weapon and flinched, recalling the sound as he'd hit the heavy weight of it against his palm.

"An excuse for everything," her husband's phantom voice echoed, exasperated. "When, really, you're just too scared, too frightened of the world to do things right. To think. Think about it!"

If he drove here, his car could be blocking the garage.

She imagined a car slowly rolling up the driveway as they slept. She pictured him waiting outside in the darkness, seeing them indoors, vulnerable, unknowing. Little players lit up on a stage through the windows. A wild thing invisible as he circled the campfire that blinded them.

"Are you *sure* you locked the doors?" her husband asked.

I—don't remember exactly? But I always lock the doors. You're the one who forgets. Who doesn't even think it's necessary. You're the one who always thinks we're safe, that I'm overreacting. Paranoid.

"You are paranoid."

If someone's determined enough, if someone doesn't mind doing some damage, taking the time, you can't keep them out. Not really.

"You know it almost never happens, a stranger targeting someone. You've got all your dark little statistics stored in there. Violence nearly always comes from inside the house."

He's here. This is real.

"Violence nearly always comes from someone you know."

She rubbed her cheek, feeling the ghost of her father-in-law's long, thin hand.

"Here you are, forcing them into this horrible place, impatient with them, hand over a mouth, irritable, incapable, telling yourself it's because you love them. *You're* the violence in the house."

You let your father-in-law into your life. And now you've let this Corner in. Something you did. Something you didn't do. And don't you remember him? There's something about him. Something familiar. Isn't there?

She knocked the back of her head against the chimney to unhinge her husband's counterfeit voice from her brain, to disrupt the dizzying swirl of blame and confusion.

Stop, stop it. It's not your fault. You want him to be someone you recognize, because then there might be some horrible thing you did, some reason for all this. And you'll come out and—what—say, "Yoo-hoo! I remembered who you are and what I did and I'm so very sorry, it's all my fault." And he'll say, "Wow, thanks, no need to murder you now, because I so appreciate the apology." It's ridiculous. You didn't do anything. It's his fault. This Corner.

"And now you're thinking of him like the kids do? As the Corner? If you weren't delusional at first, maybe you are now. At least you have to consider that."

You're not delusional. He was trying to scare you. And he did a good job, because you're scared.

"You should've grabbed a weapon," said her husband.

What weapon? There's nothing, nothing.

"The fire poker."

She felt a full-body wince of acute regret.

Why didn't you think of that? You're stupid, so stupid!

She pictured herself lying in the hidden place, holding the looped handle of the poker in one hand, its L-shaped end pointing at the hidden panel door. When it swung open, she'd have her foot against the L of the poker, her hands on the loop. She'd be strong, using arms and legs together. Boom, puncture the skull, dead.

She groaned aloud with the beauty of it. The impossibility of it. The poker was only just on the other side of the wall in the living room. But getting it would mean leaving the hidden place, going through the office and into the living room, which was visible from the stairs, the entry, the playroom, the kitchen.

So here you are. Swallowed up and fantasizing about the best ways to put a fire poker you don't even have through someone's skull. You can't get it, not with-out risking showing yourself. Wouldn't it be better to sit against the door? To use body weight and legs pressed against the rise of the chimney to keep him out? Keep him from being able to tell, even if he pushed the just right spot, that the door was a door at all?

"It figures," muttered her husband. "Your solution is to do noth-ing at all. To hide."

Sometimes the hardest thing to do is nothing at all.

She flinched, reeling back in time.

But other times the worst thing to do is nothing at all.

Unlocking the door to her dorm room at her mid-Atlantic uni-versity after a late-night cramming at the library. Her then boy-friend had spotted her from the hall, hurried behind her, and wrapped his arms around her just as she swung the door open and took the first step into the room. He'd intended it as an affectionate hug of a greeting, but she hadn't seen or heard him approach. She only saw and felt the man-arms pin her hands to her sides as they tightened. She'd registered that strength, the emptiness of the hall, of her room, the late hour, and was drowned in a wave of utter help-lessness, the surety that this was it, the primal bad.

She hadn't screamed. Hadn't fought. To her deep shame and

horror, she'd gone loose, folded into a tiny fetal ball of trembling whimper, staring blankly at the linoleum floor of the dorm room.

You can't freeze like that again. If it comes to it. If it comes to a confrontation.

Even now, her disappointment at her reaction was bottomless. She'd crumpled to protect her belly as though her attacker had been a bear instead of a man. As if a human man would be as merciful as an animal, bat her around the head and neck and try to bite her tender middle, try to kill her quickly. Certain it was a man come to push her into the room and hurt her, all she'd been capable of was melting into terrified weakness. How was that any different from compliance? After all, she couldn't even make herself say, "No." Scream for help. Couldn't speak at all. Couldn't elbow him or fight or move.

Ringing in her head were the same things she'd heard said so often, this time said about her: *Out so late, all alone, no precautions, what was she wearing?*

She rolled her head against the brick of the chimney. A wave of deep exhaustion pulled at her, and she let her eyes close.

At first, she remembered, her boyfriend felt terrible. It hadn't even occurred to him the level of fright his surprise hug might give her, the level of threat she felt in the dorm so late, when she thought she was alone.

Must be nice, she'd thought bitterly. *Must be nice to live life that way, feeling safe.*

Even though he apologized, it was the beginning of the end of their connection. Because when she told him she'd decided to take a self-defense class, the thin, closed line of his mouth silently told her, "Don't you think you're overreacting? Being dramatic over nothing."

After that, any emotion she showed—jumping in fright at a house centipede that crawled from under the bed, irritated at his being late, trying to vent about an unfair grade—he'd roll his eyes. Sigh. "Those can't bite, you know." "I'm not even that late, calm down." "What did you do wrong to get that grade anyway?" "Relax." His words made it simple to read his thoughts. *She's overwrought. She's illogical. She's just like all the others, feelings not to be trusted. Turn that dial down, sister, to something a little more little.*

"You're not taking me seriously," she told him. But his thoughts were as hard to find tangible evidence of as his breath. "What do you mean?" he'd say. "What are you talking about?" Her complaints were just another overreaction.

Easier to think that way, she supposed, than for him to accept he'd been inadvertently cruel. Easier to think she had a problem than accept how instead of protecting her, he'd terrified her. Because those things did happen. Could happen.

Those things are happening to you right now.

"Why are you so mopey? Why are you so annoyed?" As if he had nothing to do with her tears, with her irritability. As if feelings were things she picked up at random, clutched to her heart, completely separate from his small cruelties as he sought to justify himself.

The self-defense class she attended was disappointing. She'd imagined kung fu. Cool moves that would somehow turn her smallness into an advantage, like in the movies where the little lady in heeled boots takes down the big bad.

But it was mainly about screaming.

"Women are conditioned to be quiet, not to make noise," the teacher said. "Most of us are too self-conscious to be loud. To draw attention. Even in an emergency."

She couldn't scream loud enough, uninhibited enough, to please the teacher. With triumphant banshees wailing around her, sound caught in her throat and came out strangled. They learned only one aggressive move in the class, a thrust with the butt of the palm to crack a nose. A shock and awe approach that (maybe) allowed a chance to run off screaming. She had no trouble popping the defense class dummy in the face hard as she could, so hard it bruised her hand. The dummy's head barely wobbled.

"If I were you," the teacher said coolly, "if I were your size? I'd focus on making some real noise."

Well, well, well. That teacher was way off. Imagine where being loud, screaming when you saw him on those stairs, would have gotten you.

But the linoleum of the dorm room floor resurfaced, and the momentary feeling of superiority, of vindication, vanished.

No matter what, you can't unravel like that again. If it happens, if he gets in here, you kick and gouge and use your nails, your teeth—anything. Everything! Or you'd never forgive yourself.

"You wouldn't deserve forgiveness," echoed her husband's voice.

"Mommy?" said the little girl, startling her so much she gave an involuntary huh noise, a whole-body jerk. Drifting sleepily in the depths of her memory, her imaginary conversations, she'd assumed the children were asleep.

"Mommy, I need to use the bathroom."

"One or two?" she asked, thought to herself, *You're on autopilot.*

"One."

Typical, typical. You get the kids all packed up and ready to go. All buckled in. They've got a stuffed animal, a snack, you juuust pull onto the highway, and then you hear, "Mommy? I need a bathroom."

At least it isn't number two.

"Mommy?"

"Shhh, I'm thinking."

Thinking made her acknowledge she needed to go, too. Terribly.

"All right," she whispered. "Buddy, I need you to take off your diaper. Mama will help, okay?"

Before lockdown, her son had gone several months without needing a diaper overnight. But bedwetting began within two weeks of staying home, a thing she and her husband attributed to his sensitivity, his worry over their worry. The pediatrician shrugged it off. Told them to be patient, that stress-related setbacks were normal, and not to shame him. Over the summer, seemingly acclimated to the strange new world, their son's accidents stopped. But in November they resumed, more frequent than ever before. She had put him back in diapers, trying to shoo away the guilt that she couldn't shield her perceptive son from the cruelties of the world.

It was a strange dance in the dark, unwinding the blanket and helping the little boy take off his pajama pants, then the diaper.

"Gross," the little girl said as she threaded on her brother's diaper.

"I know," she whispered. "But do it anyway."

She helped her daughter take off the diaper when she was done. Took off her own underwear. Cringing, she held the diaper's clamminess against her.

Well, well. Here's an advantage to being small. Here's a good thing about it. Able to use a kid's diaper, hooray. And not nearly as terrible or disgusting as you thought it would be. Hardly used. Bigger fish to fry, larger worries.

It was difficult to put her underwear back on, her body still slicked with sweat. But she struggled into them, shooing aside thoughts of why it mattered to her so much to have them on.

She put a light hand on his shoulder, then on her daughter's, settling them back down on the blanket. The girl's arm circled over her brother.

One small hurdle dealt with. One little problem addressed.

Her breathing had evened. Her blood pulsed something close to normal. Her hands had shed some of their shake.

It had calmed her, having a physical thing to cope with, a solvable problem to capably dispatch. The second-guessing, the critical voice of her husband—cold edged and crueler than he'd ever be in reality—quieted.

She closed her eyes and watched the distant lights behind her eyelids, just for something to see. Some relief from the deep black. Listened for anything that might help indicate where the Corner was. She rested the back of her head against the chimney brick. The only sound was the rustling and breathing of the children and the wheezing of the storm through the house.

You're falling asleep, she realized. *You can't fall asleep. You need to get that fire poker. Or get help. Or at least watch over them. Bar the door.*

But sitting cross-legged, feet tucked into the hollows behind her knees to warm them, she was finally thawing. The relief of the empty bladder made her feel in control of her own body for the first time in what seemed like weeks. And descending from those great heights of fear brought a sinking, unfightable drowsiness in this dark pool that felt like safety.

It's not your fault. It's not your fault.

As she faded into her exhaustion, she felt something like a breath on her cheek, something like the drift of a cobweb.

Delicious, hissed the voice of the Corner directly in her ear, and she gasped aloud, choking on a panicked inhale of rotten air.

10

Mama! Are you okay?"

She could barely speak, her throat tightening as though an invisible hand were pinching her windpipe.

Her little girl's hand gripped her knee. She hugged her daughter close, pressed her head to the tiny shoulder.

"It's all right, Mommy, it's all right!"

"I'm sorry," she said, "I'm sorry. I fell asleep. Just for a second."

Her son whimpered.

"Come here," she whispered low. "Come here, my guy. I'm sorry. I'm okay. I didn't mean to scare you."

The little boy reached out, touched her arm, crawled into her lap. As usual, his body melted into hers.

Here you are worried about their behavior, about them making noise, and you do this? Call out like that? What's wrong with you? If he gets you, gets them, it will be your fault.

Her son nuzzled her neck. She exhaled, breathed again, absorbing the reassurance of the boy's animal love.

"Sorry," she said. "I'm so sorry."

Her son put his small, warm palms on her cheeks. She pictured his heavy-lidded black eyes looking straight into hers through the darkness.

"It's okay, Mama," he said seriously.

"What are we going to do," her husband would say, "when he gets bigger?"

They'd look at each other, horrified. Each imagining how their son's clean love, his constant need for their arms around him, would vanish. Because of course it would. It had to. That particular type of sensitivity, affection that straightforward, couldn't survive. The natural order was to hide the depth of your love, for fear that others might see it as weakness. And if that didn't happen on its own, didn't evolve organically, people like her father-in-law would work hard to shame him so that the boy hid his feelings, not just from them but from everyone, quick as slamming shut a book.

She held her little boy tight.

You have to do something. What's the right thing to do?

"I'm so proud of you," she whispered to the children. "You're being so brave and quiet. You're showing Mama how to be brave, too."

How can you help them? How can you get help? There's no way to know where he is except when he's practically on top of you.

As they sat pressed against the rough masonry, all tangled arms and unseeing eyes, she was certain that if the children had been only a little younger, if this had happened only a few months ago, they would never have been able to be this quiet. This obedient. Ready to comfort her. Able to accept that bad things could happen.

They understand that life can snap in half.

"What do we do, Mama?" whispered her daughter.

"Wait. Listen. Be quiet as we can. Sometimes the hardest thing to do is nothing."

Her son wiggled on her lap, cuddled into a ball against her chest. The rubble on the floor pressed into her where the robe had shifted off her legs.

Delicious.

You were falling asleep. It was stress. Of course it was. That voice slinking in your ear. It's only normal. Normal confusion, a normal reaction, in an abnormal situation.

Even so, she scratched a finger in her ear as if to clean the voice of the Corner out of the hollow places.

She focused on the light up and down of her son's breathing. His softness, the heaviness of his head against her bruised breast.

Her daughter crawled back to the blanket. She could hear the girl wrapping it around her, protecting herself from the cold and grime.

"Let's think," she whispered, "about what to do. Just think. Not talk. Just think for a little while, and wait quietly."

"Okay, Mama."

How long will you wait? How long can we stay? Think it through.

There's the sippy cup, full but small. There's the diaper. The blanket. The kids may fall asleep. Easier to keep them quiet longer if they do. When it's light outside, will he leave? How long has it been already?

A gust of wind blew down the chimney, clattering the dampers. She shivered.

"Due to the predicted intensity of the storm," the recorded message from the school had said, "we've canceled both morning and afternoon in-person school tomorrow. Virtual session attendance is still mandatory. We recommend all our community members avoid driving. Be safe."

Friday in-person school's canceled because of the storm. And for virtual? Even if they don't dial in, the teachers will just do what they always do—send an email they don't expect you to respond to. Then Saturday, Sunday. No one expects us anywhere until Monday. And they're out of school for Christmas starting Thursday. It's possible—probable—that the school would even assume you're isolating before the holidays so you can safely spend time around family. They might phone to scold you, but that's it. They wouldn't call the police or anything. It's just too much time. Too much time for them to get hungry, thirsty. To make noise. Time for him to search the house. Listen close. Find us.

As though she'd called out to the Corner, she heard a soft and alien weight above. Slow and even steps crossed her daughter's room. Then, a *pop!*

She was certain that the sound was the door to her daughter's armoire. It had magnets that worked overwell, making its doors difficult to pull and ridiculously noisy when opened. There was silence, then the *cling!* sound that must be him closing the armoire, the hard refastening of the magnets that would yank the knob right out of your hand.

Another thing that needs fixing.

Her son snuffled into her chest.

He's checking all the closets. Not looking for things to take. Not shouting in a scary voice anymore. He's looking for us. Looking in places big enough for someone to hide.

The footsteps were measured. Methodical. Quiet as he was trying to be, each footstep made a muted thud as he crossed the landing overhead and went into her son's room.

The little girl moved to her side and wrapped arms tight around her. She could feel the motions of her daughter's head as it lay on her shoulder, the way she tipped an ear to search out the Corner's sounds.

A cold whistle of wind came through the vent in the stairs. Had he opened a door somewhere?

Criiick! Yes, again he'd stepped on the long floorboard in the hall outside her son's room. Which meant he was likely headed out of the original part of the house, through the room above the kitchen in the old addition, back toward the modern addition that held her room, the guest room, the laundry room.

Has he noticed the attic door yet? Doubtful. You would have heard it open.

Just outside her daughter's room, the attic door was cut into the wall. The realtor had called it a jib door, a thing she'd looked up and found to be not quite accurate. The jib door images that she browsed had been of doors purposefully and beautifully hidden, cut into moldings or bookcases.

But their attic door was more visible. It was built of the same vertical boards that paneled its wall. This made the vertical sides of the door seamless with the wall itself, but the cut at the top was as obvious as a normal door. Although in the rest of the house the hinges had heavy iron strapping, the attic door's hinges were of a different type, visible only from the attic side. She'd guessed that the door might have been half-disguised in this way because the original owners hadn't wanted to be reminded of the closeness of the people they'd enslaved sleeping above, but also had been too thrifty to bother with completely hiding it. The attic door didn't have a handle but could be pulled open and fastened shut by using a small, hard-to-notice hook and eye. The door always blew open when someone lifted that hook, the strange top-floor air pressures wrenching it open. There was a dent on the wall from where the hook always hit.

You really ought to put a doorstop there to keep it from slamming open, patch the wall.

Doorstops, things to fix, what does it matter? Think of things that matter.

Has he found the basement yet? Likely.

The basement door was obvious in the entryway. She wouldn't be able to hear him open that door, not from the hidden place.

Too bad. You could lock him in the basement. It's got that heavy bolt so the kids don't go down there. Can't lock him in the attic. The hook would rattle out the minute he threw a shoulder against it.

She scolded herself over the fantasy.

Think of real things. A real plan. There has to be something. There's always something.

Except when there isn't.

She closed her eyes and pictured the house.

A rectangle, a triangle. Four windows on the left, four to the right, another above the door in the middle. Panes hatched like tic-tac-toe boards. In the center of the roof, a square stub of chimney. An idea of a house.

Yes, the house looked just like a child's drawing. Just like a house should. In her mind's eye there was a little curlicue of smoke snaking out of the chimney, drawn in gray crayon. To the children, to her, the house was a place elementally, reassuringly *home.*

She mentally sketched the house from a bird's-eye view, carefully labeled it, the grounds, viewed the floors in cross section, flew higher and higher in imagination to get a better perspective.

The rectangle of the old house. The square of the kitchen addition behind it. The rectangle of the modern addition attached to the kitchen. The long driveway that curved from the street, around the trees, past the side of the house to the garage doors in the addition all the way at the back.

She flew higher still, squeezed her eyes tighter, bracketed and labeled the distances.

Two hundred feet or so down the driveway to their street. Take a left, pastures upon pastures upon fields and then the woods, and then, only after maybe two miles, a farmhouse. So instead take a right out of the driveway, follow the road up the hill, the winding street. A football field or so past the driveway was the first house. Two hundred feet after that, another. Who lived there? In the first house, a nurse. She lived alone, and often worked night shifts.

Heading for the nurse would be a risk. How far was the next house?

You don't even know who lives there! Why don't you know them? You had plenty of time to introduce yourself before lockdown. You met the nurse, then the other neighbors weren't home. Why'd you never go back?

Too shy, too awkward, too nervous.

Focus.

She drew out the geography in imaginary pencil lines.

Yes, the houses get thick and thicker that direction. But even the nurse's house isn't exactly close in this weather. Plus there's the hill to walk up. And then, if he looked out any window at the front of the house, he'd see you. Or at least see your tracks. Be able to follow. The road won't be plowed yet. Through the snow there, you'd be so exposed.

And if you try to travel as the crow flies?

She itemized the dangers. The thick snowdrifts of the fields. The twisted bramble of the woods, filled with crawling, dormant vines of wild grape, the thorny, tangled greenbrier. The ubiquitous New England fieldstone walls traced irregularly through the forest, so difficult to climb over given their loose rocks. And there were streams, blanketed by drifts but still running underneath the ice and snow, soundless and undetectable.

Impossible. Impenetrable. Impractical.

She swiveled her mental map. Behind the house was the yard, the kids' slide and swings. Behind that, the graveyard marking the transition from grass to trees. Beyond the graveyard, through the woods, the trail.

That's it. That's the way.

The path through the woods.

I n early October the year before, not long after her mother-in-law died, she asked her husband if he'd used the leaf blower on the trail through the woods behind the house.

"No, why?"

"The whole path? There's hardly any leaves on it."

He came to see for himself. The children were running and whooping along beside him, using sticks like swords.

The forest floor was thick with leaves and pine needles. But the trail was neat and tidy. It snaked brown and soft through the forest, like something often used and carefully tended.

"There were leaves before, weren't there? I can't remember when we last took the path," her husband said.

"It's been awhile. It's strange. Do you think someone back there cleared it?"

She gestured down the two hundred feet of path in the direction of the house-studded blacktop of a cul-de-sac that began where the trail ended, about ten feet beyond their property line.

Their house had originally been the seat of a three-hundred-acre farm. Subdivided in the 1980s, most of the land was sold by a previous owner to a developer who carved it into a neighborhood of massive midnineties McMansions on enormous lots.

She found it jarring to pass their antique house and acres of rolling pastures, to walk through the graveyard, to take the path through the forest of hundred-year-old trees, to be peacefully immersed in a bygone, pristine New England—then burst out into the separate world of this cul-de-sac.

She'd squint at deep black asphalt as though it were a mirage. Out of it rose a bristling vista of demilune windows, columned porches, doorways and side doors, three-car garages, peak of roof behind peak of roof behind peak of roof. There were shiny security cameras, topiaries in urns, black mulch, swimming pools, stone on wood on vinyl on plaster, black and brass NO TRESPASSING signs. She'd find herself blinking away the illusion that the top-heaviness of these houses would cause them to capsize like poorly steered ships in their neon-green oceans of lawn.

Had someone in one of those immense homes been bothered by the unkempt path? It connected to the trim little sidewalk around the cul-de-sac that went on to intersect the town's bike path, so it was reasonable to think someone might have been irritated by its naturalness, by the way it didn't quite fit in. Had they swept it clean? Tried to sculpt it away from its primitive, wild state to mirror their precisely edged flower beds?

"I don't think they'd come on our property," her husband said. "I think it was just the wind."

"Maybe it's ghosts." Her daughter grinned.

She smiled at her daughter, wiggled spooky fingers. "Yeah! Walking the path from the graveyard."

"What, with rakes? Brooms?" her husband asked, making their daughter giggle.

"There's no such thing as ghosts!" Her son sounded confident, but then he yanked at her hand, looked up big eyed. "Right, Mama?"

"That's right. No such thing as ghosts. I was just teasing."

"I wouldn't mind ghosts who did yard work," her husband said, and she'd bumped her shoulder affectionately against his big arm.

"What a weird thing," he muttered quietly.

About a month later, she found her husband looking down the path while the kids dug out their slide, their swings, from an early snow.

"What is it?"

"It's not much snow compared to everywhere else. It's strange."

Sure enough, the trail was visible even through the accumulated snow. A depression marked its dimensions, as if someone had shoveled just before the snow stopped falling, keeping it soft but distinctly shallow.

"The trees maybe catch most of the snow?"

They'd looked up together at the web of branches arching over the path.

"But the snow is deeper everywhere else. Even in the thickest part of the forest."

"The branches must catch some, though? Or, it could be the wind. Maybe the snow in the woods looks deeper because it drifts, blown from the path."

"Yeah. Maybe the path acts like a kind of wind tunnel? Snow gets swept out. That could explain why there were no leaves, too."

They'd both stared, hands on hips, the kids playing behind them in the newly fallen snow on the other side of the graveyard.

"I wanna make it a snow *woman*," her daughter insisted.

"It's a snow*man*," her son said, sounding as though he was about to cry. "'Cause I've got a *boy* hat for it."

"Guys, don't argue." She turned to scold them. "It's not like snow people have private parts. They aren't men or women. Just snow people."

A flash of immediate regret as she saw her daughter's mischievous look.

"Let's put private parts on him!" her daughter said.

"Oh my gosh, guys, do *not* put private parts on the snowma—snowperson, please."

They giggled. She knew behind her back they'd already be sculpting snowy genitalia of one type or the other in exaggerated dimension. Decided not to further engage in this particular battle now that the kids were at least getting along.

"A couple inches of snow on the trail, almost a foot everywhere else," her husband said. "I can't figure it out."

"It's weird," she agreed.

"I *still* think it's ghosts!" her daughter shouted over to them. "At Halloween, the ghosts had those long skirts. That's what sweeps the path."

"Skirts?"

"You know, like sheets."

"You mean how people use sheets as ghost costumes?"

"Yup."

"We know you're just trying to scare your brother," her husband chided. "That's not kind."

"It could be deer?" she mused. "I remember as a kid they'd make trails through aspen groves. Wore paths right down to dirt. If there's enough of them, that could be it. Could even explain why there's not so much snow here in the winter. Deer might tamp it down."

"I bet that's it!" her husband said. "If you don't see deer around here, it just means you're not looking hard enough."

"I'm sure that's it," she agreed.

That night her son woke her with a hard tap directly between her eyes.

"I saw a ghost," he whispered.

"Let me guess," she said as she tucked him back into bed. "Was this ghost in a sheet?"

"No." The little boy yawned. "He wanted me to follow him down the stairs."

Her son woke her the next night, tiny hand squeezing her neck. He woke her again the next night with a shocking flick to her closed eyelid.

"A ghost. He wants me to play with him. Can I have the lights on?"

"He's not letting you get any sleep," her husband said. "We've got to nip this in the bud."

Unsurprisingly, her photographer husband turned to photography to solve the problem. He bought a wildlife camera designed to be Velcroed around a tree. It was motion activated, camouflage cased, solar paneled, and waterproof. Her husband made a big show of it, brought the kids out to help put it up. Pointed the camera lens at the spot where graveyard changed to trail. The next morning, they watched the video, huddled together over the small screen embedded in the back of the camera under a protective hinged cover.

The video flicked on to show deer after deer passing down the trail, silent and colorless but with their night vision–lit eyes flashing through coils of blowing snow.

Her husband tapped the screen. "You see that? Trail must act like a wind tunnel with the trees so thick there. No wonder it looks so good."

"Ghost deer!" her son blubbered, covering his face.

She squinted at the screen. With their eyes aglow and shrouded by shifting white clouds of snow, she saw with dismay that the deer had an unsettling otherworldliness.

"Great," she grumbled, wearily resting her forehead on her husband's shoulder. "Ghost deer. Is that a step up from a haunted staircase at least?"

"Look!" Her daughter pointed at the screen. "Ghosts don't poop!"

Sure enough, a buck had paused in front of the camera, lifted his tail, and let loose.

Her son brightened, then started to clap and laugh.

"Poop!" he shrieked. "Ghosts don't poop!"

She and her husband shared a discreet high five.

"Thank you," she whispered to him.

Her husband put the camera back on its tree trunk, but they never needed its anti-ghost evidence again. Her son stopped waking her complaining of a naughty ghost on the stairs, and she and her husband were satisfied that a busy deer trail and the region's steady northwest cold-weather wind explained the path's bizarre cleanliness and hollow appearance.

There in the hidden place, she felt the idea of the trail and its wind-culled snow run through her like a revelation. It was the obvious choice. All those artificial mansions were the closest possible source of help.

Stay under the eaves of the house so there's less snow. Duck under the windows to be out of sight. One hundred feet to the graveyard. Two hundred fifty feet down the path to those houses. It's a little farther, but it's much better than that uphill distance to the nurse's house. You'd be behind the house. Hardly any windows face that direction. You wouldn't be so exposed.

"Though, of course," said her husband, "you don't know anyone who lives back there, either. Never bothered to meet them. All superior because you think their houses are ugly."

She shook off the intrusion of her husband's imagined voice. Thought of how tantalizingly close she was to the old front double doors. Pictured the bar that swung on its little nail falling into place again when the door shut.

It'll lock you out.

The thought of crossing that threshold, of that little bar swinging closed, locking her away from the children, made her exhale a pained whimper.

There was the extra key in the plastic hide-a-key rock. Extremely well hidden now under the snow. So not impossible to get back in, but nearly, especially if the Corner was still in the house.

But slippers? A robe? And underneath it only underwear and an old T-shirt, drenched in sweat. Could the cold kill you?

Her brain flicked through the contents of the office. Nothing there that would help keep her warm.

But he pushed something around in the hall closet when he was searching for us before. Something made a clatter-whoosh *noise like cloth on hangers.*

She rubbed her neck above where her son's head rested. Felt the slick bite of cold air on skin.

You should just wait! Be patient. He'll give up. The sun will scare him away. For all he knows someone's supposed to visit tomorrow. Certainly he'll expect the plow. Wouldn't want the plow guy to see his car. See him.

But what if he parked somewhere else? Walked? And the plow guy wouldn't call the police, not about a strange car. He might remember a car later. After something happened. Which does you no good at all.

The three-day weekend unspooled before her, looking as clean and uncannily empty as that groomed trail through the trees. With school canceled early in anticipation of the storm, she'd prepared for a quiet long weekend at home alone with the kids. She'd felt galvanized out of her recent lethargy by the coming nor'easter. She'd made sure there was plenty of gas in the generator. She'd done all the massive piles of laundry just in case they lost power while home alone, folded it, and put it all away in one go for the first time in nearly two months. She'd ordered and picked up groceries just as the snow started falling. She'd swept the ashes out of the fireplace, out of the enormous beehive oven in the living room, remembering her husband making pizza there, all of them happy and full and warm. Brought in plenty of firewood so that they could roast marsh-mallows, make s'mores, as a special treat. She had told the children that depending on the condition of the roads, they could pick out a Christmas tree on Saturday or Sunday.

It's not like your dad would notice if he didn't hear from you. Not like your husband is going to check in. Or your father-in-law.

Yes, she'd assembled a weekend that required no other people but that she had been determined to make look like normal life.

But the Corner doesn't know that. He doesn't know no one will notice you're gone. How could he know?

He knew it was just the three of you alone here. You can't know what he knows. How long has he been watching?

She touched the knot on her head. Winced.

And you were just so pleased with yourself, getting all that ready for the weekend. Doing small and happy things for the kids after all these weeks of you being so incapable.

Another blast of cold cut through her. Involuntarily her eyes were drawn to the vent, where the wind whistled through.

She froze, throat closing. There was an undulating movement in the darkness outside the vent. Vague shapes slowly took form in the thin moonlight that traveled into the entry from the four small transom windowpanes above the front door. Round yellow eyes, unnaturally large, stared at her from the other side of the vent.

The Corner.

Even as her body stiffened, her son stayed still in her lap, breathing such that she was sure he was asleep. Her daughter's head was on her shoulder, heavy and warm. Were they both sleeping? She hadn't noticed, focused as she'd been on drawing all the possibilities for escape in her head. She didn't dare move in case she roused them. Kept her eyes fixed on the thing outside the vent.

It's nothing, it's nothing. Stress. A trick of the light. There's no Corner. And people don't have yellow eyes. It's not him. It's imagination. Nothing, nothing at all.

But it was something. After so long in the darkness her eyes could still discern little in the black of the hidden place, but outside the vent the tiny trickle of moonlight allowed her to make out a face with pale skin. A bald head with a few scraggly hairs. The bottom of the face, the mouth, the teeth, the chin and nose, receded into darkness.

The eyes blinked, massive and yellow.

12

When she was a child, her school made a fuss over fitness and survival of the outdoor type, every field trip a hike or a cross-country skiing ordeal.

As usual she was struggling to keep up with her classmates during one such hike in fourth grade. The others were always faster, as if made speedy by their shared lifelong intake of Wonder Bread and Jell-O. At each turn of the mountain trail she hoped to see other kids waiting for her, baking red under their white-blond hair as they downed handfuls of trail mix.

She sensed a vibration in the air and stopped walking. It was the exact same feeling as when she was in the car and *buzz*, she'd turn her head and meet the eyes of someone staring at her from their car. That momentary catch, the certainty, that you're being watched, able to sense it even at eighty miles an hour. It was a perception growing ever more attuned as she anticipated the curiosity over the newly whitened marks on her face; the ones that had begun appearing soon after her mother's death as though she'd left the weight of them behind for her daughter to take up.

Struck still, she looked for the source of her disquiet, taking in the trail and forest around her until her eyes met the golden gaze of a mountain lion. It was about thirty feet away across a river.

Drought lowered, the river ran at a medium-level rush around exposed boulders that would be easy for the lion to get through and over. The animal was shaded by the aspens, the light through the quaking leaves giving its yellow fur an underwater-green cast.

Despite never before seeing a living mountain lion, she knew this one wasn't right. It was emaciated. Its rib bones pushed out prominently like it had swallowed a barrel. Bald patches in its fur were rimmed with matted blood. The ears were straight and pricked, but one was half-gone, the tear in it jagged. The long whiskers sagged on the lowered head, which moved slowly back and forth like a movie cobra dancing to a tune. The hips and shoulders jutted up sharp, pulling the skin of the thing taut.

All the more disorienting was the lion's deformity. When the animal opened its jaws, its long pink tongue lolled out as though it were a yawning house cat. It drew its tongue back in with a lick of its own muzzle, a lick that swished over a whole set of extra teeth, bristling and uneven, protruding from the side of the lion's face like a second, smaller mouth.

For the first time since the markings had begun to blanch her skin, she understood that strangeness, difference, could be immaterial. Because the only thing that mattered was the way the lion's round yellow eyes were filled with pure starvation.

She remembered what she'd been taught. She pulled her backpack off and held it above her head. Tried to yell and whoop to frighten the animal, but the fear caught in her throat, and she found she couldn't make a sound.

So instead she sang, which she discovered, inexplicably, was not nearly as difficult as trying to scream. She tweaked lyrics and filled in unremembered blanks as she began moving down the trail.

"One, two, three-four-five, you're the prettiest cat alive!"

She thought such an unright creature—disfigured and cast out, and, she was sure, hurt by its own kind—might like these words. Might be happy to get a compliment for once. Might, just like she did, find itself longing for them.

"Six, seven, eight-nine-ten, please just let me go again."

She backed down the trail as best she could, working hard not to fall, eyes trained on the lion, surprised at how clear and loud her voice was growing with her fear growing beside it.

"Why won't you let me go?"

The cat loped along the opposite bank, following her so casually she understood with horror how simple it was for the creature to keep up. How easy it would be for the lion to overtake her.

Make yourself big. Don't turn your back to it. Make noise. Don't, don't, don't fall.

The animal's hunger took away whatever was left of its beauty, its symmetry. Her voice quavered as she sang, "Do you want to eat me so?"

She pulled at her windbreaker so it would flap, make her look larger.

Don't trip, don't trip.

Her fear, her focus, was such that only when she came around a bend in the trail, singing at the top of her lungs, "Please, kitty, don't you bite, this little finger on my—" and nearly stumbled over three of her classmates, who had stopped for a snack, eyes wide and mocking, did she realize how ridiculous she must seem.

"Oh my gosh, what are you doing?" a girl giggled.

The rush of heat to her face, the embarrassment, outweighed even the relief. After all, she was ten years old. She'd already felt gangly and awkward, and now her recent loss singled her out as either pitiable or cursed.

"There's a mountain lion following me!"

"What? Where?"

They stood up, craned necks.

She pointed across the river, but the animal was gone. It had retreated somewhere into the trees. She still felt its yellow eyes.

"I don't see anything."

"It's there! Somewhere."

"Oh, come on."

"You probably imagined it. They're really rare around here. *I've* never seen one."

"It was skinny. It looked sick."

"Sick? How could you tell that?"

"Was it foaming at the mouth?"

"No, just skinny. And patchy. There was blood."

"If it was sick, it would've attacked you for sure. That's what my dad says."

"It was all messed up," she insisted. "It had teeth out the side of its face!"

All three of her classmates looked at each other before laughing. "What? Teeth where?"

She rubbed her cheek. "Here! It had extra teeth sticking out. Or something."

Rolled eyes, heavy glances, giggles.

"Sure, okay. You saw a monster."

"Not a monster, just a . . . I don't know, super-messed-up mountain lion!"

"What-*ever.*"

Her heart cracked to survive such a thing, to do everything right, and have it shooed away like nothing. Imagination.

"I don't care if you believe me," she told them, told herself, holding back tears. "I don't care what you think."

But of course she did. She cared very much.

Years later, her father emailed her an article about a mountain lion killed in Idaho. Out of the side of its head sprouted an extra set of teeth and whiskers. A conjoined twin that died in the womb and stuck to its sibling, or maybe a teratoma—a tumor filled with hair and teeth and whisker, posited the scientists. A real mystery, said the article. Unprecedented.

She doubted her mountain lion could still be alive, so thought it might not be unprecedented at all. She pictured other such cats stalking the Rockies, elusive and beyond the belief of anyone who hadn't seen them.

"Your old friend?" her father had written with a smiley face.

"A mountain lion's one thing, but a cat with two mouths? Trick of the light," he'd said at the time. "Stress. Not possible."

Buried under her own stairs, in the yellow beam of those predatory round eyes, she heard the echo of her father's voice.

"Trick of the light. Stress. Not possible."

She blinked at the thing outside the vent, at its bare, bristled head. At its enormous yellow eyes.

You've lost it. You're delusional.

The shape of the thing twisted. With that movement, it went inanimate. For a moment she couldn't understand what she was seeing. Couldn't process the mountain lion eyes going lifeless yet still staring at her through the vent. But then something clicked. It wasn't a living, staring hunter, but a picture.

Her skin turned to gooseflesh, tiny hairs pulling themselves out of flop sweat.

She was looking at a drawing. A drawing of a skull with ratty wisps of hair, eyes glowing. The kind of thing that was printed on a certain type of T-shirt. She was sure if she could see more of it above the skull, above the glowing eyes, it would say Black Sabbath, Metallica, the name of some other band that toyed with painted death for purposes of coolness and album sales.

Yes, she could see now what was happening, what the explanation was.

The Corner was sitting on the stairs. His back was to her. She had seen a bit of his shirt earlier, slices of him through the vent as he'd checked those front doors, but this was a fraction of him zoomed in close. Sitting the way he was, the skull eyes gazed from the back of his shirt and through the vent at her, blinking and winking with each wrinkle, each movement.

Please, kitty, don't you bite.

She thought the pounding of her heart might be loud enough to wake her son, still sleeping on her lap.

It's impossible! How did he get there without you hearing him? Or . . . did you fall asleep again?

She didn't think so, but supposed it was possible. Her fear, her throbbing head, the way she'd flown above the house to think of escape routes were so like a dream.

But . . . all the noise he made before. The toys in the playroom, the crackly board at the entrance to the office! And no way he came down the front stairs. Even quiet as you managed to get down them, with all your practice, it would still be deafeningly loud in this hollow place.

She tried to understand. Hypothesized that he'd come down the kitchen stairs and through the living room. That he'd accidentally or on purpose avoided the loud board at the entrance to the office. That he'd sat down carefully enough she hadn't heard the stair tread crack.

He's learning the sounds of the place. How to camouflage himself.

Again she felt her mind snag and catch on something familiar, something she should remember.

It's something to do with the shirt. Have you seen that shirt before?

Of course you have. People wear them all the time, black shirts from some band with skulls on them, glowing eyes, bones.

If you could remember, it could help.

Stop it. Focus.

She closed her eyes, awash in gratefulness that the children had happened to fall asleep. Hadn't been whispering, letting the Corner come on them unawares. Certainly even whispers would be hearable through the vent, on top of it like he was. A tiny twist of chance that had turned in her favor.

"This place crawls when it's empty," the Corner had complained aloud to himself earlier. "There are voices, noises, and no one's there."

Yes, he had heard voices. And now he was searching for her and the children, tracking the source of those disembodied sounds. The Corner sat five feet away watching, listening patiently with pricked ears, his closeness a suffocation.

He knows you're here.

Stop, stop. He's sitting in this spot because from here he can hear anyone in the playroom, the office, the stairs, the kids' bedrooms. He's waiting for you to make a move, a mistake. Give yourself away.

It occurred to her that she and the Corner were doing the same thing. Both waiting quietly in the surreal present, paused between their past lives and whatever future came next.

Breathe. Think. You can't do anything. Can't control anything but how quiet and still you are. And even that you can't control. Not really. Snores, sneezes, sighs. The slightest movement from the children, and he'll hear you.

This complete lack of say in her own present, her own future, made her heartbeat calm. There were no decisions to be made. Not in this moment, anyhow. She leaned her head against the brick, felt the warmth of her children's breathing bodies, and was strangely relieved to be momentarily absolved of all responsibility.

13

She woke up confused, mouth powdery sour. A familiar sound was just vanishing at the edge of comprehension. She saw only darkness. She oriented herself, and her heartbeat ticked up with the memory of where she was.

Her eyes flew to the vent. There was nothing on the other side. Which didn't mean the Corner wasn't there. Just that he wasn't sitting on the same step.

Stupid, stupid! To let yourself fall asleep! You fall asleep now? Here?

She gingerly pressed a finger to the knot on her head. It had settled at the size of a peach pit. Still throbbing, but not sickeningly painful the way it had been. She pawed carefully with her free hand, found the sippy cup, and drank. It washed away a bit of the webby feeling from her mouth. She stopped herself from drinking more.

Save it for the kids.

Her legs cramped as she stirred. Her son's weight had cut off her circulation. She suppressed a groan of pain, the awful feeling that her veins were constricting from heel to hip, and forced herself still so she wouldn't disturb her little boy.

Through the ache of it she heard something, and realized at once it was the same sound that had awakened her, but that had then gone quiet.

Singing.

The tune was cheerful. Not far away. The kitchen? The living room? Certainly on this floor. He was humming, a vibration that came low and heavy through the wall.

He was close now. The living room?

Then the threshold to the office crackled. There was a hollow *bonk*—the sound of the guitar being picked up. Then the sound of it being strummed. A pause. Another noise. He was tuning it.

She listened wide eyed in the dark. Her daughter woke and stiffened next to her, little hands gripping, constricting around her arm, her wrist.

Through the wood came the sound of a note going up and down, settling, the familiar slide of the guitar finding a clear point on the scale. She could picture her husband's fingertips on the silver tuning pegs, the way the guitar sat gently in his lap, how small it looked against his wide chest. It was always so surprising to see someone with his wrestler's build be so gentle, coax out such beauty. When he held the guitar, it reminded her of the way he'd cradled their children in his arms as babies.

"Are you here, little one?" the Corner rasped. "Got a song for you."

He played, the sound bright on the freshly tuned instrument.

She couldn't place the song, but she knew it was a child's tune, some nursery rhyme with lyrics impossible to recall, her mind blank at the irreconcilability of her fear and the soothing sound of the guitar.

The strumming stopped.

Then, the voice of the Corner, timbre tuneless and filled with rattling nails.

"Little pigs, little pigs, let me come in."

Her son shifted. She moved slightly to give her legs some relief. Sucked her lip with the torture of pins and needles.

Don't wake up. Sleep through it, please.

The boy settled, quiet.

Her daughter's hand tightened so hard around her wrist she grimaced.

"I'm tired of waiting. You hear that? I'm not going to dress in granny's pajamas and wait around anymore. This wasn't supposed to be dull." The Corner's cockroach voice scraped and burrowed, dripping with disdain.

Her daughter's fingernails dug deeper.

"No sheep's clothing. Just me, little piggies." He paused, listening, then added, "You know, that Big Bad Wolf got lit on fire. Climbed down the chimney. Scrabbling in the bricks, how did he ever fit? Shimmied down into a pot. Boiled and eaten."

He strummed the guitar again.

"But that's not how life is, little one. Pigs are the ones meant for eating. And I'm smarter than that old wolf," the Corner said. "I'm gonna *burn* the house in."

She felt the walls cave in around her. Imagined what it would be, to be in this place, smoke filling it. To be forced out for air and find him waiting. Her daughter started to cry into her robe, whimpering, "Mama, Mama!"

"Shhhhh, shhh!"

"Buuuuurn," he hummed. "That'll flush you out, you three little piggies. Hear that? Smoke you out, *easy-pleasy*."

She startled, her spine straightening, fingers spreading out as if she were falling, about to catch the weight of her whole body.

Easy-pleasy. How? How does he know that?

That was her son's phrase. He'd heard it in some cartoon, and ever since he was about three years old, "easy-pleasy" was the only way he said "please," embellishing it with different rhymes.

Easy-pleasy-lemon-squeezy, easy-pleasy-cracker-cheesy, easy-pleasy-carrot-peasy, easy-pleasy-booger-sneezy.

She saw her son's little face laughing at his own cleverness, at his own little poems, and felt the agonizing distance between those everyday moments of happiness and the awful moments they were trapped in now.

How does he know, how does he know, how does he know that? He knows us. He knows your little boy but—

"You think anyone will notice smoke through *this* storm? At *this* time of night? Far as this fuckin' creepy place is from everything? Nah. You're aaaaall alone."

Her daughter nuzzled between her arm and robe. Her son still slept, somehow undisturbed by the noise, the threat, the music, and her fear.

He thinks he's safe. Because he's warm in the dark sleeping in his mother's arms. But the Corner knows him, he knows us, somehow—how?

"Even bricks get hot. Even hidey-holes fill with fire." The voice of the Corner luxuriated in these words, as if picturing something so beautiful it was impossible to describe. "One-two-three and the best for me. Hear that? Hear that, little pigs? Dried-up spotty sow, little pretty piggy-wiggy? I'm going to burn you up. You and this damn haunted house. Come on out now, before you fry like bacon. And maybe—" The Corner paused, as if thinking, and when he spoke, an edge of the human crept in. "Maybe if you're good, maybe then the boy can be left out of it. He was never supposed to be involved." Again, a short silence, the Corner's voice shifting to grinding, accusatory, fury. "That's your fault, old witch. That's your doing. Another one hurt by you not accepting the way things should be. Don't want more blood on your hands, do you?"

The words lapped so near to their wall she unconsciously pressed herself back on the cold chimney, away from the Corner, away from the creature that seemed to see through the wood, describe where they were, tongue licking over the words "bricks" and "hidey-holes."

The blood rushed and pounded in her ears as she clung to her little boy, and for a moment she thought it was the whoosh of fire.

More blood? What blood is on your hands? Breathe. It's okay. You're still okay. Be quiet. He'd never let your boy go. Never. He's a liar.

The Corner muttered low, talking to himself, only bits hearable. "Living room, kitchen, basement . . . closet, closets . . . where? Would've seen . . . you know this . . . where?"

She understood from these broken mutterings that he was itemizing the rooms of the house, its closets, its underbeds and cabinets. She imagined him counting out on his fingers one, and two, and three, all the places he'd searched for them. All the rooms he'd combed through, snapping aside curtains, doors, covers. Trying to think of what he could have missed. Checking the trackless snow outside the windows for any sign of escape.

He creaked back and forth through the office, a beast in a cage. He sat with a wince of the armchair, then almost immediately began pacing again. Her body stayed pinned stiff and still against the masonry. Her eyes, blinded by the darkness, nevertheless darted back and forth as they followed the source of the words, the sounds, her mind running over everything, everything she'd seen, heard, trying to understand.

Easy-pleasy, easy-pleasy, it can't be a coincidence. Think. Think! Make a list. This isn't the first thing you've thought was familiar.

She breathed in and out to try to slow her frantic mind. Ordered moments in time and memories into a mental chart.

When you first saw him, saw how big he was, there was something you recognized. Your mind went blank the way it does when you see someone you know in an unfamiliar place but can't remember their name with their body somewhere so out of context.

And then—his voice. Not the awful Corner voice, but the way he first sounded. There was something familiar, something scratching at you.

Your little girl. The Corner man from her nightmares, she said.

And when he said he just wanted money, he made it clear he knew you were alone in the house. He knows you, somehow.

And the yellow eyes. That shirt. It was familiar. It was!

Easy-pleasy. Easy-pleasy.

But these pieces didn't come together in a satisfying *click!* Nothing interlocked to give her a cohesive whole, an explanation. She hung her head, dizzied by unfocused disappointment, not even sure if she should be frustrated with the failure of her own memory or if there was nothing at all to remember.

A grating sound, a low roar she recognized as the rolling noise of snow sliding off the roof, triggered the Corner's footsteps. She pictured him rushing to the office windows at the front of the house to figure out the origin of the unfamiliar sound and seeing a curl of snow *whumph* to the ground after slipping off the steep pitch of the roof.

"Oh, shit," the Corner said, voice shifting out of its low rasp and into a higher register.

What does he see? Has he seen you?

"Holy shit," he repeated, clearly talking only to himself but so excited, so thrilled at whatever thought had come over him, that his words grew louder.

"You idiot, all this time. You didn't even think! You didn't explore enough. Didn't do what you should've. That roofline. There's gotta be an attic." He cackled aloud, clapped his hands together victoriously. "They're hiding in the goddamn attic!"

Later she'd think about how if you grasp tight at anything fragile, you'll crush it. And she'd think of how fragile memory could be. Clutching at the familiar voice, shirt, proportions of the intruder, at the sound of him saying "easy-pleasy," her mind had strangled any cohesion between these disparate flashes of recognition.

But the Corner's joy as he realized there must be an attic, the almost friendly tone he used to scold himself, the undercurrent of cruelty in that happiness, his anticipation of having them by the throats, caused every piece to fold together and set her mind alight.

It's him. It's completely and clearly him.

The realization that she knew this man, that she remembered him, burned through every vein. She started to retch, interrupted the physical response as best she could, but something vile still ballooned at the back of her throat, needing to be swallowed.

It's him.

She knew many of the worst predators weren't purely strangers. Some of them found ways to meet and interact with their prey before deciding to hunt.

It's not your fault. And there's nothing you could've done.

Hopelessness submerged her. The Corner was a lightning strike on a clear day. His choice to hunt them felt as beyond her control as her mother's death. There was no relief in it at all, no revelation in the recognition that allowed for a way out.

What are you going to do?

Through the throbbing river run of her thoughts, she heard the dissonant clang of the guitar as the Corner dropped it to the floor. He must be rushing now, agitated. The door between the office and the entry flung open with a rattling crash. *Click!* The dim light in the entry went on. It shone through the vent like a weapon, slid again through the cracks in the stairs, around the knots in the boards. Where the light touched her, it felt like fire.

BAM! BAM! BAM! the footsteps rushed up the stairs, a bit of yellowed sneaker passing quickly by the vent, BAM! BAM! BAM!

It was too much, that sound, so loud it was like being inside a pounded drum.

Her son woke up and wailed.

14

They'd taken their sandwiches to one of the metal tables sitting outside the café and brushed off the accumulated crumbs left by the previous occupants. Although their daughter was tall for eight, she was still able to sit cross-legged on her chair, singing the old preschool rhyme as she folded herself in: "Crisscross applesauce, spoons in the bowl!"

A man came to the table and stood beside it, blocking the hot August sunlight. Backlit, the sun rimmed him like a painting of a haloed saint.

"I'm the manager," he said. "Just stopped by to say welcome."

Their little girl tipped her head back to look up at his preposterous height. She gave him the hesitant lift of her child's smile.

"What a princess!" the manager exclaimed. "Beautiful."

Something about the manager's overlarge body, his wide head, his paleness, reminded her of wet sand. And yet in the intensity of his eyes sweeping over her daughter she saw a tight, rubber band energy.

"You got a cocktail there?" he asked the girl, pointing to her lemonade.

"No," their daughter said. "I'm not old enough."

"Well, I'd never have guessed!" The manager's voice had the affectation of exaggerated shock common to adults teasing children. "I know you're old enough to drive, though."

The little girl shot him a flat, bored look before silently taking a bite of her sandwich.

Though his mouth was hidden by a mask, she was sure she saw a shadow of a frown cross his face at the way her daughter pointedly ignored him.

The manager cleared his throat, said sagely to her husband, "You're going to have your hands full with this heartbreaker."

"You have kids?" her husband asked.

"Not yet."

She imagined under his mask the manager licked thick, chapped lips and rough stubble. His body, the brush of his eyes, his words—all of it repulsed her. She knew that aside from his size, objectively he was simply average. Medium features, medium hair color, medium age. And yet, some gnawing, ancient instinct curled in her stomach and tensed her neck to straightness. Warnings chittered and flashed and she thought, *Be reasonable. He didn't look at her like— like that. You're in public. It's fine.*

"And check out this bruiser!" The manager playfully mimed a boxer. "How you doin', big guy?"

"I'm great!" Their son grinned at the manager they way he did at all grown-ups. "How're you?"

She melted a little at her son's sweetness. His perpetual bright sunniness.

"Best-behaved kids we've had in yet," the manager said.

"Thank you." Her husband smiled. "How long since you opened?"

The manager glanced over his shoulder at the café behind him, then said, "Not long. Rough time to do it, of course, but it had all been set up and paid for before—you know—all this."

The manager waved his hand around as if to take in the sandwich shop, the road beyond, the town, the distant hum of the highway, the invisible infection, the months of lockdown, death itself. *All this.*

His eyes slid again to their little girl. She felt her hand jerk toward her daughter, as if to interrupt . . . what?

Stop it. It's nothing.

"At least we're a takeout operation, you know? Got the outdoor tables, too."

"Sure." Her husband nodded. "Sure! Everyone wanting to eat outside. And this is an awesome spot!"

It struck her as it always did how much her husband's personality mirrored what she remembered of her mother. Brimming with enthusiasm. Hyperbole. Easygoing friendliness. *An awesome spot!*

The whole place had grown uglier in her eyes, turned now to the background of the discomfiting man. The fake shrubs rimming the café's wide concrete patio didn't do much to hide its view of a pockmarked parking lot. On the other side of the lot's stained concrete berm was Route 23. Across the busy road was a Verizon store, a Joann Fabrics, and a Taco Bell. The café was part of a shopping center with a Starbucks on one side and an empty storefront on the other, a banner in the window half-fallen to proclaim "ns coming SOON!" Cars hurried by. Cars waited at the light. Cars spewed noise and exhaust.

She had suggested they eat their sandwiches at home, but her husband had insisted on the patio, seizing any chance to be back in the world.

It's all so ugly. We could be anywhere, anywhere in America.

"You guys did a good job spreading all the tables out. It feels really safe," her husband mused.

She frowned at how small her daughter looked in the manager's shadow.

Safe.

"Well, if you get a chance, we'd love it if you reviewed us online. Love it if you come back." The manager clapped his hands together. "In the meantime, anything I can get for you folks?"

"No, nothing." It was the first time she'd spoken since the manager arrived at the table. Her voice struck her as obnoxiously loud, yet the manager didn't seem to hear her. The strap of her daughter's tank top had slipped, looping loose over her thin upper arm. The manager hooked the fallen strap with one finger and deftly replaced it. Her daughter hunched away from him, intuitively recoiling from that touch. He withdrew his hand. All over in a moment.

Did you see that? Did that just happen?

Her insides squeezed, freezing her tongue to silence. Her mind tumbled over vague memories of that same gesture. All the times a boyfriend, her husband, had replaced a strap that had gone askew.

It was intimate. It always is, always was, every time.

Don't be ridiculous. It was only a second. Just a quick little reaction.

"Do you have coloring stuff?" her son asked the manager. "Crayons?"

"How do you ask?" she corrected automatically and winced.

"Easy-pleasy-lemon-squeezy!"

"Not that kind of operation, bud, sorry." The manager shrugged. "How about you, princess?" He leaned down as if to catch their daughter's eye. "Refill on that cocktail?"

Behind her teeth trapped words bubbled. *Don't go near my daughter. You're being illogical.*

Because what had this man done, really? Nothing, nothing at all. A swift fix of a strap. Teasing words. Eyes that hovered and crept. Men and their eyes, always thinking they were so subtle.

Have you ever been right about something like this? Not in any provable way.

She imagined saying something. Setting in motion what she was sure would be the put-on confusion of the manager, the genuine confusion of her husband, who was, after all, a good man and therefore immunized to intuition built on fear. Her mouth felt sewn shut by all the undercurrents and implications and consequences. Saying something, anything, would turn the manager into the victim. Leave her husband baffled, apologetic. She and her husband would argue. The kind of argument that turns cruel and personal, searing and scarring the skin branding iron style. An argument that cut deep because the real problem was that, at bottom, they each lived in separate, untranslatable realities.

Yes, she would seem ridiculous. She would lose any argument, easy-pleasy-lemon-squeezy.

It was one second. Did you see it? It could all be normal.

So she stayed silent. So did her daughter, chewing on the bendy straw in her drink.

"Cat got your tongue?" the manager asked the girl.

"Love?" her husband prompted. "You need anything? The man's asking."

Their daughter shook her head and slouched further into herself, not looking up at her father or the manager.

"Aw, don't hide that smile, how about—"

This, at last, broke her.

"I think we're all set," she interrupted with a brittle cheerfulness, eyes fixed dark. "Don't let us keep you."

The manager seemed to register her existence for the first time. A tightness rippled barely visible underneath his skin. She thought immediately of a fisherman on a riverbank, torn out of blissful casting by the realization his line was snagged in a tree he hadn't noticed was so close behind him.

She pressed her tongue to the back of her teeth to force a hard, lipless smile. "*Thankssomuch,*" she hissed. "*You'vebeensohelpful.*"

"Oh . . . uh . . . right!" The manager's face fell into what seemed to her exaggerated surprise and offense. "I'll let you get to it, then."

She watched him walk back to the café. Like the other employees, he was wearing black, but she frowned at his ratty T-shirt, the leering skull on the back under a band name printed in a font so Gothic it was unreadable. She took an enormous bite of her sandwich, pretending she didn't feel her husband's eyes on her.

"Why'd you have to be rude to the guy?" her husband asked.

She finished chewing. Swallowed. "I said he was helpful."

"Come on."

"He'll survive."

"He's just trying to be friendly. Get people to come back. New business and all."

"Mmm-hmmm."

Her husband leaned back in his chair. "I knew you'd have an issue the *second* he called her 'princess.' That kind of thing drives you nuts."

"Just didn't want to talk to him when I could be talking to you guys."

Her husband gave a puffing exhale.

She ran her hand through her son's black hair. Down his soft neck. He nuzzled her hand with his cheek like a fawn. Then he picked his nose.

"Stop that," she told him, "it's gross."

"I can't help it."

"Sure you can."

A woman came out of the café holding two cups. Spotting the numbered flag they'd been given at checkout, she headed to their table.

"One iced coffee and one iced chai latte?"

"That's right, thanks," she said as the woman set the sweating plastic cups on the table.

"I'll just put your receipt right here," the woman said, tucking the curling paper under the metal weight of the numbered flag.

"I like your hair," her daughter said, fixated on a streak of pink by the woman's cheek.

She held her breath the way she always did at such precipices.

"I'll tell you a secret," the woman said. "It's not my real hair! It just clips in." She paused, looking at their daughter's disappointed expression, then lowered herself down expertly in her short skirt to be eye to eye, said conspiratorially, "If I had hair nice as yours, I wouldn't need to stick fake stuff in it." The woman regarded the shining black depth of their daughter's hair. A marking whitened half of the girl's left eyebrow and turned a streak of hair ultrapale at her temple. "Really. It's something special."

Their daughter brightened and gave a shy half smile.

She thanked the woman, sharing a heavy look that made it clear what she was really thankful for. Noted how her little girl tracked the woman, how her eyes fastened longingly at the café door the server disappeared through. Filed that away.

Her husband's face was sour.

"What?" she sighed.

"I just don't get it. You're polite to the waitress, but not the manager?" *Here we go again.*

Since the estrangement from his father, her husband hadn't revisited his accusation that she might have misread the situation on the day of his mother's death; that she might have done something worthy of his father's wrath. But this new habit—her husband examining her behavior, searching for signs she was socially blunted, inconsiderate—penetrated the otherwise placid surface of her marriage to remind her,

That's right, he wants to blame you. That's right, he needs his father's approval so badly he's ready to sacrifice your reliability. And that's right, it's your fault for letting that black hole of a man into your life.

She knew she needed to sound calm. Dismissive. She needed to repress the lecture she felt rising in her throat about how she'd ignored her instincts about his father and look how that turned out, about how infuriating it was that now her husband wanted her to shuffle off her revulsion to this random stranger for no reason at all. A rant like that would show she was all the things she wasn't allowed to be. Bitter. Angry. Filled with impotent regret.

So she shrugged, asked, "Why are you making this a big deal?"

"I just don't understand why you're so weird with people sometimes."

"Look. I know you think I'm being rude or awkward or whatever. But I don't have to pretend to enjoy having him hover over us. And that woman was . . . kind."

"'Princess,' is just, like, not offensive."

"I don't like princesses," the little girl piped up. "We live in a democracy."

She gestured at their daughter as if to say, "Exactly, she gets it!"

"I like princesses!" said the little boy. "They're good at singing."

"Good point." She intercepted the little boy's hand in midair as he went to pick his nose again.

"What's a heartbreaker?" their daughter asked.

Her husband turned, surprised by the non sequitur. She feigned engrossment in helping her son blow his nose, curious how her husband would answer.

"It's when—it's when you don't love someone who loves you," her husband said. "That's called breaking their heart. A heartbreaker."

"So a heartbreaker hurts someone's feelings?"

"Sometimes. But . . . it's a compliment. The man said it to be nice."

She heard more than felt her teeth clench.

"He was using the word 'heartbreaker' to mean 'beautiful,'" she told her daughter, "because people want things that are beautiful, and are sad if they can't have them. But no one is required to love someone else. No one's entitled to your love or attention."

She looked at her beautiful daughter. So unique, so unusual, people said, wanting an explanation, uncomfortable over their longing, their need for difference to be defined. They stared, trying to reconcile what they saw as aberration with their interest, uneasy over their attraction to it, uneasy about not being able to classify. To silo her singular beauty.

The little girl glanced at the café door the woman had disappeared through.

"You understand?"

"Yeah."

Does she? Do you?

Watching the children barter their pickles, her husband conceded, "I guess the guy was a little weird."

Happily surprised at his about-face, she said, "Right? What was he, like, thirty? 'Princess, sweetheart, heartbreaker.' He's not old enough for stuff like that to seem, I dunno, reasonable. And did you notice he didn't go to any other tables? Doesn't that seem—strange?"

Her husband shrugged dismissively. "He probably already made the rounds before we got here."

"I guess." She glanced at the children, busy with their own conversation. Said low, "I didn't like how he fixed her strap. It was—strange."

Her husband bristled, and she instantly wished she could take the words back.

"What are you talking about?"

"He put her tank top strap back in place. On her shoulder."

She plucked a phantom strap, placed it on her own shoulder to demonstrate.

Her husband crossed his arms and cocked his head. "Come on. That didn't happen."

"Maybe you didn't notice, but he did it."

Her husband's lip twisted and his eyebrows lifted, the skeptical expression he always gave when he thought she was incorrectly perceiving the world. This look told her they were teetering at the edge of the argument. The one she knew she'd lose, easy-pleasy-bread-and-cheesy, because the manager had only said excusable things. Because he'd repulsed her, frightened her, in a way illogical enough, visceral enough, that she knew she couldn't explain it.

She attempted to shift into a different argument. "I mean . . . I don't get why this bugs you. You get to yell at the UPS guy, but I have to be all friendly with this guy? I'm allowed to be, like, fractionally rude when I happen to think someone is creepy or annoying or whatever."

"The UPS guy's an idiot," her husband grumbled.

She gave a snorting laugh. "True! Very true. And this guy was overly familiar. It was irritating."

Her husband's eyes widened. He lifted his chin to gesture behind her.

The manager walked toward them carrying the largest wedge of vanilla cake she'd ever seen. He set the plate down dramatically on their table, nearly upending the little numbered flag on its metal pole. The cake was a beautiful shade of cream. It was so soft, the waves of icing so deep, its sheen so matte, it looked too perfect to be real. The children stared as though they were witnessing an apparition of the Virgin Mary.

"On the house!" The manager put his hands on his hips. "For the best-behaved kids, of course."

Their little girl reached toward the cake as if she was going to touch it, make sure it was actually there. Pulled her hand back. She beamed up at the manager.

"Thank you!"

"Cake for a cupcake," he said.

Her daughter's smile faltered.

"You didn't need to do that," she told the manager. Her voice came out as clipped and cold as she'd meant it to.

"My pleasure! You've got to be a gentleman when you've got a princess in the house."

"Thank you." Her husband seemed as mesmerized as the children. "That is quite a piece of cake!"

The manager set down extra plates and utensils. He picked up the numbered flag, sending the receipt the server had tucked under it skittering across the table. He stopped the paper from blowing away with a heavy slap of his palm.

"I'll get this out of your way," he said, lifting up the flag. "Want me to toss this for you?" He waved her husband's copy of the receipt, held between two fingers.

"Sure, thanks," her husband said.

The manager shoved the receipt in a back pocket. "All right. Enjoy!"

His whole self glowed triumphant. His eyes connected with hers, and behind his mask she was sure there was a sneering smile, one that whispered, "I win."

The manager gave an obsequious bowing motion, then went back into the café.

"That's, like, a quarter of a four-layer cake," she grumbled. "And he didn't even ask if it was okay to bring it?"

"You're seriously taking issue with free food? Free *dessert*?" Her husband grinned and shook his head, well aware of her sweet tooth. "Never thought I'd see the day."

Her husband cut chunks of the cake. When he started to cut her a serving, she waved him off. "No thanks. I'm full."

"For real? You're turning down dessert?"

"Yep."

"Maybe you should be short with people more often," her husband teased. His irritation was gone, his expression one of vindication. "Guess that's what gets you free food."

"Guess so," she said.

She watched her family eat the cake. Icing coated her daughter's lips. She wiped a glob of it off her son's chin, swept crumbs from his shirt. She went into the café for a to-go box, relieved that she didn't see the manager inside. She used two forks to lift the leftover cake into the box. Couldn't close the top because of the size of the thing. Had to carry it out with the Styrofoam lid flopping. She kept the box wedged between her feet in the passenger seat of the car on the way home so it wouldn't slide, get icing on the seat, the door.

The next day while her children played outside, while her husband flew over a harbor filled with boats, their sails small as bug wings in his camera lens, she threw the cake in the trash.

"Can we have some of the leftover cake for dessert?" the children asked after dinner.

"I ate it," she said.

"What do you know," her husband chuckled. "Not able to resist free food after all."

Her grandmother's voice reverberated in her head.

"Nothing in this world's free," it said.

15

She clapped her hand over her son's bawling mouth.

"Shhhhh, shhh! Mama's here," she whispered. "Shh-hhh!"

In the light cast through the vent, she saw her daughter lean close to her little brother, whisper something, press her forehead to his.

She refocused, took stock.

There'd been no hitch in the Corner's steps, the last two stairs echoed BOOM! BOOM! before his footfalls slammed across the landing, followed by the thumping sound of him hurrying through her daughter's room.

No pauses, no hesitation.

"He didn't hear," she whispered with relief so thick it filled the hidden place. "He didn't hear us! It was too noisy, it's okay, we're okay. Buddy, I'm going to take my hand off your mouth now, okay? You have to—have to!—be quiet. We can't let him hear us."

Tentatively, she removed her hand. It was wet with his spit. It burned. In the light that seeped into the hidden place from the chandelier on the stairs, she saw her son had bitten her palm.

"Mama!" He plunged his head against her chest, crying.

"Shhh, I know you're scared," she told her son. "I know, but shhh."

"He's going to light a fire." Her daughter's voice was high pitched and desperate, her hands twisting the belt of the robe. "He's going to burn us up!"

"Shhh, shhh. He's still looking for us. Looking for the attic door. We have to be quiet."

Together, their eyes went to the ceiling of the hidden place. Scrabbling sounds, footsteps. Yes, he was searching up there. It wouldn't be long until he found the attic.

Something warm and wet slowly poured over her, a realization coated with terror.

This is it. The first little sliver of opportunity you've had to get help since you hid them away. You know he's telling the truth. You know he's willing to burn you out. Or wait you out.

In her mind's eye she saw the manager casually pocket their receipt at the café. A receipt that would have had her husband's name on it. Remembered the slither of his eyes over her little girl.

He's been planning this. Planning this for four months.

She saw the laminate floor of her dorm room, heard herself whimper. Could feel the shame of her body melting, every bit of her mind evaporating into fear.

You can't live through that again, failing like that. You've thought it all out, you know what to do. The only thing that will doom you is hesitation.

And it's not really about you.

She felt her ten-year-old dread. Heard her ten-year-old voice. *Why won't you let me go? Do you want to eat me so?*

This is no game. This is for all that matters. All right. All right.

She tried to keep her voice from shaking.

"The attic is big," she said. "It will take him a little time to look once he finds it."

She paused, pulled the children to her body tight in a rough and awkward hug. They were so perfect, their skin, their smell, their hair and stale breath.

"Where do we go," she asked, "if there's a fire? If we smell smoke?"

"Outside to the big rock."

"Very good! If you see fire, smell or see smoke, you need to get out the secret door. You need to go to the old front doors. Remember how I showed you the latch works? That little bar you have to lift?"

"Yes, Mommy."

"I'll make sure the bolt is unlocked, so if you smell smoke, if you see fire, all you need to do is lift that latch. You close those doors behind you, you try to get to the rock. If it's too cold, you hide under the bushes by the fence. It's not so far, and there shouldn't be so much snow there. You know where I mean? You cuddle close to each other. You take the blanket with you."

"But you'll take us?"

"No. I have to—I have to leave. Now."

"No, no!"

They clung to her, crying. She realized that they seemed so loud to her, but that their sounds, every sound they made, was suppressed, as though their fear unconsciously muffled their voices.

"You have to be brave. So does Mama. I'm going to go get help, okay? Or else the Corner—the man's—going to hurt us. You have to close the secret door behind me. You stay quiet. You stay out of the light, and stay together. Warm as you can. Only if there's smoke, fire, do you come out."

"No, Mama, we can go with you!"

Their despair hurt somewhere deep in her jaw. She could feel them starting to disintegrate.

"You can't come. It's too cold. There's too much snow. He'd catch us."

WHAM!

They all went silent at the noise.

"That's the attic door." Her breathing came faster now. "He's found it. I have to go. He won't hear me leaving while he's in the attic."

"Mama, no! No. Please!"

There was a live-wire force moving her that she recognized as the will to live. To make sure the children lived. Again she saw herself from the outside, wondered, *How are you this awake? Have you ever been this awake?*

"Now. I have to go *now*."

She crawled toward the panel on hands and knees, able to see where she was going this time with the light scattered from above. The children held her, followed her, grabbing and quietly keening.

She sat and faced her children with her back against the panel. They were streaked with dirt. She stared at them, their beauty, their wide, dark eyes, thickets of lashes. She swiped to softly brush hair from one face, then the other. Their hands were everywhere, trying to trap her there. She leaned toward them, kissed cheeks, noses, eyelids, fast and desperate. Hungry for every new memory. But panicking.

You don't have time for this!

"I love you," she said. "I love you more than anything in the world. Mama is going to work so hard to come back to you. You smell smoke, see fire, you leave. Don't come out for anything else."

In rushed a vision of the Corner hurting her to lure them out. She heard how frantic, how desperate, her voice was becoming.

"Even if you hear Mama telling you to come out, don't come out. Even if you hear Mama hurt, crying, don't come out, okay? I'll open the panel when I come back, all by myself, all right?"

Her daughter had the hem of the robe twisted tight in her hand. Her son was wrapped around her calf. It was as if they thought she was turning to smoke, and only their clinging was keeping her solid.

"Promise me!"

"Okay, Mama," said her daughter.

"You, too, promise me!"

"Okay," said her son, and nodded.

"You are the best and bravest and I love you. I'm so proud of you."

She tried to turn to open the panel, but they wouldn't release her. Little hands tightened, little arms gripped her the more she moved. Boa constrictors, settling themselves around her for more efficient suffocation. Instantly her mouth went tight, her vision thinned.

Why won't they do what you say? Why won't they just obey? You're running out of time!

A parent's a tyrant, a parent's a dictator. If you just did exactly what I said right when I said it, there'd be peace.

"You promised! Let me go," she said in that voice that verged on the edge of fury, the one that normally frightened them into obedience, a voice that now reminded her sickeningly of the Corner. "Let go *right now*."

But they wound around her leg, her robe, her wrists, pulling her down, and she groaned with rage.

"There's no time for this! Stop it!"

She shook them off, unlatching hands roughly, little fingers bending, gasps and crying. They still wouldn't let go. Their hands kept refastening, their desperation letting them find new purchase the second she managed any movement, little voices calling out, "Mama!"

Too loud! They're too loud.

"No!" she hissed. "No! Stop it, this is unacceptable. You've got to do what I say. Or the Corner will get us."

With both hands she pushed her son hard in the chest, and he tumbled to the dirty floor. She saw the shock on his face as it hit. Heard a crunch she hoped was the grit of mortar dust skidding beneath him.

She yanked her daughter's hands from her arm, her robe, held the girl by the wrists and shoved her backward against the chimney brick.

Laying violent hands on her children was so jarring, so unreal, that for a moment she was convinced she'd killed them.

Then they both started crying.

It's for their own good, for them.

Her teeth ground in frenzied panic, at revulsion over what she'd done, making it difficult to talk.

"*Quiet!* No crying, no sound! Or the Corner will get you."

Delicious.

They were scared of her. She'd never before raised a hand to them, and their baffled, scratched faces tried to reconcile all their memories, all her talk of love and safety and returning with how she'd hurt them. Instead of reaching for her, they picked themselves up and crawled to hold each other, watched her push the panel, watched it open into the dark office.

She clambered out, awkward in the robe and slippers. Turned around on hands and knees.

"Close it!"

They didn't move.

"*Now!*"

Her daughter leaned forward and pushed the panel closed, eyes mistrustful. She watched the children disappear, watched the panel hitch into place.

Just before it shut, she whispered a desperate "I love you!"

For a moment she stayed on all fours. She felt seasick, adrift at the separation, its violence. Tried to suppress visions of them suffocating in smoke, screaming in fire. A creeping dread rolled over her, suddenly aware of all the room's dark corners.

She couldn't get stable, couldn't stop the *flick, flick, flick* of images tearing through her mind. So much could happen so quickly. The idea of her absence. Of their calls. Of the Corner's claws. Of this being their last memory of her, transformed to monstrousness.

Breathe, breathe. There's no time. Move.

She stood and came close to collapsing on her sleeping legs. She stomped to restart their circulation and staggered forward through the door to the entry. After the darkness of the hidden place, the light from the single candelabra bulb over the stairs was blinding.

You did what you had to do. For them. Stop thinking about yourself. No, no, no one is coming to rescue you. There's no real choice. Pain and risk are coming. You're wasting time!

She opened the tiny entry closet, squeezed her eyes shut in hope that whatever she'd heard the Corner rustle through there was warm, helpful.

She opened her eyes.

"Thank you, thank you!" she said to her husband, to her mother-in-law. "Thank you!"

Hanging in the closet was her mother-in-law's old fur coat. Boxy-shouldered, outdated, mothball-smelling, floor-skimming mink. Or fox. Or, for all that she knew about fur coats, made of bunny rabbit.

"I'm going to donate it," she'd told her husband, holding it up. Her mother-in-law had pressed the coat on her during that day's care, insisting it was a gift. As though it were the kind of thing people still wore, or still valued. "It's . . . immoral."

"Well, it's not like we bought it. And wouldn't throwing it away be even worse?"

"You sound like my dad," she said, thinking of her father's piles of old magazines, broken lawn chairs, decaying, rolled-up rugs.

Her husband held the coat and smiled at the thing, a thousand memories lighting up his eyes, memories of his mother in this coat when it was new and sleek and loved. She'd sighed. Thought it ugly, impractical, unfashionable, unflattering. But knew she was power-less against the prospect of her husband's happiness.

"Maybe you'll wear it someday," he said.

"Just . . . find somewhere it won't get in the way."

So here it was. Her husband had hung it in this strange, useless little closet under the front stairs. The closet was so small that the bottom of the hanging coat pooled on the floor. Waiting for the day she wouldn't hate it. Would put it on.

Which was today.

She reached for it, hesitated.

But he looked in here. You heard him rooting around in this closet. Won't he notice it's gone?

No time. No time! It's worth the risk. Because look at you. Underwear and an old shirt, drenched in sweat. Fuzzy slippers. A clammy robe. It's going to be painful. You think you're cold now, uncomfortable now. No, no. This has been nothing at all. If you don't put this on. Hypothermia? Frostbite? How quickly do those happen?

She recalled digging out a snow shelter in winter next to her classmates, sweating away in fourteen-degree weather, the sun set-ting and the feel of that sweat-drenched shirt under her coat. She'd been unable to sleep, her soaked base layer wicking away every bit of warmth.

"Well, of course," her mother told her. "You're lucky you didn't get hypothermic keeping on wet clothes like that. Don't those teach-ers pay attention to anything? Don't they know anything?"

She stripped off the robe, used it to wipe the line of sweat between and under her breasts, her stomach. Thought a second and took off her drenched T-shirt. Left on only the underwear.

She threw the robe and T-shirt into the closet and closed it. On went the coat, heavy and reeking of mothballs. The inside was silky and clung to her damp skin. It was too long for her, ending about an inch past her feet. Her fingers were swollen with nervousness, and she fumbled with the buttons through the stiff fur, managing to fasten three of them. She paused, opened the closet again, yanked out the robe and wrapped it around her head like a turban, hoping it would help keep her warmer. Instead it upset her balance. She threw the robe back in and closed the closet.

You're wasting time!

"Ninety percent of success is preparation, the rest is perspiration," her grandmother's voice instructed.

No sounds came from upstairs.

He must still be in the attic.

She looked at the vent, squinted. She couldn't see the children. She leaned down and put her face to it.

"Shhh," she whispered. "I'm sorry. Stay quiet. I love you!"

She listened, couldn't hear a response.

That's good, isn't it?

There was a needle dragging a thread through her chest, sewing a bloody message that said, *You hurt them. You hurt them.*

No, you didn't! Not much. All you did was push them away.

The panic wouldn't stop throbbing in her throat.

No time, no time!

"I love you! I love you!"

There was a whisper of movement.

"Quiet. Stay quiet," she said. "And don't come out."

She looked up the stairs, listened again for any hint of what the Corner was doing.

Did you miss any noises? He's up there now, looking, but for how long? How long until he gets angry, starts trying to flush them out? Hurry.

She turned to the door. There was the unavoidable wince of iron on iron as she threw the bolt. Then she lifted the little locking bar with one hand, the latch with the other.

As she opened the doors, she was sliced by a blast of cold wind, by swirling ice. Already her eyes were tearing with it. Instantly her skin ached and her body shook fiercely with the shock of that bottomless cold.

She couldn't make herself step out into the storm.

Go, go!

Her body didn't budge. She clutched at the coat as her feet stayed planted.

You've been here before! There's no real choice about what will happen. There's no real choice about the pain. The pain is coming no matter what you do, will get so much worse before it can get better.

"You're being so brave!" the nurse told her, her husband told her, and she remembered knowing she wasn't brave, not at all. It was simply that she had no say in the matter. The baby was coming, labor had hit her fast, it was too late for the drugs, the end. She remembered thinking, *Maybe bravery is just enduring. Maybe bravery doesn't exist. All there is is getting through it.*

This is the same! No different than childbirth. The ball is already rolling downhill. Gravity has got you. If you stay, there's even worse pain. There's violence. Death. Not just for you, but for them. Them! So no, no real choice at all. No real matter of bravery. You have to push, you have to cause yourself more pain before the pain can ease.

There at the threshold, the agonies that could emerge from the Corner exploded in her head, infinite. What was that, compared with what was outside this door?

She breathed in and out, and at last accepted it. She stepped out of the house. As she closed the entry doors behind her, her eyes fixed on the grate in the stairs until the doors shut and the little bar fell into place, locking her out.

The point of no return.

16

Standing outside in the storm, she knew immediately it was impossible.

Who do you think you are?

She kept herself plastered to the side of the house.

Stories of superhero mothers swirled in her head. Mothers who'd lifted cars off their trapped babies. Who'd fought off bears, tigers, snakes. Pulled children from the mouths of alligators. Shot to kill. Screaming, righteous, winning.

What a bunch of bullshit.

Years ago she'd jumped into a calm part of a river where the water was deep and smooth. There'd been a late August sun, hot, dry air. But the water was fresh-melted snow from the Wasatch, and on hitting it she'd gone into shock, inhaled, only kept from drowning because she'd gone straight to the bottom and had involuntarily pushed up off the river rock hard enough that she broke the water's surface.

This cold was the same. So painful, so sudden, that she choked. Her muscles spasmed, her jaw twinged like glass had been plunged under her ear to the bone.

And this, all this, even with the coat.

Thank God for the coat.

The storm was raging, snow swirling, making things visible, invisible, dark, white.

You should have gotten the fire poker. Waited for him. Hit him. This is too much.

She looked down at her shaking body, at the way the fur coat swallowed her feet.

No. These odds are better. And you're here now. You've got no choice. If you don't move, something will move you.

"That's all being an adult is," said her grandmother's southern drawl. "Doing one thing you don't want to do. Then doing another thing you can't the best you can."

She breathed the aching air, carefully stepping in places close to the house and protected by the eaves. The snow dusted into her slippers, melting on her feet.

When she turned the corner, the wind ticked down a notch. It was the lee side of the house, the snow shallower. Even so, her face, her head, throbbed with the cold. She took one hand out of her pocket to press to her cheek, her nose. Did the same with the other, alternating sides to warm herself as she moved slowly forward.

The coat smelled worse the more the snow hit it, the moisture doubling the stench of mothballs, neglect, and animal musk.

She had to be careful not to trip on the hem of the too-long coat. Air and ice crept up her legs, whispered through the gaps between the buttons, breathed down her spine, froze the moisture still collected on the notch at the base of her neck.

The coat's warmth was preternatural. The only spot of hope in the dark, miserable, unfair, and frozen world.

She peeked through a window into the living room. There was no sign of movement. The room sat so still, so empty, it looked colder even than where she stood in the snow. She felt acutely how alone she was, without the children. She hurried past the windows, feeling unseen eyes on her.

One step, another, yes.

She ducked under the kitchen windows, wind howling, cold moisture now seeping through the slipper soles. After she'd passed beneath the windows, she peeked through a pane of the antique, wrinkled glass into the kitchen.

The Corner was coming down the stairs, tilting his head to the side this time where the ceiling cut low to avoid hitting his head again. He appeared watery through the glass, every bit of him distorted and in motion.

Blood filled her ears to pounding deafness and she recoiled from the window, flattening herself against the siding.

Did he see you? He's down from the attic, down already. They're alone. Alone! He's going to start a fire. Smoke them out. Alone!

She groaned, the pull of helplessness yanking out something unseeable from where it was embedded in her bones. The fear, the back roll of her eyes as she imagined her children suffering, made the cold fractionally more forgettable, a little less painful compared with the horror of the Corner's potential.

Move. Move! You're past the windows now but . . . if he spotted you, he'll follow you. He'll catch you. You have to go, now. If you stay you'll never forgive yourself. No one will forgive you.

You wouldn't deserve forgiveness.

"This is it," her husband's voice scratched through her brain. "You can't lose. You're not allowed to."

She ran. Ran alongside the house before plunging into the driveway. The snow was deep there, unprotected as it was, deep enough she gasped at the crystals cutting her calves, her knees. She had to step like a doe through the drifts, the snow pushing the coat up, ice tearing her skin, filling the slippers until each step was frozen.

Don't lose the slippers. Keep your hands warm in your pockets when you can. Don't lose your balance.

Thank God for the coat.

The coat's satin lining claustrophobically adhered to her skin, wettened by the blowing snow sneaking down her neck. She registered a chest-constricting irregularity in her heartbeat. The heart of a prey animal under the animal skin of the coat.

The trees above and ahead cut the storm with a *woosh*. Even through the torture of the cold, through the heave of her burning lungs inhaling ice, the dark line of the forest frightened her. It loomed, hiding things, looking too vast and angry to let her through.

In a distant way she noted that she couldn't see any car, that there was no obvious way the Corner had arrived.

You never do the right thing, you left them—left them! Should've run for the keys, the car, the gun.

Ahead were the graves, off kilter and snowcapped.

Yes, yes! The trail. Almost there. The trail will be easier.

Her feet were perforated by a thousand cuts, each step requiring she fully will it into reality. The cold penetrated her calves, crawled up her inner thighs, grabbed at her privates in a way that made her think someone had skimmed a blade from knee to groin and was pulling out the lace of arteries and veins through her muscles the way she might pull a weed, lift the stringy tangle of roots from dirt.

Unbearable! You need to stop, you need to warm your feet.

No. If you stop, you'll never get up again.

She reached the graves, picked through them by memory, most just lumps in the snow, completely covered.

Don't trip, don't trip on them!

But she already had. She fell over the smallest one, hidden under a snowdrift. The headstone of the eight-month-old, date of death just prior to the Civil War.

She caught herself, hand clutching the snow-dusted winged skull on the tallest stone.

"Mother, Father, I will meet you in heaven," read the epitaph of the grave she'd stumbled over.

She remembered it. Had read it many times, her brows knit as she stood over that tiny marker, imagining what that must have been like for that particular mother and father.

See? This is nothing. Nothing compared to that. You have to get through this. So that doesn't happen. No little graves.

Her legs were ripped apart. Her feet were useless.

All those stories, all those movies, lies. Lies and more lies about what people could take. What a mother could do. How much pain the human body could live with. The final girl beating down armed men, outrunning monsters.

It's like childbirth. No choice.

That's right. And women die in childbirth. And you'll die, too, if you don't move.

She stood, moved forward, her progress slower after her stumble. Some part of her had twisted such that pain traveled from her ankle up to her back teeth.

Her feet were nothing but pained stumps. Her body shook such that the cold seemed to penetrate her marrow, curling to make a home there.

Shouldn't your feet be numb by now? When will they go numb? How can you hardly control them, yet still feel every little bit of awfulness?

Her hand was wet in her left pocket. She pulled it out, looked at it. In the darkness her blood was black.

It's just a cut. A cut from catching yourself on the gravestone.

The amount of blood disturbed her. The cut slashed across the round part of her whitened palm. Blood pulsed out of it, thick over her wrist where the pearlescent marking met pigmented skin. The blood slickened the fur of the coat.

She stuffed her hand back into her pocket. Closed her wet fist in the lining, sticky warm in the middle but quickly chilling to freeze at the edges.

Don't look, it's not that much blood.

Hurry—hurry! It's been too long since you left them. How long has it been?

She kept moving, eyes on the trail ahead. The trees bent over it, heavy with snow. It looked like a tunnel dug by some great creature, round and dark. The home of devils and unknowable things.

Stop it! The devil is what's behind you. The woods are just the woods.

There was a scratching in the air.

Smoke?

She whipped around to look at the house, terrified that it might be on fire. But there was nothing. No licking flames. No sign through the blowing snow of any smoke against the black sky. No smell, either.

Your mind playing tricks on you.

But it wasn't. It was that same feeling of being watched she'd felt under the yellow gaze of the deformed mountain lion. The same one that tugged her eyeballs to another car racing down the highway to meet the look of someone staring back at her. The twinge of someone gawking.

She squinted through the swirling snow, opening and closing her bloodied fist in her pocket. On the second floor of the house, a light was on in her bedroom, dim through the storm.

Outlined there was the figure of the Corner.

She knew that view. It was the only window that gave a clear line of sight across the driveway, where her deep tracks cut through the snow. That window was the one and only place that let you see all the way to the entrance of the path where she stood now, staring back at the house.

The silhouette vanished. The light went out.

He saw you.

The fear rolled down her throat. She screamed but there was no sound.

Why can't you ever scream?

She hiked the coat up awkwardly in her arms, turned, and fled down the trail.

Her eyes blurred with the cold, the wind, the speed. Her feet were somehow still moving, but they were uneven, one barely able to hold her up when she put weight on it. Her heart cracked her ribs. Her lungs burned with ice.

Don't look back, don't look back!

There's blood on the track.

She stared just ahead, trying to see what was coming through the darkness, what was under her sodden, aching, frozen stump feet. The snow on the trail was thin, that same uncanny thinness as always, just enough to hide tree roots. To hide slippery, decaying leaves. She stumbled, lurched. Again and again her legs staggered sideways, slid backward, and still she kept forward momentum. She slipped on a rock under the snow and fell. She scrabbled up, yanked the coat high to free her legs, and let them run.

The air was thick and strange, difficult to breathe, her body in a new dimension between the earth and water.

Are you moving? Are you running? Everything is so slow. Why can't you move faster?

The tunnel of the path narrowed, distorting the distance ahead as if the end of the path grew ever farther away.

It's because the path is haunted. That's why it looks funny. That's all. All the ghosts with their skirts making the air curdle. Keep moving.

Something tore at her coat so forcefully her shoulder made a cracking noise, her mouth a *huh!* sound as she was pulled bodily backward.

Don't look back! Go!

She pulled, she ripped away. She wrenched herself forward, freed. From a branch? A hand? Again she ran.

Then there was a slap her across her cheek, her eyebrow, her forehead. The shock of it made her reel back a step and fall to the ground, stunned. One eye went dark and bitter and bloody. She wiped the drip of it with her unhurt hand. Something black arched in front of her, vague and without depth as she looked up at it with her one working eye.

Just a branch. You ran into a branch. Weighed down and low with snow.

No, no, it's the Corner, it's a claw.

It hovered above her, razor taloned, and as she stood it became a branch again.

Keep moving. Don't let him grab you! He'll use you against the children.

"Delicious," wheezed the Corner.

Everything was uneven now, ground tilting at odd angles. Trees circling. The woods were whispering.

Go back, go back, there's blood on the track!

You've sucked in snow and ice and it cut and bloodied your insides, that's all.

Her lungs opened like butterfly wings, red and soft, organblood spattering the snow with a steam and freeze.

Bloody eye, bloody hands, bloody feet. Don't you make a tasty treat.

Delicious.

She recognized, dimly, that her brain wasn't working quite right. That her eye wasn't, either. That her slippers were gone. Was she frozen? She looked down. No, her legs were still moving. She swiped at her eye, saw through the clotted lashes the black open end of the trail, so close all of a sudden, so all at once!

She threw herself out of the trees, floundering in the snowdrifts that deepened where the path stopped. She tried to scream, and blood came out. She coughed it into the snow. She was swimming, swimming through the snow.

The houses were dark. Sleeping giants, barely visible now through the thickening blizzard, unprotected here with the way they'd clear-cut the trees, planted small, shapeable things.

Where is he? He's nearly on top of you, he must be, you can feel him. Don't look!

The coat was heavy, so horribly heavy, catching all the snow. She pulled it up again, forced herself forward, legs wallowing dark against that whiteness. Her exposed thighs screamed with it.

With one eye open but foggy at the edges and the other swollen to blindness, she flailed toward the dark outline of the nearest house.

Time was broken. Space didn't look right; it kept rolling and shifting and the house had run away.

A floodlight.

"Help!" she mouthed, silent.

It was like her nightmares. She saw the linoleum floor of her dorm room. She tried to scream and no sound came.

Shame on you! Call for help, do it!

Out came air and metal, the taste of tinfoil between teeth.

A door, there! There's a door, get to the door.

The coat was difficult to hold, kept slipping and binding her legs, the lining slick and soggy.

Through her unhurt eye, she saw she was at a door, its brass knocker shaped like a pineapple.

She reached out. It was hard to use the knocker. So heavy. She saw a white box with a button, held it down, pumped it. Heard a distant chime.

A light nearby. She leaned her forehead against one of the long, thin windows that flanked the door. Vague somethings swam behind the glass. Then a face peered through, white and pale, eyes growing big.

She saw her reflection in the glass, dark, bloody, unrecognizable.

The face disappeared, then peeked through the window again.

She pressed the doorbell.

When the door opened, when her hand fell away from that little white box, she saw she'd left it smeared with blood.

"Hullo," she heard herself say. "I'm your neighbor. Can you help me, please?"

17

S he'd been only nine, but she clearly recalled that her mother's killer was balding. The sight of the back of his head as he sat facing the judge stuck deep in her memory. There was a little quiver of his cheek visible if he turned even slightly. He had a big belly, flat butt, arms that looked especially scrawny given the size of his middle. What hair he had was getting a little gray. He looked to her like a white blob. The middle-aged man she saw everywhere. The policeman, the lawyer, the doctor, the accountant, the politician.

She hated him. Stared daggers at his doughy body. The man who had obliterated her mother, erased that beautiful voice, the milk of her skin, the fingers that braided hair, the consistently sour breath, the too-loud voice—he'd wiped all that from the face of the earth. He'd annihilated now and forever all the mother's love she would have gotten, and had left all the love she still had bottled up with nowhere to go.

Even so, she had a difficult time remembering the killer's face. He was too similar to the rest of them. Same puffy, faceless man who thought the things he had were things he deserved.

It felt like a betrayal of her mother that she found the trial horribly boring. It was duller than being trapped in her third-grade classroom, as tedious as the church services it so precisely mimicked. Like church she had to wear her uncomfortable dress with the shiny black shoes and the tights that never sat right in the crotch. She had to stand when the big guy stood, sit when he sat. Listen to the preaching. Blah, blah, blah, Mercy. Blah, blah, blah, Justice. In the words of so-and-so. Let us now read from. As in church she stared at the statues. Discreetly checked the clock. Sat by Grandma on a long bench. And just like church, her father had begged off with one excuse after another.

"Let him stay home," Grandma said as they drove across state lines toward the trial. "Everyone reacts differently to grief."

She decided she liked church better than the courtroom. At least at church there was singing to wake her up and a snack toward the end. At least at church everyone asked forgiveness.

The words that reverberated through the courtroom were even less penetrable than readings from the Bible. Instead of murder, they said manslaughter, though the man slaughtered was, in fact, a woman. Instead of saying plainly what actually happened, instead of describing the immolation of an entire life in a single moment at the hands of this drunken little man and his too-big truck, instead of talking about the soft places crushed, hard bone turned smithereens, precious things irrevocably broken—instead of all that, it was talk of traffic lights. Timing. Little maps, pointed at here and there with an extendable metal rod. Speed limits. Left-turn signals. Blood alcohol.

She glowered at these antiseptic charts. Already at nine she was a list maker, an organizer, had learned at her mother's side how to take machines apart, how to fix them, splice wires, and use a soldering iron to melt bits of circuit into amenable pools. There was a time for technical discussion, for analysis at a remove. And then there was this place, which should have been filled, like her mother's funeral, with faces stunned to stiffness or contorted with tears.

With people saying they didn't understand, how could it happen, it was unfair, horrifying, all of them kneading the cold from their hands, lightly touching their arms, their chests, as if to check that yes, they were still alive, somehow, despite her mother being whisked off the board.

But on droned the men at the front as she scratched at the dark stone lodged in her muscle and bone, the unbearably heavy one that slipped from heart to stomach to throat to the core of her brain, whispering, "None of this matters because she's gone, she's gone, she's dead. Some things can't be fixed. Some things are unfixable. The world can snap in half."

It took three days. Three days of watching the nondescript man in court, sitting slumped and trying his best to look repentant, but mainly appearing bored the same way she was, as irritated with the procedures as she was.

He was sorry, so sorry, will live with this his whole life, such an awful burden. Upstanding citizen, already punishing himself. Already in a program. *And*—mitigation. Contribution. What had *she* been doing, what was she thinking? Remember, it was a rental car. She was an out-of-state driver. Of course she was distracted. Unfamiliar car, she must have been frequently looking at maps to navigate. Yes, her driving record was good, but let's face facts. Where she was from there are more cows than people, everyone's a teetotaler, everyone's record is good. Sure, his blood alcohol was high, members of the jury, but—he looks just like you. Your husband. Your father. Looks like everyone you know. Poor guy. About your same age, isn't he? Just made a little mistake, unlucky timing. Tell me you've never made a mistake? Maybe even that same mistake. And that out-of-state woman, the one whose face is different, isn't quite right, a woman, here, alone on business? Isn't that somehow odd? The one who, well, an illness like that, being marked like that, it's somehow suspicious, isn't it? Think about her actions. Her mistakes. Her strangeness. Why ruin his life?

Grandma had introduced herself to the prosecution and the police that first day, thanking them for their hard work. By the next morning she was tap-tap-tapping their shoulders, southern politeness turned to steel. "It's incompetence, is what it is. How dare you? He'll do it again. Maybe to someone you love next time. You saw what he did. To a young wife. A young mother."

But from the police, the prosecution, there was only indifference, rising smoky and insidious.

"Please, calm down, ma'am. We work with the facts we have."

"Calm down—the gall! They're supposed to speak for your mother," Grandma seethed. "That's their whole job. If it'd happened back in Utah, you can bet it'd be different. I'm no fan of the Saints, but there's some things they understand, and alcohol is one of those things."

She couldn't understand why her grandma insisted the lawyers and policemen should feel a responsibility toward her mother. Couldn't Grandma see they were diodes, capacitors, transistors, each an essential part of the circuit of this place where her mother was reinvented as irresponsible, culpable, suspect, unrecognizable?

The killer was someone in charge of something mildly important in that particular place. And of course he was someone living, and therefore had the advantage of being able to exist. To be looked at, considered, sympathized with.

And her mother was a dot on a chart. Her mother was absence. She could feel that nothingness. There was an infinite, empty place her mother's love used to fill when she held her, tucked her into bed, packed her lunch, let her push the shopping cart, her mother squeezing her hand as they walked—*bum-bum, bum-bum*—like a heartbeat, a secret way to say, "I love you," her mother saying, "My beautiful girl, how'd I get so lucky that you're mine?" Even these little things had been turned immense in loss, memories that made her tuck her knees to her chest under the covers and fold around her newly hollowed center.

As the judge read the not-guilty verdict, she wondered if the jury needed to believe her mother had done something wrong, had somehow deserved to be violently, painfully destroyed. Because that would mean what had happened to her mother could never, would never, happen to them. Maybe that one was self-consciously scratching at a hairline, that other picking at a cuticle, all of them avoiding looking in her and Grandma's direction, because somewhere inside they heard a little voice whimpering, "That could've been me. That could've been someone I love. Someone who loves me."

The jury didn't want to see, the way she did, that invisible threads, delicate and easily torn, lay beneath everything. A distant breath of random chance, a choice made by a stranger, could split them, ends floating like cobwebs while precious things tumbled through to darkness, unrecoverable.

Some things can't be fixed. Some things are unfixable. The world can snap in half.

"It's an injustice, is what it is," Grandma lamented.

But justice wasn't possible. Justice would require the jury return her mother, whole and alive. Only the possibility of sanitized vengeance was on offer, and even that had failed.

After the verdict, Grandma pulled her into a hug, whispering, "His ways are not ours."

But there was no possible reason she would ever accept, no larger meaning possible, in the horror of her mother's death. To survive it, she clung close to the memory of her mother's effusive joy over everyday things. The hummingbird at the feeder, the precise twist of a wire, snowfall, a perfectly cooked egg, to all these simple things her mother would say with genuine wonder, "Isn't it beautiful? Isn't it just beautiful?"

Curled under the covers around the well of her grief, she remembered her mother's fingers running through her hair. The squeeze of her mother's hand saying, *Bum-bum, bum-bum, I love you.* The uneven bend of her smile. She saw that even the odd angle of her top pinkie joint, the way she constantly hummed to herself, was special, important, and all of these small, wondrous fragments let her form a scaffold of meaning, a will to go on. Life had to be beautiful, because her mother had said so. Life had to be precious because it was delicate, could so easily disappear into absence. Yes, she had to survive desolation, because although her mother was no longer there to bear witness to the world's beauty, its tenuousness, she still could.

She watched the magnetic, swirling loveliness of the dust motes dancing in the courtroom sunlight as the judge sentenced the man to fifteen months. Not for murder, not for manslaughter, but for the lesser, guilty charges of driving under the influence. Of leaving the scene. With time served, twelve months. The benign little killer was out on parole in eight months. Less time in jail than her mother had taken to create her life; create her entire existence.

Other people expect them to sprout horns. Other people think evil knows it's evil. Other people say, "He's a good man, really."

But no. She and Grandma had that front-row seat to see that evil can look like a little nobody, a little anybody, shedding his crocodile tears. Evil can be a saggy, slumping man, who, when the judge read the sentence, couldn't repress the satisfaction brimming his eyes. Eyes that said, "Yes, see? Justice! I'm not so bad after all. I'm no worse than anyone else, just as I always suspected."

Even though, of course, he was worse. Unrepentant, unreformed worseness, unable to understand the vastness of what he'd taken, the fundamental importance of a life that wasn't his. Evil's face so forgettable in its everydayness that not even she, whom it mattered most to, could hold that man's features in her mind. Just recalled the balding head on the pudgy body. The graying, thinning hair. The sense of relief radiating out from him after the long, boring process of injustice.

Nine months after the trial, Grandma sat her down. She'd gotten a call. The man who destroyed her mother had been less than thirty days out of jail when he and his wife were killed in a car crash. The man's blood alcohol, Grandma said, "was higher than a light pole."

"God set it right," Grandma insisted.

She didn't agree. Though she knew it would disappoint her grandmother, she no longer saw a higher power as an unquestioned given, certain her mother's death proved any god inadequate. After all, if God had set it right, then God must also have set it wrong. Maybe he had stepped out of the picture altogether. Maybe had never been in it at all. She didn't pretend to know.

"I do pity his poor wife," Grandma sighed. "I suppose she made her choices, but it doesn't seem she deserved that end."

The wife, who'd sat immediately behind the killer during those three days. The wife, who'd fidgeted and squirmed nonstop. The lady she'd caught staring at her several times before quickly looking away. The woman with Krystle Carrington hair and jewelry and long-sleeved flowered dresses. The unquiet face of that woman, now dead, she remembered perfectly.

18

The pale, gray-haired man standing in the doorway wore pajama pants and a T-shirt. He didn't invite her in, just stared slack-jawed.

"Honey? What is it?" called a woman's voice.

"Some lady!" he yelled back, not taking his eyes off her.

"What?" shouted the woman.

"Hullo," she said again through her metal teeth. "I'm your neighbor. Can you help me, please?"

"Shit." The man winced. "What happened to you?"

She started to fall, caught herself on the brick of the exterior wall.

"Sorry," she told him on seeing the bloody mark left by her hand. "So sorry."

"Jesus . . . come in?"

She stepped into the house and slipped, her bare feet soft jelly things, wet and slick on the tile. She landed hard. The neighbor reached down as if to help her up, then thought better of it, and pulled his arms close to his chest. She dragged herself forward with her hands, feet useless and knees constricted by the fur coat, crawled like a baby until the neighbor was able to shut the door against the storm. He rubbed his hands together, cold from the brief exposure.

She pressed her cheek on the square tiles.

Just a little nap. That's what you need, a little kittycatnap.

"What happened? Are you all right?"

There was movement farther in the house, a woman hurrying down the stairs.

"Christ!" the woman exclaimed. "What the hell?"

"I dunno," the neighbor said. "Call 9-1-1, she's hurt."

"She might be . . . *dangerous*?" The woman mouthed this as though only the man would be able to understand.

"She can't even stand up. Just call the cops already!"

The woman's mouth pursed into a tight red O.

The electricity in the house burned her good eye. The tiles were so white. The rug beyond them oatmeal. An enormous crystal chandelier blazed above the stairs. Light wood furniture was visible in the darkened house. Mirrors in the entry, the other rooms. Everything bright and reflective. The woman wore a long pink robe that was liquid behind her as she hurried back up the stairs. Silk.

"What happened?" the man repeated.

"There's someone in my house," she said. "He's trying to kill me. He's trying to get my children."

The neighbor had noticed her skin now, was staring at the traces of white.

"Are you contagious?"

"No. It's . . . genetic. Please, he's trying to get my children."

"What?" The neighbor squinted at her.

Maybe your voice isn't working. Maybe you aren't hearable through your lips, filled up with blood.

"Can you sit up?" the neighbor asked. "I can barely hear with you talking into the floor."

He reached a hand to help her and she extended her own, but again he withdrew it. She vaguely wondered if he was more afraid of the blood or the whitened skin of her hands and wrists. She pushed herself up until she sat against the wall. She swiped at her swollen lip to try to clean it. Touched her eye and immediately snapped her hand away from causing herself such pain.

"Someone broke into my house. My children are hiding there. I need help."

"I've got the police!" the woman called out as she came back down the stairs, pointing at the cell phone in her hand. "They said they're coming. They want to know who she is." The woman stopped short. "What's wrong with her skin?"

"She said someone broke into her house. That her kids are still there," the neighbor said.

"Ooooohhhh!" The woman's eyebrows shot up. She repeated this into the phone.

"What's your address, hon?"

She gave her name, her address.

"I think—I think he followed me."

"What?"

Both the neighbors rushed past her, the man locking the dead bolt before they each sprung to one of the narrow windows on either side of their front door, cupping hands around faces to peer outside into the storm.

Her feet stuck out at strange angles from the coat. Their skin looked like the fur of the mountain lion, partly torn away, bloody at the skinned places.

She leaned against the wall for support so she could make her voice louder, hearable.

"They have to get to the children, my kids, they're hidden, they have to go to my house, please!"

"She says the intruder might have followed her," the woman said into the phone. "But I don't see anyone. Do you see anyone?"

"No," the neighbor agreed. "Nobody."

"Someone's in my house," she repeated.

"We don't see anyone," the woman told the phone. "But it's hard to see anything in the dark with all the snow."

They seemed so close; their voices hurt her ears.

"Did he do . . . that . . . to you?" the woman asked, looking at her.

"He's going to start a fire," she said. "He's going to smoke—"

"Did this man who broke in do all"—the woman pointed her finger at her, waved it in a circle—"*that*?"

"I'm gonna get the first aid kit," the neighbor said. "Google hypothermia, yeah? See what we should do?"

"I'm putting you on speaker," the woman said into the phone, "so I can look up hypothermia. To see if she has hypothermia."

She licked her lip and tasted iodine. The neighbors' manic energy, their excited discombobulation, increased her sense of exhaustion, her need for sleep.

"I hid my kids," she told the woman. "I hid them from the Corner. The man in the corner."

"You hear that?" the woman said to the phone she was simultaneously typing into. "She's really out of it. She's talking gibberish. And her face is all messed up, like someone hit her. And she's barefoot. In a fur coat."

"A fur coat?" a tinny voice said from the speakerphone.

"Yes," the woman told the voice. "Just showed up in a fur coat, but barefoot in the snow and all beat up."

"Where did she come from?"

"My house." Her voice was a faraway thread. "My house!"

"You hear that? She says she came from her house."

"What's the address?"

She mumbled it, and the woman repeated it loudly into the speakerphone.

The neighbor reentered with a first aid kit, towels, and a steaming mug. He snatched the phone from his wife.

"Look," he said. "It's hard to understand what she's saying. But it sounds like she thinks someone's in her house, that whoever it is is after her kids, who're still there." He listened. Asked, "How old are they?"

She told him, and the neighbor told the phone.

He'd put the first aid kit, the towels, and the mug on the floor next to her. She gingerly wrapped a towel around her cut left hand. Its fingers were thick and unbendable. She couldn't work the zipper on the first aid kit.

The neighbor looked so tall standing there, talking on the phone. The woman was staring out into the night again, wringing her hands and peering through different windowpanes as if the view might change from one to the other.

She put her uncut hand on the mug the neighbor had put beside her, its warmth miraculous. She took a sip that burned down her throat, and she felt a wave of gratefulness to feel anything warm, to feel anything at all comforting again.

"I still don't see anyone," the woman said.

She forced herself to enunciate.

"Let. Me. Talk. To. Them."

"She wants to talk to you," the neighbor told the phone. "I'm gonna set the phone down next to her so you can hear her better."

"My kids," she rasped. "Five and eight. I hid them from him. He said he was going to start a fire. Smoke us out. You need to get to my house. Help them."

"Ma'am? Hello?"

"Five and eight. He's going to light a fire. Help them."

"Do you feel safe where you are now, ma'am?"

Through a wave of dizziness she said to the phone, "He's going to smoke them out, the Corner."

She floated, distant from the room. The neighbors were silly, running this way and that. She took a sip of the hot drink, then another. The taste was so present. So warm.

"I'm sorry, ma'am, I don't understand what you said. Are you feeling all right?"

No. I'm broken and blinded and my feet are going to have to be amputated, and I can't breathe right and the Corner's waiting to eat them alive and my skin is going to fall off and my heart isn't beating evenly and my brain is stuffed with cotton balls and I'm dying.

But when has that mattered? You know this song, you've been here before. On the airplane's the only place they say, "Put your oxygen mask on before assisting others." Mostly you're on that bed and they've got a scalpel and the right answer always is, do what's best for the baby. And if you say, "Hey, maybe spare me a minute, spare me a little pain, I have a few questions," there are frowns and "Reallys?" and finally "That's not advisable for the baby, baby, baby."

"Get my kids," she said.

The burning liquid was the only warm thing in the entire world. The only source of comfort. She closed her eye for a little rest.

Delicious.

The neighbor snatched up the phone.

"You better send an ambulance, too. She looks like she's been out wandering in the snow after being used as a punching bag."

Wandering. Just a little stroll, a little jaunt. Red Riding Hood following the forest path, tra-la-la.

The woman wasn't at the window anymore but was leaning over next to her, arms full of beach towels.

"The internet says we're supposed to take off wet clothes and wrap you up dry, okay?"

When she shook her head, it was full of water that went side to side.

She reached for the phone again but then saw her hand was

wrapped up with a towel. The blood was so bright in this slick white-tiled place. It throbbed red through the fabric. The blood down her arm was dried in muddy brown rivulets. She turned her arm right and left, awed.

"I'm going to just sleep a little while," she told the woman.

"She's bleeding, yeah. All swollen," the neighbor said, then listened before announcing, "They say they're on their way."

"Where?"

"Here."

"Hon, won't you let me wrap you up warm?" the woman asked. "This coat is soaked."

"No! No! Go to my house."

Her voice was far away.

"She wants you to go to her house," the neighbor said into the phone.

"They're going to both," he recounted after listening at the phone. "Here and your house."

"What about the snow?" asked the woman. "Can they get here?"

"Oh, yeah—so! What about the storm? We live in a gated community and the private road hasn't been plowed yet."

Even through the neighbor's panic, his excitement, she heard a ringing note of pride when he said "gated community." When he said "private road."

The woman was tugging at the coat buttons, and she swatted at her. Knocked some of the hot liquid out of the mug and onto the floor.

"Fine." The woman held up her hands as if surrendering. Then to the neighbor she said, "She won't let me help her."

The lights were pulsing even brighter now, and she closed her one working eye again to still them, to give herself a little relief from how present, how aglow, these people were.

"They said they'll get through the snow fine," the neighbor told her. "They say they know where your house is. They say they've been there before."

Of course they remember the house. Of course they do.

"Why were you there before?" the neighbor asked quietly into the phone. Paused. "Fine. Whatever, don't tell me. Just thought it might be relevant."

The floor was so comfortable. She traced her hand along the grout lines, all the squares so reassuringly even.

Wait. This isn't where you're supposed to be. You need to get up, get home. Because—because of something.

She put down the mug. Tried to stand. Her feet wouldn't get under her. The coat was so heavy. It twisted around her legs.

"Hey!" the neighbor called out. "Calm down! Just relax."

His words poked a tenderness at the base of her neck, stoked an anger that made her struggle up more doggedly, her feet sticky with dried blood now on the tile.

"Sit down!"

"I have to—"

What do you have to do? Something important. Late, late, for a very important date.

She tried to take a step. Her legs went bendy.

The neighbor reached out to support her. The phone clattered to the floor.

"Little help here?" he said to his wife, grimacing.

The woman hurried from her post at the window and helped sit her down.

"I don't see anything out there, okay?" the woman told her. "No smoke, fire, nobody following you, all right?"

She sagged against the wall. The woman handed her the mug, and she drank until it was empty.

So warm it burned.

You are alive. This is real.

"Hey." The woman snapped fingers in front of her face. "Hey! I don't think you should fall asleep."

"Hay is for horses," she scolded in her grandmother's voice.

The neighbor picked the phone up again.

"Yeah, still here, sorry. Dropped the phone. She's losing it. Trying to get out into the snow to get her kids. Hysterical, you know?"

"WebMD says we're supposed to get you warm," the woman said. "At least let me cover your feet."

She nodded. *Slosh, slosh*, went the water in her head.

The woman briefly hesitated before touching her torn, dappled skin, then wrapped a beach towel around her feet, pink and orange Hawaiian flowers.

She looked around at the white tiles, white walls, white faces. The red blood turning brown.

"Is this a hospital?" she asked the woman wrapping something around her feet.

"No," said the woman. "We're your neighbors. You came to us for help."

"No," she sighed. "I don't know you. I don't know you at all."

19

The man and woman were turning red-blue-red-blue, colored lights flashing through the windows. She heard excited voices, saw hands flapping like birds. She sipped her refilled mug, and the warmth of the drink felt impossibly beautiful.

"And *then* she said he'd followed her, but we didn't see anything."

"And *then* she said there was smoke, but we can't see any smoke."

"She said her children were hiding, that she'd hidden them."

"She wouldn't let us take off that coat even though it's wet. Wouldn't let us help her. She's probably hypothermic."

"They said on the phone you'd been to her house before."

"Do you see? Doesn't it look like someone hit her in the face? Her eye all swollen?"

"Maybe it was her husband. Isn't it always the husband?"

"It wasn't her husband," a new voice said. She turned her head slightly to see a policeman. He squatted down next to her.

"You okay, ma'am? How are you feeling?"

He was young, and she blinked to try to make him older.

"There's something in my eye," she told him.

The boyish officer nodded. "Yeah, you're pretty torn up."

"My kids?"

Another policeman appeared out of the bright light of the entry, blue-red-blue-red flashing at his back, and likewise squatted down beside her. It was the same thing she did with the children. "Getting on their level," the parenting books called it.

"You remember me, ma'am?"

She looked into the smooth blue eyes over the blue paper mask. Took in the graying blond hair.

"The sergeant," she said.

"There's an ambulance on the way."

"I need to go to my house," she muttered.

"You think you can talk a little louder?" the sergeant said, leaning toward her.

"My kids."

"Yeah, I've got a car at your house now. You say someone broke in, is that right?"

The neighbors spoke at the same time.

"That's what she said! That someone had broken in and—"

"Someone was after her kids, she said, and she hid them 'cause he was going to—"

The sergeant put up a hand in a practiced "stop" gesture, like he was directing traffic.

"Ma'am, let her tell it. So," the sergeant said evenly, "someone broke in, is that right?"

She nodded. "A man. I hid—I hid with the children."

"All right. Was this man armed?"

"He had something. About—" She set the mug beside her and held her hands six inches apart. "This big. He—" She mimed the Corner's motion, the way he'd whacked the weapon into his palm. "It made a noise. It was . . . loose."

"How can a weapon be loose?" the woman asked, and the neighbor shushed her.

"Any gun?"

"Huh?"

"Did this man have a gun?"

"No. I don't know."

"You didn't see a gun? A knife?"

"No."

"And is there any way my guys can get in the house? Any key under the mat or the like that might make that easier?"

"In the rock," she said.

"What?"

"The rock. But it's all snowed. Snowy."

"I don't understand, ma'am?" the sergeant said.

Her head was heavy. She closed her eye.

"Ma'am?"

There was a loud crackle of the radio, a beep, fuzzy words.

So tired, just so cold and so tired.

"You have a blanket we can use?" the sergeant asked the neighbors. "We need to get her out of this wet stuff, warm her up. There's some major accidents out there. And with the surge, everyone's short staffed. Ambulance is gonna be a minute."

"I tried to help her change, she wouldn't let me."

"That's fine. Now we'll try, all right?"

"We gave her a warm drink there," the neighbor told him.

"Good. You have any electric blankets, hot-water bottles, that kind of thing?"

"I think we have a hot-water bottle somewhere."

"Get it. Hot water, but tap hot, not boiling. Don't want to burn her, yeah?"

"Okay."

"Let's get you out of this coat."

She felt hands on her, fumbling with the coat's buttons, and their uninvited movement forced her to thrash and kick at the hands pressing on her chest, legs, hips.

"No—no!"

"Calm down, we're trying to help you, we can't warm you up with this wet coat on. Ma'am. Calm down."

She flailed blindly, connected with something soft.

"Shit . . . just . . . hold her arms, all right?"

The air crawled down her chest as they unbuttoned her coat. The officers parted the coat wide and then lifted their hands away from her when they saw her naked breasts, stomach, legs, the symmetrical white markings butterflied from groin to belly button. She thrashed, tried to scream, but only gasped again and again.

She saw linoleum. Tried to draw her arms and legs in to protect the soft places.

You ran all this way, you did all that, and it's happening anyhow. He got you anyway, that's what this is.

She started to cry, to weep, and the salt stung.

This is a mortuary. White tiled and bright, and you're on the slab and they've scissored open your skin to see what made you stop ticking.

"What—what are you doing?" The woman sounded shocked.

Hands released her, and she was at last able to curl fully into a ball, forehead to knees, lying on her side atop the wide-open coat.

"We're just trying to help. To get her dry. Get the coat off."

"Here," the woman said. "Cover her up, Jesus." Lightly, worriedly, the woman added, "She's skin and bones."

Fabric covered her naked body, went over her face. She opened her eye to see a pink blanket, to see the white tiles.

"Hey. Can you give us some privacy? You can see she's scared. Let me help her?"

"We're helping her. We need to talk to her."

"Of course, I'm sorry, I didn't mean anything. Just, maybe she'll be more . . . comfortable? With a woman helping her? Just for a minute?"

"Fine. A minute."

The woman sat by her, blood soaking into the pink silk of her robe.

"Hey," the woman said. "They're gone for now. Some privacy, right? Let's get you dressed, huh?"

"Your—your robe. The blood."

"Oh, it's all right."

The woman looked away.

"Men," she said. "They don't think. Helping!" she scoffed. "I'd be just as scared as you, they undressed me like that. Wish you'd let me take that coat off you in the first place. I've got a sweater, sweatpants, socks. It'll help. You won't win any beauty contests, but should warm you up."

She let the woman help her sit and button on a huge sweater. The woman gently pulled drawstring sweatpants up her legs, put big chenille socks over her swollen feet. She couldn't feel any of it, skin at last numbed to deadness.

"Are you sick?" the woman said, face tense with concern.

"No."

"You're just . . . honey, you're so thin. And your skin! Is there—is there anything you want to tell me? Do you feel safe at home?"

She strangled on a laugh, tasted blood again.

"You done in there?"

"Why were you naked?" the woman whispered.

"To stay warm," she said.

The woman's eyes swept over her pityingly.

The policemen reappeared, took her elbows to help move her onto a chair that hadn't been there before. There was gauze around her hand, a hot-water bottle in her lap. A blanket draped her shoulders. She swallowed the last of the warm drink and remembered that they were wasting time.

"We have to go," she wheezed.

The radio chirped. "We're at the house, Sarge. No vehicles. No tire tracks. No footprints except for some going across the driveway at the back of the house. Likely your girl's, 'cause they head your direction. House is dark. We clear to go in?"

"One minute," said the boyish policeman into his radio.

"Okay," said the sergeant. "Little better now, yeah? You look a little better. Sorry if we scared you. We were just trying to help warm you up, all right? You were kind of fading there. You okay? You think you can help us out?"

She nodded.

"Now, is there a key hidden somewhere?"

"In the rock, under the snow."

"Ma'am, you said that before, and it doesn't make sense, understand?"

"You know, I bet she's talking about one of those hide-a-key things!" the woman chimed in. "Looks like a rock but it's plastic? They've got a little compartment thingy? That you hide a key in?"

"Is that what you mean?" the boyish policeman asked her.

She nodded, head so heavy with its liquefied brain.

"Where is it?"

"By the entry door. The left side."

"Oh-kay, ma'am," said the sergeant.

"There are too many doors," she muttered. "Every room has so many doors, and he didn't like it."

The sergeant wandered away into the brightness of the house, talking to whoever was on the other end of his radio.

"No tire tracks, huh?" said the neighbor to the boyish policeman. "No footprints but hers? What d'you think that's about?"

The boyish policeman ignored him.

"Is the intruder the one who hurt you?" the boyish officer asked her.

She shook her head.

"How did you get hurt?"

"The snow, the ice." She gingerly licked her lips. "I think I ate blood."

Three sets of eyes stared at her. Every time she blinked her unhurt eye, the hurt one tried to blink, too, and pain shot across her face so deep she was sure she was irreparably broken.

The sergeant reappeared, stood next to the boyish policeman.

"Ma'am, my guys are in your house. They've done a sweep. There doesn't appear to be any intruder."

"Fire?"

"No fire."

"My children?"

"They haven't found them yet. But you said they were hiding. Where are they?"

"Behind the wall," she said.

"You . . . put your kids behind a wall?"

"Yes. In the hidden place."

The entry hushed. It had echoed like a canyon, and now everyone was so still and silent it made her ears ring.

"I don't understand," the sergeant said.

"Behind the fireplace. In the office. I left them there."

"Are they all right?" asked the sergeant.

She felt herself start to cry and tried to stop it, but the tears burned through her bloodied, swollen eyelid, seeping into her cracked skull. She swiped at them with the hand that wasn't wrapped in gauze.

"They're so little," she blubbered.

"Were they all right when you left them?"

She thought of her son's soft cheek hitting the floor, her daughter's head against the brick. The little fingers that had to be forced and pried away. She choked on the memory, on her own snot and tears.

"They were scared, so scared!"

The sergeant's face was level with hers now. He was on one knee like a football player in a huddle.

"I need you to focus," he said softly. "I need to know exactly where your kids are."

"My head," she told him. "There's something broken."

"Just tell me what you can," the sergeant said.

"He's very, very big, the café manager. He said we were delicious. Said he would find us."

"Okay, all right. That's . . . helpful. Now, where are the children?"

"In the office. Bottom right panel. It opens up if you push the just right spot. A hidden door."

"Tell 'em," he said to the boyish policeman, who relayed this into a radio, crackling and beeping back and forth instructions.

Even kneeling the sergeant's posture was precise. She wondered at how the edges of his stiffly pressed uniform stayed so rigid under his coat. His eyes were blue and blank, locked on hers until she closed her good eye and drifted.

The boyish policeman whispered something to the sergeant.

"Ma'am," the sergeant said, shaking her lightly on the shoulder as if to wake her. "They're not finding an opening. No hidden room. They've called out for the kids. Nothing. Where are they?"

Yes, they were brave children, good children. They were still hiding. Hiding from all those male voices calling out. "Don't even come out for Mama, not even if you hear Mama screaming and murdered. Don't come out unless there's smoke, fire. Mama will come to you! Mama will open the panel." Wasn't that what she'd said?

It has to be that, because otherwise . . .

She heaved, sick with panic.

What if? What if they can't find them because he took them?

The sergeant gently dabbed her face with a towel. His voice was stiff as he asked quietly, "Ma'am, did you hurt them?"

Her thoughts thickened. She'd popped their little fingers away from her arms, her robe. Knocked her son into the dirt. Her daughter against the brick. Grit and crack.

How did he know? How'd he know that?

"I don't—"

"Did you hurt them?"

The room was so hushed and the sergeant's voice so low even the walls seemed to tilt toward them, listening.

She touched her swollen lip and her finger left a depression. She felt it slowly refill, like her face was made of sand and seawater.

Did this sergeant have children? The last time, the first time you met him, didn't he say he had kids? Hadn't he offered that up, hadn't he said, "I'm so sorry, so sorry, I'm a father myself"?

If he was a father, he'd know how ridiculous this question was. Of course she'd hurt them. Not just tonight, enraged and frightened that they wouldn't let her help them, no. She'd hurt them in a million accidental, stumbling, impatient ways.

You're a horrible mother.

The time she'd left her daughter on the changing table and the baby had slipped off, gotten that cut on her head that left a scar just under the eyebrow. The time she'd stepped on her son's pinkie toe and broken it, had to tape it to the one next to it to heal. The time she was cuddling her daughter and stood up, ripping out a clump of toddler hair that had somehow gotten caught around her shirt button. She could still hear that scream.

A horrible, horrible mother.

Then there were the uncountable hurts they'd caused her. The baby fingernail that scratched her retina deep enough she'd seen blurry for months. The kick to her chin that slammed her tongue between her teeth so hard she'd lost a small chunk of it. Pregnancy, the months of vomiting, constipation, cramps. Childbirth, being split and sewn up and left with her muscles so torn apart she couldn't control her bowels, so broken that her intestine peeked through her stomach, round and tender and needing to be cut open and shoved back in. The sleeplessness that made her say, "Now I understand why sleep deprivation is considered torture. Now I understand why people lose their minds."

Never ending.

You're not a good mother.

"I never hurt them on purpose," she said, weeping quietly.

"Of course not," the sergeant said, low and brittle. "But you hid them? In the wall of your house?"

"Yes. Yes!"

"How about this," he said. "How about we get you in our truck, we all go to your house, and you can show us where they are? And then we'll get you to that ambulance? Can we do that?"

She felt a rush of relief.

"That's all I've wanted."

"Behind the wall?" the neighbor whispered loudly to his wife.

In a single motion the sergeant lifted her out of the chair. One arm hooked under her bent knees, the other behind her shoulders. Instinctively she wrapped her arms around his neck to support her weight, then pulled them protectively back to her chest, the gesture too bizarrely romantic.

The neighbors backed away deeper into their house, faces turned long and blanched.

"Get the door," the sergeant said, and the boyish policeman held it open.

"Thank you," she called in the direction of the neighbors when the sergeant turned sideways to fit them through the door together. "Thank you."

The boyish policeman followed them out into the storm.

"Oh my God," said the woman, voice fading away behind them as the officer closed the door. "Oh my God."

20

The vehicle wasn't a police car but a big white truck with a light on the dash, washing the snow with alternating color until the sergeant flicked it to darkness. The road wasn't plowed, and the tires kicked snow up high on the windows as they drove. Almost immediately they were at her driveway, creeping slowly between the reflective plow markers poking through the drifts until they stopped near the garage.

Again the sergeant swept her up like a man about to take his bride across the threshold. She was dizzied as he carried her to the front door, the boyish policeman following along behind them. Inside were two more policemen waiting in the mudroom.

So many eyes.

"This way," said one of the new policemen, and she was flown through the house. When they passed the steep kitchen stairs, she felt the sergeant hesitate, step wide to avoid a spot at the base of the stairs the way visitors walked around the places bodies must have rotted under the graveyard dirt.

"You need any help, Sarge?"

"Nah, she doesn't weigh a thing."

Every light in the house was on, the living room ablaze as they walked through it. But there was only the little desk lamp in the office. Her husband liked to work in the semidarkness, said it made the images on the monitor clearer. Her eye rolled to the shadows at the edges of the room, searching for any movement in its corners. Her vision was so flattened, so limited, that every bit of darkness beyond the lamp's small beam vibrated, alive and menacing.

"See? See here? Nothing."

One of the men had a flashlight, was pushing on different wall panels, rough and impatient.

"Oh-kay, ma'am."

The sergeant set her down next to the wall, and her knees went soft, slowly folding until she sat on the floor. The sergeant nodded to an officer who was holding up his phone. Its light was so bright in her one eye that she cringed.

"You ready there, man? Yeah? All right, ma'am, why don't you show us where you put those kids. Can you show us that?"

She moved awkwardly to position herself in front of the panel. It was difficult to find the just-right spot with her fingers still numb, with her hurt hand bandaged. She shook out her good hand, tried again. Ran fingertips around the edge until she felt the telltale indentation in the wood. Pushed.

The door to the hidden place swung inward. Officers jostled behind her, one saying quietly, "What do you know!"

She stuck her head into the black nothingness.

"Loves? It's all right, come out, the police are here, come on—"

Before she could finish speaking, she was shoved aside, a yelp of pain and surprise strangling in her throat. The sergeant and the policeman with the lit-up phone were all at once between her and the panel, and she fell backward, felt her calf crushed under the pressure of one of their legs as they went to hands and knees to look through the secret door. She used her forearms to drag her body away from their tangle of booted feet and heavy limbs. The sergeant held a large black flashlight, whipping light in and around the hidden place.

Then came a *click* that brought every little piece together in her swollen brain.

They think you hurt them. They think you buried them in the wall.

She closed her eyes. Swallowed big.

But you didn't. They're going to be there, and they're going to be okay. Aren't they?

Her head was buzzing; her brain was jelly. The whisk of the flashlight back and forth pained her.

They shoved you aside so you won't contaminate the scene. Isn't that what's happening?

But the children must be all right. You saw them, and they were all right? Your son's face in the dirt, your daughter's head on the brick, but they sat back up. No matter how many times you've lost your temper, put them in the crib and walked away and covered your ears to give yourself a break, you would never . . .

She didn't want to leave that moment. The not knowing. It was so much better not to know. To close her eyes, lean deep into her brain's hum of exhaustion. To not know if she'd done something irrevocable. To not know that they'd been suffocated by the bulk of the Corner. Vanished, hurt, hurting right now, because she'd abandoned them. Or hurt them.

It's your fault.

The sergeant pushed farther into the hidden place, only his legs visible. "Hey, it's okay! You can come out! It's all right. We're policemen."

Thin and distant came her daughter's voice.

"Mama?"

The relief was a euphoric drug so intense she thought she would fall asleep right there, forever happy.

The sergeant backed out, sat on his haunches. Stared at her.

"Maybe they'll come out," he said, "if they see you."

She couldn't speak, her lips were too flabby. Her lacerated skin stung with tears she hadn't realized she'd been crying.

The sergeant reached out a hand. She refused it, managing to crawl forward on her own.

The policemen parted to let her through. She put her head into the hidden place. She didn't have a flashlight, couldn't see anything.

"Time to come out, okay, loves? We're safe now."

"Mama! Mommy!"

She sat back into the room and waited. They crawled out, streaked with grime. Her daughter gorgeous and shining in her red nightgown. Her son round tummied and soft, melting into her.

"Hi, hello," she said. "It's all right now. It's okay."

"Mama," said her daughter, leaning back, regarding her, "you look *awful*."

She turned away from them and vomited on the nicest rug in the house.

21

Two months earlier her son had dressed as a bat, her daughter a witch. Trick-or-treating was canceled county-wide because of the pandemic, so she took a page from Easter and hid candy in the yard. She and her husband watched the kids dash around with their plastic pumpkin buckets.

"Look, Mama! Look, Daddy!" they shouted anytime they found a piece of candy.

Her son flapped his arms to extend his bat wings while he ran.

"I'm flying!"

Their daughter dragged her witch's broom between her legs. "Me too! I'm flying! We're flying! Like Daddy! Look!"

After dinner the children fished through their loot, traded it, ate candy as quickly as they could.

"Can we trick-or-treat this way every year?" their little girl asked.

"Why?"

"You don't have to say, 'Trick or treat.' You don't have to say, 'Thank you.'"

"Those aren't good reasons," her husband scolded. "You need to be comfortable talking to people."

"I thought we weren't supposed to talk to strangers," their daughter pointed out.

"Well . . . that's true. But you're always with a grown-up trick-or-treating, right? Talking to adults is an important thing to learn. You don't want to be too shy."

"*Mommy's* shy," her daughter grumbled.

She felt a bubble of resentment. "I can talk to grown-ups just fine, thank you."

Of course her daughter had said something about her being shy. Of course her husband's comments over the last year now knit through the little girl's understanding of her mother. The girl had registered the judgmental tip of his head when he said, "Do you know you interrupted that guy?" "It was awkward when you didn't . . ." "Why are you acting so nervous?" Little pinpricks that showed Mommy's social ineptitude, an oblique collection of evidence that she'd misunderstood her father-in-law, that she'd misread the situation, reacted ineptly, because that was what she just did, had just done, didn't she see that?

His father drops him alone in the woods again and again, and he's still trying to find his way back with bread crumbs.

When she met her husband in a life-drawing class senior year of college, his open friendliness, his unselfconsciousness, had interested her. He'd been so comfortable tracing the soft curves of the naked bodies that the professor scolded him for his frequent joking with the models. She never managed to cork her embarrassment, had to imagine the subjects as inanimate as the wooden hands they'd sketched in the first week of class. But her quiet focus had seemed to fascinate him.

His lopsided smile was beautiful as he watched her work.

"I don't think I could come close to drawing something that good."

She'd never met a man who so readily admitted she was better at something, let alone one who seemed happy about it. His ease, his appreciation, reminded her so much of the way her mother had made her feel—smart, special, capable—that falling in love with him seemed like fate, a connection to something elemental she'd thought was gone forever. Then there had been the steadiness of his eyes on hers. His gaze didn't jump from marking to marking the way she was used to. When he traced their lines, he called them—called *her*—beautiful.

"Was there something you did?" he'd asked, and she'd felt the first fissure in their marriage. Now, each time he criticized her behavior, desperate for his father's approval, love, vindication, she felt a chisel lightly hammering, *tap-tap-tap*, hairline fractures invisibly weakening the keystone of respect that held up all they'd built.

"You know what I miss about trick-or-treating this year?" she asked the children.

"What?"

"Seeing the costumes! And the houses decorated, too. Maybe we can drive around, see what people have done for Halloween?"

"Yes, Mama! Do you think they'll have the skeletons out again?"

"Yeah, remember that?"

"And the puffy dragon!"

"That's right. That one house had a big inflatable dragon."

They piled in the car and cruised slowly along the streets of the most popular trick-or-treating neighborhood nearby. Took their place in a line of cars likewise filled with dressed-up children plastered to car windows, looking out at the decorations.

Their daughter's witch's hat grazed the roof of the car. Their son smiled vampire bat teeth. They waved at costumed people sitting bundled on lawn chairs, watching the cars of kids go by.

"This was a good idea," her husband said, happy at even tangentially being able to touch the outside world. "How'd you know this was going on?"

"I didn't. But what else are people going to do?"

"Good point," he said, smiling at her, and she reminded herself that most of the time, this was how he was. Most of the time, just like before, when he looked at her, she knew he thought she was clever, creatively fun.

Their daughter spotted a little coven of striped-socked, pointy-hatted scarecrow witches positioned around a fake fire, fog pumping at their feet.

"Look! Witches like me."

"Oh yeah," her husband said. "That's clearly a cool crew there. You know them?"

She'd given a snorting laugh, teased, "Why would you think all witches know each other?"

"Daddy, are witches real?" their daughter asked.

"No, but people used to think they were."

"Are bats real?" their son chimed in.

"Yes."

"Vampire bats?"

"Yes. They don't live around here, though. And they drink animal blood, not people blood."

"Gross!"

"Yup."

"And unicorns aren't real, but narwhals are real."

"That's right."

"And Santa's real?"

"Mmmm," her husband hummed noncommittally.

"But ghosts aren't real."

"Correct."

"Are dragons real?"

"No, dragons aren't real."

"But dinosaurs are real!"

"They were real."

"And they left their bones."

"Yes."

"But there are no dragon bones."

"That's right."

The children thought about this.

"It's confusing," their daughter said.

"Yeah, it is," her husband agreed. "I always thought maybe a long time ago people found dinosaur bones and invented dragons to explain them."

"I'm going to be a dragon next year," their son said. "I wanna breathe fire."

The little boy roared, pretended to spew invisible flames.

"Ew, Mommy, he's spitting on me!"

"Don't spit on your sister. Anyway, for now you're a bat, remember? Bats can't spit."

"Really?"

"Have you ever seen a spitting bat?"

"No."

"Well, there you go."

"Just 'cause you haven't seen something doesn't mean it doesn't exist," her daughter said.

"That's true," she admitted. "You're too smart for me."

"You can't see gravity," her daughter said.

"Or air!" her son called out.

"That's right. And you can't see love, either," her husband said.

"Sure you can," she told him, and when he smiled at her, she squeezed his hand. Felt a tiny break mend.

As they drove home in the earliness of autumn dark, it started to snow. Now her husband was the one excitedly plastered to the car window.

"Look at that! Look at that! All the maples are so red now, and with the snow on them? If I can get some shots of this—well! Those are the bestsellers, the fall foliage stuff. And especially if the sun comes out, lights it up right? What do you think? You okay to entertain the kids by yourself tomorrow? Because I've gotta leave before five to be in the air by daylight."

"Sure! Of course. It's supposed to be beautiful tomorrow."

"Fingers crossed!" Her husband held up crossed fingers in the rearview mirror, smiled at the kids crossing theirs, holding them up for him to see.

When they got home, her husband loaded his car with cameras, equipment, and food, preparing for a predawn start. He was in bed before she'd wrestled the children out of their costumes.

When she told her daughter it was time to put the witch's hat away, time to take a bath, the little girl shrieked, "I don't want to!" swung a small open hand, and hit her on the edge of her chin.

She gave her daughter a time-out, reeling with how much the girl had looked like her grandpa in that moment.

"It's hard when things are over," she told her daughter as the little girl snuffled regretfully, rubbing her forehead against her mother's shoulder. "It's difficult when something fun ends. But that's no reason to hurt someone. Especially your mommy. Your family. Your family is your team."

"I'm sorry, Mommy."

"I know, angel."

She read aloud to them from *Charlotte's Web*.

"Are they really going to kill the pig, Mommy? Are they really going to eat him?"

"We eat pig."

"We don't eat talking pigs."

"Very true."

"But are they going to eat Wilbur, Mama?"

Their sugar highs had melted away, holiday hyperactivity transformed into tiredness. They looked at her with big eyes, worried for the radiant, terrific, humble pig.

"Oh, honey, no, I'm sure they won't eat the pig."

"Charlotte wouldn't let it happen," her daughter insisted. "Charlotte will help him live forever."

"Nothing lives forever," she told them. "That's what makes living things special. But Charlotte is smart. She'll help make sure they don't eat Wilbur."

"Wilbur-bilbur-silber-pilbur," her son rhymed sleepily. "Can we get a talking pig, Mama?"

"Tell you what. You find one, we can keep it."

After tucking them in, she went downstairs to lock up and turn out the lights. In the darkness she saw the snow had stopped, that the yellows and reds of the fall leaves were coated with a thin layer of white. The temperature was below freezing. She crossed her fingers the way her children had in the car that the weather held.

In bed she inched her feet into the circle of warmth her husband's body always made, pressed her forehead to the spot between his shoulder blades she liked best. When he was sleeping, when his warmth and smell surrounded her like this, she could believe that someday the edges of her hurt would soften. That someday he would understand the way he'd smashed things, atone for suspecting she'd somehow induced, was at fault for, her father-in-law's violence.

After all, she was full of broken pieces that had mended. Even if they'd knit together at odd angles. Even if they were still tender. Unlike the old saying, her broken places hadn't healed stronger. But so far they had always come together enough to allow her to function.

And her husband still wasn't speaking to his father. That had to mean something. That had to be a start.

What tortured her most thinking back on it later was how happy she'd been to hear her husband leaving in the dark hours of that morning.

Each day her husband needed to feel he'd gotten things done. He was incapable of being in a good mood otherwise, yet everyday chores—the laundry, the dishes, the picking up after children—didn't sate the "get things done" thirst. No, each project had to be something finite but showy and, most irritating of all, had to be the center of her day, too. If she didn't help him move the woodpile from over here to over there, fix that door, replace a cracked tile, didn't assist with the dullest parts of his work, reviewing his just-received prints for flaws, didn't sign his name on them as he happily told her, "You do my signature better than I can!" he'd mope—a mood that could last for days, souring every interaction. She suspected that mainly he wanted her close more than he wanted her help. But she resented that the everyday chores still waited, and she was left to do them alone once he was finally able to relax, things done.

So there in the darkness, she curled comfortably in bed, knowing she'd be in charge of her own day. She could get the thankless work out of the way while it was still daylight.

She contentedly cowled the blanket over her head, muttered, "Fly safe," as he closed the bedroom door. There was a muffled rattle-pop from downstairs, and she lightly frowned that he'd slammed a door so hard, remembering his endless complaints to the children: "Guys, don't slam doors, stop being so noisy, why are you always so hard on things?"

When she woke again, it was light outside. She grabbed her phone, saw it was after seven. How long did she lie there? From bed she peeked outside at the snow-crusted, sunlit beauty of the new day. She imagined her husband circling above in his little plane.

Thinking about how brutally icy the air must be up in that other dimension, she snuggled in deeper. She scrolled on her phone, enjoying the luxury of time wasted. Finally, she got up. Brushed teeth, showered, dressed, started gathering a load of laundry. Didn't dare peek in at the children for fear she'd wake them.

Ever since lockdown began seven months before, winding down into an unscheduled summer followed by partly remote school, being alone had become a rare and precious thing. She'd grown to savor any sliver of silence. There was hardly a single recent moment she could remember being actually, physically, by herself. Hardly a waking hour where her family wasn't asking her for something, pulling at her, needing help, to "get things done" or be soothed or fed or amused or helped or taught. For the past seven months she'd walk down the stairs, and all eyes would turn to her, saying, "What do you have for us today? I need, I need, I need. I want, I want, I want."

Exhausted by the constant violation of even the last vestige of her privacy, she'd put a bolt on her bathroom door, high up enough that the children couldn't reach it and accidentally lock themselves in. Even then they scrabbled at the door. "Mama? What are you doing in there?" She'd rest head in hands, say, "What do you think I'm doing in the bathroom?" She'd hear them pad away, then her husband would give a crisp knock. "Honey, you okay in there?" She'd look at her phone. Never more than four minutes had passed. With eyes closed she'd reply, "I'm fine. I'm coming out."

Heading to the stairs, she was thinking about having the whole coffeepot to herself, unloading the dishwasher while watching the kind of guilty pleasure television she'd never dare stream when her husband was in the house. She wondered if she would enjoy these shows so much if his disapproval didn't give them an air of the forbidden.

"How can you stand that trash?"

"Just something to watch while I fold the laundry," she'd say, and shrug.

She couldn't explain to her husband why she was fascinated by the women in these shows. They had long ago learned the exact dollar value of their beauty, yet their carefully tended surfaces showed how impossible it was to always be your most attractive, most intriguing self. Understanding the size of their stage, they buckled at even the slightest criticism, exploded spectacularly, and were then embraced by an audience who lived vicariously through that fun-to-watch losing of shit, the viewers able to only dream of being allowed to show such anger. And when these women became wealthy, famous, beloved, when they were sure they'd got their fingertips on the brass ring, their husbands, boyfriends, partners, left them. Every time. After all, their men had never learned how to be supporting players.

Later, the fact that as she came down the stairs she'd been thinking about these husbands, these needy reality show husbands, gnawed at her.

The scene at the bottom of the kitchen stairs was so out of the ordinary she paused midway down, confused.

"Love?"

Her husband was on the floor by the big pine table they used as an island in the kitchen. He was on his side in a fetal curl, hands clasped tight and tucked under his chin. It was the same way their son always slept, looking like a tiny, praying angel.

"Are you—are you okay?"

He was resting on a blanket she didn't immediately recognize. It was so smooth, so cleanly reflected the light through the kitchen windows, that she thought it was silk. A beautiful color, darker at the edges than at the center where he lay. Just outside its perimeter, she saw his phone on the floor.

The screen was shattered. Seeing the jagged destruction of that glass, she was finally able to understand.

She called 911. Said "husband," said "stairs" and "bleeding." They told her not to move him. To stop the blood if she could. The blood that pooled around him in that shining blanket was coming from somewhere between his skull and the floor, but she was afraid she might irreparably hurt him if she lifted his head. She pressed a towel over his hair and lay behind him. Put her arm over him as the towel turned red. Told him everything was going to be fine, just fine, as she felt the shallow lift of his lungs under her palm.

The medics put her husband on a white plastic board. The police asked her questions. Their voices traveled distorted as if through a tunnel.

"No," she told them, "I didn't see how he fell. I was asleep. Showering. Getting dressed. I didn't think he was still home."

She walked next to her husband as they lifted the board, headed for the ambulance.

"Ma'am, I'm sorry, you can't come with us."

"But—"

"It's policy. Not even family in the ambulance. They're not going to let you into the hospital, either. No visitors."

"Can I—"

"We have to move."

"Please! Let me say goodbye."

She reached for her husband's hand, soft and pale and bound to the gurney. Squeezed it.

"I love you," she said. "I love you!"

Her husband exhaled a small bubble of bloody saliva that popped like chewing gum. And then he disappeared.

22

She woke up in a yellowed room. Everything was dulled and flat.

Someone told her she was safe. She knew from the pain this was a lie, and closed her eyes.

There was sunlight through a window, and agony. The person talking wore blue scrubs covered by a yellow paper gown, his face disguised under a mask and plastic shield. He, or someone who sounded like him, kept coming and going, repeating the same things, words that ran over her body and washed down a drain, easy to forget. *Orbital fracture, basal, swelling, surgery, drained, edema, frostbite, stitches, scar, nutrition, sprain.*

The room swung side to side.

"Where are my children?" she heard herself say, voice slurred.

"I don't know."

"Can I see them?"

"There aren't any visitors allowed right now."

She pulled at the tube in her hand.

"Hey—ma'am, hey! Don't do that!"

"I need to find them," she tried to say.

"Ma'am, stop! You're going to hurt yourself."

"Where are they?"

Pull, pull, pop, pop.

Then there were hands, and beeping, and darkness.

She woke again to find the sergeant sitting in a chair next to the bed, staring at the muted TV mounted in the corner. She clutched the blanket and pulled it up over her chest, feeling his hands under the fur coat.

"Where are they?"

He was startled by her voice. She was, too. It sounded as if she'd taken up a pack-a-day habit and years had passed since they'd last seen each other.

"Wha—huh?"

"Where are my kids?"

"They said you were awake. I was hoping we could discuss the break-in."

"My kids?"

"They're with your father-in-law."

"No," she croaked. "Nope."

She tried to push herself up, sit higher on the bed. Looked around for her phone to call someone, anyone, else.

"Hey, relax. They're okay. A caseworker's checking in on them."

She pulled at the tubes, heard a beeping start.

"I don't think you're supposed to—ma'am, stop that!"

Pull, pull, pop, pop. Hands, dizziness, and darkness.

She was alone in a half-lit room. She didn't know where she was.

Just float away and find them.

She sat up, put her legs over the side of the bed. They were wrapped in gauze, her feet cocooned huge and white. She stood up and then went weightless. Felt her cheek meet the floor with a crack in a vague, distant way.

When she opened her eyes, she understood she was in a hospital bed. The pain was a living thing, squirming and shifting. Her face had become a swollen rift. She tried to lift her hand to her head to touch it, assess the damage, and found that she was restrained. Padded Velcro cuffs held her wrists to the bed. One hand was bandaged. Tubes came from her arm, tangled like a sterile spiderweb. She couldn't reach to pull them out. She could only barely reach a button printed with a lady in a dress.

"Yes?" came a disembodied voice.

"Help!"

"What do you need, ma'am? You hit the nurse call button."

"I'm tied up. Please help me!"

"That's for your own safety. You fell out of bed. You've been pulling out your lines. Just try to rest."

She thrashed.

"Stop that, ma'am, just—"

The voice went dead. She threw herself back and forth on the bed and was exhausted so quickly that by the time the nurses arrived she was still and weakened.

"It's okay, ma'am. You keep trying to walk and pull your tubes out. This is so you don't hurt yourself."

"My children?"

"Yes, we've told you, they're with your father-in-law."

"No. No."

She started to writhe again, to pull the softness of the restraints into pain. And then there was a face hidden by a mask disappearing into her eyelids.

The next time she swam up to consciousness, she stayed still. She could feel that she was badly injured. Vaguely remembered the word "surgery." The word "fracture." She hit the nurse call button, and when someone arrived, she rasped out, "It hurts."

"All right, hon, you just press here. See this little device I'm putting in your hand?"

She pressed a round, red button, and there was a swell through one of the lines. It wasn't relief, exactly, but a rolling carelessness that made the pain bother her a little less.

"When can I leave?"

"You've got a bit of a road ahead of you, hon. But you're doing great. Already talking, already getting it together, I can tell. The main thing is to rest."

The hospital never got dark. Day and night were all mixed together. Days, or hours, later, she asked a different nurse, "How long have I been here?"

"A little under forty-eight hours."

"That's all?"

"That's all."

The nurse cocked her head. Her expression was hidden behind a mask and face shield. But her voice was full of curiosity.

"It says here you got hurt in a home invasion?"

That's it, that's what I need to tell them. I need to tell them about the Corner.

"Can you—can you get the police? I need to tell them who it was."

"Who was it?" the nurse asked. "Who did this to you?"

She shook her head, couldn't quite pull her wiggling thoughts out of the sucking drain of her cracked head.

Remember, remember. Don't forget.

The sergeant was back in the chair next to the bed. Again he stared at the muted TV mounted in the corner. Again she tried to cover herself with the blanket, but this time couldn't move her arms to do it, wrists quietly rattling in their cuffs. The thinness of the hospital gown, the grip of her restraints, made her feel simultaneously exposed and suffocated.

The sergeant's fist clutched wilting yellow flowers.

"For me?" she said.

"Oh! Huh? These? Yeah." He set the flowers on the table next to her bed.

The sergeant didn't seem to know where to look, and neither did she. She resisted pressing the red button, afraid she'd fall asleep again with the floating feeling the medication brought. Her eye itched horribly, bandaged with gauze that wrapped around her head, matting her hair.

In her new voice, scratched and aged, she asked, "My kids . . . are they safe?"

"Yes."

"The Cor—sorry, the man—he might look for my daughter. He might—"

"Ma'am, please, calm down," the sergeant said. "Your children are safe. There's no one after them."

"But he, the man who broke in, he was looking for my daughter. How can you know she's safe?"

The sergeant sighed heavily, and she saw herself the way he must. One eye wild with fear, the other bruised and broken. Shackled to the bed. Her words scraping and slurred.

"It's not like television, ma'am. Criminals don't go back for victims who got away." He paused, seeming to internally recognize this wasn't always true. "Unless this person had some kind of . . . family connection? Or a romantic one?"

She shook her head at the idea she was related to the Corner, had had an affair with him, and the fervor of the movement spun pain down her skull and neck.

Maybe he's right. Maybe they're safe. But—

"Are my kids still with that man?" she asked.

"Your father-in-law? Yes."

"I'll get someone else. Call someone else. Do you see my phone?"

"Your phone's in evidence. Their grandpa was the only relative we could find nearby."

"You—I told you what he did, didn't I? When we talked about my husband's fall?"

"Yes."

"And you still gave him my kids?"

"The alternative is family services."

"What?"

"They'd stay with strangers. Or in a group home. Likely be split up."

She saw her father-in-law sneering, heard his voice saying, "You need to stop babying him. It's one thing for the girl to be a tomboy. But you're going to turn him all wrong, too."

"I'll find someone," she said.

"You have some other relative I don't know about?"

She imagined her children wedged among her father's stacks of neglected things.

"In Utah. But . . . I'll think of someone."

She had friends, of course she did. But she'd let communication lapse over the last two years, dominated by their move, her mother-in-law's illness, then the illness of the whole world, its isolation. And none of the friends who were left lived nearby.

Why? Why'd you let them slip away from you? Is there anyone, really, that you're close enough with? Who is close enough to take them?

Anyone would be better than him.

"A relative's preferred," the sergeant said.

"Not one who's dangerous."

Again the sergeant exhaled in a way that implied she was use-lessly panicking, didn't understand the facts. "Ma'am, he denies he did anything to you. You never pressed charges. And a man who just learned his wife died? It's understandable he might act . . . out of character."

"Out of character," she repeated, feeling the sting of the ser-geant's rationalization, her body cast aside, shoved by the sergeant the same way he'd done after she'd opened the panel. Again came the melting confusion of that realization—*they think you hurt the chil-dren.* And again the understanding, *He doesn't believe you. He believes your father-in-law. Thinks you're lying. Or at least exaggerating. Hysterical.*

Her head ached and her memory went crooked. Everything fuzzed together, overlapping. The sergeant shifted into the past, be-came one of the suited men in that long-ago courtroom, one of the diodes in that circuit who said, "What we need to consider is this woman's active, contributory fault."

"Rest assured," the sergeant went on, voice indulgent now, "we're aware of your allegations, and your children are regularly checked on. And as far as moving them"—he cleared his throat, looked away from her—"now that they're with their grandpa, he may not want to pass them along to someone else."

She rattled her unhurt hand in its cuff to focus herself.

"He's never shown any interest. He'd be happy to get rid of them."

"No, ma'am. He's holding his own."

He wants control. Your husband's gone, your mother-in-law's gone. His grandchildren are all that's left. He wants to throw you away and keep them for himself. Maybe you should call a lawyer. But no, the way he is, he's probably already tired of the kids.

"I saw them myself just this morning. They were fine. Happy. How are you feeling?"

Her legs crawled with fire. Her eye pumped blood. She couldn't close her left hand.

"Peachy," she croaked. "But . . . school?"

"He's hired a babysitter to help him and handle all that dialing-into-class-remotely stuff. It's almost the Christmas break anyway. No big deal. He's got it figured out."

There was a tickling in her head, somewhere unscratchable. She tried to scratch it anyway. Felt her hand stop short in the cuff.

Man up. Stop crying.

"Now, getting to the reason I'm here? They gave me a call. Said you could ID the guy."

She licked her lips. It felt like they were made of softly chewed gum. The room was swimmy and thin.

The sooner you get out of here, the safer they are. The sooner the police catch him, the safer you'll be. And the sooner you can get them away from that man. Focus.

"Ma'am?"

"Sorry, it's—my face," she said. "It's painful."

"What can you tell me about the person who broke into your house?"

She tried to pin down her thoughts, everything scrambled by worry over her father-in-law.

Focus.

A yellow skull. Old shoes. Long laces. Tall.

"He's from that new café."

"What's that?" the sergeant said, leaning close.

"From the sandwich shop. Bakery. On Route 23, by Starbucks? The new one."

"I know it, yeah. You recognized him from there?"

"He's the manager there."

"So you know him."

"No."

"Sorry, it was this manager or not?"

"It was him."

"So you do know him."

"I only met him once."

"Once?"

"Once," she repeated.

"When?"

"Back in August. This last August."

"Okay. But you recognized him?"

"Yes."

"Can you describe him?"

Her brain was leaking, yet her eyes were dried out, were being sucked into her skull from the inside.

"Big," her mouth tried to say. She shook her wrist in the cuff. Closed her eyes to see the Corner better in memory. "White guy. Dirty blond hair. Very tall."

"How tall? Ma'am?"

He's too fuzzy for you to speak to. Wait for him to tune into the right station.

"Ma'am?"

"He wore black," she said. "He had old Reebok sneakers, white. Gloves. A shirt with a skull on it."

"A skull?"

"A yellow skull. Yellowed shoes, yellowed skull. Tall. Big. Huge. He hit his head. Will you—can you call my children? I want to talk to them."

She felt herself fading, her body pulled physically into sleep, but remembered something important, said, "Do you think he'd go after her again? He was after my daughter. You have to watch out for her, he could get her now, he could—"

When she opened her good eye, the sergeant had been blinked out of existence.

A nurse made of pointy edges was poking at her here, putting something around her there, pulling at a bandage, lifting the cover on her eye, switching something under the blanket.

"Was—were the police here?"

"I dunno, hon."

Then she saw the yellow flowers wilting on the side table. The sergeant hadn't put them in water.

Relief let her release her hands, gone to fists in their cuffs.

The sergeant was here. He's probably arresting the Corner right now. And then you'll get the children from your father-in-law, and he hasn't had them long, it will be okay—

The pain woke her next. She clicked the little red button and nothing happened. There was no light out the window, but as usual it was bright in the room, the door open to the hall. She called the nurse and told her the red button wasn't working.

"Sorry, honey, that means you'll have to wait. It'll work again when it's safe. But this is good timing, you're due for a blood draw."

Vial after vial. She looked the other way.

"Can you untie me?" she asked the nurse.

"Sorry, hon. It's for your own safety. Anyhow, that decision's above my pay grade."

"Can you help me call my kids?"

"It's the middle of the night, hon. Plus, I don't think the number's right. Man that picks up always ends the call right off."

There was a crack in the ceiling. Maybe her memory of calling had slipped through a crack like that. She looked at it, thinking about the blue-scrubbed man who faded in and out to lecture her about the damage to her head. *Orbital fracture.* He repeated words but never explained them. She pictured a cartoon cat hit on the skull, stars rotating, orbiting, around a massive bump, the cat staggering and black eyed. *Please, kitty, don't you bite!*

That sounds right. That sounds exactly right. Cartoon stars. Fractured orbit.

A blood pressure cuff hissed around her arm.

"Why don't we sit you up? You're looking better. Swelling's already down."

The nurse flipped the blanket off of her legs, slowly unwound a bandage.

There were strips of skin torn from her foot, her ankle and calf. Toenails were missing. In their place was raw skin the color of coals.

She flailed her destroyed legs.

"What did you do? What did you do to me?"

This is no hospital.

Another nurse hurried in, held her good hand gently in its cuff.

"Hon, you stop that now. We're changing your dressing, okay? It's to help, to get you better. I know you want to get better, see those kids you keep talking about, right?"

She stopped moving. Looked up at the nurses. Both were hidden behind their masks and plastic shields. Pinned to their scrubs were photos of what they looked like underneath it all. Smiling faces that resembled these figures not at all.

"What did you do? To my feet?"

"It's from the frostbite. The doctors removed the dead skin, and debrided the injured areas. It should grow back just fine. Might look a little odd, but it should grow back. Your toenails should regrow, too. That takes time."

She looked away as they changed the left bandage, then the right.

"I'm sorry if I kicked you."

"No, dear, I'm all right. You had a shock, that's all."

"Where's the policeman?"

"Oh, he'll be back." The nurse's voice hitched into feigned casualness as she asked, "This all happened during a break-in?"

"Mmm. I went through the snow to get away. Got help."

"Well, aren't you brave? Looks like it was a lot to put yourself through."

"My kids were in the house. He was after them."

The nurses lifted their hands away from her, as if such a curse might be contagious.

"Was this man who broke in—did you know him?"

They want it to be your fault.

"A stranger," she said. "Someone I'd only seen once before."

"Who would do such a thing?"

A monster.

"Just a man."

"Why'd he do it? Did he take things?"

She felt her children's hummingbird hearts, closed her eyes, and said, "He tried."

23

She sat down next to the entry door the paramedics closed behind her husband. Wrapped her arms around her legs and rocked back and forth. This made the world go as unsteady as her mind until she was moving in time with it, bringing everything level again.

Her hands, her cheek, were sticky with his blood.

"I don't know what happened," she said again and again to the police standing above her. "He said he'd be flying by daylight."

She complied limply as the police took photos of her. Stood with a female officer in the bathroom. Peeled off her bloody clothes, placed them in plastic bags the woman held out for her. Was briefly ashamed of the tattered condition of her underwear as the officer deftly zipped them in a bag.

They gave her permission to shower, to get dressed, to leave for the hospital they all knew she wouldn't be allowed inside of.

Looking back, she must have explained some of it to her children. She must have gotten them ready, left down the front stairs and out the old front double doors so the children wouldn't see the blood on the kitchen floor. She must have driven away. She knew she must have done all that because she found herself in the parking lot of the hospital, holding her children's hands as they were told they couldn't come in.

"Please. Can you please at least give us an update?"

She paced back and forth, the children's hands gripped in her own until a man came out and introduced himself as a doctor.

The first thing he said was "I'm sorry," and it buckled her knees until she was looking up at him from the concrete, the *woosh* of the hospitals automatic doors opening and closing and opening again with her weight.

The doctor sat down next to her as though sitting on the ground were a normal thing.

"We'd like to speak to you about organ donation," he said.

For this, they were allowed into the hospital. In a small, private room, the doctor told her there were no miracles possible at this point. This was brain death. It wasn't like the stories on the news of people waking up after years or decades. There were no stories, no instances of someone ever traveling back from the place her husband was now.

The children clung to her as this doctor took an ice pick to their reality. Daddy dead but not dead. Daddy gone but still here.

"I don't need the speech," she told the doctor. "He would want to be useful."

She signed away her husband's still-beating heart, his liver, his kidneys, the lungs that were filling and emptying on a breathing apparatus, his pancreas, tissues, corneas. His bone and skin and blood.

"Can we see him?" she asked the doctor. "Can the children see him? Before? To say goodbye?"

"No visitors are allowed on the patient floors. Because of the surge. But we've been doing video calls."

She didn't argue. She'd seen the news. She understood she wasn't special, that she was now joining the legions of families kept from their loved ones to interrupt the furious spread of disease. On the screen her husband's mouth was opened disproportionately wide to fit a tube. His head was partly shaved. His eyes were taped closed.

"Daddy's left his body behind," she told the children. "We need to say goodbye."

"But he's right there?"

"I'm sorry, loves. That's just his body. His mind, his . . . everything else . . . is gone. But at least we can say goodbye to his body. At least we get to see him one more time."

"We love you, Daddy," her daughter said quietly. "I love you!"

"Air hugs," her son called out, miming a hug. "I'm giving you air hugs, Daddy. See you soon!"

"Sweetheart, you won't see Daddy soon. This is—he's not coming home."

"Okay, Mommy." Her son nodded, humoring her.

The nurse holding the phone in her husband's room was practiced. Talked soothingly before disconnecting, knowing they, the family, would never hang up.

During the drive home, she told the children a story, hoping to make it true by saying it aloud. Daddy hurrying down the steps in the dark, looking at his phone, so excited! So happy. Checking the weather, checking the time until sunrise. But he tripped, fell. It's like turning off a light switch. He didn't suffer. And most of all, he didn't mean to leave you.

She didn't tell her children that it was her fault, didn't tell them about the long slow tick of time wasted.

The police were still at the house when they returned. She had the children wait at the old double front doors while she went around to the entry, went past the police, the pool of blood, and opened the latch, holding up the bar on its little nail that had swung down behind them when they left. Together they went up the front stairs. She put the children in her office with a TV show blaring on her computer. She instructed them in her strictest voice to not go downstairs.

"The hospital let us know," the sergeant said. "I'm so sorry for your loss. I'm a father of young children myself."

He handed her a card.

"This is a forensic cleaning service. You'll want to get in touch with them."

He handed her another card.

"Contact me if you think of anything else. Anything that might be important, anything you forgot to tell us. We're nearly done here. Is there anything else we can do?"

"Could you—could you tell my father-in-law? What happened? We're not on speaking terms. I can give you his information."

"Of course. Of course we can do that."

When they left she stared at the blood. It was crackled, had dried like the Utah deserts of her childhood. She called the cleaning company. An abrupt woman told her they weren't taking on new clients. No one was. Too much risk, too much infection.

Over the next three days she cleaned up the blood herself. Before landing on the floor, her husband's head had hit the old table that functioned as their kitchen island. The blood bleached out of the table easily. The floor was more difficult. Blood had dripped between the old boards and was quickly discovered by tiny, nibbling ants. After wiping and scraping, she was left with an irregular stain soaked into the porous pine. She brought out the orbital sander, obliterating ants and creating wood dust filled with aerosolized blood.

She called her father and told him the version of the story she'd invented for the children.

"What a thing!" he said. "I always liked him. You want me to come out there?"

Of course she did, but she knew her father well enough to pause, let him finish the thought.

"Though I suppose I can't, can I? Risk getting on a plane or driving that far through a surge and all. Plus, it's against the rules, isn't it? Though if you want to come home . . ."

Again, she stayed silent.

"Well, that'd be just as bad, wouldn't it? You three having to get out here during all this. And then quarantine and everything. And you know I don't have the space."

It was exactly what she'd expected, had learned to expect, from her father. Even so his apathy, the sting of his indifference, forced her eyes closed.

Don't cry.

"We'll stay here, Dad. I just wanted to let you know."

An exhale of relief through the phone. "All right then, okay! Well, you keep in touch."

"I wish Grandma was still alive." Her voice welled with a sob. "It would be good to talk to her, you know?"

Her father was silent. She heard him shifting the phone.

"Yeah. Well. Huh. Anyways, I love you, and I'm real sorry." He hung up.

After sanding, the pine went back to its natural pale yellow. Only the gaps between the floorboards showed bloodstain. She carefully brushed on polyurethane, coat after coat. It dried cleanly.

If you didn't know it was there, you'd never know it was there.

With the blood gone, her husband turned to ash, box stored in the corner of his closet, there was nothing left to do.

She didn't change her sheets. Didn't touch her husband's pillow. Sometimes she lay open eyed, staring at the indentation where he'd laid his head.

What shall you do now? What shall you ever do?

She allowed the children into the kitchen again. She logged them on to remote school. Shuttled them to and from their half days. Their voices were hard to make out, sounded submerged. As they watched television, she'd nuzzle their skin, kiss their bellies. Holding her children in the blare of the television, in its blue light, was the only time it was easy for her to fall asleep.

"He didn't suffer," she told the ones who called, trying to make it true. "It was quick. No, we can't have a funeral now. Maybe a memorial later? I'll let you know. No, there's nothing you can do. Thank you, thank you for thinking of us."

Within a month the sympathy tap was exhausted and the calls stopped. Until the article about her husband came out, of course, but that was different. The people who contacted her then had an eagerness, a thrill in their voices at their proximity to death. Their nearness to even the tiniest hint of fame.

24

The psychiatrist didn't start by discussing the break-in. Instead, he sat in the chair in her hospital room and asked about her weight. Listened to the litany of her losses. Calmly labeled her thinness self-harm, destructive, a sign of depression.

As if these are things you don't already know. As if they matter.

She didn't deny any of it. Told him she agreed. At last said, "When it came down to it, though, turns out I want to live."

"Yes." His eyes darted over her bandages, her bruising. "But you have a lot of work ahead. Trauma doesn't end when the trauma ends. Everyone's past forms their present."

"That's true," she conceded, eyeing him with more interest. "It's all still here, the past. What happened to my husband. The grief. This Cor—" Her voice cracked. "This man, breaking into my home. I wish none of it had happened. But it did. And in my head it's still happening."

"You need to grapple with what you've been through."

"And help my kids."

"They're not the only ones who went through this. If you don't look after yourself, what will they have? If they can't depend on you?" The psychiatrist clasped his hands together in his lap. "Do you really want to stay where you are now?"

"No," she said, understanding the psychiatrist wasn't referring to the hospital, but to the way her mind was stuck in a dark well, clawing uselessly at distant light. "I don't."

She'd treated coming back to herself like a jigsaw puzzle, flipping and turning the pieces on the table, analyzing them, until she was able to arrange each memory—*something hit you in the face on the trail, you saw him open the front doors, those sneakers*—among the rest to form a complete picture. So as the psychiatrist asked her about the Corner, her frenzied flight through the woods, her physical injuries and how she'd incurred them, she answered as well as she could, picking up this or that puzzle piece, and when something took time to mentally arrange, she explained, "It gets jumbled. Bits of it slip away, then kind of spring on me. Images. Feelings. It's—disorienting."

"It's only been four days," the psychiatrist said. This seemed impossible to her, since in the odd twilight space of the hospital, she'd just arrived, yet simultaneously was sure she'd been there for weeks. "You may find that your memory isn't what you'd like. That you have intrusive thoughts. Or that you're reliving this person hunting you. That's normal. A normal response to trauma." He shrugged, added, "Sometimes people can't remember everything, even with time. The mind can protect itself by sealing things off."

"I guess I wouldn't even know if that was happening," she mused. "And I keep thinking that this . . . person . . . who broke in will try and find my daughter. But then, that would be illogical, wouldn't it? Risky for him?"

As best she could—puzzle pieces not quite fitting, often having to force them together—she described the way the Corner had hunted her little girl. His behavior at the café. After all, if he'd tracked her down after four months, why wouldn't he try again? And then there were the dangers of her father-in-law's custody. The psychiatrist slowly drew out their history. Discussed her limited options.

"These are all reasonable worries," the psychiatrist reassured her. "And I do think you're correct. You getting home, you speaking with the police, helping them catch this man—those are the most efficient, effective ways to address these problems."

The psychiatrist's serious face, his measured words, "reasonable," "efficient," "effective," "normal," were a balm. They soothed her more than a press of the red button.

"Are you willing to continue counseling after you're discharged? I can provide you referrals. And I do specialize in, publish about, post-traumatic stress. If you wanted, we could make sure you have an appointment with my office."

Her broken face managed a smile. "I'd like that," she said.

When she woke it was morning and the cuffs were gone. She rubbed her wrists in relief, sure that this small modicum of freedom was thanks to the psychiatrist.

Guess that means you're sane after all.

She touched the bandage around her head, her eye. Patted her snarled hair.

It's all still happening. It always will be.

"Hello," the sergeant said.

This time she was able to pull the blanket over herself, yanking it up to her chin.

"I'm sorry. I didn't mean to startle you."

He took up a lot of room, legs splayed wide, elbows sticking out from the armrests of the pink upholstered hospital chair near her bed.

"I just—I didn't see you."

"You've got limitations." He tapped his eye to indicate her half-broken vision.

"I thought visitors weren't allowed?"

The sergeant shrugged. "Cops are an exception."

"Right." She started to breathe normally again. "So. Did you get him?"

The sergeant shrugged. "Not yet."

"You couldn't find him?"

"Looks like he doesn't work at that café."

"He quit?"

The sergeant shrugged in a way that made clear he couldn't, or wouldn't, give details. "Something like that. We're trying to track him down."

Her throat swelled with anxiety.

"But if you can't find him . . . are you making sure my daughter's safe? He was—did I tell you? He was after her. He made that clear."

The sergeant's face darkened. He tap-tap-tapped a finger irritably on the arm of his chair.

His politeness, his belief, is conditional on you not questioning him.

"You told me." The sergeant's voice was clipped. "You ID'd the guy as a stranger. And like I told you, a criminal like that, it just doesn't happen that he'd go after a victim who got away. It would guarantee he'd be caught, for one. And your father-in-law lives in a busy apartment complex, where cops are checking in on him and your kids. All right? Now, you feeling up to talking? Might help us get the guy."

Her eye burned under the bandage. She ached with fury at the sergeant's impatient dismissal of her concerns. She could smell her body, its reek of vinegar and old grease. Her jaw hurt. Speaking still scratched her throat. Her whole skull was soft around the edges and ragged from the pain. But they'd freed her arms. She could move her legs. Wiggle her toenail-less toes under the blanket. Think a little more clearly.

Remember what the psychiatrist said. You're reasonable, efficient, effective, normal. Helping the police catch him is the quickest way to help the children.

Help yourself. And maybe the sergeant's right that the kids are safe. That the Corner wouldn't go after them again. The sergeant would know that kind of thing, wouldn't he? About crime? The facts, the numbers?

"Ma'am?"

"Right. Yeah, sure. I can answer questions."

You're as ready as you can be. You have to convince them. They have to catch him.

But she needed to see the children. To reassure herself they were safe. To read on their faces how their grandfather was treating them.

"Can we call my kids first?" she asked. "A video call? They've tried for me here, but my father-in-law won't pick up for me. He might for you."

The sergeant gave a resigned grunt. "Sure. Okay."

Her father-in-law picked up on the first ring.

"Hello, Officer, what can I do you for?"

The sergeant told him. She could picture her father-in-law's expression going sour from the change in tone.

"Fine, I'll get them."

The sergeant handed her the phone, and there were her children. Beautiful, shining. Worried.

"Mama, you look soooooooo bad," her son said.

She laughed and it hurt. She cried and it stung.

"Don't cry, Mommy!"

"I'm just so happy to see you two."

"Your eye is all black. Like a raccoon." Her daughter squinted closer to the screen at her bruises and eye patch. "Half raccoon, half pirate."

"Yeah! A raccoon pirate!" her son agreed, as if this was exciting, a great compliment.

"That's me, raccoon pirate Mommy." She lightly touched the bandage over her eye. "How are you guys? I miss you so, so much!"

"When are you coming to get us?"

Her daughter's eyes slanted to the side. She was sure her father-in-law was just off screen, scowling as he overheard the little girl ask the question.

"The second I get out of the hospital, I'm coming to get you. I promise. I'm working really hard to get better."

"Okay, Mommy."

"How have you guys been doing? You feeling okay?"

"Yes! We have a babysitter. She's real nice. Her hair is *so* long."

"You like her?"

"Yeah. She plays family. And we made cookies. She has Legos!"

"That's wonderful, guys. Have you had good behavior for Grampy?"

The children looked at each other.

"We're trying," her daughter said, then whispered close to the screen. "But it's hard to be quiet enough."

I bet. I bet that man wants you quiet. Wants you invisible.

"Okay. You keep working hard to have good behavior. I know it can be difficult. Have you been doing remote school?"

"Mm-hmm," her daughter said. "The babysitter dialed us in this morning. And now it's break!" She paused before adding, "They say he isn't real?"

"Who?"

"Grampy, the policemen."

"They say who isn't real?"

"The Corner."

"Grampy says the monster's a pigment," her son said. He was pulling silly faces, and from the angle of his eyes, she could tell the little boy was looking at his own image in the corner of the screen, making faces to entertain himself.

"A *figment*," his sister corrected him. "A *figment* of imagination."

"Oh, loves, do you remember? We talked about this. There was no ghost, no nightmare man. No monster. Grampy's right. It was just a person."

"He's a pigment," her son insisted. "Grampy says so." Then he leaned closer, said conspiratorially, "But he might be a ghost, Mama, 'cause the police say he doesn't even have feet!"

Her eye felt so swollen it might burst through the bandage, and she wondered if her injuries or the usual difficulties of trying to get the children to focus, to communicate well over the phone, were at the root of how hard it was for her to understand what they were trying to say.

"Sorry, love, why are you talking about feet?"

Her little girl was looking away from the screen now, and she was certain her father-in-law was doing something to draw her daughter's attention. The girl's visible nervousness was contagious, and she stammered out, "You know what . . . never mind. Don't worry about that. There was no Corner, okay? Just a man, talking in a scary voice."

"There's a lady who wants to know all about us." Her son was back to distractedly making faces, looking at his own image on the phone.

"The babysitter?"

"No, a brown lady. She gave me butterscotch!"

"She gave us *both* butterscotch," her daughter said.

Maybe her father-in-law was dating someone. Someone curious about her. But . . . dating a brown lady? It would be a cold day in hell for that man. A policewoman asking questions, maybe? The caseworker the sergeant had mentioned?

She stared dumbly at their beautiful faces. "I can't wait to give you hugs," she said.

"Are you coming back soon?"

"Yes, love. I'm working hard to get better, and then we'll all be back at home together."

"Daddy didn't come back," her daughter said.

Their big eyes lowered to shatter her. She read in their faces their fear that she'd been plucked away from them, had disappeared into the vastness of the hospital like their father, would return to them only as memory and ash, a longed-for specter haunting the woods.

"I'm—I'm so sorry to be away from you."

Her voice was strangled, weak.

This is not about you. They need to know you won't disappear.

She cleared her throat.

"Remember when we were in the hidden place and I told you I'd come back?"

Their little heads nodded, little faces fastened tight to her through the screen.

"And I did, didn't I? This is like that. I'm working really hard to get back to you. And then we'll be together. Okay?"

"For Christmas?" her son asked.

What day is it? What day is Christmas?

Her daughter saw her confusion.

"Christmas is day after tomorrow," the little girl said. "Mommy isn't well enough to see us then."

"Are we going to miss Christmas?" Her son's face started to break, teetering on the verge of tears.

"Oh, no, honey, we'll have Christmas! I—I won't be able to see you. But we'll have a late Christmas, okay? It will be extra special because you'll get two Christmases. One with Grampy, one with me, okay?"

"But what about Santa?"

"Don't you worry about that guy." She nodded as sagely as her injuries would allow. "If he knows when you're awake, knows when you've been good, he certainly knows when your mama's in the hospital and he has to come a little late, right?"

Her son's face brightened at this reminder of Santa's omniscience.

"Okay, Mommy. I—"

A flash of her father-in-law's chin and cheek appeared, and then the video cut off. She handed the phone back to the sergeant and leaned back on her pillow, dazed.

"He hung up," she said.

"Yeah."

"Thank you. He would never have—thank you."

After all that, all that, and you can't even hold them. This will be their first Christmas without you.

She turned away from the sergeant to hide her tears, wiping them with the corner of her blanket.

25

You up for those questions now?" the sergeant asked.

She noticed that the boyish policeman sat near the door. She gave him a lift of her hand and he returned the gesture.

"We were hoping you could walk us through everything you can remember."

"You're sure he won't come back? For my daughter?"

The sergeant rubbed his temple as if the question pained him. "Okay, ma'am. How about you explain why you're so focused on that."

A man like the sergeant whose first thought is that a mother buried murdered children in her walls? He must already have some dark ideas about motive.

"The Cor—this man, broke in because of my daughter."

"Can you explain why you believe that?"

"He was strange toward her. At the sandwich shop. And he mentioned her specifically when we were hidden."

"What exactly did he say that night?"

"He kind of—called to her? 'Little girl, come out,' that kind of thing. And he—" Her voice wavered, she tried to keep it under control, forced a cough to regain her composure. "He said he was a wolf. He called her a—" She swallowed deeply, then was able to choke out, "Called her a little pig. Said she'd be . . . delicious."

The sergeant didn't respond, which made her keep talking despite herself.

"It sounds, I don't know, silly, saying it now?"

"Silly?" The sergeant scribbled something in a small notebook.

"I just mean . . . it sounds silly, but it was scary. Even for me, an adult, you know?"

Again the sergeant stayed silent, but this time she did, too. At last he asked, "And how did this man behave strangely at the sandwich place where you first saw him?"

She shifted uncomfortably. The memories made her skin itch.

"He was . . . inappropriate. He called my daughter princess, sweetheart. Kept staring at her. She had on a tank top. He—the strap of the shirt had slipped down, and he put it back." She mimed the motion. "It was the—the," she stuttered, "way he did it? I dunno. It bothered me."

"You said this was back in August."

"Yes."

"And your husband?"

"Yeah, he was there."

"And what did he think?"

She looked down at her hands. Made herself release the edge of the blanket she was twisting.

The sergeant already thought you were capable of killing your children and walling them up. Don't let him know your husband thought you were overreacting.

"He agreed the guy was creepy."

"Did this man seem threatening?"

"When he moved that strap? He did. To me he did."

"How'd your husband react to that?"

"He didn't notice."

The sergeant's face and tone flattened. "Didn't notice?"

"No. I guess he . . . happened to be looking the other way."

Again the sergeant wrote something in his notebook. "Anything else you remember?"

"He—he took our receipt from the table. It must've had my husband's name on it. So maybe that's how he found us?"

The sergeant tap-tapped on the arm of his chair. "When he broke in, didn't you say he headed toward your room first?"

"Yes."

"But you still think he was after your daughter."

"Yes."

His eyes narrowed. "It's a pretty extreme thing, to assume he was after a little girl."

"Is it? Ask the women you know what it was like being a little girl."

A dark cloud passed over the sergeant. Faded.

"You don't think that this man's behavior at the restaurant could have been innocent? That you read into it?"

"I mean, I guess? But it was odd enough that it stuck with me."

"I see," he said, but his expression reminded her of her college ex-boyfriend, dubious over the way she saw the world.

"Not all men are good men," she said.

"Right." The sergeant nodded. "Fair enough. Was he wearing a mask when you saw him at the sandwich place?"

"Yes."

"But you're confident that the man you saw in your home and this café manager are the same person?"

"Yes."

"One hundred percent?"

Why if someone asks you something enough times do you always start to doubt yourself? And of course you're not one hundred percent sure.

"One hundred percent," she lied. "And that's why I want to make sure you're looking after her, that he isn't still—"

The sergeant held up a weary hand to interrupt her. Set his note-book aside. "Ma'am," he said, "even with all you just said, what I told you stands. It's not likely. A relative, an abusive spouse, a spurned partner—those are the people who keep pursuing their vic-tims. But someone who breaks in? They don't go back. They know they'd get caught. So please . . . believe me when I say your daughter is safe. You do not need to keep revisiting this."

Just because it's unlikely doesn't mean it couldn't happen. Everything you've just been through is unlikely.

"He was . . . frightening. And so I want to be sure she's safe, that you're watching, that—"

"We're watching them, ma'am. She's safe. They're safe."

The sergeant's face was hard, allowing no room for questioning.

"Okay," she said.

Of course they're not safe. You have to get out of here.

"So. Why don't we start with what time you went to sleep on the night of the break-in," the sergeant said.

She closed her eye, leaned back.

You have to help them catch him.

"Ma'am?"

You can do this. So what if your father-in-law thinks you're full of shit. That it's all a "pigment." Screw him.

"All right, okay," she said.

Slow and steady she walked the sergeant and the boyish officer through the shattered memories she'd carefully dusted of their ter-ror and reassembled to try to separate fact from panic. She tried to keep it linear, but the sergeant insisted on circles, asking her to re-peat things, the same questions again and again. She described the Corner once, twice, a third time. What he looked like at the top of the stairs. What she saw through the vent. Was she sure about the shirt? The weapon? The shoes? And how could she be sure? Wasn't it dark, wasn't he far away? What did his gloves look like? The weapon? Again she mimed its flop. Tried to imitate its *thwack*.

The memory of that noise penetrated her spine, even through her pain.

She tried not to flinch as the sergeant asked her to justify her failures, then justify them again. Why not go for her car, the gun, her phone, a weapon? Why not take the children with her? Why was she so thin? Did she normally wear contacts or glasses? How had she been able to fall asleep in the hidden place, if it was all so frightening? How had she hit her head? Was she dizzied? Did she lose consciousness? How had she gotten so hurt in the woods, just running down a path? Was she sure of the intruder's description? It was an awful lot of detail for someone she'd seen for seconds. Why hadn't she recognized him immediately, if she was so sure it was the man from the café?

Each question sheared her confidence, highlighted how she'd been illogical; each explanation she gave felt horribly insufficient. Her brain went ever more liquid, swimming with whys and hows.

He's right, it's strange, it doesn't add up, your memory is frayed. You made so many mistakes, why didn't you think? How could you fall asleep? Why did it take you so long to recognize him?

No, there were no prescription drugs in the house. No, no illegal drugs.

Even the things she thought she'd done right, been smart about, were difficult to explain. The sergeant had her describe in detail how she'd gotten her children into the hidden place so quickly. Walked her through the order of what she'd grabbed when (Fuzzy-doll, water, son, daughter, Pinkbunny, blanket, pillow) multiple times. The sergeant's children couldn't stay quiet for five minutes, how had hers managed for hours? She hadn't known the fur coat was there? Well, wasn't that lucky?

The sergeant's interest perpetually rotated back to the Corner and his frightening voice. Around every bend in questioning lay the central strangeness of his behavior, his words.

"Why would this guy be speaking out loud? Why would he let you know he was headed to the attic, for example?" the sergeant asked.

Why would he? Why would he do that?

She swallowed heavily through her thickening throat. The sergeant was looking at her the same way as when he'd said, "Why don't you show us where you put those kids?"

Her hands began shaking like they had in the hidden place as a thought licked like fire across her brain.

It's not that he blames you. He doesn't believe you. He doesn't believe what you're saying about any of it.

She swallowed, as if she could rid herself of this realization by gulping it deeper. "Like I—like I said," she told him, hesitant now that the sergeant had transformed into someone she had to prove things to instead of someone who would prove things for her. "I think he was trying to scare us. He wanted to get us to make noise, give ourselves away, by sounding scary and saying scary enough things to frighten the kids."

The sergeant's steady gaze made her squirm.

He wants to unsettle you. That's what cops do. Just tell him how it was. No matter how strange. You have to make him understand.

"He also seemed to believe what he was saying? He half explained it. He thought he should have—deserves—whatever he can take. Because he's superior somehow. That he can ignore the rules, step over them, he said, and take whatever—whoever—do whatever he wants. The disdain was—you could feel it. Like we weren't human beings to him. And that voice?" Again she stilled her hands from clutching and releasing the blanket. "Yeah. It was frightening. He meant it to be."

"Your kids . . . they have a lot of ideas. They seem to think this 'Corner' was a monster, or something from a nightmare. Or a ghost."

The kids know. The kids were there. He has to believe when there's three of us.

"Yes. The scary voice he used was confusing."

"What did it sound like?"

Metal and teeth. Barbed fingernails scraping a chalkboard. Steel wool scouring a pan bare.

"Raspy, I guess? Like you'd do a villain's voice when you read aloud to kids."

"So he was doing an act."

"I mean, yeah. And it kind of fell apart, eventually. He realized the house had to have an attic. He got excited about that, thought we were hiding up there. And when he got excited, he sounded more normal, you know? All for show."

The sergeant pulled a sardonic smile she could sense even through his paper mask. "You think he had multiple personalities?"

"Isn't that fake? Just a movie thing?"

The sergeant shrugged. "You think he was crazy? Talking to some voice in his head?"

She distractedly traced a finger along the path of her skull's deepest hurt. "I mean, is anyone who could do that totally normal? But it was scarier than him being crazy. He seemed calculated? Like he'd thought out exactly what he was doing. And that frightened me." She thought a moment. "He did say he was bothered by the house. Something about it being creaky. Having too many doors. But that doesn't make him crazy, I guess. Lots of people are afraid of my house. People think it's haunted because it's old."

"And you don't consider yourself superstitious?" the sergeant asked.

"No."

"They say as many people in this country believe in ghosts as believe in Jesus," the sergeant said, writing in his notebook.

Her head ached. Her eye made everything milky.

"Guess God and ghosts are about equally believable," she muttered.

The sergeant's head clicked up, eyes narrowing. "Excuse me?"

"Sorry, I—I just meant . . . religion's a belief in the supernatural, too. Something beyond our understanding?"

Careless. You've offended him.

The sergeant's eyes were cutting above his mask. "I guess you couldn't believe in ghosts, to live in that house," he said.

Again she realized she was twisting the edge of her blanket as though she'd worry it apart. "He did—he did quote the Bible. That bit about women learning in submission? My grandmother was religious, and she raised me, so I recognized—"

The sergeant gave a dismissive wave, and she stopped talking. He handed her a paper sketched with a basic floor plan of her house. Another with the property as a whole. "These look right?"

Her professional self frowned. *Proportions all wrong, lines unconfident. Labels missing, no detail at all.*

She gestured for his pencil. He handed it to her and rolled the hospital table she used for meals so it cantilevered over the bed. She drew swift lines, wrote additional words.

"Here."

"Huh, whatdayaknow. That's actually better."

They went through the map. She marked where they'd heard footsteps. Where she knew the Corner had traveled. Valuables the police had found were itemized, their locations noted on the map—jewelry, safe, ammunition, her phone, the computers. It didn't look to her like anything obvious was missing. They traced her escape through the woods. Put *x*'s over the graveyard and a spot on the trail, marking where she thought she'd been injured.

"Do you think he followed you out of the house?"

"That night I was so afraid I thought he might have, but no. Looking back, I don't think he did."

How can you not be sure? You should know that. Do you just not remember?

"So." The sergeant consulted his notebook. "You heard this man for some reason say aloud that he was headed to the attic. You decided to go for help. How did the children react?"

The sergeant leaned back in his chair, but his eyes hooked to her, hungry as the mountain lion's. She felt sickened, immediately sure the children had told him she'd pushed them off her. Hurt them.

"The kids, they were upset, didn't want me to leave."

"But you did leave. How did that work?"

He already knows. So tell him how it was.

"I told them I was getting help. They were terrified. It was awful." She blinked back tears. Swiped at her eye with the blanket corner knotted in her hand. "I had to push them off me. I just kept thinking how it was maybe their last memories of me, and they'd remember me pushing them away. I had to make them listen. Make them let me go."

The sergeant nodded, taking notes. "You pushed them? Physically? With your hands?"

"Yes. They wouldn't let me loose otherwise. It was—"

"One of them bit you."

It wasn't a question. She balked, had forgotten her son's teeth in her palm, such a tiny thing compared with all her subsequent pain.

"Oh, oh no, that was, that happened when I covered my son's mouth when he woke up. The Corner going up the stairs was really loud, and that woke my son. He bit down."

"The Corner?" The sergeant arched an eyebrow.

Stupid, so stupid, why'd you say that?

"Sorry. The kids, they called him that, so—"

"All right." The sergeant lounged back in his chair again, but she tensed. Something about his casualness appeared feigned. "Did you have anything to drink that night? Alcohol, I mean?"

She recalled sitting on the kitchen stairs after midnight two days after her husband fell, drinking wine directly from the bottle and staring at the half-cleaned blood. The wine was the only thing she'd consumed since her husband's death that she could fully taste; her senses had gone numb in loss. She'd felt just fine, disappointingly sober, even, until she stood up. The sway of drunkenness caught her, and she barely managed to clutch the banister as she fell. She slid down one stair, just one, tailbone landing hard. The wine bottle crashed down and came to rest not far from the bloodstain. She made it to the toilet in time to be sick. Was sick for hours, vomiting every time she thought of what had nearly happened. Since then, just the idea of alcohol made her taste her stomach.

"No, nothing to drink. I gave it up after my husband died."

"Gave it up altogether?"

"Yes."

"So, you're sure you didn't have any alcohol that night?"

She felt like there must be a trick here, this repeated question about alcohol, but couldn't find it. She hadn't had anything to drink.

Unless your mind's protecting itself by forgetting something, like the psychiatrist said.

"I didn't have anything to drink," she said.

She felt the pain of that months-ago fall, and realized she'd gone too long without hitting the red button. Pain was the price for clarity, but that was starting to turn. The room was shrinking down to her injuries. Her heart beat in a long line down her forehead and around her eye socket.

"Ma'am?"

"Sorry. My head hurts. What were you asking?"

Why had she done this thing and not the other? Why did she go this way and not that one? Identifying marks? Why was this "easy-pleasy" phrase, that T-shirt, so key to recognizing this man, hadn't she seen his face? Hadn't that been enough? Was she sure she'd seen her phone in the man's pocket? Describe him again.

She saw a small black object on the table next to the sergeant.

"What's that?"

"That's the recorder? You gave us permission to record this interview."

She searched her memory, couldn't recall anything to do with any recording.

"Oh. Right."

"You remember that?"

"It's just . . . my head," she said. "It aches."

"You all right? You're looking pale." A crawl of pink embarrassment spread across his cheeks. "Not . . . pale . . . obviously, with your, I mean. Skin? I just meant . . . you don't look so good."

"I'm not feeling so good," she wheezed through aching teeth.

"Hm. Well. Let's go back to when—"

The crack in her skull was widening. Her jaw strained, her eye was a taut and bloody drum pounding beneath the bandage.

They don't believe you.

She hit the red button and drifted, heard herself mumble, "He stepped over."

When she woke to an empty room, she instinctively reached toward the bedside table for her phone. With a confused swell of realization, she sat up. The sergeant had said her phone was in evidence, had asked if she was sure she'd seen it in the Corner's pocket. And her phone had been on that list of valuables, with a notation that the police had found it on her bedroom nightstand. Which meant— what? That the Corner had put it back?

Why would he do that? Or . . . were you wrong? Did you actually see it? Did he take it at all?

She stayed awake for hours, rearranging the puzzle pieces of her memory again to try to fit this new fact, wondering and worrying over what else might have escaped her.

26

The haunting began two weeks after her husband died. Walking past the living room windows, she felt the pull of the mountain lion eyes, the slow stretch of its double mouth. The wrinkled glass showed a flicker of movement, a figure sliding behind the trunk of her husband's favorite tree, the massive old pine that sat at the pasture's edge. She hurried outside, arms crossed against the cold, to get another angle.

But there was only empty pasture, the sway of grass and trees.

After that, she slowly grew aware of a steady drip of inexplicabilities.

The children played on the swing set behind her as she looked down the forest path. Something seemed different. She squatted down, examined the dirt, soft after snowmelt. Had the sense a great number of feet had traveled over it. She quickly stood up, feeling ridiculous, recognizing the way she was pantomiming trackers she'd seen in movies.

The hide-a-key rock wasn't in its usual place by the door. She spotted it next to the woodpile five feet away. Returned it to where it was more camouflaged among the other rocks of similar size.

"Don't move the key rock," she told the children.

"I didn't."

"Me either."

"Fine. Just—don't move it."

"Okay, Mommy."

As she watched the children eat breakfast, her daughter eyed her, hesitant.

"What is it?"

"I think I saw—I saw a man again. Watching me, from over there."

She gestured out the window, toward the old pine.

"Again? When?"

"Last night. When you were sleeping."

"Love, why were you walking around in the middle of the night?"

"I just woke up. I was at the stairs. I saw him out the window."

"You were sleepwalking?"

Why didn't the monitor wake you up to help her? You must have slept through it. What's wrong with you?

"I guess. But, maybe it was Daddy? Daddy always liked that tree."

Her heart swelled, understanding that hope.

"Angel, it wasn't Daddy. Daddy isn't here anymore. You know that, love."

Later she checked the baby monitor's transceiver. It was switched off. She turned it back on. Told her daughter, "Love, please don't turn the monitor off. Otherwise I won't wake up if you're sleepwalking."

"I didn't turn it off, Mommy."

"I know you're a big girl. I know you're responsible. But it's dangerous if it's off."

"I didn't. I didn't do it."

Maybe you did it, and forgot? Maybe your husband did it, before. Maybe he thought it wasn't necessary because it had been so long since she last sleepwalked. Maybe he's trying to tell you something.

Like her daughter, each bit of strangeness triggered the thought, *It's him! He's come back to us.* It was her husband, still not quite solid enough to use it, who'd moved the hide-a-key. It was her husband, trying to reach them, who'd vanished from behind his favorite tree, who'd left the path looking tamped down, traveled.

Stop it. You're imagining things because you're exhausted. Even when you sleep you don't rest. Because you miss him. It's so impossible that he's gone, it's easier to think he's here. And because of the article.

She knew, objectively, that the uncannies began at the same time the feature in the city paper was published. That was the logical explanation for why she and the children felt her husband had been wrenched back into reality. Daily, she ignored emails, texts, calls, and voicemails from seemingly everyone they'd ever met. Most messages leaked the sender's glee at his or her proximity to fame, seeped superficial pity about her proximity to death. Only a few shared her fury, shared their sympathy, asked how she was, given the way the article made her look.

It was the gallery's fault. Or hers for hiring them. She was tired of calls from interior designers, pained by their palpable desperation for artwork instantly made more valuable by death, their condolences impatient. So when a gallery tracked her down, gave her a convincing pitch for representing her husband's work, she signed on the dotted line. Recalling the hundreds of prints stored in her husband's office, she told them that of course she had signed photos, lots. She had a rare night of restfulness, thinking how the money would allow her time to find more clients, or even a job at a firm. Even so she woke sickened at the world for recognizing her husband, caring about him like this, only after he was dead. Her one consolation was that she had absolutely no signed prints. All those vultures would unknowingly be paying for her hand writing his signature.

During lockdown her husband had leaned out of his tiny plane to photograph miles of empty highways. Had taken shots of Boston, New York, Providence, Hartford, abandoned, postapocalyptic.

These had not sold at all.

"I'll take them off the website for now," her husband had said. "But just you wait. Once people can look back on it, say, 'Remember when we survived that?' they'll be interested. Until then, it's just too fresh."

Or maybe people just don't want their beach house decorated with a four-foot-tall photo of a plague city.

What she'd said aloud, though, was also true.

"I think it's your best work."

The gallery had agreed, the representative almost salivating over the scans she sent of these pieces. The article had been the gallery's idea. It featured quote after quote from the representative about this "new period of deeper work, historic and insightful," along with much speculation regarding her husband's derring-do in the airplane to achieve such shots and weepy hand-wringing about what a loss it was to the artistic world.

No one had contacted her for comment. But they'd found her father-in-law. She recalled the old man spitting, "Photography's for girls. And men who don't like girls." But there he was, misty over how he'd nurtured his son's artistic skills, so obvious even when he was a child, at least to an attentive father. How he was inspired by good old dad's love of airplanes. How masculine he made art by involving said airplane. A quote, pulled from the article large and bold, felt the same as that awful slap across her face.

"I think the investigation will show his death was no accident," her father-in-law said.

"You couldn't ask for better publicity," the gallery representative gloated. "A little mystery? A little hint of foul play? Your father-in-law may have just doubled your net worth. Oh, don't say that, honey, no! I'm sure no one would ever think he meant you had anything to do with it. Honestly, I assumed it was something about the airplane. Oh, sweetie, you know how it is, we told them not to bother the widow for a puff piece."

That's what she was. *A widow, widow, widow.*

So no wonder, she told herself, *No wonder, signing his name, seeing his name, hearing it again and again—of course it feels like he's near, with all that.*

A shriek from her son and she ran out of the house, terrified he was hurt. There was her little boy, laughing and muddy on the cold November ground beneath the swing set, and she could breathe again. A chain hung loose, the other side dangling with the swing still attached.

"Are you okay?"

"It broke, Mama, look how messy I am!"

She examined the swing, the chain. How was it possible? The screw-type carabiner that had attached it was delicately undone, its metal clasp securely locked open, not a thing that could have happened unless done deliberately.

"Did you do this? Unscrew this?"

The children shook their heads.

"I mean it. Did you? This is dangerous."

"No, Mama."

"Well, someone did. And it wasn't me, which means it was one of you."

"No."

"Don't lie!"

"I didn't!"

"Me either. Really, Mama!"

"Maybe it was Daddy?" her daughter asked.

The fine hairs on her arms crept with a macabre hopefulness that mirrored her daughter's tone, filled with wistful longing.

Maybe he was trying to fix it. He always fixes things.

"Daddy would have never done something that might hurt you. Don't do it again. Please."

Sleep was elusive, every creak and whine of the house startling her to wakefulness and then wide-eyed worry about the next day, and the day after that, and everything she should have done better. After the incident with the wine and the stairs, she didn't dare drink to help her sleep. Alone in the house with the children, she'd never take a pill. When white noise failed to do anything but annoy her, she tried earplugs, which made it easier to drift off yet still let the sound of the baby monitor through.

When she managed to fall asleep, there were only three ways she woke up.

First, to the children, sleepwalking, poking, frightened.

Second, eyelids snapping open, mind wound tight with terrifying questions and dark answers: *How long can you believably keep forging his signature? Is there a way to print more photos without anyone catching on? Are the children ever going to be okay after this? Will they remember him? How are you going to be able to do it, all this, all on your own? How can you get through this, again, again! You'll never feel normal again, you learned that much from your mother.*

And third, she'd wake up after a bout of sleep paralysis. Prior to her husband's death, she endured the disorienting horror of these episodes only once a year or so. But now she'd regularly wake, unable to speak, move, or even blink, her eyes peeled to track the shadow man who walked across the room, a not-her-husband man who got in on her husband's side of the bed, voice slippery through the sound of her hammering heart as he said, "This has to happen," before vanishing. Only then could she at last move again. And despite the recurring nature of these nightmares, only then was she able to understand the shadow man had been a dream.

So as much as she wanted, needed, to sleep, sometimes the inevitable terror of waking meant she didn't sleep at all.

In late November, two deer stood in the snowy pasture, stock-still and staring into the forest. One spread its front legs slightly and hissed in a way she didn't know deer could. They waited, then together ran in the opposite direction of whatever they'd hissed at. She went outside and looked into the woods for the source of their misgiving. Saw only the weave of leafless branches.

"Where's your hat? The new red one? If you're going outside, you need a hat."

"I dunno, I lost it."

"First your mittens, then Monkey, now your hat? You have to take care of your things."

"I do, Mama, I do! They just keep disappearing."

Everything felt askew. Everything seemed touched by invisible hands.

She knew that on the surface she was doing things. Signing photos. Emailing former clients, desperate to increase her workload. Bringing the kids to and from school, trying to keep things as normal as possible for them. But she also recognized new hollows and bones emerging from her body as though she were a drying lake. Her skin hung differently from her face. Her sleeplessness darkened her reflection, making her mind buzz. It was as though grief were a thing she'd swallowed, a parasitic worm that didn't allow room for food, for proper functioning, for anything but itself.

The sergeant showed up at the door again a month after her husband died. She made a pot of coffee as he sat at the kitchen table. She noticed he picked the chair farthest from the stairs.

She considered telling him about all the strangeness. Maybe there was something there. But, a missing hat, the baby monitor switched off, the carabiner unscrewed, hissing deer?

No, you'll sound crazy. And even if you didn't, none of it is much of anything.

"Are you all right?"

"Yes and no," she said. Seeing his concern she smoothed her hair, forced a smile, and asked, "Do I really look that bad?"

He shot her a panicked glance. For once she found him completely readable. He thought she was being coy, flirting, and was clearly horrified.

This was the first thing that she could remember thinking was funny since her husband had called the scarecrow witches "a cool crew" on Halloween.

"Not bad? Just, um. You look tired." He cleared his throat, avoided her eyes. "You know, my *wife*"—he said the word so pointedly she suppressed a grin, thought, *Yes, you must look very, extremely, super-duper bad*—"my *wife* swears by this one kinda tea to help her sleep? I'll have to ask her about it for you. She's real good with all that stuff. The herbal medicines? Essential oils and things? Does her own research. No chemicals and all that."

She felt her expression going flat. She wondered if the sergeant understood the code of the things he was saying, understood he was letting her know their worlds were irreconcilable.

She poured a cup of coffee, slid it across to the sergeant. He took off his mask to drink it, and she realized this was the first time she'd seen his face. He looked exactly as she'd imagined he would. Roman nose, square chin, clean shaven, handsome. A regular Captain America. *Not your type at all*, she thought, a pang of inappropriate-for-the-setting lust welling up as she thought of her husband's ruggedness, his crooked nose, his broad chest, dark liquid eyes, freckles. She poured a cup of coffee for herself and took a sip. Felt its warmth buzz straight from her empty stomach to her head.

"Your father-in-law," the sergeant said, "brought up some concerns with us."

"Oh yeah?" She sat down at the opposite end of the table, legs weakening with surety this was going to be about the foul play implied in the horrible article.

"Yes. You said you weren't on speaking terms. Why not?"

"He didn't tell you?"

"He did, but I'd like to hear it from you."

She took another sip of coffee. Paused to mentally diagram her husband's little family, break it down to its essentials.

"I took care of my mother-in-law when she was ill last year. My husband was too frightened to see her that way, and that man? He couldn't be bothered. Acted like her cancer was mainly an inconvenience she was forcing on him. Not that she helped on that front. Apologizing for being sick. Always blaming herself for everything. She died just about four months after we moved here to help out. I was the one who found her. I sat my father-in-law down and broke the news to him. He hit me in the face. Right here." She tapped her cheek. "He hit me hard enough he knocked me down. So no, we're not on speaking terms. And I've got no interest in ever seeing him again."

The sergeant's blue eyes stared at her, firm and direct.

"You press charges?"

"No. Just stepped out of his life with my husband and children." She took a long sip of her coffee. "Is that the story he told you?"

"No."

"Did he say he hit me?"

"No."

"What did he say?"

"That he thought you were trying to create a wedge between him and his son by not speaking to him. Said you were after money."

She scoffed and shook her head. "He made it crystal clear from the time my husband and I were in college that he wouldn't be helping us out financially in any way. He didn't approve of my husband pursuing photography. So we had zero expectations there. And we don't need anything from him anyway."

"So financially, you're . . . comfortable?"

"Yeah," she said, not knowing if this was true, not sure she could do all this alone, trying to convince herself. "For the first years we were married, I made triple what my husband did, easy, while he was trying to break into the art thing. He did okay, and then after a while he did well. His photos have been our main income for the last five years or so. Now he's gone—I'm going to have to figure it out. But I've got clients. Savings." She kept her voice even as she thought of the forged signatures on her husband's photos, adding, "And there's still lots of my husband's art to sell."

"No life insurance?"

She shrugged. "I've got some that covers me, but he didn't have any coverage. It was too expensive because of all the flying he did in that awful little plane. They wanted to carve everything out of the policy to the point it didn't seem worth paying for."

"I see."

"Turns out, I guess, we should've paid for it anyway, since the plane had nothing to do with it." She paused. "I worried all the time that plane would kill him. Seems ridiculous now."

The sergeant's eyes bored into her, searching, until at last he said, "Your father-in-law thinks *you* killed him. Pushed his son down the stairs."

Even prepared for this as she thought she was, her hands shook.

"Christ," she said, surprised at the sting of hearing this out loud, proof that her father-in-law could think this of her. She wiped her sweating palms on her shirt. "Did you see that article? About my husband? He said something that implied that's what he thought. He really does hate me. Thinks I'm . . . disfigured."

She slid her eyes to the sergeant to see how he responded to this. But he'd gone back to his factory settings, expression impenetrable.

"He said you were having problems. Marital problems."

She shook her head. "Our only problem was him. Unlike with you, he couldn't pretend he never hit me when it came to my husband. Because of the bruising and all. But he tried to convince my husband it had been my fault. That I'd been mean or rude when my mother-in-law passed, which was a lie. And my husband, well. Fathers and sons, you know? They're complicated. My husband . . . he wanted to find a way for us all to get along, I think. And that just wasn't on the table for me." She chewed on her lip. "Anyway, my father-in-law wouldn't know about any problems. He and my husband weren't talking."

The sergeant cleared his throat. "They were, actually. Talking. Even spoke the day before your husband died."

She felt this hit her in the stomach. Had to force herself to breathe.

"Is that what my father-in-law said?"

"Showed us his call log."

"He called my husband?"

The sergeant shook his head. "Sometimes. But your husband called him, too."

She rubbed her temples with her knuckles as if to knead knowledge of this betrayal from her brain. Imagined her husband calling from the tarmac, the car, the poison of her father-in-law's voice trickling into his ear somewhere far from home so she'd never know. And he must have deleted the call records. There'd been no call with her father-in-law listed when she'd picked up her husband's phone to take condolences, then absentmindedly scrolled back in time on his call log, mistily picturing him calling this or that friend.

Maybe he called his dad to yell at him. To test him. See if he'd apologize. Guess you'll never know. Because you certainly can't believe anything the old man says.

She tried not to cry.

"I wish he'd told me they were talking. His dad's approval meant a lot to him, you know?"

"Aside from . . . tension . . . with your father-in-law, any other issues?"

She shook her head. "That was the big thing. But . . . you're married long enough, and some of the things you used to find endearing get to be annoying, you know? He used to like that I was shy. It let him be the outgoing, social one. And I used to like how adventurous he seemed, flying around. But over the years? He wanted me to be more extroverted. Fit in better? I wanted him to be safe, get a different plane. Help with the chores more. With the kids."

She looked out the kitchen window. Saw a robin on the stone wall, unseasonably fat. Felt the painful roots in her chest where her husband's voice still whispered, "Was there something you did? Something you maybe said that set him off?" Wished desperately that her husband were there now to explain himself. That he were there not helping with the chores, insisting whatever he had in mind was more important. Capable and interested and trying to lure her into the sun. He'd tell her the truth. He'd extract the painful, spreading growth of this betrayal.

"I just . . . I miss him. I miss him more than . . ." She looked down at her hands, clenched in her lap. "We were happy," she said. "Now that he's gone, every argument seems so . . . small."

"Did you push your husband down the stairs?"

She thought it was important to look the sergeant in the eye when she answered.

"No," she said quietly. "I didn't."

"Well," the sergeant said, settling back on his stool, "I hope it's some comfort that we've ruled his death an accident."

"Oh," she said, taken aback by the unexpected speed of the resolution, that these questions had been the last steps and not the first. "Did you tell my father-in-law that?"

"Yeah." The sergeant shook his head, edge of a sardonic smile flickering. "He wasn't too happy. Told us, 'Absence of evidence isn't evidence of absence.'"

"He was a lawyer, once upon a time."

"He mentioned that, too."

"He always does," she said. "How'd you determine that? That it was an accident?"

"The body. The way he fell. The blood. The way your stairs are laid out, nearly impossible to give someone an effective shove from the top. Especially given how small you are. It's not a big flight. A fall down your steps wouldn't normally do that kind of harm. Just a freak thing he hit the table here on the way down." The sergeant tap-tap-tapped the side of his head to indicate point of impact. "Catching the edge of the table's what did it. And, of course, because of what your children said."

She jerked her eyes to his. "You talked to my kids?"

"Sure, day of. You don't remember that?"

"It's kind of a blur."

"Of course." He nodded, but underneath she sensed a shimmer of judgment, a tremble of "what kind of mother forgets about her children on a day like that?"

"What did—what did they say?"

"Same as you. Their dad was going to leave early. They were asleep. You and your husband got along. Happy family. Then, of course, there was your reaction." She must have looked confused, because he added, "You were upset. But cooperative."

She remembered rocking back and forth, covered in blood. She remembered having to strip naked. Remembered their taking photos as she tried to stay standing, the strength all gone from her legs, her spine. And apparently she'd let the police sneak upstairs and speak to her children without her there. She wondered what, exactly, had been so correct, so unsuspicious, in all that.

They sat in distanced silence for a little while, each sipping their coffee, thinking about her father-in-law spitting accusations. About the twists and angles of the stairs. Falling bodies.

She surprised herself, blurted out, "I can't stop thinking about it—him all alone. Maybe he was trying to call for help. Could hear me moving around upstairs. Paralyzed. He must have been so afraid. It would have been torture."

"You don't know that's how it was. He was probably unconscious the whole time." Flatly, the sergeant added, "It's not your fault."

She was sure that he knew as well as she did that of course it was her fault, because there was the possibility that she'd had, for a little while, the power to make everything different.

She quickly wiped the corners of her eyes with a sleeve.

"Your kids at school?"

"Yeah."

"How're they doing?"

"Not great. They don't seem to understand he's gone. They keep thinking they see him. Out the window by a tree he liked, or in the woods. They have nightmares. It was all so quick. So unreal. They wouldn't let us see him at the hospital. We had to say goodbye over the phone. It was like watching a TV show. Not getting to hold him, say goodbye to . . . someone so important. They recommended a counselor through school. A grief counselor. They meet over the computer."

"I'm sorry," he said. "And you? Bad dreams and all that, too?"

She shrugged. "I get sleep paralysis sometimes."

"Oh? What's that?"

"You wake up, can't move. Some people see a figure, like a dark figure, in the room. After a while it disappears. And slowly you get so you can move again."

"Well, that sounds gawd-awful."

The sergeant's eyebrows were knit, his expression a mix of pity and revulsion.

"It doesn't happen often," she lied, bothered by his reaction and falling into the old habit of hoping that saying something out loud might make it true. "Hasn't happened in a long time."

"Are you one of the people who sees a figure?"

She lied again. "Sometimes. Not always."

"What does it look like?"

"Just a man. The silhouette of a man."

"But frightening?"

"Yeah. Frightening."

The sergeant gave another slow look around the old house, let his eyes catch on the blood still staining the gaps in the floorboards. His gaze tripped up the steep steps.

"It's really common," she said, feeling a need to reassure him, reassure herself, that such a thing was normal, that she was normal, that there were no ghosts, no living shadows, in the world. That sometimes things fell, sometimes they were lost, knocked askew, broken. That anyone would imagine strange things, things appearing, vanishing, after feeling death so close, after seeing death perched hungrily on someone they loved.

"They think maybe that's where all those alien abduction stories come from," she told him. "Why those stories are all so similar. You know . . . can't move, can't speak, see figures with glowing eyes, then all of a sudden you're back in bed again? That story. Just people with sleep paralysis. Not little green men beaming them into spaceships and doing experiments where they can't move or whatever."

"Huh." The sergeant nodded. "Interesting."

They sat in silence. She thought about the swept-clean path, the movement behind the trees. The way the children's voices lilted with hope when they suggested Daddy might have been watching, might have done this or that. The way objects seemed to travel lately, as if their property, their land, their house, were subject to a different gravity.

"I guess there are simple explanations for most things," she mused. "Even the ones that at first glance are the strangest."

"Yes." The sergeant rubbed his chin heavily. "I tell myself that all the time."

27

She forced herself awake in her hospital bed whenever she saw daylight. She tried her best to pretend she was comfortable with the constant stream of masked strangers coming in and out of her room, giving them cheerful "Hellos!" and stretching painful smiles. Tried not to startle so visibly each time they woke her. She strained every bit of herself to prove to the vast, interchangeable mass of white coats and scrubs and masks that she was better, better, better—time to go!

Time to get the kids away from that man.

Someone changed the dressing on her eye, and she saw light through its swollen lid.

"A good sign," a doctor told her.

"You better believe it!" this happy-and-feeling-better self said.

On Christmas, nine days into her stay, a nurse helped her hobble through the halls on socks with sticky bottoms.

"You're doing great!"

"Damn right," she agreed, nearly convincing herself she was the kind of person who would lightly swear in front of others, grin at them, fun and plucky.

"Do you think you'll be discharging me soon?" she asked the psychiatrist.

"That's not up to me," he said. "But I'll sign off on it. And we'll be seeing you regularly, as long as you're still amenable to that?"

She nodded.

"Last time we talked, you gave me your consent to speak with the police about your mental state. You remember that? Because they'd asked about if it was safe for you to go home?"

"Yes. So I could get a kind of . . . psychiatric sign-off."

"Exactly. Given your low weight and that you told them your injuries weren't caused by the intruder, they were concerned about your safety. Concerned about self-harm."

Her heart beat hard with worry. "What did you tell them?"

"I told them you were making immense progress and were agreeable to, even excited about, following a treatment path. I told them you have the struggles anyone would who went through what you did. That mentally you're ready to go home."

"Thank you, Doctor," she said, trying not to cry. "The police . . . I don't think they believe me. It's like you said, I can't tell the story well? It's . . . mixed up. Did they give you the—I don't know— impression that they thought I might be imagining it?"

The psychiatrist tipped his head. "Do you think you imagined it?"

The baby monitor turned off, the broken swing, the deer braying into the forest.

"No," she said as firmly as she could. "I know what I saw."

"Well, then. There you are. They asked if I'd observed any signs of delusion or psychosis. I told them I hadn't. I told them, just as I told you, that you've experienced a major trauma, so it's normal that it may take time to recall things cohesively, if you're able to at all."

She nodded, tears finally leaking out to sting her damaged face.

He believes you. And he must know, because he's a psychiatrist. And he says you're normal, normal, normal. Even if you don't feel normal, if nothing feels normal, it is. And you are.

She asked the doctors, nurses, everyone, "Can I use your phone real quick? Do you mind if I call my kids?"

Her father-in-law never answered.

The pain was a constant throb, but she found ways to function despite it. Fearful of dependence, of gaps in memory, of not being able to move her limbs enough to strengthen them, she'd stopped pressing the little red button. Took far smaller doses in pills.

"When do you think I'll be able to drive?" she asked the doctor who told her to look up, down, left, right, her hurt eye following his commands from between its puffed lids, from under its stitches.

"Once your surgeon signs off, I think you're ready to be discharged," the doctor said. "You should be able to drive just fine as long as you're not still taking meds."

Given she could see only dim shadows out of her broken eye, she assumed he was joking, and gave a mirthless laugh. He looked back at her, puzzled, and she realized they all had a common goal.

They want you out of here, too. You're just one more person to look after. The whole place is overwhelmed, has been overwhelmed for almost a year. Of course they want you out.

So she started to sing for the surgeon. "Any idea when the surgeon's coming, any idea when I'll be discharged?"

"Really?" asked a friendly nurse. "If it was me, I don't know if I'd want to go back without help. Let alone go back to where all that happened."

"I called a locksmith. And an alarm company," she said. "If I do a subscription service, if I let them run electricity outside, they can put cameras everywhere, alarms on every window."

"That's not what I mean, hon. All that with your husband? I don't think I'd be comfortable sleeping where I knew someone'd passed."

"Maybe," she said, wondering how this nurse had managed to

work in a hospital where people died as part of the job, managed to live her sixty-odd years believing someone hadn't died in most homes. "Maybe," she said, surprised anyone would suggest she leave the only place that still held memories of her husband, the only place where he still existed.

"Maybe you're right," she told the nurse.

This was what she said to everyone, the thing all human beings wanted to hear. "You're probably right, what do I know? Aren't you smart, what a great suggestion, you're so right, right, right."

"Your kids are doing fine," the sergeant said on the phone. "One of my people saw them yesterday. A caseworker was there this morning. Hasn't she called you? Why don't you call her? You left her a message? Well, she'll call you back. Be patient."

Finally he told her with a brittleness she knew meant he was serious, "You need to stop calling me about this."

"This" being her children. The injustice of it, the proof of her father-in-law's awful possession, made her sob into the thin hospital pillow. A new woman came into the room, interrupting her tears.

"Are you a nurse?"

"I'm a PA."

"What's that mean?"

"The physician's assistant? For your surgeon."

She had no idea what the hospital ranking system was, but at the word "surgeon" she wiped her face and sat straight, knowing she had to appease this extremely young, extremely blond person. The woman had her lift arms, squeeze hands.

"Sorry I assumed you were a nurse," she said. "A friend of mine? A doctor? She says that happens to her all the time. But not to male doctors."

She had no such friend, but didn't see this story as a lie. Because of course that's how things would be.

"Yeah," the PA sighed. "It happens a lot."

"Are you the one able to sign off on discharging me?"

"Yep."

"Great! So great. I'm ready to go."

"Do you have a place to stay?"

"Sure, of course."

"It's just"—the PA gave her a sympathetic shrug—"the police said you couldn't go to your house without their sign-off. Your exams are good, so we're ready to discharge you, could do it tomorrow, but you need a place to go. And a ride home."

She called the sergeant. He answered with a curt "What?" assuming, she guessed, that she was calling about her children again.

After you've been so good, after you haven't called him at all for two whole days. About your own children.

"They say I'm being discharged, but said something about you needing to give me permission to go back to my house?"

"Oh, right," he said, voice relaxing. "We'd like to walk through the house with you before you move back in there. It might trigger memories, or else you might notice things that are out of the ordinary, moved or missing or different."

She was exhausted at the idea of going through it all again, the endless questions, having to walk through those violated spaces with the sergeant.

Maybe bravery is just enduring.

"Yes," she said with forced cheerfulness, "of course! Can we do that tomorrow? They said they could discharge me tomorrow. Then if we do that, I can go after and bring the kids home."

The sergeant paused, and she imagined him looking at a calendar. "Yeah, I can do tomorrow. Tell you what. You call me when they're ready, and I'll be your ride home."

"Thank you, thank you!"

She passed the rest of the day fueled by purpose. She confirmed appointments with the locksmith and the alarm company for the next day when they'd reopen after the Christmas holiday before closing again for New Year's. Left a voicemail telling her father-in-law she would be discharged tomorrow, would be picking up the kids.

She barely slept. Hit the nurse call button as soon as light trickled in, and asked, "Am I discharged? Can I go?"

But no. There was paperwork, forms, visits from nurses, scheduling of follow-up visits for plastics ("You don't want scars if you can help it!"), to see the surgeon (she realized she wasn't sure if she'd met or even seen this person whose hands had patched together her skull), to confirm regular virtual visits with the psychiatrist ("Looking forward to talking with you again"), the ophthalmologist ("Don't want to go blind, after all, ha ha"). They gave her a ream of prescriptions for pain, to help her sleep, to stave off infection, to help with nausea caused by the other medications. It was so much human interaction in just a few hours that her head reeled with it, her face ached with her put-on friendliness.

Finally she called the sergeant and told him she was ready. An orderly rolled her to the hospital doors in a wheelchair. She wore the clothes the neighbor had given her. They smelled of fabric softener. She suspected one of the nurses had taken it upon herself to wash them. She wondered vaguely where the fur coat had gone.

"You see your ride?" the orderly asked.

"Not yet. But it's all right, you just go."

"You sure?"

"Yes."

The minute he was out of sight, she stood and walked out the doors, her injured feet clad in her sticky hospital socks. She made her way slowly but capably past the spot where she'd crumpled at hearing her husband was brain dead. The air was frigid, the day overcast. She sat on a bench under an overhang and waited.

It was a beautiful, beautiful thing to be outside. She looked out happily at the bare, windy parking lot with its sad little trees, one step closer to her children.

28

The sergeant drove with the boyish officer in the passenger seat. She noticed other drivers staring at her in the back seat of the police cruiser, imagined them wondering, *What did she do? Why'd she get arrested? Why is she all beat up?*

"How long do you think this will take?" she asked.

A half shrug from the sergeant. "Probably a couple hours."

"And after that, can I stay in the house?"

"Depending what you see, we may need more time there. You may want to stay with a friend tonight."

"Sure," she said, thinking of nearby hotels that might have room for her and the children.

She caught the sergeant's blue eyes reflected in the rearview mirror.

"I was reading online," he said, "about your condition."

"Sorry—what?"

"Your father-in-law told us about how your mom had it and all."

She rubbed her forehead, looked out the window.

I bet he did. I bet he had lots to say about me.

She could feel the sergeant's eyes on her skin, could feel him thinking the usual thoughts. In the sergeant's gaze, she felt his creeping unease at her difference, her uniqueness.

"It's interesting stuff," the sergeant said.

"Is it?" She stared pointedly out the window.

"Sure. Must've been hard, it starting so young."

The usual exhaustion rolled over her at the sensation of being a specimen sliced and pressed between glass. And despite telling herself, *Just stay quiet*, she muttered, "Yeah. It wasn't great. But you get used to it."

"Mmm," the sergeant hummed, eyes flitting to the rearview mirror for another look, an all-too-familiar glance that said, "How could anyone ever get used to *that*?"

People are creatures who can get used to anything. That's the best way to define us.

She leaned her cheek against the cold window. Tried to focus on that chill through the blasting heat of the cruiser.

They pulled into her driveway. The sergeant shut off the engine and turned to face her through the Plexiglas partition of the police car.

"I understand you're still dealing with some"—he waved a hand in her direction—"medical things. So if you need help, need a minute, just say so. The point here is for you to tell us if you see anything out of the ordinary. Anything that isn't yours, that's out of place, that's missing. Something that's been moved, anything that makes you remember anything new. Anything at all, oh-kay? And that means outside, too, all right?"

"Sure, right."

He drove up the driveway slowly, looking back at her to make sure her head was on a swivel, checking out the trees, the snow.

"It's plowed," she said. "I hope my plow guy didn't mess anything up. Evidence or whatever. He's scheduled to come super early if there's snow."

"Don't worry about it. We took a look at the driveway before it was cleared. We'll start inside."

They parked. The path to the door hadn't been shoveled, but boots had tamped the snow into an uneven walkability. The boyish officer went into the house and came back with a pair of her boots. She tried to hide the pain of putting them on her ruined feet.

They started in the garage, where the officers told her that her husband's car battery was dead.

"That likely died awhile ago if, like you say, you hadn't been using it," the sergeant told her. He pointed out that her car, parked in its usual spot in the garage, had a flat tire. "We made a note of this. But it doesn't appear to have been done on purpose, see?" The sergeant tapped a spot on a back tire. "Looks like you caught a nail."

At least you didn't run for the car, at least that turned out to be a good choice. But . . . the Corner must've done it?

"I used my car earlier that day, though, and everything was fine. You don't—" She cleared her throat. "You don't think he did that? Seems like a pretty big coincidence."

"It's possible, but no way to know. Had a flat myself last week. It happens."

Going inside, she first felt the too-bigness of the rooms without the children. The house had its same smell, same not-quite-warm-enough temperature. But there was something unplaceable, distant, that felt crooked. An open window letting in the wet, maybe. An unquiet that meant the mice had been active.

The Corner.

Stop that. Focus.

She sat down to take off her boots, looked around for her slippers, and remembered that they were lost somewhere in the snow. She left on the sticky-bottomed hospital socks, hoping the tour of the house wouldn't take long enough to aggravate her feet, still unruly in their swollenness.

"Can you please take off your boots?" she asked the officers. They exchanged a look but complied.

Together they went into the basement, damp and spider-webbed as always.

"I wouldn't really be able to tell if anything was different. I never come down here unless I absolutely have to. It's too gross and dark." She paused. "Wait—I smell—do you smell cigarette smoke?"

The officers raised their noses like bloodhounds, then shook their heads. "Nah," the sergeant said. "Hope you've got a dehumidifier somewhere down here, though. Musty."

In the kitchen, the antique pine floors, the ones she kept pristine, the ones she'd cleaned of blood, were deeply scratched. She gave a mournful "Oh!" over the damage.

"Yeah, sorry about that," the sergeant said in a voice that struck her as not sorry at all, lip service to what he saw as an overreaction to something unimportant. "That's from my guys walking through."

Don't lecture them. You need their help.

Filling the silent spaces while she looked through the house, they asked new questions ("Anyone you can think of who might have had a grudge? Is this door always bolted?") but mainly they repeated the same questions the sergeant had asked her in the hospital ("Any prescription drugs in the house? Why didn't you go this, that, or the other way? Why didn't you do this, that, or the other thing?"). Her pounding brain, eager for the painkillers she was denying it for purposes of lucidity, of being able to drive to get the children, started to think that they were stupid, forgetful, asking and re-asking in a slightly different way.

On they marched. They repeated their prompts: "See anything? See any changes? Anything missing? Anything different?"

"No," she said again and again, "nothing, nothing, no."

She tried to avoid going up the stairs ahead of them. She always felt so exposed and vulnerable going up a staircase with a man behind her. But they wanted her to have the first look at things, so her legs traveled level with their eyes as they climbed. A pit hollowed her stomach when she remembered they'd seen it all before, could look right through her clothes to their memories.

The attic dust she'd been sure would hold footprints, helpful evidence, was widely scuffed.

"From our guys again." The sergeant shrugged. "The priority was looking for the kids. Making sure they were safe. And making sure there was no intruder in the house."

She didn't dare ask for an apology, didn't dare accuse them of incompetence.

You told him exactly where the kids were.

Upstairs, little things crawled out sneakily, only barely catching her eye. Changes so tiny she nearly missed them. Every time she pointed out damage to a rug, a floor, they said, "That was us, that was our guys." The unapologetic tone, the dismissal of all their destruction, made fire burn in her throat. She clamped her lips together tight to suffocate her temper.

The first change she saw was in the kids' bathroom.

"This toilet seat is up," she told the officers.

"So?"

"So? There are no men living here."

"Well, there's your little boy." The sergeant sounded concerned, like she might have forgotten her son's existence.

"He sits down or else he makes a mess. Because he's still so little."

"I have a young son, ma'am. A long time ago I was a little boy myself. And I can tell you no little boy in the world always sits down, every time, no matter what he tells his mother." The sergeant and the boyish officer nodded to each other, eyes giving away the knowing smiles hidden under their masks.

"Well, my son sits."

"Mmm." The sergeant hummed. "I'll make a note of it."

But instead he stared at her, not writing anything, as if daring her to call him on it. She breathed through her nose and counted down from ten.

Her daughter's room held the most notable changes. A piggy bank was on the floor when it was usually on the dresser. And things were missing.

The officers exchanged looks as they wrote down a list of the absent items as if to say, "This doesn't seem like anything at all, I'm sure these things are just misplaced, but I'll write it down because she's watching us."

A T-shirt from YMCA camp, red. Teddy bear, six inches tall, red bow around its neck. Days of the week underwear, Monday and Thursday. One pair ballet tights. The small tin box shaped like race car, red, approximately six by four by two inches, contents assorted marbles, barrettes, pebbles.

She steadied herself on a dresser. The seasick taste of acrid bile crept through her throat and into her mouth as she thought of why he'd chosen these things, pictured the soft fabric of those tights, the polka-dotted cotton with the cursive "Monday" and "Thursday" hanging limp in the Corner's immense hand.

"We'll look at the list of what your daughter packed. She may have taken these things to her grandpa's. Or they could be in the laundry bin or something."

She tried to blink away the image of the Corner's flat thumb rubbing that fabric, the tin box the little girl filled with her most valued things.

She swallowed down her nausea. "You don't understand. My daughter loves that box. You know how kids do, saving little things? Erasers, special rocks? She wouldn't have lost that. And she never takes it with her anywhere. It belongs here."

"Right. We'll check."

The charger cord snaking across her bedroom nightstand reminded her to ask when she'd get her phone back.

"Today, when we're done here," the sergeant said, as if she were a teenager who had to earn phone privileges.

"Where did you find the phone?"

"The far side of that table there."

"But that's not where it goes. That side is—was—my husband's side of the bed. That's his charger."

"You're sure? Sure you didn't happen to plug it in there?"

She was sure. Sure, sure, sure.

"Oh!" She exclaimed seeing the little screen propped on the nightstand. "The baby monitor! My daughter sleepwalks, so we use it as an alert, so we can—I can—intercept her. Not sure if it records but worth—"

"It was shut off," the sergeant interrupted her.

"But I never shut it off?"

"It was off. At the camera end, little switch turned to 'off.'" The sergeant mimed flipping a switch.

Then she remembered she'd found it shut off that way before, after her husband died. That her daughter had insisted she hadn't touched it. That she'd thought maybe her husband had done it before he fell.

"I—I checked and it was on just a few weeks ago. The man must have switched it off? Though—maybe my daughter did?"

"Mmm." The sergeant scribbled something in his notebook.

In her husband's closet, they hovered nearby as she struggled with the safe's combination. Finally the boyish policeman took the paper with the instructions and the combination on it from her, had it open in seconds as she fidgeted, embarrassed over her own ineptitude. Nothing was missing. The gun sat snug in a nylon holster next to her husband's wedding band and the three golden eagle coins her father had insisted she take after her last visit to Utah, "For when everything falls apart."

She'd accepted them to appease him, but after the last year, she had to admit to herself that though her father was paranoid, he might have a point. Life, society itself, felt more tenuous than she would have ever believed a year ago.

The sergeant slid the gun out of its holster. "Smith & Wesson M&P 2.0," he noted, verifying the magazine was empty. The matte blackness of the thing, the metal sounds of the magazine sliding and clicking against the body, made her nervous.

"Oh, well, my husband had it forever. From before we moved? It was a hobby, he—"

"Ammo stored separately?" the sergeant interrupted.

"Yeah, up there." She pointed to the top closet shelf, and the sergeant pulled down the box, inspected it, and returned it to its place.

"Box is full." He tucked the gun back into the holster. "You a licensed owner?"

"My husband was."

The sergeant nodded, unsurprised. "Have you filled out the online form? You've got to notify the state when you inherit a firearm."

"I didn't realize. I'm not really into guns," she said.

He squinted in a way that made her feel the need to justify herself.

"It's just, with the kids in the house, statistically it's actually less safe—"

The sergeant waved her off. "Right. You can surrender it, if you'd rather. But the state offers classes. This model's easy. And it isn't cheap, so, up to you."

As much as the sight of the gun made her squirm, as often as her husband had said, "It's just a tool. Any tool can be used in an unsafe way," as often as she'd disgustedly responded, "The purpose of most tools isn't to kill someone, though," she recalled her longing for any weapon in the hidden place. She shook her head at her own train of thought.

As if having it did you any good. As if you would've magically become a sharpshooter if you'd managed to get to it that night.

"Can't hit the broadside of a barn," her grandmother's voice muttered in memory, watching her father try to teach her how to shoot at age eleven. Like nearly everyone she'd grown up around in Utah, her father owned not just one gun, but many. She chewed her lip, recalling her dad coming around a corner, rifle aimed at her, thinking she was an intruder during one of her overnight trips down the hall to the bathroom. She'd refused to go anywhere near a gun since, and it had bothered her that she couldn't persuade her husband to get rid of his handgun.

Maybe until the Corner's caught, you keep it. Safely. It's a machine. You can deal with machines.

"I'll—I'll hold on to it for now," she told the sergeant.

He gave her a quick, unreadable nod, and locked the gun back in the safe.

They marched downstairs.

In the playroom, her daughter's Lego creations were in pieces, fragments scattered through the room.

The officers scanned the uniform mess, asked, "Are you sure the intruder broke these things? How can you tell?"

"We heard him that night. He . . . smashed them. Threw them against the wall."

"Mmm," the sergeant said.

At the door to her husband's office she paused, looked to its corners, realized her jaw was cramping, her teeth clenched tight.

The office was as bright and cheerful as its dim spot in the house ever got, afternoon sunlight streaming through the windows. The panel to the hidden place was open, inside inky black even in the daylight. A stale human vinegar smell led her eyes to the pool of her own vomit. It was dried and dark. No one had cleaned it up. This struck her as cruel and inconsiderate, though she knew logically cleaning up wasn't—shouldn't be—the officers' job.

"Why didn't you try to contact 9-1-1 online?" the boyish officer asked, lifting his chin toward the computer. She told them her husband kept it disconnected, the better to focus on work. They nodded, and she understood they already knew it was offline, and she wondered why they'd wanted to test her in this way.

"I bet you've got a lot of spooky stories about this place," the boyish officer said.

"She doesn't believe in ghosts," the sergeant said. "Doesn't believe in the *supernatural*."

She winced. Her flippant comment about religion had clearly lodged deep.

He wants you to apologize for saying all that about religion and superstition being the same. Wants you to apologize again. Sorry, sorry, sorry is all you ever say. Don't you dare apologize again.

"The real world's scary enough for me without ghosts," she said as evenly as she could.

29

I s that—that's every room now, isn't it? Are we finished?"

"We need you to take a look around outside," the sergeant said.

This did not sound in any way possible. Physically, she had been trying to ignore the pain, the sluggishness of her own blood. Mentally, she'd been trying to push away the sense that these officers had been next to her for days, had asked her the same questions hundreds of times, that they would never leave and she'd have them hanging around her neck forever.

But the light outside was only just beginning to transition to its evening yellow. Not so much time since she left the hospital. Not so much time searching the house, answering questions, looking at their blank eyes.

"It's just—I'm tired. Can we do that another time?"

"How about a little break, then we see how you feel?"

It was bizarre, being ushered to take a seat on her own couch, in her own house.

"Need a glass of water or anything?" the sergeant asked, as if it were his house, his glasses, his water.

"Can you call my kids? He picks up for you."

"Um . . ."

"Please."

"Sure, yeah, all right."

The sergeant dialed. Her father-in-law picked up immediately.

"Officer, thanks for calling me back. That lunatic woman left a message saying she's picking up the kids today. Over my dead body will that crazy bitch—"

"It's me."

Her voice sounded thin and exhausted, though she'd aimed for strong, snide, something that would embarrass him.

Her father-in-law sputtered, then said, "What do I care? You are *not* coming here. You convince them some goddamn demon is in your house, gonna burn and eat them? Jesus Christ, no wonder they don't think you're—"

"Sir?" the sergeant interrupted, voice urgent in a way that she couldn't unpack. "Sir? That's enough now, I've got lots to discuss with her, all right? So put the kids on."

"With all due respect, Officer? No," her father-in-law sniped, and hung up.

"He really can be an asshole, can't he?" the sergeant said flatly.

Her hand in yours, that little hand. She's still so little. His stocky legs, that baby pudge. His cheeks, the one dimple. Her knobby knees, her dark, shining eyes. Their dad's light scatter of freckles, his same broad forehead.

She sighed. "Yeah. Well. The sooner we get this done, the sooner I can see them, so, let's get this over with, okay?"

The boyish policeman couldn't meet her eyes. The sergeant gave an awkward cough.

"Mmm-hmm, right. Then let's take that walk, yeah? Let us know if it gets to be too much for you."

From the sergeant's tone, it was clear that telling them it was too much wasn't an actual option.

She struggled back into her boots, fumbled at the zipper of her coat with her wrapped hand. The sergeant reached out to assist, and she recoiled.

"I've got it," she said, turning away from him, zipping it up.

"We're going to follow a track we made through the snow, all right?"

"Sure."

"So that's where you came out?" the sergeant asked, indicating the front double doors.

"Yes."

"Those there." He pointed. "Those are your footprints?"

She squinted at the soft indentations. It must have snowed since, or at least blown snow, because they only had slight dimension.

"I guess so."

They followed her footprints at a remove along the side of the house, past the living room windows, the kitchen, around the corner of the garage, across the yard to the graveyard. They asked her to describe her escape again, and she pointed out the window she'd looked through and seen the Corner coming down the stairs, the path she'd made through the snow.

She felt tender inside, hurt in places that were normally concealed. When she stumbled, the boyish policeman gave her his arm. She didn't want his hands near her, said she didn't need help, but thanks.

"You said you fell around here?"

They were standing in the graveyard.

"Yeah, cut my hand. There, I guess? That's probably my blood, that dark spot on the front of that gravestone? Where I caught myself."

"You don't remember for sure?"

"It was dark and I was running."

The sergeant pointed at the house. "So, am I correct in saying you were standing here when you saw someone in that window up there, looking out?"

"Yes. That's my bedroom window."

"You know, it kind of looks like someone is standing there now, doesn't it?"

She was bothered at how the sergeant's voice seemed filled with practiced thoughtfulness. She squinted at the window in the fading evening light.

"Does it? It's hard for me to see with my hurt eye."

"Yeah," the boyish officer agreed in a way that again struck her as rehearsed. "The pattern on the curtain, lit up like that from inside? It looks like a person."

"You know, I'm pretty sure the curtain wasn't closed at all, not that night. So . . . something for your list? That's changed?"

"You're 'pretty sure'?"

"I'm sure."

They turned to look down the path. As usual, there was less snow there. She shivered, felt the wind blow down the trail, turned her cheek so it didn't hit her full in the face.

"So, there's your footprints," said the sergeant. "And on this other side of the trail is where my guys walked through later on so they wouldn't disturb your tracks. Anything strange, unusual, out of place?"

Barely discernible was her stagger of imprints in the snow. Running parallel to it were windblown footprints the sergeant said had been made by his officers. Around and between these footpaths, the snow was punctured by the small, distinctive tracks of the deer.

"It seemed—it seemed so much farther. Further?"

"Far enough if you're only wearing slippers."

"So, he didn't follow me? I didn't think he had, but wasn't sure. Or could he have followed in my tracks?"

She looked at the officers inquiringly. Their arms were folded, faces stony. She turned, took in the blank smoothness of the snow in every direction, broken only by the plowed driveway, the police-flattened track they'd followed, the small trace of her path and the footprints of the officers, made night of.

"I don't understand," she said. "Where are his footprints? Were there tire tracks from his car? From when he left?"

Still no response, no movement from the police.

"Did he park somewhere else?"

Her son's voice reverberated in her head. *The police say he doesn't even have feet.*

"It's a good observation," the sergeant said. "There were no tire tracks. No footprints other than yours."

"How is that possible?"

"We were hoping you might be able to explain it."

"Me?"

"Yeah. Like maybe this place has a secret entrance, same as it had that secret room."

There was something knocked loose in her skull. She resisted the urge to scratch a finger into her ear canal to try to pull it out. He's *a pigment*, her son's voice said.

"There's nothing like that," she told them.

"So how do you think this man managed to get out here, get into your house, with no tracks? No car?"

"I don't—maybe—" She saw the floors in her house, scratched, grimy. The attic dust scuffed. "Maybe your guys drove over his tire tracks? Walked through his footprints?"

The sergeant shook his head at her, his eyes hard blue marbles. "Nah."

"How can you be sure?"

"My guys took photos when they got here. Snow-covered driveway, no tire tracks. No footprints when they did their initial sweep."

"He could've walked here. Parked somewhere else? Then his tracks got snowed over. Blown over."

"Your tracks are still here, though. We checked that night, and there were no larger tracks over yours. Checked the perimeter of your property, too. Nothing disturbed but your tracks out the front door and down that path."

A choking panic welled up from her belly.

"Maybe he's—could he have come earlier? Been waiting in the house for us? Hiding?"

"It's possible. But there was already snow on the ground before the storm. So there should have been a sign of some disturbance, some tracks. Did you see anything? Notice any signs, footprints, that day?"

She thought back. She'd logged the children in to their remote morning school. Left the house at twelve thirty, as usual, to take the kids to afternoon in-person school. Ordered from the grocery store. Picked up the kids, picked up the food. Watched them eat, her own appetite still lacking.

"I don't remember any footprints. But I wouldn't have noticed. People come all the time, you know? To deliver packages, or just 'cause they're looking for another house and get turned around."

"So you didn't see anything?"

"No, but . . . like I said, I might not have noticed."

"Mmm-hmm."

"Could he . . . have hidden in the house? After? Waited for you all to leave?"

This earned her a stern look from the sergeant. "Any more secret rooms in there?"

"No."

"Then there was no intruder in your house when we got there. We searched the whole place. Thoroughly."

"Right. Of course."

She tried to make a connection, find an explanation, and failed to. Her thoughts sparked and faded out, sparked and faded out, live wires briefly touching and then pulled apart as she tried to understand how it could be possible.

No footprints. No tire tracks. No sign at all but the smell of cigarette smoke. The toilet seat up. Your daughter's missing things. A lowered curtain. A flat tire. Maybe.

"Okay," the sergeant said. "How about we go back inside? There's a few more questions we're hoping you can help with. No need to do that out here in the cold."

She looked around her as she slowly walked through the snow back to the house. It was all so impossible, the flat plane of that snow. Its sparkling evenness was a betrayal, somehow, another thing unexplained and unexplainable. Like the clean beauty of the path. The baby monitor, shut off, useless. Her phone returned to her bedside.

The sheen of the world had an incongruity to it that made her go soft with fear that her mind was irretrievably damaged.

30

S he tried to massage the pain out of her hairline, but it only made the fissure in her head groan, bone rubbing against bone like a biological fault line.

The sergeant sat a distance away from her on the couch, the boyish policeman in a nearby chair by the fireplace.

"Is there anyone other than the guy from the café you think might have targeted you? Anyone who you hadn't paid, say, or who you turned down for a date? Anyone who would've thought you owed them money?"

"No," she said over and over. "Nothing like that."

She answered more questions, endless questions, mournfully looking outside to see it was already dark.

At this rate the children will be asleep by the time you get to your father-in-law's apartment.

With a shudder she realized she couldn't get the children at all, not with a flat tire.

Why didn't you think of that before? Right away? What's wrong with you?

She interrupted the sergeant midsentence, blurting, "Can you put a spare tire on? I want to be able to drive, to get the kids, do you think you could help? I don't know if I can do it by myself."

The sergeant grunted, said, "Ma'am, how about we focus, all right? Then when we're done here, we can discuss all that."

She felt the sting of his dismissal, the sergeant again seeming to see her children as a distraction, an insignificant detail, her heart plummeting, shrinking, at the realization that she wouldn't see them tonight. Even if the spare were on, she couldn't drive all the way to her father-in-law's house on it, given the distance and the age of the spare.

"I'm sorry to ask, but maybe you had a bad breakup, an affair? Or your husband might have had an affair? Sometimes people feel they're owed something, after that," the sergeant said.

At this idea her dismay over not seeing the children was whipped away by outrage and she sputtered, "No! No affair. No."

"All those long days he was away flying? Nothing suspicious?" the boyish officer chimed in.

They made an affair sound inevitable, obvious.

Are you sure? Would you have known? How do people know? You didn't even know he was talking to his dad.

"Are you trying to tell me something? Have you found someone?"

"No," the sergeant said in his cryptic way. "It would be normal for you to have suspected something, is all. Most married people have suspicions at some point, yeah?"

"Well, I didn't. I never did."

The sergeant looked at her like she was touched in the head, and she found herself covering her face, covering her biggest marking with a palm, feeling its whiteness flare with insecurity, with the implication that of course her husband might have had an affair, because look at her.

"Mmm. Okay," the sergeant said. "Now, I brought a couple things here to show you." He unzipped a duffel bag and laid out two items next to her on the couch. They were sealed in large clear plastic bags.

"Are these the shoes the intruder was wearing? The shirt?"

In one bag was sealed a pair of fresh white Reeboks, men's size 9. They had a black stripe and brown gum soles. In the other bag was folded a black T-shirt with a photo of a diamond-encrusted, black-eyed skull printed on the front.

"These are my husband's things." She set the bags back down, pointed. "The shirt, he got that at a museum. See the writing? The shirt the Cor—the man was wearing, the design was on the back, not the front. The skull had messy hair, yellow eyes. And the sneakers are my husband's, too. The man's shoes, they didn't have this black part. They were older, cracked. All white. But yellowing. And they were high-tops. Did I tell you that? Plus, you know . . . bigger. He had to walk sideways down the stairs his feet were so big."

The sergeant gave a curt nod, then put the bags back in the duffel. "Not sure if you noticed as we've been walking around, but there's no signs of forced entry. No broken window, no doors kicked in, no locks messed with."

"Oh, I . . . right." Her mind tripped over their walk-through, trying to recall the state of the windows, the doors.

What's wrong with you? How out of it are you that you didn't notice?

"How do you think someone might have gotten in?" the sergeant asked.

The pain was trickling behind her back teeth now. She stretched her mouth wide, then closed it again.

"I—I don't know. I locked all the doors. Windows. How did the police get in? That night?"

"The door was unlocked," the sergeant said coolly.

She could almost feel her brain skitter over this new piece of information, trying and failing to grasp it.

Impossible.

"Wait, what? Which door?"

"The entry door. Maybe you forgot to lock it."

Sometimes she'd jerk up to sitting in bed, thinking of open doors. Couldn't sleep until she threaded her way downstairs in the darkness, trying not to wake her husband and have to listen to him saying, "You're paranoid! Who cares if it's unlocked?" The reason she needed to check, needed to make sure, was that she could never actually remember locking up. It was a thing so automatic, such a part of her routine, that she wasn't conscious of it. Like a person who commutes every day, but can't recall anything about their drive that particular morning.

"It's not possible," she said. "I never leave a door unlocked."

"You remember locking them that night?"

No, she thought.

"Yes," she lied. "But maybe he found the hide-a-key?"

"That rock thing?"

"Yeah."

The sergeant shook his head. "Nah. We found it buried in the snow where you said. Undisturbed. The key was in there."

"It's just, this is going to sound—" *Crazy.* "Strange? But after my husband died, after an article came out about his art? I felt like—I thought—someone might be watching us."

"How so?" The sergeant and the boyish officer exchanged a darting look.

It felt like my husband was still here, watching over us. Trying to get home.

"Um. Well. I think I mentioned to you, back then, how the kids thought they saw someone, a man? I assumed they were just hoping it was their dad, but maybe not? A couple of the kids' things—a hat, a stuffed animal—just vanished. And I thought I saw someone out in the pasture. So did my daughter, a different day. Then the swing set? Someone had messed with a carabiner. And—"

She hesitated. Thought about the baby monitor switched to "off."

Deer braying into the forest. That same sense of the yellowed mountain lion's eyes.

How paranoid, how haunted, do you want to sound?

"And the key rock was moved, once. Over by the woodpile, instead of by the door. It's possible he could have copied the key?"

The sergeant laced his fingers together. "And you didn't report any of this."

"No. I mean, what am I going to report, that I can't find my daughter's hat?"

"It wouldn't be all that unusual," the boyish officer mused, "for someone to watch a house before a break-in."

"Wouldn't be unusual for kids to screw with stuff, either." The sergeant leaned back, asked, "So you think this man was watching your house?"

A sense of loss washed over her as she recalled the way she, the way her daughter, had hoped that the strange sights after her husband's death were little indications of his still-hovering presence. Ridiculous, of course, but oddly comforting. A feeling diametrically opposed to the possibility that the Corner had stalked them, close and silent.

"That's all I can think of. That he was watching us. Planning. He knew, that night, he said it? How it was only the three of us in the house. So he must have been watching. He must have copied the key."

"That's a lot of effort," the sergeant said.

Unsure how to respond, she stayed silent.

"All right. Now, there are some inconsistencies we need to clear up." The sergeant waved his hand dismissively. "Just little things."

"Inconsistencies?"

"Yes. You said you didn't have anything to drink that night. No alcohol."

"That's right."

"This is not a thing to lie about ma'am, right? Drinking's legal. No big deal."

"I know that." She tried to keep her irritation out of her voice. Glanced impatiently out the window, at the way it showed time slipping away.

The sergeant wiped his palms on his thighs where his pants hitched into tight awkward folds around his bulk. His eyes thinned.

"Now, see, that doesn't inspire a lot of confidence," he said. "'Cause when you came into the hospital, you had a blood alcohol level of—" He grabbed his notebook from the coffee table, tried to look like he was searching for something. But the page he stopped at was obvious, flagged with a yellow sticky note.

"Okay, here it is. Blood alcohol level of . . ." He squinted at the page, then looked up at her. "Point oh seven five."

"Sorry, I don't know . . . is that a lot?"

"It's not nothing," the sergeant said.

"Could it be from using mouthwash? Sometimes I use mouthwash."

The sergeant gave a sardonic chuckle. "No, ma'am."

Something's wrong up there, isn't it? Something rattling around and buzzing. Maybe you dislodged something in your brain that night. Can't you feel it moving?

"I don't understand. It's not possible."

"These numbers?" The sergeant held up his notebook. "Your blood? It doesn't lie."

"But, I didn't," she protested through the humming doubt deep in her ears. "I didn't have anything to drink."

Under the unwavering eyes of the officers, flanked by their large and uniformed bodies, she sensed the weather in the room had changed. She crossed her arms for warmth, heart fluttering.

"Okay, then. Moving on. There's nothing taken—"

"The stuff of my daughter's—"

The sergeant shook his head. "Which she may well have misplaced."

"Not her treasure box," she insisted, shaking her head vehemently. "That race car-shaped box? That's got her treasures. That's what she calls them. My treasures."

"Children lose things."

"Not that! She wouldn't."

The sergeant gave a deep, put-upon sigh, and started ticking off items on his fingers.

"No fingerprints, no footprints, no tire tracks. No sign of a car. No forced entry. No injuries inflicted by this person."

"He wore gloves. White ones. Plastic." Her voice sounded breathy, and she tried to bring it back to a normal register. "He could've been waiting, like I said. Hiding in the house until we went to sleep. I know it's not a lot to go on, but . . . I told you who he was! And then there's the toilet seat that was up. The flat tire. And the kids saw him, too. That night."

"You said he manages the sandwich shop."

"Yes, that's right."

The sergeant's eyes were hard and cold. "We talked to the lady who owns the place, ma'am. She's never had a manager there. Just her and three girls running things. She's never even had a man on the payroll."

Her mind was sucked back to that August day, replaying her memories as if fast-forwarding a film, the things the manager said, the way he introduced himself, his staring. Her visceral, instinctual fear.

It was him. It was him.

"It's impossible, he must've said he was the manager even though—"

The sergeant leaned closer in a way that made her shrink from him. "You see where I'm going with this?"

Yes, she thought.

"No," she lied. "He was here. I saw him. The kids saw him. What did my kids say?"

The sergeant crossed his arms and leaned back. "That you told them there was a monster. They say this 'Corner'"—the sergeant put air quotes around "Corner"—"came straight out of their dreams. They said that's what you told them. 'Monsters are real, and there's one in the house.'"

She hung her head, stared at her bad hand clenching and unclenching. She imagined the children looking up at the sergeant, at their grandfather, so hopeful. She understood their longing. *Maybe it wasn't real*, they were thinking. *Wouldn't that be nice? Maybe it was a dream. And we were safe all along.*

"The kids heard him, they saw him," she muttered. "No matter what their grandfather's managed to convince them of."

"They mainly remember you," the sergeant said. "They said you were frightening. Violent."

Her face clicked up to him, mouth open.

"No!"

"Ma'am, you admitted that yourself."

"I didn't hurt them. I just . . . pushed them away from me. So I could get out. Get help."

"That's not how they remember it."

That's not how you remember it, either. It was awful. So awful.

Her throat thickened.

Don't cry! They'll never take you seriously if you cry.

She rubbed her good eye with her bandaged hand.

"It was real," she said to the sergeant, to herself. "He was real. You believe me?"

They don't believe you.

The sergeant's voice aimed for softness, but still came out crisp.

"Look. You've been through a lot. Losing your husband, I mean. You haven't been well. No one to talk to, not eating. You'd been drinking."

"No, I hadn't."

"Fine. But even so." He tapped his notebook. "Your blood alcohol doesn't lie. Your ID of this person was way off. It makes it hard to trust you. Or, I guess I can say, it makes it hard to trust your memory."

It unmoored her, the blood alcohol. That the café had never employed a man. It was possible the Corner had copied a key, but how had he vanished, leaving no tracks in the snow?

The sergeant could be lying about the blood alcohol. About the café. They can do that, can't they? The police? To try and get you to say you made it up.

Her mind reeled through this possibility.

But these things . . . they're so specific. They'd want to find the Corner. They must've talked to people at the café. And the blood alcohol. Why would they invent that? Maybe the hospital made a mistake? Mixed up your results with someone else?

She tenderly touched the side of her face. Adjusted the wrap around her hand. The pain reassured her that she was present. That her mind was registering the physical world.

You were hit on the head. Things slip through cracks. The psychiatrist said you might not be able to remember things right. To remember everything. He was here.

She knew she hadn't had anything to drink. Could clearly remember the Corner, outlined in August sun, introducing himself as the café manager.

They don't believe you.

But it happened. It all happened. Somehow. How? You need to think. To rest.

"You told me, back when your husband died, that you see things as you're waking up sometimes. Hallucinate. Is that right?"

Her head snapped toward the sergeant so quickly a tight line of pain traveled from clavicle to hairline.

"No—hallucinate?"

"You told me back then you'd see a dark figure in your house. Of a frightening man."

"That's—no, that's just a dream. A sleep condition. Not a hallucination."

"You said you saw a frightening man."

"In nightmares sometimes, that's all," she muttered. "I'm—I'm so tired. And my head. It hurts. Can we talk tomorrow? Can we do that?"

"No, ma'am," the sergeant said. "I'm afraid we're far from done here."

She leaned her forehead into her good hand. Remembered her daughter saying, "He watches me from the Corner when he thinks I'm asleep."

With a fingertip, she tapped the agony of her hurt eye to focus herself. To make the pain overwhelm the panicked thought that maybe the Corner had been in the house before that night. That maybe one of the shadow figures who had visited her after her husband's death could have been real—the Corner watching her sleep.

31

The sergeant cracked each knuckle on his right hand with his thumb.

"You heard of Occam's razor?"

She nodded, flinching at the noise of popping joints, at the condescension in his voice.

"It's a theory says the simplest explanation is likely true. Now, that's absolutely right, in my experience doing this job. Simplest thing is generally on target."

You told the sergeant that there's simple explanations for most things. But a conclusion can't be verified solely by its simplicity.

"Let's talk this out. You miss your husband," the sergeant continued. "Then a man appears on the stairs your husband fell down. Plays your husband's guitar. Wears things that are in your husband's closet."

They must have looked for things they thought could discredit you.

She started to respond, and the sergeant put up a hand in a "stop" gesture. "Then there's the lying, ma'am. And yes, you *are* lying. Those blood alcohol levels are simple fact. I have to ask myself, 'Maybe she's so troubled by her husband's death, not eating, not sleeping, that she forgot she drank?'" He tapped a finger to his temple to indicate how her brain might have unraveled.

He's trying to make you doubt yourself. Just because you can't think of an explanation doesn't mean there aren't any. Just because the whole night felt unreal doesn't mean it was. Your pain is real. Your flat tire is real. Things are missing. It all happened.

"No, that's not—"

"Even aside from the drinking, ma'am, aside from the fact no man has ever worked at that café, you told us he stole your phone, which we found on your bedside table. You say you always leave the baby monitor on. It was off. Not the kind of thing an intruder would guess at, that you had a baby monitor for a kid so big. You weren't even sure if he followed you when you ran out of the house. You say you were terrified, but that you fell asleep when he was sitting on the stairs. Your kids are small, scared, but you want us to believe they did just what you said, didn't make a sound to give you away. Want us to believe that you got them, their toys, water, a pillow and blanket—everything but the kitchen sink, pretty much—into that hiding place in what you tell us was probably five minutes. That sound plausible to you?"

"Yes, I—"

"Then every time we talk to you, you're solid ice. No feeling at all, even after something that traumatic. That kind of experience would make most people have *some* kind of reaction."

But you've been crying so much. Crying all along.

"I have—"

"On top of that, ma'am, your kids tell us a different story than you do. That you're the one who told them there was a monster. That you're the one who was scary. The one who hurt them."

The shame soaked her as if she were reliving it.

How could you? How could you do that?

"Then this *weapon*." The sergeant said the word with such skepticism it was as though weapons didn't exist at all, were impossible to conceive of. "Flexible, small? Not a knife, a gun, not even a rope? A little floppy thing?" He clutched this imaginary ridiculousness, waved its invisibility with a limp wrist.

"It made a sound, a heavy—"

"But most of all, ma'am," he interrupted her, "what confuses us is that we tried it out. I went in that hidden room. My guys walked all around and I couldn't hear jack shit, frankly. But you? 'Oh, I heard him go into this room and yell. Heard him go down these stairs. Heard him kick some toys. Heard him open this wardrobe a full floor above me.' You've got some *supernatural* hearing there, ma'am."

That word again, "supernatural." He is holding a grudge, he is! Because he must have heard something. You heard so much.

"Not to say this was on purpose," came the calm voice of the boyish officer from the chair by the fireplace.

The sergeant took a deep breath. Rubbed his legs and cracked the joints of his fingers again as if to let out pent-up energy, to re-mind himself to be kinder, to give her the easy out of declaring herself mentally damaged instead of criminally deranged.

"Right. Right! I'm not saying any of this was on *purpose*. I mean, you've gone through the ringer. Clear enough there's lapses in your memory. Your shrink confirmed that. Couldn't remember giving permission for us to record your first interview, for example. Maybe you forgot about drinking. Drink enough, that's easy to do. And your kids, they tell us you've been real out of it. Most folks I know, sure, they've been scared of getting sick. But you? Lost your husband, so of course you haven't been acting normal, thinking clearly. Maybe a little stir crazy. Drinking too much. Lonely. Hallucinating those shadow figures at night like you told me about, worrying for your kids." He held his palms out in front of him as if to preemptively de-fuse her protests, said, "Understandably, now, understandably."

She stared down at her hurt hand to avoid looking at the officers. She felt simultaneously heavy and drained.

How is it possible? How is any of it possible? The sergeant unable to hear anything from the hidden place, your blood alcohol, the unlocked door, no tracks, no manager at the restaurant, no—

"Then this intruder. Real chatty, yeah?" The sergeant's voice bristled with scorn. "Blabbing about how scary your house is, how scary he is. A fairy-tale Big Bad Wolf right on your doorstep. And looky here, you're the only one who can keep your kids away from all that badness. But even you admitted, even you said, calling himself this Corner, that it was"—he flipped to a page of his notebook, pointed at a word he'd written in caps and underlined—"silly. See that, ma'am? You said it was silly, that he'd call himself that. That he'd be talking aloud."

She recognized that despite his efforts to stay calm, the sergeant was sliding deeper into agitation. She scraped her memories, but couldn't recall ever calling the Corner "silly." Her shoulders hunched around the growing fear in her chest, her inability to make herself heard, understood, believed.

It happened, it happened, don't listen to him. It was real. Things missing, the toilet seat, the smell of cigarette smoke, the flat tire—

The sergeant's voice slipped into a lower, growling register. "You set yourself up to be the hero, didn't you? You've got a fur coat stashed in that front closet. Probably didn't count on how bad it would be, though, going through the snow. Didn't really think things out about footprints, forced entry. But now, you've got attention, right? Me, my guys, doctors, nurses. Big hero to the kiddos. Little lady fighting the Big Bad Wolf. A pretty simple thing, don't you think?"

"It's easy, given what you've been through, to get confused," the boyish officer said soothingly.

The sergeant cleared his throat.

"Exactly. And you're all alone. No family nearby, except that asshole father-in-law. No friends in this new place. And you clear enough weren't dealing well with things. Skin and bones. Had to be cuffed in the hospital."

"But the psychiat—"

The sergeant plowed over her protestation. "Not the first time you've seen a strange man in your house, is it, with the shadow men you told me about? And you're always awake, pacing the house constantly, your kids say. Letting them watch TV all day. Clinging to them, they said, getting hysterical over every scraped knee. And you 'pushed them away,' as you put it, when they were scared."

You're a terrible mother.

The sergeant leaned close, elbows on his widespread knees, chin resting on his knit fingers. The ice blue of his eyes lanced through her.

"You see how all this happened, ma'am? How simple it is?"

"He must have lied?" She shook her head, wishing she could make her voice louder, stronger, as her mind plucked at straws, at the thinnest wisps of possible explanations. "About being the manager, he—"

The sergeant didn't pretend at patience now.

"Ma'am, the fact is, you were wrong. You made it up. Dreamed it. You're lying to us. You're not in your right mind. You wanted attention. Can't you see how that's clear?"

He hovered so close now she could smell him. Spray starch and raw onion under cologne.

Her mind folded inward, wending its way through a story from a psychology class she'd taken in college. Once upon a time, the story went, a man whose neighbor accused him of returning a teakettle broken replies that actually, it was already damaged when he got it, and really, he'd returned it undamaged, and truly, he'd never borrowed it anyway. It was to illustrate the way people think in dreams. *I was in this place but it wasn't this place. I was talking to you but it wasn't you.*

That illogic perfectly matched the sergeant's contradicting arguments.

Actually, you're crazy. But really, you purposefully set it up. Truly, you're lying, but also, you just imagined it. In actuality, you weren't good at staging a crime, but at the same time, you didn't mean to. You're paranoid, hysterical, but not emotional enough. Your story is too linear, but you make no sense. You calculated how to make yourself a hero, but also forgot every detail that would have let you get away with it. You're dysfunctional, cutting yourself off from the world, but all you're after is the attention of strangers. You're certain you're the only one who can protect your children, but really, you hurt them.

All those contradictory realities could not exist simultaneously with each other, but all of them nevertheless entwined to support the sergeant's main point.

He thinks the Corner doesn't exist. He doesn't believe you.

"I'm the teakettle," she murmured. Her hurt eye felt as though it were dissolving, turning to liquid that was filling the spaces under her skin. "I'm the teakettle."

The sergeant and the boyish officer exchanged a look she knew meant they thought her mind had, at last, fully flown. All the familiar things, her belongings, backgrounded these strangers. There was a small stuffed horse under a chair by the fireplace. There were smudges of ash on the rug.

You can't win. You're playing a game with stakes, but you can't win.

"Why don't you tell us the truth?" The boyish officer was working hard to infuse his voice with kindness. "It's all so understandable."

The pain was terrible. The confusion, the sense that her brain was a skipping record, missing pieces of itself, overwhelmed her. How could she refute the seemingly endless contradictions, all the facts and alternate facts and maybe-facts the sergeant had just thrown at the wall to see what stuck? How could she do that with her skull so soft and battered?

"This can't be happening. This is a nightmare." She cradled her head in shaking hands.

The sergeant crossed his arms, his opinion of her shattered somewhere long ago. Maybe when he first saw the blood alcohol test. First found out there was no manager at the café. Maybe when she'd dismissed religion as supernatural. Maybe, just maybe, the second he'd set eyes on her back in November.

"A nightmare," he said sternly. "That's exactly right. Thank you for admitting that. Now, you're smart. You're a smart lady. That's exactly it. It didn't happen."

He said the word "smart" the way her grandmother sometimes had, as a sarcastic response to back talk. "Well, aren't you *smart*."

"It happened. It's your job. It's your job to believe me," she murmured.

The sergeant gave an unamused huff.

"Frankly, ma'am, people lie to us. It's our job to listen. To follow facts and evidence. This may have seemed real to *you*. But it doesn't mean it happened. Like you just said yourself, it was only a nightmare."

She desperately wanted to shut her ruined eyes and go to sleep.

"No," she said, her voice a distant whisper, "it wasn't a dream. It really happened."

Think of the treasure box, think of what you saw, think of the children, standing there in the office, listening with you. They heard and saw him, too.

"It wasn't a dream," she said again, louder. "The flat tire, the toilet seat, the missing things—"

"Ma'am, first you say it was silly, a nightmare, now you're saying it happened? Come on now." He shook his head slowly as though he were a disappointed teacher. "Stop this."

The sergeant paused, then released a long exhale that rattled her, given how it seemed designed to create a sense of foreboding, to impress upon her that he was about to play an important card.

"I didn't want to bring this up, but frankly, I have to. Maybe it'll help you understand how important it is that you level with us." She looked up at him, at the sky-blue glass of his eyes. "A report was filed with Family Services. They'll need to evaluate you, evaluate your home, before you can get your kids back."

The pounding swell of her cracked eye socket, her pained skull, surged outward.

"What?" she said, voice strangled. "What?"

He talked slowly, deliberately. "Family Services will need to assess you, the kids, your home, before you get them back."

"I don't—what?"

There were bright spots in her vision. She tried to see the sergeant through them, blinked rapidly to clear things up.

"My understanding is this is just a first evaluation to see if there's a case for escalation."

"Escalation?"

"To see if there's any need for supervision, or a change in custody."

She felt her arms around her children in the hidden place. Heard them desperate and scared, calling out *Mama!*

"How—why?"

"Someone reported you as possibly unfit."

"What—who?" she stammered.

"That's anonymous."

"My father-in-law?"

"I can tell you that he's disturbed by the way you harmed them that night. So he could very well have reported you. But it could be someone else. From the hospital, say. One of the kids' teachers."

The casual way the sergeant listed the people who might find her unworthy to be a mother clarified her understanding.

This was planned.

"Could it have been a cop?" she asked.

The sergeant gave a half shrug, but his stare bored through her, daring her to accuse him. In her eyes he was transformed to one of the officers in her mother's courtroom, part of a many-headed whole that efficiently discarded victims and survivors.

They make it your fault because that's easiest for them.

"Officers are mandatory reporters," the sergeant said coolly. "The point is, us being able to let them know you cooperated, were truthful, that you've got a grip on reality? That'll go a long way in your favor."

Yes, it's blackmail. The police, your father-in-law, all working together to take them from you.

Just as it had in childhood after her mother died, after her husband was rushed bloody out the door, her body curled up unbidden around the aching longing in her chest. Her arms wrapped her ruined calves, her forehead met her knees, and her eyes closed reflexively.

"Trauma doesn't end when the trauma ends," the psychiatrist said.

"Ma'am?"

You promised them—promised them! You'd come get them. And now, now what?

"I don't understand," she heard herself mutter.

You do understand.

The sergeant's tone was low and calm. "There'll be a letter waiting. You'll get a call from the caseworker. I tried to tell you. She's the one you should be calling about your kids. But it's early days. Plenty of time to get the ship righted again. Near always, the mom gets the kids. And you've got a nice house. You're well off enough.

You'll be okay. You'll get them back. As long as you just think it over, like I said. See what makes sense."

She kept her eyes closed, her body closed.

"You want some water? Anything I can get you?" the boyish officer asked.

Her stomach started to heave with panicked despair. She held herself tighter so they wouldn't hear the start of her mourning, see her falling into nothingness.

"You think it all out, yeah?" the sergeant said. "There's bound to be some answers, explanations, when you think it over."

"Leave."

"You sure? Nothing else you want to say?"

"Get out."

Another sigh from the sergeant. "All right. We can talk later."

She didn't answer.

"You understand, ma'am? You'll be all right? You get down, you can always call that shrink, or call us, yeah? I know it seems rough now, but—"

She looked up at him then, her fractured face twisting around all the anger she was never allowed to release.

Her voice cut out of her in a hiss. "Get. Out. Now."

For the briefest of moments the sergeant's eyes registered surprise. "Right," he said. He gathered himself. Pulled something from the duffel. "Here. Your phone. I'll set it right next to my card here for you. We'll be in touch."

The boyish officer eyed her with concern as he trailed the sergeant out of the living room. She overheard him say as they put their boots back on, "Should she be alone, you think?"

"Not on us. Psychiatrist's the one who discharged her. Anyway, it'll give her a chance to think."

She heard the door close. Heard their car roar down the driveway. She turned to scream deep into a pillow. Frustrated by the way she'd been trained to suffocate herself to silence even when alone, she threw the pillow across the room.

She wailed, mouth opened to an animal sound, a deep, primordial reverberation.

32

*A*fter all this time, you could finally scream.

She was hoarse. She wasn't sure what would happen next, but had the nauseating sense she was riding a wave that would lift her up and crash her down without her getting a say in the matter. She drifted, exhausted in the way only an explosion of emotion could make her. Yet every time she'd start to fade, she heard the Corner. Would click her eyes open, look for ragged claws, a forked tongue wrapping around a doorframe.

You're scared because it happened. You're scared because it was real.

She stared at where the police had tracked ashes along the floor, grinding them deep enough to stain the rug. It reminded her that her husband's ashes were in a box in the closet. A flame of fury began licking at her throat, and in her anger her thoughts rattled disjointed.

Children gone, husband ashes, ashes everywhere. Everything important burned after all. He thinks you lied. Are crazy. Blames it on drinking you didn't do. He doesn't understand how it was. How was it? How was it really? "Female obstacle" the Corner called you. And that's what you are to that sergeant. Inconvenient, insisting on your own sanity. This happening here makes him look bad. The strangeness, the awfulness, makes it even easier for him to dismiss.

Her anger burned brighter as the sergeant, the Corner, the

forgettable murderer in the courtroom, the ones who defended him, who failed to defend her mother, intertwined.

That murderer hadn't been able to rein in his worst impulses. The Corner was proud of his own disregard for the rules. And yet both were protected by the same institutions and mores they so clearly disdained, so clearly felt themselves somehow above. The same written and unwritten codes that the sergeant and the others like him upheld.

"All these things they do to make you soft, to make you a sheep," the Corner had said. "But I step over."

The fact that the Corner was in the world and her mother, her grandmother, her mother-in-law, her husband were all gone was a rock in her heart, a furious understanding of unfairness and responsibility.

It's just you left. This is for everything that matters. None of this is unsurvivable. None of this is finished. The shrink was right. The goddamn Corner was right. You're the only obstacle.

She sat up. Wiped her face with her sleeve.

They look at you and think they know you. But they don't see you. They can't. They think they're better. Know better. But there's no "better." There's just people, making choices. Coping with the hand they've been dealt. And you're going to choose to use your advantages. Choose to hire a good fucking lawyer. You're going to choose to fight. And you are not going to let anyone make you question your own mind. Because if you'd done that, if you'd done it when you saw that mountain lion, if you'd done it when you saw the Corner, you'd be dead.

She took her phone from where the sergeant had left it on the coffee table. There was only one voicemail, left by someone from the state. "Per our letter contacting you regarding the two minor children . . . assessment . . . screening . . . contact us at . . ."

It was too late to call them. She pulled on snow boots and a coat.

Despite her determination to do something, to fight, she hesitated as she reached for the door.

He could be out there.

She peered out into the semidarkness through the window in the entry, but the reflection of indoor light on the glass made it difficult to see outside. She turned off every light and waited. There was no movement outside. No new footprints in the snow.

The sergeant is right. The Corner probably wouldn't come back. It's too risky.

She slowly made her way down the driveway and emptied the mailbox. As she walked to the house, cradling the accumulated envelopes, magazines, and slick junk mail, her good eye caught something out of place in the pasture to her left. Her heartbeat surged until she understood what it was. A doe and fawn stood stock-still in the snow, soft ears swiveled toward her.

The fawn was small for this time of year. A late-born arrival trying to survive its first winter. Which was already a difficult one.

After the deer regarded her for a beat, some invisible current in the air caused them to run. They moved simultaneously as though there were a tether between mother and child. She watched their white tails fluff against brown backs, their grace as they leapt through the snow, past the graveyard, and vanished down the path.

See? Even now, things are beautiful.

"Good luck," she said aloud to the deer.

She frowned, overtaken by the sense she'd forgotten something, as though she'd gone into a room and couldn't recall why. She tried to grab at the tickling thread that said, *Remember? Remember?* but it kept dancing away from her until she thought, *Stop it, stop it. You're torturing yourself thinking you've forgotten things. Are forgetting things.*

She went inside and locked the doors. Double-checked that all the downstairs windows were latched. Only then did she sift through the mail. She read the letter she'd been looking for once, then again.

"You have been reported . . . care and protection of the minor children . . . assess if there is need for escalation . . ."

She tucked it under her arm. Brought the letter, her phone, and the bag of hospital prescriptions upstairs and set them on the bathroom counter. Checked to make sure all the upstairs windows were locked.

No one in the house, she reassured herself. *No one in the house but you.*

Without the judgmental eyes of the police hovering over her, the safe was simple to open. The gold coins, her husband's ring, and the gun sat in a line.

She ran her fingers over each item, as if she might absorb their power.

All these things you're storing for safety, security, in case of emergency? All of them are cold metal. Nothing soft, nothing warm at all.

One of the coins sat askew, and she straightened the stack. The gun's holster had a metal clip so that it could be attached to pants or a belt. The sergeant had set the holster with the clip facing down, tilting it at an odd angle that had caused the gun to slide halfway out of the holster. She took both items from the safe. The gun looked ridiculous in her jittery cupped palms. She thought of the easy, competent way the sergeant had held it, his practiced click of the magazine, how small it had seemed. The grip was uncomfortably large for her. The gun wasn't metal at all, she realized, but molded polymer, grip rough but without any rubbery give that might make it easier for her to hold. She fiddled with the magazine release, annoyed at how inept she was compared with the officer.

She shakily managed to remove the slide and magazine and calmed as she stepped into the familiar role of inspecting the mechanics. Though the outside was resin, the innards were metal. In her hands, disassembly was self-explanatory. She squinted closely at the exposed springs, screws, and pins. It was a simple machine. Pulling the trigger lifted a bar that struck the bullet and caused it to fire.

Methodically, she reassembled the gun, fingers competent and calm. Dissecting it had relaxed her. It made the gun seem less a live thing, a little less an unpredictable animal crouching in wait and more a simple bit of elegant engineering, albeit designed for horrific purpose. She slid the gun securely into the nylon holster, set it down, and took her husband's wedding band out of the safe. The ring was too large to stay even on her thumb, but she set it on the counter anyway. She locked the safe, the gold eagles from her father glinting before they vanished.

All your worrying about money, all that surreptitious signing of your husband's photographs, yet isn't it interesting how money's the least comforting thing now?

She rummaged through bathroom drawers. The only Band-Aids she could find were ones she'd bought for the children, decorated with the happy face of SpongeBob SquarePants.

That's nice, though, the colors, the reminder of the kids.

She wrapped one bright Band-Aid around her husband's platinum band and put the ring back on. Had to wrap another around the first until the ring at last clung snugly to her middle finger, clacking reassuringly against her own wedding band. She rubbed the platinum shine of it with the pad of her thumb. Pressed the primary colors of the toothy cartoon sponge.

See? A little softness. Not so cold. Not so alone.

She gave a wry grin, imagining the gun wrapped the same way, softened by cartoon characters like the ring. Pictured the sergeant's frowning disapproval if he'd pulled the weapon out of the safe to find it decorated with stickers like the Trapper Keepers and lunch boxes of her childhood. Wondered why she was sure even a tiny bit of color would, in fact, make her less edgy around the cold matte blackness of the thing.

In the guest room, she laid out a huge piece of paper on her drafting table. Beside it she neatly set a compass, pencils, erasers, templates, a ruler, and a T-square. Although she did most of her drafting on the computer, she liked to begin every project in pencil.

When she sat down, she felt the open door behind her like a cold breath. She realized that as she'd checked the safe, wrapped her husband's ring, she'd unconsciously stood with her back to a wall.

So no one could sneak up behind you.

The drafting table was surprisingly easy to move. She shoved it such that she could sit facing the door to the room. This time when she sat, the hairs on the back of her neck stilled and she was able to focus.

She drew a grid. A color-coded list of concrete steps (*hire a lawyer*), and uncertain ones (*prove you're telling the truth*). Her capability, the confidence of the lines she drew, the clear architectural lettering, all spoke to her in a way that said, *You are not crazy. It was all real. You can get them back. You will get better. You can protect them.*

Things already scheduled she put a dotted line through. The alarm installers, the locksmith, would arrive in the morning. The new problem of the immobile cars had yet to be dealt with.

She forced down a microwave meal of indeterminate age. Then she gathered pillows and a blanket from the guest bedroom and locked herself in her bathroom, the only room in the house with a door that bolted from the inside.

Her hand lingered for a moment on that bolt with the memory of installing it, desperate for some barrier between her and her family, for some tiny moment alone. It seemed like a desire sprung from another life, such a contrast to her current all-consuming longing for them.

She wound a nest of bedding in the cast-iron bathtub.

Another hard thing softened.

She downed her medication. Put in her earplugs. Surrounded by the walls of the tub, she didn't so much fall asleep as fall completely unconscious.

The first dribble of light through the bathroom window woke her. Her muscles were horribly twisted. The small of her back ached as though she had spent the night lying on a fist. Even her finger with her husband's ring on it tingled, unused to the band.

That's what happens when you sleep with metal things.

She checked her phone. An hour until the locksmith and the alarm installers were scheduled to arrive. Standing as still as she could, she listened to the sounds of the house. Pressed an ear to the bathroom door. No creak of stair treads. Nothing but the sound of the wind outside. Even so, there was something about the depth of her sleep that made her nervous about leaving the bathroom. She was still too close to dreams for courage. She showered, brushed her teeth, and then, sitting on the edge of the tub, made call after call, leaving the same voicemail.

"Hello, I've just been notified that family services will be looking into my situation, and I see online you have experience with assisting parents. I'm in need of immediate representation. . . ."

In between each call she thought, *The hospital could have made a mistake about your blood alcohol. You know the tin box is missing. The teddy bear. Her clothes. You did feel watched. He could have copied the key. Put a nail in the tire. And maybe he did hide, somehow. Snuck out somehow.*

She had left sixteen messages by the time she heard a knock downstairs. She slid open the bathroom bolt, peeked out at the still and empty hall, and listened carefully, pressing the Band-Aids circling her husband's wedding ring to reassure herself no Corner stood in the shadows, waiting to strike. She left the bathroom, dressed in a loose shirt and one of her husband's sweaters, pulled soft sweatpants over her tender legs, and fumbled as she made sure the drawstring was tied tightly. She hoped the baggy clothes hid the state of her body with its bruises, its swelling, its hard, unnatural lumps. Downstairs she apologized to the locksmith for making him wait. He was followed quickly by the team of alarm system installers.

"All the locks," she said. "Every camera, every window, every door. Yes, run whatever electricity you need. Sure, wires there are fine."

The noise and motion of other people in the house allowed her to wander with a sense of safety, a sureness that the Corner wouldn't spring out at her, that he couldn't do anything to her, surrounded as she was by workers seeking her out, asking their questions. "Where do you want the new panel? Should we hook into the generator, too?"

Carefully but efficiently she put her hands on everything in the house, looking for any signs the Corner had left of his existence. Anything to fill that void on her chart that said *evidence*. The other that said *proof*.

He existed. All living things leave traces.

In the basement she smelled cigarette smoke again. Asked one of the alarm company men working there if he smelled it, too.

"Oh yeah," he said. "I quit a year ago, and it's like I got a sixth sense for it now."

This acknowledgment, this verification of her own senses, made grateful tears spring to her eyes at the same time she felt a ripple of resentment.

You know what you smell. You shouldn't need someone else to tell you it's real.

If there were any other signs the Corner existed, she didn't find them. He was an absence. A smell with no source, vanished objects, memories. He was displacement—her phone on the wrong table, the toilet seat open, the baby monitor switched off. If he'd left footprints in the attic, the basement, they had been obliterated by the police during their search of the house, dust scuffed by different treads of many sizes.

The cops were messy. Sloppy.

Discouraged at finding no evidence, she changed gears. By early afternoon she had stacked several heavy-duty garbage bags' worth of trash and a box full of old clothes in the garage, bringing her home a step closer to being combed and tidied after months of grief-induced neglect.

She imagined a caseworker coming into the house, seeing it lived-in but clean and shining. "Oh yes," the pretend woman said. "This is a lovely place for children."

But no evidence. Only things missing. Things set askew. A smell.

He's a ghost.

She hired the first attorney who called her back, appreciating the woman's matter-of-fact tone and derision of the police.

"Cops," the attorney scoffed. "They show up again—and they will, I promise you that! You don't say a thing. You give them my name and number and that's it. I'll get in touch with the family department, try and light a fire, make it clear this is one they can get off their plate quick. But I'll warn you, they're as backlogged as everyone else, understaffed with people calling in sick. It'll take longer than you want, and longer than it should, to get your kids home. In the meantime, meet with that psychiatrist. You want to show you're getting help. You'll want someone willing to attest to your competence."

The locksmith snuck looks at her battered, marked face as she wrote his check, but asked no questions. The alarm installers walked her through the new system. Was she sure, was she really sure, she understood it?

"So, you had a break-in?" The team leader eyed her damage with open interest. "What happened?"

"Guy broke in." She shrugged.

"Betcha wish you had put all this in *before*, huh?" he asked. "Bad guy wouldn't've tried anything. And worst case, you would have gotten him on camera."

"So what you're saying is it's my fault he broke in," she said lightly, watching for his reaction as though he were a bug in a jar. *Tap, tap, tap.*

"Oh, well, no, no! Not saying that of course. No one deserves . . ." He waved his hand in midair as if to circle her body, her injuries. "But it's true what they say, ounce of prevention, pound of cure!"

"No one ever thinks what you've done is enough, if something bad happens," she said.

"I didn't mean to upset you."

She cocked her head at him, said coolly, "Do I sound upset?"

"Maybe—is your husband around? Want me to show him the system?" His eyes flitted behind her, hopeful a man might appear, someone reasonable.

"He died," she said.

"Holy shit," the installer said, eyes at last turning human, seeing her. "In the break-in?"

"No."

The installer shifted uncomfortably, looking around like the house might be infected, flinching as his eyes skated over her markings, and asked, "Was he sick?"

"He tripped and fell."

"That killed him?"

She saw an opening that would let her take advantage of the man's pity, his guilt, his clear opinion she wasn't quite competent.

"You know how to jump a car? Or how to put on a spare tire? With him gone, hurt like I am, I can't do it myself."

Within twenty minutes her car had a spare, and her husband's car battery was alive again. The alarm installers left, puffed up with the sense they'd helped a damsel in distress. She activated the new security system, locked the house with her new key.

More metal. More safe metal.

As she drove under twenty miles an hour to the repair shop to avoid blowing the ancient spare, the furious honking of the cars behind her, the yelled expletives from the cars that passed her, were just so much background noise. She sang along to the radio. Smiled about how the doctor had been right, after all, her vision repaired enough that she felt safe. At least on such a familiar road. At least going so slowly.

She wondered if life would always be this way. Panic and fear that a window might have been left open, listening to the sounds of her own house with her heart racing, clinging to metal comforts to sleep, to function, but everything else? It all seemed so simple, so easy. How had she ever cared about irritated drivers? About the condescension of the contractors she paid? About what anyone thought of her? She sat up straighter in the driver's seat to relieve the aching pressure at the small of her back. Thought with longing of the way her husband used to massage her shoulders, kneading out the kinks.

It would be better now, with the alarm installed. With the new locks. She had to make it better. She gripped the steering wheel tight.

You can't let the Corner take your home from you. Don't let him take that comfort from you. Pollute your memories.

The past two years spun through her head. The kids jumping in leaf piles. Her husband's endearing but baffling obsession with perfecting the grass of the lawn. Her daughter eating tomatoes out of their summer garden. The children's snow forts, pillow forts, blanket forts. Cooking pizza in the beehive oven. Winter fires in the enormous fireplace.

No. He won't get that. You won't let him take that.

At the repair shop, she drank cup after cup of coffee, noting but choosing to ignore the woman behind the desk gawking at her. It was oddly preferable to assume people stared because of her injuries rather than at the skipping white traces of her vitiligo.

While she waited for her new tire, she flipped through a magazine from December of the year before.

The star on the cover posed with hands on hips and a forward slouch, quote superimposed over the photo reading, "I always want things dangerous."

She leaned back, chair pressing the hard knot at the small of her back so uncomfortably she readjusted herself. How safe the world had to have felt to say such a thing. She couldn't remember it ever feeling that way.

By the time she got home, the sun was orange, tangling low in the trees. Approaching the garage, she spotted the doe and fawn at the head of the trail just past the graveyard, perfectly still but for the puffs of steam out their wet black noses.

Her husband told their old joke, "If you don't see deer around here, it means you aren't looking hard enough."

The alarm installer said, "Worst case, you would have gotten him on camera."

Her mouth went dry as she was hit by what had gnawed at her the day before, the memory she hadn't been able to grasp when she'd seen the deer bound away down the path. She turned off the car, hand trembling. She'd failed to put it in park, started to roll backward before she slammed the brake, wincing with the way the impact hurt her injured foot. She stared out the windshield at the mother and her baby.

The wildlife camera was still somewhere out there in the woods, pointed at the forest path.

It would make sense, that the Corner had approached the house by using the path. There'd been no car, no tire tracks. He had to have walked. It would have been easy to park back on the cul-de-sac of McMansions unnoticed, and cut down to the house along the forest path.

Don't get your hopes up. It'll probably show nothing. It'll probably be out of batteries. It's been up how long? Over a year. And even if it works, he probably never went that way. But maybe. Maybe, maybe, maybe.

She pictured the Corner watching the house from the woods. But no matter how long he might have stood waiting, watching, he never would have seen the solar-powered wildlife camera in its camouflage case, hidden against a tree ten feet off the path.

But that camera might have seen him.

33

She parked in the garage and hurried into the house to exchange her sneakers for snow boots, almost forgetting to disable the alarm so that it wouldn't alert the monitoring services, the police. The installer had warned her that in the first weeks people often forgot.

"You got a wife coming in from shopping, yeah? Hands full of bags, all excited to crack 'em open, next thing she knows she's missed a phone call from us, and the police are there."

"I'll remember."

"Sure, course," he'd said, and she'd disinterestedly clocked him looking askance toward his buddy, both of them pegging her as hopelessly damaged. Endlessly stupid.

And here you are, she thought, and smiled to herself, *nearly proving them right.*

Her excitement helped her move quickly despite her unhealed body. She walked out of the open garage door and toward the trail. Compared with her shoeless midnight race through the forest, without the weight of the officers by her side like the day before, using the trampled path the police had made felt light and easy. Under the low evening sun she traced carefully through the gravestones, recalling her previous fall. Made her way to the entrance of the path and tried to remember exactly where her husband had mounted the wildlife camera.

It was windy. Clumps of snow fell off treetops with each gust, leaving divots in the snow that made the woods, the path, even the pastures and graveyard behind her look as though an odd-footed army had moved through, gaits irregular and broken.

She left the shallow snow of the trail and moved into the drifts of the darkening forest, bits of ice slipping into her boots when she went in too deep. In her excitement she at first moved haphazardly from tree to tree, swearing at the hidden sticks and branches catching on her sweatpants.

You don't remember where it was. That's okay. It's been, what, over a year? It must be out of batteries. Out of memory. Even with the solar panel, it couldn't have lasted. Don't get your hopes up. Be methodical.

She imposed an imaginary grid over the general area where she thought her husband had mounted the camera. She followed its lines, marched precisely as possible, her tracks growing into an appealingly even web behind her.

As she started to worry that her husband might have taken the camera down and failed to tell her, she saw it. The device blended in well with the tree trunk it was strapped to, but there it was, just below eye level. Her heart sank, seeing how the solar panel on top was partly covered in snow, how flakes had collected in the rim around the camera's eye.

She wrestled with the thing, finally taking the mitten off her unhurt hand to allow her to pull the Velcro from around the tree.

Please, please, please, she prayed to no one in particular, *let there be something, anything!*

The device was similar to a digital camera, with its own two-by-three-inch screen in the back behind a hinged cover. It was more intuitive than she remembered, and smaller, easy to hold. She hit the "OK" button and the screen lit up, making her heart pound with hope.

She hit the button with a printed arrow pointing left and the most recent video played. The recording had been triggered by the motion of her own staggering self walking back and forth, searching, time-stamped 4:08 p.m., small digits indicating it had a twenty-minute run time.

She was so excited she had to stretch her fingers wide, shake out her hand, breathe deep to calm herself, before immediately clicking backward in time to see if she could find the Corner.

The next video was time-stamped 4:02 p.m. The doe and fawn, running away from her car. They were only partially obscured by the snow on the camera lens, leaping high and out of frame. She looked up at the sky, its near darkness. Had difficulty believing she had searched for the camera for only twenty minutes or so.

She went to the next video, stamped just two minutes before the doe and fawn. There was no motion, no animal that looked to have triggered it. She peered closer at the tiny screen. There was only an empty view of the trail, the trees, a corner of the pasture with the massive old pine at its edge. Maybe the falling snow had made it turn on? A squirrel?

Or else this dumb hurt eye isn't doing as well as you thought. Probably the snow falling off the branches was enough motion to trigger it to record.

She looked up, looked around, heard the *whumph* of falling snow around her, the cracking noise of frozen wood in wind. The branches were black against the sky, which had turned a deep navy.

It doesn't matter, what does it matter? Get to the day it happened! That's what matters.

Overeager, she hit the button twice in quick succession to scroll backward in time. But what flickered and then vanished as she clicked past made her stop breathing, made her ignore the fawn and doe slowly strolling past the lens at 9:00 p.m. the day before.

"What was that?" she whispered to the woods. "What the hell was that?"

She clicked back to a video time stamped 7:03 a.m. that day.

The Corner was carefully picking his way toward the house down the footprinted path left by the police on the trail. He went out of frame at 7:04 a.m.

He came to the house. This morning.

Frantically she looked around her, breath instantly coming fast, hands making the camera shake.

Where is he now? Did he get into the house? Is he here?

The swell of her blood was so loud she couldn't hear anything but its pounding. Everything in the forest was turned to shadow but the dim blue tint of the camera light. She clicked once more to the second, more recent, video she'd skipped.

It was time-stamped 7:28 a.m. Right about when the locksmith had arrived. When she'd freed herself from the bathroom.

The Corner ran into frame. He slipped slightly in the snow, recovered himself, and stopped. He turned around, craning his neck in the direction of the house. She imagined him watching the locksmith, the alarm company truck, parking in the driveway.

That means—what? Maybe he was trying to get in—maybe he got in? Then he heard the locksmith coming and ran without being seen.

For eight minutes, the Corner stood in the camera's frame, moving sometimes as if to get a better view. She fast-forwarded, desperately skipping thirty seconds at a time to see what he'd been doing, to find out how the video ended. She had to force herself to breathe. It was as though a nightmare that should play only in her head had been filmed.

Did he try to get in the bathroom? He could have, given his size. He could have knocked the door down if he wanted. Why didn't he? Was he searching for your daughter? Seeing if she was back home again? Did he get in?

Her heart seized, imagining what could have happened if she'd been brave. Reasonable. Hadn't bothered with changing the locks and putting in an alarm system. If she'd slept in her own bed. If she hadn't gotten so tired of the children constantly bursting into the bathroom when she was using it that she'd screwed in that bolt, up high, out of their reach. It was so many things coming together all at once that even there, frozen and terrified in the snow, she felt lucky. Grateful for the bolt. For how frustrating the children had been. For whatever bizarre impulse, logic, or horrifying, stomach-churning biding of his time had kept the Corner from breaking in, breaking the bathroom door down.

On the screen she stopped fast-forwarding at a sign of change. Watched the Corner straighten himself to his full, massive height. He stood in profile. His mouth moved, and in imagination she heard the rasping voice seethe between his teeth.

He made a fist, pounded his chest as if knocking the Corner's rattling malice from his lungs. His mouth kept moving. Swearing to himself, making a plan?

Cold sweat trickled down her spine, settling metallic and frozen at the small of her back.

The Corner turned and walked away from the camera. He traveled just inside the tree line, hidden from view should anyone look his way from the direction of the house. He easily passed through the snow in long strides before disappearing behind the massive pine at the edge of the forest some eighty feet away from her.

After thirty seconds of no more movement, the video ended. She clicked, frantic, onto the next video. It was the scene of emptiness, of the pasture, the tree, the forest, at 4:00 p.m.

This time as she watched, she had eyes only for the pine. She stared at it, pixelated and distant on the tiny screen. Not even daring to blink, she saw motion.

Her daughter's voice rang out in memory, pointing out the window at the old pine. "Maybe it was Daddy? Daddy always liked that spot. By the tree."

Through the wavering glass of the kitchen window, she'd seen movement near that pine. Gone out to find nothing.

But he was there. That's where he watches.

On the screen a dark blotch that must have been the Corner moved out from behind the tree. For a moment the blotch stilled, then vanished behind the tree again. It was too far away to tell what he was doing. But she knew. She knew.

He was watching. He was there the whole time. He ran away from the house when he saw the workers coming up the driveway. He waited. Saw them leave. Saw you leave. Stepped out, only just now, when you came back from the repair shop. He saw you come out here. Right here. Into the woods.

Trembling, she clicked the "off" button and hugged the camera to her chest to hide its residual glow. She swallowed cold air so quickly it burned. Blinked into the darkness, eyes blinded from the dim light of the video, empty gray spots obscuring her vision.

Where is he? Has he been getting closer this whole time? Stalking you? He's on top of you, that's where he is, he'll murder you any second.

The snow was bluish white under the first wisp of moonlight. Her skull ached as she opened her hurt eyes as wide as possible, trying to see where the Corner might be, but still slightly blind from staring so long at the screen. She strained to hear his footsteps through the snow, twigs breaking as he charged through the forest. But there was only the black of branches and the white of snow, the crack of wind through iced trees and the slow, heavy sound of snow knocked from treetops.

What's he waiting for? He must have seen you. What could he be doing? Where could he be?

Just as the doe and fawn had frozen on seeing her, at first stillness seemed the only safety, the only thing that might allow her to think, assess if she was being hunted. Every bit of cold air that slipped across her neck made her startle, sure it was smooth glide of a knife.

Slowly her damaged eyes adjusted to the darkness. Tree on tree on tree stretched before her. She couldn't see any outline of a human figure in the moonlight. No one reaching out to grab her. The small of her back, wet with cold sweat, itched as if eyes were on it. She whipped around to look behind her, fearful the Corner might have circled around, but the only movement was the wind catching the high branches. She pressed her lower back, but the awful feeling didn't go away.

It came to her all at once, shamed her that she hadn't thought of it before.

Call 911! What are you doing? Call the police!

She reached for her phone. It wasn't in her right pocket, where she could have sworn she'd felt its weight. She set the wildlife camera down on the snow and frisked herself, frantic.

Where is it? Where is it? It's not here, it's not here! Did you drop it?

She hiked up the coat to feel the pockets of her sweatpants. With gratefulness bordering on answered prayer, she found the phone. The light from the screen was painful. Did it light up her face for the Corner to find her? Her hand wavered so horribly that the phone wouldn't unlock. She squeezed her husband's wedding ring tight against her palm to calm herself, and at last held the phone still enough it recognized her face and unlocked. She dialed.

"Nine-one-one, what is your emergency?"

The voice was so chipper that her mind turned blank, unable to meld it with the dark forest, the threat, her terror.

"Hello, what is your emergency? Hello?"

The irritation slipping into the voice on the other end of the phone wakened her.

"Yes, yes! There's someone here. He's after me. Please!"

"What is your address?"

She told the dispatcher, repeated it, gave her name, and at the end of every piece of information heard her dry tongue rasp out, "I'm in the woods. Behind the house. Please, send someone. Please, he's here, he's back, please."

The woman kept asking questions, told her to stay on the line, but it became increasingly difficult to speak as fear swelled her lips and tongue. The risk of standing there, phone alight, swelled through her brain, her whole body shaking now, trembling beyond her control. She didn't hang up, but she clicked the phone screen off, turned off the ringer, and put it in her pocket, unable to bear the light, the sound.

At first she thought her shaking was caused simply by the sheer terror of her position, her panicked mind not knowing what to do. But as the forest continued to surround her dark and quiet, she realized she was cold. Extremely cold. For twenty minutes she'd walked the snowdrifted forest. For the last fifteen minutes she'd been standing still, hatless, with a mitten off, on her frostbitten legs. Standing in a snowbank that was sifting ice into her boots in the dark woods.

She dazedly picked up her mitten. It had fallen onto the snow during her search for the phone. She put it on her frozen hand. Made a fist inside of it, like a child does, to warm it.

What now? What now? What do you do? Where is he?

Nothing moved. Anytime she shifted, looked around, all she could feel was the freeze of inhaled air, a consciousness of the sweat-slicked chill of the sore knot at the small of her back.

Wait. Wait for the police. Sometimes the hardest thing to do is wait.

She picked up the wildlife camera from where it lay near her feet, half sunken into the snow.

Stupid to leave it. Don't lose it. You have to protect it. It's proof.

She cursed her fractured eye socket, how dusty her vision was at its edges, especially in the darkness. She felt herself a tiny, broken thing under the eye of the Corner. He'd come up from behind her with that otherworldly weapon, the one too small and soft to exist, and the last word she'd hear would be "delicious."

Light swept over her, cut to shards by the trees, and at first it was the beam of a flashlight, it was the Corner, trapping her, blinding her, in that spotlight, no escape.

But then she heard the metal squelch of a car door. A voice.

"Hello? Ma'am? Where are you?"

Relief punched her in the gut, and she ran and scrambled through the snow toward the sergeant.

34

He's here, he's here!"

Even in the dark, even through her panic, she saw the hardness of the sergeant's expression. He wasn't wearing a mask, and his jaw was so taut with anger she stopped short of where he stood by his cruiser.

"Ma'am. You've got to stop all this."

She looked around frantically.

"Where's the others?"

He crossed his arms and tipped his head at her.

There's no backup. He thinks you're lying. Hysterical.

"I was headed home anyway. Told them I'd stop by. Why don't we go inside, yeah?"

"But he could be in there. He could have gone inside. When I left, I left out the garage, see?" She gestured wildly at the open garage door visible from where they stood. "That means I left the house unlocked, and when I went to the woods, I didn't reset the new alarm. I wasn't thinking, I was—he could be in there!"

You sound crazy. Slow down. Explain.

But she couldn't slow her tremor, couldn't choke out a decent explanation. "He was here!" her thickened, desperate voice said. "You can see—look, look!" She shakily pressed the camera on the sergeant.

He stepped away from the camera like it was a thing diseased. "What is this?"

"I got him. I got him on camera."

The sergeant took the device in his hands. Turned it over. The screen lit up, and she watched him fiddle with the buttons.

"Use the arrows. Click past me. Click past the deer. You'll see."

He stared down at the camera as she twisted around, eyes searching the darkness for the Corner. It was useless. The lights of the house cast her and the sergeant in a yellow circle that blinded her to anything outside it.

Wild things are invisible as they circle the people around a campfire.

The clench of the sergeant's jawline loosened. He looked up at her, then clicked again, watching. Clicked a third time, then raised his head slowly, eyes connecting with hers.

"I think we'd better go inside," he said.

"B-but—he could be in there! Don't you get it? I left the garage door open."

The sergeant didn't say anything, just turned and walked into the garage.

She didn't follow, trapped by fear in the liminal space between her home and the woods. "He could be in there," she called out.

The sergeant paused and turned to face her. He pointed to the camera, said calmly, "You saw the video, right? Looks from this like whoever was here is still outside. Camera would've caught him going back into the house."

Her mind *flick, flick, flicked* through the videos. The last sign of the Corner was him vanishing behind the pine as she pulled in the driveway at 4:00 p.m. Instinctively she looked in the direction of the tree, but only its swaying top was visible against the night sky. She knew she wasn't thinking logically, jittery with terror and cold.

Are you missing something? It feels like you're forgetting something. But the sergeant has to be right. He has to be thinking more clearly than you are. The Corner's outside, and that's where the danger is. Outside!

The darkness immediately seemed more threatening, the lights and warmth of the house like safety. She followed the sergeant inside, hit the button to close the garage door. She locked the entry door to the garage behind her and hurried to peer through the window by the garden door, reminding herself of the neighbors searching the night for any sign of the Corner. She couldn't make herself sit down. Nervous energy, adrenaline, forced her to shake out her hands, to pace tightly but erratically back and forth in front of the door, checking that the doors were locked, that the alarm was activated, glancing again and again into the night.

The sergeant sat down on the small bench in the entry nearer to the kitchen, oblivious to her agitated pacing fifteen feet away from him. He stared down at the little screen, wide thumb gentle over the buttons. He sagged into himself as he scrolled, didn't look up as she tried to explain, babbling at him from the opposite side of the entry.

"I remembered the camera, in the woods. To see the deer? The animals? My husband put it up. Last year? For the kids. I'd forgotten. Then I saw him. On the video? So I called the police. You see the time stamp? He was there, waiting, hiding behind the tree. I think—I think he has to be close now. Behind the tree? Or in the woods? He could be anywhere. I don't know. I don't know where he is."

"Okay," the sergeant said softly, eyes still fixed on the screen. "All right." His face was drawn, growing older as he accepted what he was seeing.

"Shouldn't you call someone?" she asked. "Shouldn't you— find him?"

The sergeant looked up at her. "He's there," he mumbled. "He was really here."

She didn't say anything, but the sergeant's tone was so changed, sounded so like a lost child, that she paused her nervous pacing.

"And you—those kids. Christ." He shook his head. "Shit. Just, all right."

As if the images on it had made him physically weak, the sergeant limply placed the camera on the bench beside him. He took out his cell phone and hesitated a moment before dialing.

"Yeah, hey, it's me," he said to the phone. His elbow propped on a thigh, he leaned his head heavily into his hand and rubbed his forehead. "I need everybody out here." The sergeant listened. "Yeah. I know. I know what I said, but." He breathed deep. Exhaled. "You won't believe what I'm sitting here looking at. She's got a goddamn vid—"

Behind the sergeant, the Corner stepped out of the darkened kitchen. A scream froze in her throat at the sight of such an impossibility, the figure of the Corner so massive over the officer he looked like an entirely different species. Indistinct weapon in hand, in a single step he stood beside the sergeant. With no break in his motion, no hint of hesitation, the Corner hit the sergeant once, twice, three times in succession on the crown of his skull, *tap-tap-tap*.

For a moment, the sergeant stayed upright on the bench, mouth forming a silent O. Then black blood slid thick down his face. The hand that held his phone dropped to his side, loosened, and the phone clattered to the ground, the sound of it hitting the brick floor of the entryway preternaturally loud. The sergeant listed to the right and crumpled onto the bench. His body settled shrunken over the camera, as though something so essential being taken had hollowed him.

She couldn't move. She was rooted to the spot by terror, unable to understand.

But he's outside. You're safe.

The Corner turned to look at her. Immobile, stiff, and conscious only of the hard, icy knot at the small of her back where all her fear-induced sweat had pooled, she watched as his lips pulled back into a smile.

"You," he snarled. "Don't you move."

It was simultaneously a command and a simple statement of fact. Every bit of her felt frozen, any motion completely impossible.

Just like in your dreams. But this is real. How is this real?

Staring at the Corner, at the body and blood of the sergeant, she understood that if either she or the sergeant had watched the full twenty minutes of video recorded as she searched for the camera, they might have seen the Corner sneaking in the background toward the house to lie in wait.

This is your fault. You didn't think. Think!

The Corner looked down at the sergeant, reaching for the wildlife camera. With a jolt, she understood that this was why he'd revealed himself. Why he'd killed the sergeant instead of waiting for him to leave the house. He had overheard their conversation. He knew the sergeant had seen him. He knew his image was on this camera.

First the sergeant, then the camera, then you. He's destroying witnesses in order of believability.

Small and empty as the sergeant now appeared, the Corner struggled to pull the device from under his wilted body. The sergeant's blood had pulsed over the camera, pooled on the bench, was already dripping to the floor. The Corner couldn't seem to grip the slickened camera. He was shoeless, had come upon them quiet in stocking feet, and blood from the floor soaked bright red into a white cotton toe. He grunted as he shoved the sergeant with one gloved hand, trying to yank the camera from beneath the body with the other.

The sight of the Corner's awkwardness, his human annoyance, the small hole in his sock next to that reddening toe, the way his pale fingers slid from any grip on the camera, shifted something unidentifiable in the air that made her muscles contract. An ancient part of her brain flooded with the understanding that the Corner was mortal, that prey could escape, that though everything was all at once wrong, it wasn't over. Her whole broken body tensed, filled with instinctual certainty that only movement could save her now.

She whipped around, unlocked the door behind her, opened it, slammed it closed the same way she had hundreds of times before, and fled into the night.

Her legs were weighed down by injury, by the snow. Her lungs, her muscles, were so exhausted it was as though she were traveling through air turned thick and viscous. All things were flattened ahead as her hurt eyes tried to see in the dark.

Go. Run. Don't look back.

There's blood on the track.

She bolted in irregular leaps along the foot-trodden path toward the graveyard and the trail, willing herself to go faster, to break through the pain, the drifts, stop the horrible softness of fear bending her joints in ways unnatural. The choice of direction was unconscious; she was a hunted creature running for the primordial shelter of the woods.

Through the *woosh* of wind through trees, through the sound of the frozen air scraping in and out of her lungs, she heard a laugh, the mocking voice of the Corner screeching, "Run, run, fast as you can!"

Can't catch me I'm—

But she knew how that story ended.

Delicious.

Don't look. Just run.

As she pushed her blood, her muscles, to do more, more, more, she remembered that she, the sergeant, the camera weren't the only witnesses. Weren't the only ones who had seen the Corner.

The children. They're next. Why else would he come back? And he'll come back for them.

This shift into thinking of a larger purpose forced her brain away from acting on pure instinct. She felt it slip into its most trained groove, mapping distances, deconstructing space, variables, options unfolding, spinning out in imaginary dimensions and possibilities.

You can't outrun him.

How far was he behind? How long had he been held back by his surprise at her flight? He would have had to put boots on before chasing after her. Had he delayed long enough to destroy the camera? Probably not. Probably he'd left it behind to pursue her. Probably he was close. Very close.

He's at best fifty feet behind you. Likely closer. This is it. You're all alone. No one can help you now.

Run.

Ahead was the trail, its snow-laden trees wrapping around the opening to form a black mouth.

Funnel him in. Swallow him up. Get him where you can see him. This is it. You're not allowed to fail. This is it. Go.

As she plunged past the gravestones and into the greater, sheltered darkness of the forest trail, she tore off her mittens and let them fall to the snow. She yanked up her coat, not trusting her injured hands to unzip it without slowing her down. She pulled up her sweater, her undershirt, until the skin of her belly and back were exposed as she ran.

He's just a man. Too confident in his own strength. His superiority. And what he doesn't know can hurt him. You can do this. Because there's no choice. Because you're not allowed to fail.

She stopped abruptly at the darkest point of the trail, the low branch of a huge white pine shadowing her even from moonlight, and whipped around to face the Corner. He was at the opening of the path between thirty and forty feet away, loping so easily, so casually, through the snow toward her that for a moment she saw the mountain lion, the ease with which it, with which this predator, could catch and destroy her. How in a fraction of a moment he could rip apart her hastily sketched plan, her body itself.

"Wait!" she called out, and though her voice was thinned with fear, weakened by exertion, the Corner stopped running at the sound of its plaintive exhaustion. In the darkness she couldn't see his expression, but outlined as he was by the now-distant lights of the house, she registered a curious tilt of his head, a moonlit spark of the yellow lion eyes on the blankness of the face. She had a flashback to the first time she'd seen him, rimmed in August sunlight.

Around their still figures the cold wind blew through the forest, dropping snow from high branches around them, flakes spinning down her collar and melting on her neck, melting on the awkwardly exposed skin of her stomach and lower back, her coat and sweater and shirt feeling like an odd life preserver rolled up around her middle.

Can he see you? See you enough to wonder what you're doing?

"Good girl," he said. "No point in running."

The Corner began walking toward her.

"I remember you," she said.

There was a long pause, only the sound of wind between them, and she wasn't sure if he had heard the whisper of her voice through her heavy breathing, through her asphyxiating terror.

"Sometimes people do," he said at last, sounding both dismissive and disappointed.

"People?"

His dark form was about twenty-five feet away, still moving slowly. A huge hand extended visible against the white of the snow, the Corner holding it out as though he were approaching a skittish horse. She reached behind her to the cold, hard place at the small of her back.

Can he see? Can he see?

Wait until you can see.

"People," he echoed. "It's my height. My size. It makes me memorable. It's . . . inconvenient. But it hasn't mattered."

As he spoke, she wrapped the shaking fingers of her unhurt hand awkwardly around the cold grip and pulled. With a soft pop the gun came out of the holster clipped to her waistband at the small of her back. She held it tightly, sweaty and warm on the side where it had pressed against her skin while she slept in the tub, while the locksmith and alarm company secured the house, while she drove to and from the repair shop. The gun felt frozen colder than cold where pulling up her clothes had exposed it to air, except for the spot on the grip where she'd stuck one of the yellow and white Band-Aids.

She brought the gun slowly to her side, keeping it as close to her leg as possible to hide it from the Corner's sight in the shadows. The shakiness of her hand worsened the closer he inched, trembling so violently she saw the linoleum floor of her dorm room. Felt it press against her cheek.

No. Not again. Hold on. Hold tight. Fear is just a physical reaction, as real as a slap to the face, a blow to the skull. You've taken that and more already. You have to do it, or you'll lose, you'll die. And so will they. This is not about you. He is very, very serious. This is it.

Her thumb pressed the Band-Aid. The feel of that soft stuck-on thing, the knowledge of its bright colors, the reminder of the children, their clean love, made her awful tremor kick down the slightest of notches. Her grip tightened. And still he moved closer, still he might lunge.

No. He's enjoying himself too much to be quick.

Eighteen feet away. Fifteen.

"That's right. You wait there. Useless." The Corner's purr again gave her the sense he saw her as a jumpy, unpredictable animal. He moved cautiously, slowly, but with the upright confidence that he was the superior creature. That he was at the edge of desire fulfilled.

Thirteen feet. Twelve.

"How many people? Remembered you?" she asked, hoping to distract him, hoping that the sound of his voice would help her aim.

He was close enough now that when the moonlight caught his features, she saw the unblinking intensity of his eyes, the twitch of excitement that lifted the corner of his lip.

"Some," he said with a tip of his head.

"How many . . . didn't?" she stammered, her words filed down to essentials, barely audible.

"More." The word was drawn out sensuously, viciously. "But it doesn't matter. They're all mine now." He paused, straightened himself with pride, and added in an instructive tone, "That's how it works."

In her mind's eye, she saw him the way he saw himself. His shadow dragged the pain he'd inflicted, the power he'd wielded, behind him like a cape. She watched him wrapping himself in it, fabric threaded with ghosts he'd made, trapped, nostalgically stroking the tin box he'd stolen from her daughter, things he'd stolen from others, with flat fingers.

And then the image was gone. There was only the snow. The woods. Only her and the Corner.

"No," she said, the word light but matter-of-fact. "It doesn't work that way. They aren't yours."

He stopped moving toward her, momentarily surprised. "And you think you know how things work?"

She saw her mother's face, the way her markings whitened a patch of eyelash, of eyebrow, felt the heat of her smile, the squeeze of her mother's hand as they walked—*bum-bum, bum-bum*, a heartbeat; a secret way to say "I love you," the same as she now did with her own children. She watched her whitened hand sketch clean lines and angular letters. She felt the panel of the hidden place click shut. Saw the spinning beauty of the bees' perfection. Gravity pulled the gun down heavy in her hand, the parts of it disassembled, reassembled in imagination as she visualized its mechanics, the steps to set it into motion.

"I know how things work," she said, hearing the space she'd unconsciously left between the words, as if each were its own crucial sentence.

"Then you know you're . . . incidental."

She breathed deep and thought of the downy fuzz behind her daughter's ear. The miniature jelly bean birthmark on her son's thigh.

I love you. I love you.

She opened her eyes.

"No one is incidental," she said. "There's time. Care."

He stayed still, regarding her, and she wondered if he understood what she meant, had any sense of cost and value, the effort life took to create, to cultivate.

"You know who I'll visit next," he sneered. She felt, vibrating through the air, his need to see her react to the threat of precious things ended, his eagerness that she acknowledge her helplessness so that he could bathe in it.

When she didn't respond, he began moving again. His steps were steady and his stare unwavering, as though he was savoring the anticipation of the inevitable moment his hand would at last curl around her throat.

Nine feet. Eight feet.

Her mind narrowed to a pinpoint.

You're the one who watches. You're the one who watches over the children. You're the one who knows how things work.

He thought he saw you. He never did. But you see him.

Her whole body clicked into acceptance.

You're the Corner.

She lifted the gun and inexpertly pulled back the slide. It moved smoothly into place with a precise *click*. A hitch of silence followed the unexpectedly loud noise, both of them stunned to stillness. She broke the moment, shakily using both hands to point the gun at his immense, darkened form to steady the weapon as best she could.

He lunged, blotting out the whole world.

"No," she exhaled. "No."

35

Despite the sergeant's murder, despite the Corner's existence provable to anyone morbidly curious enough to glance into his hospital room, she still had to endure a home visit and interview with Family Services. To get permission to retrieve her children, she had to wait for the police to find an explanation for her blood alcohol level, for them to at last interview the neighbor to discover that the hot drinks he'd given her that night had been spiked with whiskey.

"To warm her up," the neighbor explained, "like they used to have rescue dogs wear barrels of brandy? It helps."

"The sergeant was concerned," the boyish officer said sheepishly. "It was genuine concern. You hurting the kids, and he thought you were drinking. Lying about it. It wasn't—he didn't report you to Family Services to force you into saying anything. He wasn't like that. He was a good cop. A good man."

She was sure the boyish officer had convinced himself this was true.

Although at last required to return the children, her father-in-law still wouldn't pick up his phone when she called. She'd appealed to the caseworker and the boyish officer for help, worried about what might happen when she showed up at his apartment to retrieve them.

The officer promised to drive her to get the children himself.

"I want to help. I need to do something good," the boyish officer said with a sad smile, a distant look.

She chose to believe his stated motives, even though the police were clearly being helpful to appease her, worried not only that she might sue them for their failures, but also that she might talk to the reporters who swarmed hungrily around the hospital, the police station, and at the edges of her property line.

Deafened by the gunshots, she'd felt surrounded by a roaring tide as she watched the police help load the Corner into the ambulance, watched them photograph the scene. She saw them find and bag the black, weighted leather weapon she'd later learn was called a sap, the long, heavy object the Corner had used to murder the sergeant. After sign-off from the paramedics, the officers had left her at the station, waiting for her hearing to return to properly question her.

The boyish officer had gone on to the hospital, had recited the Corner's rights before pulling his hair out by its roots, swabbing his body for evidence. She imagined the Corner's hands paralyzed by his sides, powerless to stop them.

The invisible strands of his DNA linked the Corner to bits of himself left all around New England. In rural Maine, two grandparents killed by blows to the head, their ten-year-old granddaughter still missing, a shoeprint on a windowsill. In Hyannis, a dead mother, vanished girls. In northern Vermont, a living mother, a dead girl. A whole house on the Rhode Island coast clean and empty. A single matching hair. The tiniest trace of fluid.

Then there was the flood of possibly connected unsolved crimes with no physical evidence at all. People who'd told friends they'd felt watched. That small things had gone missing. Before murder. Before a child disappeared.

She recalled the pride in the Corner's voice as he'd hissed the word "many." Wondered if as his DNA was being collected he'd been excited at the prospect of being the center of the world's macabre fascination. Maybe he'd enjoyed thinking about new avenues of control opening to him. How he'd toy with law enforcement. Keep his bodies hidden, hint vaguely at the horrors he'd left behind. Give interviews, deny them. Watch the pain of the survivors and relive his savagery.

But when she fired at the Corner, when she aimed at his very center, aimed to kill him, her shaking, injured hands, her inexperience, the physics of the gun itself caused the weapon to kick as she pulled the trigger three times, sending the bullets high. If he weren't so tall, if she weren't so short, she would likely have missed him altogether. But he was very tall. And she was very short. So a single bullet hit him at the base of the neck and instantly severed his spinal cord. He would almost certainly have bled to death had the sergeant's interrupted phone call not galvanized an unusually fast and concerned response. The police and EMS had stanched his blood, had carefully pried the gun from her hands so soon after she fired, so soon after he fell, that she'd sat stunned on the snow, deaf and unmoored.

Online she sought out scans of spines, learned what vertebrae she must have nicked for that particular result. She lulled herself to sleep diagramming the probable path of the bullet, the recoil of the gun, the way the Corner had realized what she held in her hands, the way he'd turned slightly away from her as he'd charged, making that particular injury, making his survival, possible. Her mental illustration of the scene's physics soothed her after nightmares. Calmed her when she heard an unusual noise in the house.

The Corner was paralyzed from the neck down.

How quickly had he accepted that? How long had it taken for

him to understand he now required money, help, close and constant care? That she'd turned him utterly vulnerable? If he was anything at all like she was, every morning he'd wake thinking he was in his old world and be plunged into remembering what he'd lost. But he was not like her, so maybe he'd adapted much faster. The boyish officer had hinted that the police had left the Corner alone, asked the doctors and nurses to safely do the same, to demonstrate his complete dependence on the system. After that, the officer implied, the Corner seemed to understand his new reality. He answered questions. Described crimes. Although he was drawing things out. Giving only little bits and pieces at a time. Which, she thought, was characteristically logical. The longer he was useful, the longer he could be used to close cases, the safer the system would keep him. And when he stopped being useful? Though the system had been cruel to her, she coldly acknowledged it was far worse, his fellow criminals would be far worse, when it came to someone newly vulnerable who had owned up to such evil.

A few reporters violated the restriction of her property line.

"Ma'am, did you know him? Why did he target you? What would you have done differently? Do you know anything about his family, job, background—"

In this she heard, "What did you do wrong? Please tell me, so that I can tell myself nothing awful will ever happen to me. How did he become who he was? Please tell me, because he's more important than you are. I need to tell myself I'd be able to spot him, prevent him, never cross paths with him. Me, me, me. Him. Him. Him."

She waited. Mentally she graphed what always happened with terrible men and their horrific crimes. Y axis, public interest. X axis, time. One line for the victims and survivors. Another for the monster. By her estimate those lines were just about crossing, hers and the children's and all the lost and devastated souls fading downward to vanish as the Corner's line swept ever upward. Within a week the majority of the reporters had already decamped from her street to the charming New Hampshire town where the Corner had lived, a safe place where he had apparently committed no crimes at all.

The stories of the others he'd haunted, targeted, and destroyed showed her an alternate reality filled with annihilation and unanswerable questions, a place separated from her, from her children, by the thinnest of curtains.

She stopped asking the police about any cases but her own.

Despite his likely ulterior motives, she was grateful the boyish officer drove her to get her children. Waiting outside the senior apartment complex, her father-in-law stood over the children crossarmed and spiteful. But the old man softened at seeing the police car pull up. He gave the officer his condolences over the sergeant as she knelt on the sidewalk, hugging the children.

The pain of the cold concrete on her knees helped her understand it was reality. Helped her accept that their smell, their hair, their breath were close again. Hers but not hers.

They don't belong to you, either. That's not how it works.

"I missed you, I missed you, I told you I'd come get you!"

She let the children trace their fingers along her healing face, ask questions about her eye, her yellowing bruises.

In his hard gaze she thought she saw the old man say, "I know you must have done something to deserve this," saw that despite his losses, he still didn't understand that suffering and misfortune fall as wide and uniformly as snow, melting out of visibility but leaving their pain behind.

Drinking coffee back at the house with the boyish officer, she heard the children's happy hide-and-seek screams trickling down the kitchen stairs and tensed involuntarily.

Trauma doesn't end when the trauma ends.

"Right now we need them for evidence," the boyish officer said, "but at some point we'll be able to return your daughter's things. That he took."

She thought of the clothes, the teddy bear, her daughter's underwear and ballet tights. The tin car treasure box. The Corner contaminating it all.

"I don't want anything back but the treasure box."

Some things are replaceable. Some aren't.

She talked to the boyish officer about chance. Her son's fear of ghosts, her husband putting up the wildlife camera in response, the device's solar-paneled long life, the fact that the Corner had turned one way instead of the other at the top of the kitchen stairs, the one in a million path of the bullet. She could come up with a near infinite litany of chance that had saved her. Chance that formed the thin little wisp of fabric separating her from the devastation of those other families.

The boyish officer cleared his throat, fumbled with his coffee cup. "It wasn't just luck, you taking him out. You're a fighter. Don't sell yourself short." He shrugged. "Things happen for a reason."

She didn't challenge the boyish officer, aware that she was naturally uninclined to think well of herself. That unlike him, she didn't see some skill, some force that had helped her yet failed all those others. She wasn't better than they had been, wasn't more deserving of survival. So she stayed quiet, knowing how deeply people hated to admit or recognize the oversized space chance takes up in life. And, worse, in death.

"And after all," the boyish officer went on, "you had some bad luck, too. You were dealt a bad hand. Your husband. This guy fixating on you. We can't figure out how he made his . . . choices. He can't seem to explain it himself. And then—no evidence, no tracks, fingerprints? Your blood alcohol." The boyish officer shook his head over the series of events that had made her unworthy of belief. "Figuring out explanations? Even after we had him in custody? It was difficult. That neighbor of yours, putting whiskey in your drink to warm you up that night. Who would do that? Who would even think to ask? That he pretended to work at that café, so you misidentified him? The sap? It's just not a weapon we see. Yeah. Some bad luck you dealt with, too."

Her teeth gritted. She tried to force her voice into an even tone, but couldn't help sounding clipped and cold. "Most of that wasn't just bad luck, though, was it? Because there was the nail in my tire. The cigarette smoke. My daughter's missing things. The way the hide-a-key had been moved. How we felt watched. The lifted toilet seat. My phone in the wrong place. The baby monitor switched off. Ignoring all that, setting that aside, that was a choice."

Easier to believe a woman's lying than that bad things happened on your watch. Easier to believe the simplest thing is always correct. And it's simple to say a woman is crazy.

The boyish officer winced. She wondered what admissions he was allowed to make. What instructions he'd been given. What he could admit to himself.

"It was . . . unfortunate," he said. "An unfortunate series of . . . unexpected, unlikely, things." In a clear effort to change the subject, he asked, "You think you'll let your kids visit their grandpa? He seemed to want that."

"I thanked him. I'll mail him a check to cover the time they stayed with him."

"I mean, he did step up. Maybe give him a chance?"

She tipped her head at the boyish officer, momentarily baffled at how her father-in-law's keeping her children from her, accusing her of murder, of child abuse, the constant beratement, the not-so-whispered comments, the assault, could be outweighed by a few weeks of looking after his own blood. But then, of course, she remembered that although she felt utterly, completely altered, the world around her hadn't changed.

"It's not enough," she told him. "Not even close."

The boyish officer looked like he was going to scold her, then thought better of it.

"So, there's some developments in your case." He tapped nervously on his coffee cup, and she was struck with a sense of déjà vu, recalling the way she and the sergeant had sat together a few weeks after her husband's death drinking coffee, sitting in these same seats. "The smaller thing is we figured out where he must've hidden."

"Didn't you already tell me? In the basement?"

"Well, that's not a hundred percent. But we think he hid in the basement day of. Given the . . . cigarette smell you and the alarm guy mentioned."

"Mmm."

"So. Because we recovered the SIM card from your camera, we know he got to your house just before noon the day he broke in. Waited for you to leave with the kids on schedule. Then, like I said, probably he hid in the basement. We haven't found the copy of your key among his things, but safe assumption he copied the key from the hide-a-rock—impossible to know when, but sometime before it snowed. Based on your timeline, he probably came upstairs around midnight. Call came in from your neighbors around five a.m. And of course, the video shows him again the next day around two a.m. leaving down the path, hiding his tracks by walking in the footprints left by you and our guys." The boyish officer's brows knit at these acknowledgments of police fallibility. "That means he left twelve hours after we finished searching. I mean, after seeing that secret room, it was a pretty intense search. But what we figured out was he climbed into your beehive oven. Hid there. We found a hair, and sure enough, it matches."

She recalled that as she'd sobbed on the couch, devastated, she'd noticed ash smudged around the fireplace and ground into the carpet. Thought it simply another sign of police carelessness in her home.

"Is that even possible? The beehive oven door is tiny."

"Yeah, exactly!" The officer nodded vehemently. "That's why we missed it. How does a guy that size hide from a police search that thorough, you know? Finally we thought . . . maybe in there. Then we searched and found that hair. One of our guys, big guy, volunteered to try and get in that oven. It was a tight squeeze, but he managed. Said it was claustrophobic as hell. Getting out? That was a scene." The boyish officer chuckled. "Nearly got stuck. We thought he was going to pass out. Still . . . he did it. At some point we'll get to interview him about your case again and confirm all this. It's just that now, with these other cases—"

"Of course," she said, ceding priority to the missing, the dead, the shattered, even as this information caused painful strobe light pulses of imaginings. *Flash*, the Corner folding his limbs into the oven like a cave spider. *Flash*, him hearing her children in the hidden place. *Flash*, him gnashing his teeth, wondering if he had time to get to them.

"That means he must have heard the kids, doesn't it? That night. After I ran? They were hiding right there."

"It's possible. I mean, it couldn't've been for long, I guess? That they were all hidden in the fireplace? But he certainly would've heard us find the kids. Would've heard us searching for him. Must've scared the shit out of him, given he stayed in the house for so long after we left."

"Didn't scare him enough to not come back," she said.

The boyish officer shook his head, chastened. "It didn't. But, best we can tell, he didn't mess with that bathroom door while you were in there." The boyish officer shrugged. "Who knows what he was thinking? Who knows why he came back?"

She rubbed the painful spot between her eyebrows. "He came back because he wanted to see if my daughter was here. Probably planned to hide and wait for her. Hurting me—it would have proved he existed. He wouldn't have wanted to ruin his chance to get to her. And that night . . . he told me I was incidental. You understand? He wasn't here for me."

The boyish officer nodded, then cleared his throat. "So. The bigger thing I wanted to talk to you about." He slid his eyes to the side in clear discomfort. "How much of the video did you see? From your wildlife camera?"

"Not much. I called 9-1-1 when I saw he'd been hiding behind that pine tree that day."

"Well. There's . . . other videos. Videos on your camera go back until September or so. It still had space after so long because when it ran out of room it wiped the card, then started filling it up again. So we don't know about anything before September? But he does show up on your video back in mid-October. He was heading toward your house. Which means he was watching you. And that he might have broken in. Before that night."

"I don't understand," she said.

But she did. She remembered the boyish officer saying someone watching a house before a break-in wasn't unusual, the instant cold creep of her realization that it hadn't been her husband haunting them, but the Corner. She'd understood it again when she read in the papers that other targets had told people they felt watched, that things had gone missing. She'd thought of the baby monitor, inexplicably turned off. Of the way her daughter had recognized the voice and shape of the Corner.

But speculating that he had stalked them and, worse, that he had broken in before, was a shadow of knowing there was photographic proof.

She pictured the Corner hovering over her, watching, a sleep paralysis specter made manifest. She heard her daughter say, "But I know him. I know that voice. The man in the corner. From my dreams." Saw her little girl point toward the pine tree, say, "I saw a man again. Watching me, from over there."

It was real. You were right. It was him all along.

"We have him, on the video, coming and going. He did it with the others, too. Breaking in. Poking around a house. Sometimes he did that kind of thing a long time, going in and out of houses. Stalking people. From what he says? He got off on it. I . . . wanted you to hear it from us. Before you hear it . . . somewhere else."

"How many—did he say, how many times he broke in? Before?"

"He's on the video once in October. Once again in November. Then last month, one time—three nights before everything happened."

She took a moment to steady herself.

"But . . . he hit his head on the stairs? And he didn't know about the attic. Wouldn't he have known, if he'd been inside before? And I just—I normally wake up so easily, and the noises of the house, he would have woken me . . . everything's so loud."

The boyish officer shrugged. "Maybe that night he was louder. And maybe you're a deeper sleeper than you think."

Maybe, maybe, maybe. You use earplugs to help you sleep, after all. But your daughter saw him. Remembered him. Watching from the corner. Maybe he wasn't wandering the house at all. Maybe he was just watching her. Maybe if you hadn't been awake, he would only have watched that night, too.

"I don't like thinking about that," she said. "I don't like that at all."

You should've believed her. You should've believed your little girl.

The boyish officer nodded heavily. "Yeah. But you're safe now."

Safe.

"There's . . . one more thing. It's probably nothing."

Her stomach cratered. "What?"

"Well, some of the guys are wondering if it might be possible? If he might've pushed your husband down the stairs. The feds did ask him. He denied it. But . . . he shows up on the video back then. Not on the day you found your husband, but in October, like I said. He could've come onto your property from another direction, though. Could've come to the house more times than the video shows."

"But the sergeant said my husband couldn't have been pushed?"

The boyish officer tilted his hand back and forth in a so-so gesture. "More like concluded you couldn't've pushed him. But a bigger guy? They're talking about reopening it. Even though like I say he denies it."

She wrapped her hands around her coffee cup, thinking.

"He did say something about how he'd let my son go if we showed ourselves, otherwise I'd have 'more' blood on my hands. What 'more,' though, you know? Could he have meant my husband? Blamed me for some reason?" She shook her head. "But . . . what does it matter? He's . . . incapacitated. My husband's gone. It's done. We might not ever know for sure. Life's unsatisfying when it comes to knowing the truth." She sighed, thinking of the unknowns, the questions the Corner might never answer, the ones no one even knew to ask. "Either way, without my husband, he thought we were vulnerable."

"His mistake," the boyish officer said, and she thought she heard pride in his voice.

"I was wondering? The sergeant said when he was in the hidden room, he couldn't hear anything. Couldn't hear people moving around. That that's why he thought I was lying. Partly, anyway. I don't understand how that could be. It was all—all the sounds were so clear to me, at the time."

The boyish officer scratched behind his ear, as though what he was about to say made him itchy. "Yeah, well. After we saw your video, after . . . what happened? I tried it. Some of the other guys tried it. We got in there, made noises out in the house, and we could hear all right. Not as good as you, but you know the house better." He paused, saddened. "I think it was the sergeant's hearing. I think maybe he was losing his hearing and didn't realize. How else could that man've snuck up on him?"

Unless the sergeant could hear just fine, and lied about it to pressure you.

"I didn't hear him sneak up on us that night, either. He was . . . silent. It's just that he happened to be closer to the sergeant than he was to me. That made the difference."

They were quiet for a minute, listening to the children play upstairs.

In a small voice, the boyish officer said, "Maybe he's crazy? And that's why he did these things?"

She drank a slow sip of coffee and sighed. "When it was happening, I remember thinking, 'Doesn't anyone who would do something like this have to be insane in some way?' But he wasn't irrational. He chose us, way back when he saw my daughter at the café and pretended to work there. He took our receipt, probably got our name from it. Then he watched us. Stole the hidden key and copied it. Planned ahead. And apparently he even broke in before." She took a moment, rubbed her temple to soothe the internal pain that acknowledging this new information caused. "But what I keep thinking about is that when he realized I'd escaped, gone to get help, what did he do? He must have calculated the probability of catching up to me. He must've figured out the likelihood that he'd leave evidence behind if he ran. He sat right in this house and did all the math. So he put my phone back. He put everything, or nearly everything, back to normal. He hid. So well that you searched the whole house and didn't find him. He waited for hours with all of you looking for him. Waited half a day after you left. Then finally he followed your tracks out through the snow. Left so few signs you didn't believe he existed. You see? He thought it all out, all the contingencies, right there on the spot."

The boyish policeman nodded.

"It's just. Imagine. Imagine the presence of mind. To do all that. How can you be crazy, and still do all that? And that's just this once. He's gotten away with this, hurt others, for a long time. He might be sick. He probably is. But he chose to do what he did. Not just on the spur of the moment. He thought he was entitled to things that don't belong to him. That can't belong to anyone. And he went after them."

The boyish officer wrapped his hands around his warm cup. With surprise she heard a quaver in his voice.

"I want to believe he's crazy, you know? Rather than that someone would do, would want to do, those things."

It reminded her again of how young he was. Reminded her that despite his uniform, despite the way her own naivete had been ripped from her by her mother's death, experience strips away innocence at different paces for different people.

"Those things happen every day," she said. "Just to other people. In other places. And mostly the danger is from people they know better. Evil doesn't have to mean deranged."

He nodded again. Took a moment to collect himself before asking, "You think you'll sell this place? Move?"

"No," she said.

"Why not?"

"It's our home. It protected us."

"But all the memories? Don't you think it will be hard? For the kids?"

She felt the flat bitterness of her smile.

"No matter where I took them, they'd have to deal with all they went through."

"Yeah," he said without conviction. "I guess so."

She let the children share a bedroom that night. Remembering that the next morning was trash pickup, she put on her coat and rolled the bin down the plowed driveway. Even in her boots her feet prickled painfully; permanently sensitive to the cold where the frostbite had cut deep.

The physical injuries were easiest to face. It was unlikely all her toenails would grow back. Her eye, the doctor had warned, might never regain its former clarity.

But the Corner had left deeper damage. Panic would unexpectedly seize her heart, leaving her breathless. The children had the nervous watchfulness of rabbits, worried no place was truly safe.

Maybe other people were right. Maybe she and the children *should* find a new home. Somewhere unviolated, where reminders of their ordeals wouldn't hover nearby.

She left the trash bin at the road. Walking up the driveway, the house came into view between the trees. She paused, her memories superimposing over one another like film stuck in a camera, exposure piled on exposure. Her husband mowing the lawn. Her children chasing each other through the yard. Meals, cozy fires, glasses of wine. The quiet comforts of daily life. Profound happiness.

That was the problem, wasn't it? Leaving might distance them from bad memories, but it would also take them away from the good. And there was so much good. She squinted up at her home, recalling the way the chimney sweep had seemed so disturbed by the place, insisting that it had to be haunted.

Yes, she could see it now. A kind of blackened aura, old wisdom, pulsed from the place in the white light of the moon. Through different eyes, it might seem menacing. But for her that ancient riddle echoed—how much of a thing has to be replaced before it's no longer what it was?

Because certainly the house was not the thing it had been when first built. So much had been damaged, repaired, restored. Whole rooms culled, joists sistered, wood consumed to dust by insects and replaced.

But her home was more striking, more alive than others because her human eye saw how it was haunted by those thousand human touches; evidence of how many had gone before, had tended to and loved the place. It vibrated with those traces. And she understood that just like the house, she and the children would be transformed not just by damage, but by mending.

She balled her hurt hand into a fist around the scar on its palm, resolved.

Tomorrow she'd introduce the children to the neighbors who had helped her. Even better, they'd make the effort to meet all the neighbors. Then, just as she'd promised, she'd take the children to get a Christmas tree. They'd pick out one of the unbought, unchosen things she'd seen stacked behind a nearby garden center. They'd bring home any wreaths and garlands still there all this time after the holiday, filling the house with smells of life strong enough to stay green in midwinter. Together they'd draw comfort from the lights they'd string, from the memory of the husband and father they'd lost. Together they'd watch the days grow longer.

And tonight she'd go inside the home that had protected them. Tonight she'd fall asleep in a place that had stood for centuries, proof of the beauty born of survival.

ACKNOWLEDGMENTS

Many thanks to Helen Heller, whose enthusiasm for this book from the very first time we spoke changed my life. Her insight, ideas, always on-point criticism, and unflagging support have meant the world to me.

I've been incredibly lucky to work with editors Jeramie Orton and Harriet Bourton. Their thoughtful comments never failed to impress, and made this book what it is. Thank you both, truly, for your candor, your kindness, and your faith in this story.

Thanks to Pamela Dorman for welcoming me into a genuinely wonderful publishing family.

Saliann St-Clair and the Marsh Agency team, thank you for your tireless work on the international front.

To everyone at WME, I so appreciate all you've done representing this book.

Thanks to Jane Glaser for all of your support.

My early readers, in no particular order—Courtney Stephens, Nachel Mathoda, Liz Wendell, Sian Gilbert, and Jamie Sogn—your feedback was integral, and I couldn't be more thankful.

ACKNOWLEDGMENTS

To Christine Pride, Laurie Edwards, and Rakesh Satyal, your patient encouragement and advice to this stranger in a strange land was crucial to me in my most panicked and discouraged moments.

Yvette Yun and Marith Zoli, my amazing mentors. You taught me so much, and were the first people to pick my writing out of a pile and see some potential. I'll be forever grateful.

To my writing community—you know who you are—we went through the ringer together, and some days you were the only thing that kept me moving forward and getting words on the page. Thank you, always.

Rye, your kindness, encouragement, and ability to invariably make me feel better prove that I've got the best sister in the world. Thank you for being not just an amazing person, but an insightful reader.

To my dad, Robert, who held on to all those books I wrote in fourth grade, and who made sure I'd know exactly what to do when I encountered a mountain lion. You've given me a lifetime of support and laughs.

Thank you to my in-laws, Ruth Anne and Randy, for always bragging me up and for never failing to step in and assist with anything that needs doing, from babysitting to pouring concrete.

My grandmother Lil and my mother, Catherine, were lifelong, voracious readers who inspired my love of books and all things fiction. I know they're both looking down saying, "I told you so," as they see me wondering about choosing that whole lawyer thing. Right as usual, ladies.

On the inspiration front, I have a few thank-yous. First, of course, is my house. You're impossible to heat, but you are a stunner who has aged beyond gracefully. If you're haunted, your ghosts are benevolent ones. A big thanks-but-no-thanks to the contractor who started me worrying about what I'd do if someone ever broke in.

And, of course, many thanks to my anxiety. I knew you were good for something.

Thomas and Eleanor, if you're reading this before the year 2032, you're too young. Please reshelve. But know that I love you and am in constant wonder over how I got lucky enough to get to be your mom.

And finally, to my husband, Jason. The smartest thing I've ever done is realize that I got love right at seventeen. Thank you for this beautiful life.